MAY 2010

*Glenda
Hope.
into the C
y. Gary Shaw*

Outsider Cops

The Caribbean Case

by J. Gary Shaw

RoseDog❦Books
PITTSBURGH, PENNSYLVANIA 15238

RoseDog Books
585 Alpha Drive
Suite 103
Pittsburgh, PA 15238
Visit our website at *www.rosedogbookstore.com*

ISBN: 978-1-4809-7868-3
eISBN: 978-1-4809-7891-1

Acknowledgements

This book would never have been written and published if I had not been encouraged by the wonderful friends and associates listed below:

My wife, Marie, who stayed patient for the sixteen months it took for me to write the story.

Holly Sroka - She got me started.

My sisters Sheila and Jackie urged me on and contributed financial support.

My son Clyde supplied airline information.

My son Tom offered helpful suggestions about the Caribbean

Detective Chief Superintendent. (Rtd.), Don Gibson, supplied UK information.

My best friend Dale Neily who commented as the story progressed and contributed financial support.

My friend Barb Taylor, an honest critic.

Nime Dean, Don Drinkwalter, Marcel and Lou Salley, Winton Derby, Sylvain Côté, great friends who have stayed loyal for many years and contributed financially.

Friends - Taylor Hill, Bob Lauer, Harry Bush and Mary Jane Mimbs who continually urged me on.

Contents

Prologue

Curtis Cole was raised in Little Harwood, a small village in Devon County on England's southern coast. As a boy he marveled at how the tide rose and fell in the estuary where at times the fishing boats floated freely, and at low tide they sat stranded on the sandbars. He loved the ocean and the forest nearby where he spent countless days fishing and camping. Those experiences taught him the benefits of being patient, and how acts of nature can affect a person's best laid plans.

He always remembered his dad telling him about the Allies invasion of Normandy, France because on June 4, 1944, "Force U" sailed from Salcombe, a nearby village. June 4, 1944 was also the day he was born. War stories of local heroes left him with a lifelong impression that contributed to his fearless demeanor as he mature into manhood. He loved to read articles and books on British criminal history.

After achieving top scholar and athletic awards over the years of academic attendance he chose to enlist in The Royal Air Force. After three years he was motivated to leave the RAF to become a police detective when a six year old girl and her seven year old brother were abducted, and brutally slain in Little Harwood. Being married to Victoria Stone his college sweetheart, and raising a family, he felt that he must become a law enforcement officer. The skills and patience learned as a boy gave him an upper hand when solving complicated cases involving murders and white collar crime. Because of this he was assigned to increasingly difficult cases throughout the UK and the British Commonwealth, and he moved up the ranks the most senior level.

He was assigned to The Caribbean Case because The British Foreign Office knew that only New Scotland Yard's best detective could bring justice to The Palm Islands, a British colony. Cole, nor his superiors, had any idea of the scope of the crime and corruption that existed in the land.

Chapter 1 | Clouds

Forty-five year old Chief Detective Curtis Cole had bad memories of the eighteen murderers and psychopaths that he had tracked down over the years and brought to justice. Those successes prompted his promotion to his current rank putting him in command of about three thousand policemen. He was ready to retire when The Governor of The Palm Islands requested help, from the UK Foreign Office, to solve several recent suspicious deaths. When contacted, Cole thought, *'I'm in. This job will be exactly what I need - sun, sea and sand to sooth my jangled nerves. How hard or dangerous could this assignment be when the Island is only about 20 miles long, and with a population of less than twenty-five thousand people?'* Regulations required him to select a partner and he chose forty-two year old Sergeant William (Bill) Strong, an up-and-coming very smart detective. Both men were six feet tall, handsome and muscular, but Cole had eyes that could pierce the soul of any criminal. Those who had been interrogated by him in England swore that their blood turned to ice when they were forced to look into those steely blue eyes.

On Monday, November 20, 1989 Cole and Strong flew from London to Grand Palm Island in the Caribbean. The itinerary included a change of airline in The Republic of Calvert, an island country two hundred miles west of

Grand Palm. The detectives had been booked simply as tourists, in order to conceal their real identity, and to facilitate clearing Calvert immigration without any hassle. The Palm Islands consisted of Grand Palm, the main island, which was flat and had several lovely beaches, and Rocky Palm, about seven miles away. It projected out of the sea with four prominent hills. It was not attractive to tourists or residents.

When given the chance to declare independence from Britain the citizens of Palm Islands chose to remain as a British Colony with certain independence and elected officials. Calvert, on the other hand, declared independence from England. Palm Islands became an international financial center and tax haven. Its economy flourished under the tutelage of Premier Samuel Bruce Westwood who had been appointed by the Queen for a lifetime term. Calvertians were upset by the success of Palm Islands, and quite often delayed British officials by interrogating them until their connecting flight had departed – unless, of course, they paid a 'fee' to the Chief of Calvert Immigration.

On arrival in Grand Palm the detectives were whisked through immigration and customs inspection at the 'command' of the Commissioner of Police, a Mr. Warton Sylvester Black, who met them in the immigration center. He drove them in his Land Rover to the residence of the Governor, The Honorable Jeffery Dale Neily, who was expecting them. The Premier, Samuel Bruce Westwood, was also there - much to the surprise of Police Commissioner Black. They chatted about the trip and exchanged other pleasantries. No plan of investigative action was discussed.

After thirty minutes or so the Commissioner said "I booked you into a cottage at a complex named Sandy Shore Resort. Let's call it a day so you two gentlemen can unpack and unwind. I'll be available tomorrow to meet and discuss what I have for you."

The Governor agreed, but said, "Wait a minute. I've got a welcoming gift for you." He handed Cole a bottle of *Pirates' Best*, while saying, "This is the finest rum that money can buy. It's made right here on the Island."

Cole thanked him and said, "I'll keep you posted on our activities."

As they exited the Governor's house Cole saw a second vehicle parked behind the Commissioner's Land Rover. Commissioner Black, noticing Cole's surprise said, "That Ford Taurus has been assigned to you by the Governor. Here are the keys. Follow me."

They followed the Land Rover along the sea side road called Bay Road. It was nearly four o'clock. Traffic was heavy in both directions. Black's right turn signal started flashing, and the Land Rover entered a driveway that led to the Sandy Shore Resort and its nine cottages. Each cottage had its own short driveway. The Commissioner stepped down from his vehicle and beckoned Cole to park at cottage 9. It was located farthest from the office. Cole parked the Taurus then he and Strong walked back to meet Commissioner Black. He opened the office door for them and they approached the reception counter. The clerk at the counter was an elderly fellow named Josh. He showed them a big happy smile.

"What a great pleasure it is to see you again WB - the nickname affectionately used by some locals. I'll make sure your guests get the royal treatment."

"I have no doubt about that," WB replied. Addressing Cole he said, "I'll leave you two in Josh's capable hands. We can meet about eleven tomorrow morning in my office at headquarters."

"Until then," Cole replied. "Thank you for making our arrival so pleasant."

The Commissioner departed without comment.

Josh checked them in, gave each of the men a key to unit 9, and said, "Just call me if you need anything at all."

Cole and Strong got their baggage out of the Taurus and entered the cottage. It was quite nice, clean, and furnished with rattan furniture. It was right on the beach so the men had a great view of the sea. They quickly unpacked their bags. Cole made a bee line to an inviting, padded lounge chair, stretched out, and took in the view of the sea. Strong made tea in the microwave with the Tetley Tea bags that came as a freebie.

Now, as he watched the sun struggle to shine through a strange cloud formation, Cole had a struggle of his own. As he sipped his tea he did not want to acknowledge that this could this be an omen of what might be in store for him. He had been on the English coast many times, but never had he seen such a dark and menacing sight. Blocks of white were turning into black and gray streaks. They looked like they had been shot from a large gun and the blast was headed toward Grand Palm Island. Chasing that mass was another cluster of cloud that appeared to follow the same trajectory. 'Strange,' he thought, 'but I've been right about things like this before.'

•   •   •

At dusk he and Strong would meld into the Island scene. They would not be alone on this job as a team from the United States Drug Enforcement Agency was coming to join them. The DEA knew of suspicious individuals connected to international drug cartels, but their officers could not operate openly in the British Colony. Cole, lounging on the lanai, wondered how the land mass about five miles across the sea might figure into the crimes. That island was considered to be out-of-bounds by the local citizens. Folklore had it that four evil spirits existed there, one for each of the hills that seemed so out of place on an otherwise flat terrain. Also, ghosts of dead pirates were reported to appear on the full moon nights. The DEA agents had nicknamed the place *Four Tops* but they had not been able to investigate there. Cole had an eerie feeling. In Cole's mind it could be a perfect place for drug cartel operations.

"Hey guv," Strong said. "Let's get busy. We have to meet the DEA team at The Cricket Club at 7:30. Are you sure we should be seen together? Guess we can fudge the relationship for a few days," he stated.

"Righto Bill," he replied and he rose slowly from his comfortable lounge chair. "We'll get there a little bit early, but we'll have time to try their world famous conch fritters. By the way, have you ever seen clouds as strange as those blocking the sun? My gut says they are an omen. They bother me. I was expecting perfect sunsets over a glittering sea."

Strong did not comment, but he knew Cole often operated by gut feel and more than once it paid off. They proceeded to the Ford Taurus. For security reasons they walked single file with Strong in the lead.

"Did you move the car?" Cole asked.

"Not I." Strong replied. "I thought you parked it beside that hibiscus bush."

"I did and it sure as hell did not drive itself to this spot. Seems someone else has a key. I'm going back in and calling the Governor. He's the one who supplied it. Maybe he sent someone to fix something. Cole returned from making the call and said to Strong, "We have a problem. The Governor had nothing to do with supplying a car for us. He said the P I Police were to provide a car. Let's talk to Josh."

Josh told the detectives that a police officer did stop by to bring a second set of keys. "I told the officer to just put them on the dashboard as you men were likely resting. He probably made sure he had the right keys and started the car and moved it."

"Thanks Josh. You're probably right. Let's go Bill," Cole suggested.

Cole looked inside of the car and he could see the keys on the dashboard. He told Strong, "Stand back while I unlock the door." Strong moved quickly to get behind a huge Casuarina pine tree. Cole did not use the electronic button to unlock the car, but inserted the key into the door and popped the locks of the navy blue vehicle. He opened the door. Strong was still standing aside as he started the motor, and put the car into gear with no problem. He waved Strong to get in and grunted, "Okay, let's go."

Strong got in, and they proceeded onto Bay Road. Driving along the busy street, the Chief ordered Strong, "Tomorrow, I want an answer to who moved this car and I also want a different vehicle assigned! If I wasn't jet lagged I wouldn't have even got in. Pretty clumsy thinking on my part but it turned out okay."

His partner nodded as the Chief parked the Taurus at the far edge of the Cricket Club's large parking area.

Cole's mind flashed back to the cloud scene. He was beginning to think that the assignment might not be a holiday after all. They entered the Club and found a table near the far exit.

•   •   •

Suddenly, there was a deafening explosion. Metal smashed against the cement block structure of the club. Debris flew in all directions. Flames and smoke reached for the sky. The entrance door blew in. Cole and Strong dived for the floor and crouched under their table. They could see flames bursting in multi-colored hues. Acrid smoke filled the room. Staff and customers staggered about as they grabbed napkins to cover their mouths. It all happened so fast that Cole had no time to panic. Patrons were stunned and in shock. Cole peered outside and saw that the Taurus had been blown to pieces. Strong looked and said, "Some bastard just tried to kill us. Are you okay, guv?"

"Okay, yes." then added, "Getting here early seems like a hell of a good thing. We would have been in the car if we were on schedule. An inside job for sure. I guess we aren't welcome."

"Bastards," Strong repeated. "I'll get us a car tomorrow."

As the smoke cleared Cole surveyed the room. Tourists and locals were trying to gather their wits and get out of the place. The DEA men were supposed to wear NY Jets caps and pose as scuba divers. Cole looked around and there was no sign of them. "Crap," he blurted out to Strong, "Some holiday Bill! What the hell kind of mess, are we into?"

They had worked together on major murder cases in Liverpool, Plymouth and London to name a few. On only one occasion was their vehicle targeted and blown up, and that was not an inside job.

• • •

Constable Wilbur Black, of the Palm Islands police force, was the first constable to arrive. He had seen the flames shooting into the night sky as he patrolled the residential area close by. He immediately radioed the P.I. Fire Department but they could not respond because they were required to be at the Island airport when flights were landing or departing. The airport was only two miles away. The Fire department had only one truck. At the time of the explosion PalmAir flight 1643 was arriving from Tampa. It had been delayed by one hour due to an altercation with a passenger in transit from Canada. That flight was the one the DEA agents had booked.

Cole beckoned to the Constable to pick them up. "So far a screwed up deal and my guess is that it's not going to improve," Bill Strong uttered, as they got into the Constable's car.

"Constable, what the hell is going on here?" Cole queried. "Who would want to blow up the Taurus?"

Constable Black recognized Cole as he had seen him with the Commissioner earlier that day. He answered stoically: "Don't know mon. Lots of nasty stuff happens on this Island. That's why you are here. Solve it!"

• • •

Strong sensed the unfriendly tone and so did Cole. Years of detective work trained them to tune into sarcastic retorts. Cole nodded to his partner and he knew there would be no more conversation with Black. Back at their accommodation they thanked Black for the ride and wondered what the next surprise would be. Surely the unit would be in the same shape as they left it earlier. But maybe not; so Cole told Strong to walk around the left side while he took the right side of the cottage.

"All clear over here," Strong signaled.

"Okay on this side too," claimed Cole. He carefully opened the door hoping all was okay on the inside.

'*Why didn't the builder put a light switch inside the main door?*' he thought, as he fumbled in the dark feeling for a wall switch. A few seconds later he found a switch, turned it on, and light flooded the main room. He said, "Thank God the place is clear, Bill."

"Hey boss, I guess they were trying to kill us first, and then search this place. It looks like tomorrow I'll be looking for a new place —- and a new car."

"For sure," replied Cole. "We need a place of our own. Then we can install our own security system and not have to wonder who lives on the other side of our walls. Who knows what happened to the DEA pair but my guess is that they know how to take care of themselves." Bed was going to feel good.

Cole locked the doors, and retired to his room.

Chapter 2 | DEA Agents Arrive

Tom Oakley and Willie Patton had boarded the PalmAir BAC111 flight 1639 that was scheduled to leave Tampa Florida International Airport at 5 PM. It was to arrive in Palm Island in time for them to meet their British cohorts. They dressed like real tourists with their T shirts emblazoned 'Dive or Die', the motto of their Key west dive club. Their baseball caps that bore the logo 'NY Jets' just added to their anonymity.

"Attention, this is the captain speaking," blasted loudly over the plane's scratchy intercom. "Flight 1639 will be delayed. A further announcement will be made in 15 minutes."

Tom looked at Willie and said "I hope the Brits get this flight info. The buggers may turn up the whole place trying to find us. We can't phone them. Crap!"

After an unpleasant wait the Captain announced, "We apologize for the delay. Security had a bit of trouble with a passenger, but all is clear now. Our estimated time of arrival has been changed from 6:30 to 7:30PM."

"Think we'll make the meeting at the Cricket Club?" Willie asked.

"I don't think so but there's a slight chance," Oakley replied. "Let's relax and get some ZZZs".

. . .

It seemed like only a few minutes but it was really fifty minutes when the announcement woke them. "This is your Captain speaking. Please return to your seats. We have begun our descent into Palm Island International Airport. Your chair backs must be in the upright position and your seat belts fastened. Carry-on items must be place under the seat in front of you. We should be on the ground at 7:35. Thank you for your patience. Have a wonderful time."

As the plane descended, the flight path paralleled the west side of the island. The plane would have to turn left to align with the single runway. Just as the turn started, Oakley saw a huge explosion on the ground.

"Look Willie, what the hell exploded?" he blurted.

Willie leaned over and saw the tower of smoke and flames and said, "Do you think maybe another drug courier just got fired…. no pun intended! I guess we'll soon find out."

There was no announcement from the flight deck as the BAC111 touched down for a perfect landing. All passengers seated on the left side had seen the event, and those on the right were asking about the explosion. The flight crew offered no information. The passengers disembarked onto the tarmac and proceeded into the immigration building. Immigration officers did not comment about the blast when Willie quizzed them. Blank faces answered him.

The clearance went without a hitch and the two agents flagged a taxi. The diver was an older man named Alvin Whiteacre. He introduced himself as he loaded the scuba bags and carry-on cases into the trunk of the Toyota Camry, then Oakley and Patton climbed in.

"We just had a car explode at the cricket Club. Did you see anything from the airplane, Whiteacre asked?"

"Sure did," said Patton. "What was that all about?"

"A bomb blew up a car at the Cricket Club. Don't know more than that. I've been here for 58 years and nothing like that ever happened," the driver replied.

"Shit." Oakley whispered to Patton. "Our guys were supposed to be arriving there about 7:30."

"Where to?" asked Alvin.

"The Beach Hotel," replied Oakley.

They sat silently as Alvin chatted about the solitude on Palm Island and how safe the visitors are at any place in the country - as if nothing had just happened. It took about fifteen minutes to get to their destination. The Beach Hotel looked very inviting as they proceeded up a long entrance driveway that was lined with King Palm trees, each about fifty feet high. Pretty lights lit up the façade of the three story hotel. They were checked in by an efficient desk clerk named Walter, given two keys, and wished a happy stay. Malibu lights provided low illumination for the walkways throughout the complex. There was a four foot high hedge of orange and pink hibiscus lining the path from the walkway to their unit.

Whitacre placed their scuba gear bags and their suitcases at unit 114, and he too wished them a happy stay. Patton forked over a $20 tip in US money. That lit up Alvin's smile as he thanked them and left.

Oakley had the key and opened the door to their unit and said, "Needs a little oil," as the door squeaked lightly. Patton smiled as he joked, "Hey man this is not the Four Seasons Miami. We've been in a lot worse." Once inside they were pleased to see a bright clean main room with a bedroom on either side. Both had ensuite bathrooms with a shower and a tub. A small kitchen was at the beach side of the room. Sliding glass doors enclosed the 20 foot beach-side wall of the main room.

"Take your choice of bedroom," Oakley said. Patton chose the one on the right. It was nicely painted in Caribbean hues with the usual prints of seaside scenes hanging from the walls. "How are your digs?" Willie shouted across the main room.

"Looks like I won the draw," he replied laughing. "This could be the Four Seasons! I love it! Lots of room, desk, chair, easy chair, king bed, big bureau, TV, flower drapes on the window." Drawing them open he got a tourist's delight. There was a full moon shining over the rippling sea. And the window was a full ceiling to floor sliding glass door leading to a small patio. The beach was only about 10 feet away. It sloped to the water not more than another 60 feet away. "Hey Willie, c'mon over to my resort," he shouted. "Too bad you chose a closet."

Willie appeared and was impressed. He said, "What the Hell. We aren't here on a holiday for God's sake. Let's get serious. How are we going to contact the Brits?"

"Relax man. We'll sort that out in the morning. Our backup plan is to have breakfast at the Seaview Grill if we didn't connect as planned. I thought you knew that. Your C.O. at Forensics was to inform you."

"That asshole doesn't like me. No wonder I'm clueless."

"Not to worry, let's bunk down and dream about this sweet assignment."

Oakley checked that the doors were locked, shut off the lights and laid down in his dark room.

Chapter 3 | Meetings

The morning sun was peeking through the curtains in Cole's room and he arose to open them. A cloudless sky let the sun turn the sandy beach into a golden hue, and the blue Caribbean Sea completed the rest of the picture. The ominous clouds were gone. People were walking along the beach. Sure looked like a tourist paradise.

"Hey partner," he shouted across the room, "maybe we'll have a decent day today. We'd better get our ass in gear because we have to get to the Seaview Grill."

Strong acknowledged by grabbing the door key. "I've been ready for thirty minutes. Let's get going. We have to tell the front office that we'll be checking out later."

At the front desk they were greeted by a smiling Palm Islander. She looked to be about 30 years old, brown skin and beautiful by all standards. She spoke clearly with a slight accent. In a somewhat sensuous tone she welcomed the guests. "Good morning gentlemen. My name is Eisie. How may I help you?" She was not teasing the men but Strong could have interpreted it that way if he wasn't so serious about finding the DEA agents. '*Another time*,' was his thought.

"We need a taxi, mam," Cole interjected.

"Right away, sir," as she picked up her phone and dialed . . . then asked, "Bluewater Taxi?"

A voice with a Calvertian accent was heard: "Wuz up?"

"I have two passengers. Come now, please."

Strong could have listened to that sexy voice all day.

It seemed like in less than a minute the cab appeared. A smiling driver jumped out and greeted his fare as he opened the cab door. "My name is Harris. Where to?"

"The Seaview Grill," Strong said. "Is it far?"

"About fifteen minutes. It in Southbend, a town on the South shore. You get good view of the ocean and Four Tops, the other island."

They got in. Harris drove onto Bay road.

"Tell me about Four Tops, Harris," said Strong. "I can see that island from my room."

"Palm Islanders afraid of place. They say ghosts of bad pirates live there."

Strong asked, "Are you afraid of the place?"

"No Mon. I Calvertian. I fish over there many times. Big wahoo and tuna swim there."

"Maybe you could take us fishing there?"

"No problem," Harris replied as he looked in the rear-view mirror. "My boat is small, but if three go, I rent big boat from Mr. Bodder at Clear and Deep Dive. Call me." Reaching back he offered, "Here's my card with number to call. There is no taxi company here and each driver pays government for a license. Maybe I be your driver a lot?"

"Thanks, but we will be renting a car today. Sometimes though, we'll need a driver. Do you care what time we call?" asked Strong.

"Anytime, mon. I hard worker. I need money to send to my parents in Calvert. Very poor people there. I have wife named Bara, and two boys, here in Palm."

Harris drove along Bay Road, then through Kingtown the capital. Many people waved as he honked a greeting to them.

"Harris, it seems like you know lots of folks here," Strong said.

Harris smiled.

"The town seems active," Strong said to Curt.

"It should be busy," Curt replied to him. "Tens of millions of dollars pass through this country daily. It's no wonder crimes don't get solved. Payola is alive and well here."

They exited the capital and the traffic thinned out. The road hugged the ugly shoreline of fossilized grey coral. Casuarina and seagrape trees grew between the road and the shore. About a mile from town the road was more inland and there were small, but neatly groomed properties with colorful houses.

"Almost there," Harris said. "I drive you back?"

"No," Strong said. "We are meeting some old friends here, and they will have a car."

The Seaview Grill appeared up ahead. It was perched on the edge of a cliff about one hundred feet above the sea.

"The place was a sugar mill," claimed Harris. "It shut down when Island became tax haven and people started to work in construction. That why I have resident permit. I did construction labor and saved money to buy this car. Good money for me now. It too bad Clifford Scott, the original owner of the mill, kill himself. At least that's the rumor. The cops didn't let out any details."

Cole looked at Strong, and they stayed silent.

Harris parked the cab. Strong got out. Cole stayed in the vehicle. "Wait until we see if our friends are here Harris. This might be a return fare!" Cole said.

Strong entered the restaurant and he immediately spotted the DEA agents. He opened the door and waived an okay to Cole.

"Thanks Harris." Cole said. "How much do I owe you?"

"I take fifty dollars American, or forty Palm Isle dollars. I prefer American."

"Okay my friend, and thanks," Cole said. He slipped Harris an extra twenty. "We'll call you for sure."

Chapter 4 | Getting Down To Business

The two British detectives walked over to the table where Oakley and Patton were looking out over the sea. A few feet away Cole said in his true British accent, "See any ghosts out there lads?"

Oakley wheeled around, "For Christ sake, we thought you were dead! How the hell are you? Am I ever glad to see you Brits standing on your feet."

The Agents got up and the men gave hugs all around.

Patton smiled as he said, "I thought we might be having smoked Cole and Strong for breakfast!"

"Up your bloody American ass with the snide comment," said Cole. "Good thing I was hungry and we parked before someone blew our car into a million pieces."

"So that's what happened," commented Oakley. "Son of a gun, we all could be dead because if we'd been early, we were going to surprise you with a visit."

Cole assessed the men with their NY Jets ball caps and skin tight T-shirts. Both were wearing shorts so it was easy to see that they were in top physical shape. Oakley was about six-foot two and Patton about five foot ten. No doubt they would pass as tourists on a dive holiday. Cole and Strong sat down and beckoned to the server.

"Good morning gentlemen," the dark-skinned waiter said. "My name is Kenneth and I'm here to serve you. Would you like to order now or do you need a few minutes? Here's our menu. Can I bring you some great Blue Mountain Jamaican coffee, or Tetley tea?" he asked, as he handed them a couple of menus.

Both men ordered coffee which Kenneth quickly served. The DEA team had refills.

"We'll order now Mr. Ken," said Strong. "Bring two slams with bangers, eggs over easy, and toast, no chips."

"I guess we'd better get a plan together," Cole said. "How about we talk on the beach where there are no ears. Willie, aren't you staying at The Beach Hotel?"

"Sure, and the place is not too busy right now, so four o'clock would be good for us."

All men agreed. They finished their coffee, paid the bill and jumped into Willie's Jeep to head into Kingtown.

"You can drop Bill at the Toyota dealership and take me to Police Headquarters," said Curt.

"Okay," agreed Willie. "Tom and I want to visit a couple of dive shops and get some idea of who owns them and how they operate."

Strong was dropped off first then Cole was taken to Police Headquarters.

• • •

The P.I Police Headquarters was a two story cement block structure a block off of Bay Road. The perfectly landscaped outside parking area could accommodate about twenty vehicles. Flowering periwinkle plants edged the hibiscus and croton border. The pink and white building could pass as an upscale residence. Police Commissioner Warton Sylvester Black was serving his fifteenth year in office. He was trained in London and after five years he decided to return to his homeland. There were now twenty officers and staff, and of the twenty, six men and one female had the same surname as that of the Commissioner.

The unit had one detective, Herman Spikel, a Canadian born, sixty-four year old, former member of the RCMP Interpol forensics squad. Black was not consulted in the process of hiring Spikel and the two clashed from time to time. The foreign Office had told Cole that WB may not be too friendly but to get him onside early. As for Spikel, they suggested that Cole should befriend him after settling in with Black. The Governor had reported that Black seemed to rule the Island. Any untoward events of a serious nature had to be reported to The commissioner first and he would determine which officers would be assigned to investigate them.

•　　•　　•

Cole entered the Headquarters building and was greeted by a pleasant, but plump, receptionist. She was expecting so she immediately buzzed the Commissioner, gave him the info, hung up and said to Cole, "Commissioner Black is waiting for you. Take the stairway to your left and his assistant will show you to his office."

"Thank you," Cole said, "and by the way, what is your name?"

"Audrey Black," she replied.

"I see that you have a sign-in register, but I need not sign in?"

"Yes. Commissioner Black told me not to bother you about signing in."

"What a nice gesture. Thanks, Audrey. No doubt we'll see more of each other." Cole proceeded to the stairway.

A trim, six foot two, uniformed man met Cole at the top of the stairway and beckoned for him to follow.

"Hello," Cole said, "nice facility you have here. I guess the Commissioner is pretty busy these days as the Island seems to be booming." Mr. Trim did not respond, but led Cole down to the end of the hallway.

As was Cole's natural instincts, he observed several doors that had no names, signs or numbers on them. 'How strange', he thought.

Mr. Trim knocked twice. The sign on the door showed COMMIS-SIONER of POLICE.

A deep voice said, "Enter."

Mr. Trim entered and said, "Detective Cole, Sir."

Cole entered the Commissioner's large office.

"Thank you George," Black replied. "Have a seat detective. Glad you are here."

Cole thought, as he sat down in one of the two padded chairs, *'well at least Mr. Trim has a name.'* "Good to be here Commissioner," he said. "Okay if I call you WB?"

"By all means use it."

"Before we get down to business solving old issues, have you learned anything about the car explosion last night?" queried Cole.

"No, I have nothing to report today. My forensic detective is still working the scene. Your arrival here at Grand Palm was no secret. We are questioning our immigration agents for possible leads."

"From my experience I'd say that it was C-4 explosive, set off by a timing device. Let me know if your guys find residue. Is it normal to have C-4 on the Island?"

"Not normal, but Stephen Keith has a project underway at North Side. He's been blasting over there to build a golf course. He may have imported some C-4. Usually they use dynamite."

"Okay. I'll talk to him," said Cole.

"I've arranged for you to have another car." said the Commissioner.

"That's appreciated but we have rented one from Island Toyota, so I'll take a rain check on that," Cole replied.

WB did not show any reaction but said, "Let me give you a few historical facts."

Chapter 5 | Who's Who

The Commissioner started by explaining that the Island was once a penal colony. "First, Black is the most common name here. Our clan was named by slave merchants and the easiest thing was to name us the same as our color."

"The second most common name in the Palm Islands is Scott. The first Scott immigrants came from Wales where they were farmers. In 1870 Clifford Scott was convicted of stealing money from his church. That unforgiveable sin resulted in him, his wife, four sons, and two daughters being shipped off to Palm Island. Using his knowledge of farming, Clifford began growing sugar cane and built a flourishing business. The sons and daughters mixed well with the local population and one hundred years later the Scott clan had reproduced into fifty families. Due to their hard work and thriftiness, by 1989, the families owned many parcels of land. As for the sugar mill, it was converted into a restaurant named The Seaview Grill."

It was no secret to the Foreign Office that WB resented the Scott dominance in land holdings.

"Keith is the third most common name here," WB said. "Kirk Keith's great, great, grandfather was shipped to Calvert along with about three hundred other German convicts. Kirk Keith built a boat for fishing and used it to get to Palm

Island where he married one of Joshua Black's daughters. The couple had three sons: Donald, Harold, and Stephen. They grew up in the family boat building business. Two of them became seamen and worked for International Steamship Cargo Line. By watching and learning and saving their money, together they bought a 140 foot cargo ship and controlled the shipment of supplies into Palm Island from Florida. The business was so profitable they got into importing goods, warehousing and retailing. They operate as Palm Shipping Ltd. Donald handles the shipping side of the business and Harold manages the warehouses. The other son, Stephen, became a land developer and builder."

The Commissioner continued. "In 1973 the boys tried to get exclusive rights to air routes into Palm Island, but the Foreign Office got involved and squashed their attempt. The Palm island Government originated the airline instead, and I was named the Chairman."

On the other hand, the Governor knew that WB had cozied up to the Keith clan, a fact that WB did not divulge.

"That's good information WB. I am sure I'll trip over some of them as Strong and I proceed."

"So to carry on, there are eight unsolved cases," said Black. "They involve two Canadian tourists, two Islanders, two Americans, and two Calvertians. The Canadians were robbed and beaten to death. No motive could be established. My men found their bodies on the beach. The Islanders were from North Side. They had been at the North Side Bar and reportedly had left about midnight. A witness said they were very drunk. It seems like they missed the dead end road sign and drove right off of the cliff where the road split. They smashed through the directional sign and rolled down the eighty foot bank. The vehicle burst into flames. The bodies were thrown from the vehicle. Both men had crushed skulls. The men worked as dive boat hands."

"As for the Calvertians, their skulls were cracked and their bodies were slashed by a machete. A tourist found them in their small fishing boat that was anchored in shallow water of Smith Sound. Whoever did that job likely took off by boat."

"We identified the two Americans as stockbrokers. They worked for a Canadian stock brokerage firm, West Coast Brokers Inc. that has an office in Tampa. Immigration told us that those two had made ten trips over the last two years. They were scuba divers and liked to go on night dives."

Black sounded somewhat bored as he finished by saying, "All of the names are in the files. Let me know when you want to review them."

Cole had looked intently at the Commissioner during his talk. He felt no bad vibes, but noticed that Black glanced about many times.

"Good briefing WB. When I see my partner we will plan our next steps. He'll be picking me up any minute now," Cole said, as he glanced at his watch.

WB's phone rang. "Yes Audrey, what is it? Oh. Okay. We are finished. I will tell Detective Cole." Turning to Cole he gave the message – "Your partner is here. When do you want to meet again? Give me some notice. I'll make sure you have a private room and the files are there."

"Can I call you on that?"

"Sure. If I'm busy just tell Audrey, and George will be here to look after you too."

The two men shook hands. WB showed Cole to the door, opened it then said, "I look forward to working with you and getting to the bottom of things."

Cole left the room and walked quickly down the stairway while thinking, *'It could have been worse!'*

Chapter 6 | Moving to *Enchanted*

Strong was waiting at the reception counter. "Thanks Audrey. See you again soon," he said. Turning to Cole, Bill said brightly, "Got us an almost new Camry with tinted windows. Best of all I think I found us a place for and the DEA guys. It's a four bedroom, four bath residence right on the beach. The man that owns it also owns the restaurant across the street. Want to see it now?"

"Why not?" replied Cole. "How much?"

"It's a steal, only $3,000 a month."

"When I told the owner who we were he shook my hand, smiled, and said, "For you men, half price." He also commented that we might get some leads because Island rowdies were doing drug deals in his lounge, and he was afraid to report this to the P I Police."

"You should get a raise buddy!" exclaimed Cole. "I told you that the cloudless sky was a good omen. Let's go."

On the way to the potential new living setup Cole filled in Strong on the details of his meeting with WB.

"So when do you plan on us reviewing the files?" asked Strong.

"We'll probably start tomorrow. First we'll talk with Oakley and Patton, as planned. We have to show them where we hope to stay. If they like the place we can skip the beach meeting and have it where we are going."

The traffic was heavy on the two lane road so Cole had time to view the area. The main intersection in Kingtown had the Post Office on one corner and three four story buildings on each of the other three, all bearing a Canadian bank logo. Canadian banks were prominent throughout the Caribbean as historically there was much commercial shipping out of Halifax, Nova Scotia. A short block away was The Palm Bank & Trust building. The detectives felt that all four banks would be targets of their investigation.

Continuing north, and on the sea side of the road, he observed several smaller businesses including a dive shop, restaurants, and several small hotels. The Holiday Place was the only major hotel name on the Island and it was about another mile up the road near the Cricket Club.

As Strong slowed down and signaled to turn he said, "This is the place. It was a private residence - and a guy whom you'll meet – bought it along with the restaurant across the road. He also owned the twin of this place next door. They each sit on 250 feet of beach and the lots are 200 feet deep, - ocean to road. The house is 80 feet wide and 30 feet deep so we should be pretty safe here." A thick, high, oleander hedge blocked any view from the road. Strong turned into the circular driveway.

Cole was blown away by what he saw. "Have you been inside?"

"Of course," said Bill, "and it gets even better. There are two bedrooms, two baths on each side, a phone in every room, and a forty foot main room with floor to ceiling sliders on the sea side. The beach is right at the door. The water is not fifty feet away. I've got a key so get out and take a look."

Curt climbed out of the Toyota onto a paved circular drive. The main entrance was only a few steps away. Bill opened the door and Curt couldn't believe his eyes. He thought, '*Am I at the Ritz Carlton?*'

"How the hell did you find this place, Bill?"

"On a hunch I called that driver Harris whom I thought was a straight arrow. He seemed to be wired into this Island so I asked him if he knew of a place for rent."

"Damn good work Bill. You've outdone yourself!"

"Thanks guv. I'm calling Oakley and maybe they can come over here now."

Curt dialed. Oakley answered, "Hello, who's this?"

"Hey guy, it's me, Bill Strong. I'm with my boss. We found a place to settle into. Can you come over now to see it?"

"We just finished our tour, so okay. Where are you?"

"We're at a residence called, *Enchanted*. There's no street numbers here, just names. It's across from the Hibiscus Restaurant on the main road. And let me say this, the oleander hedge out front blocks the place so the only thing you'll see from the road is the start of a curved driveway and a small sign with the name, *Enchanted*."

"I can find the place," Oakley replied. "A guy at the beer store told us they serve great food at Hibiscus, but the ambience sucks. Patton and I will be there in ten minutes. "

"You'll see our Camry parked in front of the house. We'll be inside. The door is unlocked."

Chapter 7 | Information Exchange

The agents arrived in the rented Jeep, walked in, and Patton shouted, "Hell's bells, this is awesome!" They toured the house with Strong as he bragged about his discovery.

Cole and Strong smiled and asked, "Do you want to move over here?"

"I know there's lots of room and the place is gorgeous but we should think about it overnight," said Oakley. "It might not be such a good idea if someone tries to blow up the place like they did with your Taurus. We'd all be dead! Besides we have to remain under cover so the less we see of each other the better."

"Okay, you get a raincheck. Bill and I still have to meet with the owner so we'll do that now," said Cole. "Make yourselves at home. We won't be gone for long."

• • •

The Hibiscus Restaurant was owned and operated by Gart Webber, a Canadian entrepreneur, and his wife Louisa. Gart had Permanent Residence status. That qualified him to own a business in the country. The security system was a ninety pound red Doberman named *King* - a trained guard dog. Prior to Webber's ownership the place was just a 'watering hole' for rowdy drinkers and pot dealers. The presence of that crowd kept respectable locals and tourists from patronizing the place. He was still trying to make the place respectable. Gart welcomed the detectives as they entered.

"Hi there," said Gart. "Is this the partner you told me about?"

"This is him, Curt Cole, the best detective in all of England!"

They shook hands as Cole said, "Glad to meet you. How long have you owned this place and the houses?"

"About two years," Webber replied. "No problem with owning the houses but it's hard to get customers through these doors because of some characters who think this is a drug store. The customers who are brave enough to come here, say that Hibiscus has the best food on the Island so they put up with some distraction. We have a simple menu. We offer a high quality mix of Caribbean and Italian dishes. We sell lots of pizza for takeout. Our customers keep giving us compliments and they return regularly."

"Bill tells me that you want $3,000 a month rent for the house. Is that correct?"

Webber replied, "That's right if you promise to eat here a few times a week."

"Hey – if the food is as great as you say it is, we may come more often than that. Let's make a deal. Send the rent bill to Governor Neily and we can move in today. By the way, what time does The Hibiscus close at night?"

"We open the dining area at noon and close it at 10 PM, but my bar and lounge remains open until midnight."

"Sounds even better," said Cole. "We never know when we can eat if we get onto a hot lead."

"Then it's a done deal. I'll make sure you can get fed anytime up until we close the bar. I gave a key to Bill and I'll get another for you. Drop in later for a free meal and I'll give you the key."

Cole and Strong returned to *Enchanted* to find Oakley and Patton on the beach patio, soaking up the sun.

"Great scenery," Oakley said when he saw the detectives. "The beach parade looks like there is a Sports Illustrated swimsuit convention here in Grand Palm."

"Don't get yourself all worked up, buddy. Sex is not what we came here for," said Cole. "Let's get down to criminal busting."

The great room had a table that could accommodate ten people. The four men had lots of room to spread out papers and maps. Oakley and Patton had a picture of each of the leaders of the gangs that they were investigating. Patton went out to get a packsack that contained more pictures of their suspects. He handed the pictures to Cole.

Pointing to a couple of head shots Patton said, "This is Carlos Quintia. This other one is Angelo Suarez. They run drug cartels in Mexico and Columbia, and they are key players in the huge Central American Magdalena cocaine operation. We know some of their tactics but, we want to pin down how the money changes hands. We can't break the secrecy laws here. I understand that you can open them up legally. We need you to find out where the money gets banked or moved to Columbia and Mexico."

Cole replied, "We'll have to get approval from the Governor. We know he is anxious to help but even he has to deal with red tape. It will take some time but it can be done."

Cole also told the group what he had found out from the Commissioner of Police.

"WB was weak on details," he said. "Even though he acted cooperative, he offered only sketchy details and no forensic information that flowed from the investigations. I'm keeping a low profile until Bill and I get into the files. Otherwise I might have to bring a legal action to see the police files. Also, there is a forensic detective, Herman Spikel, who we want to interview before getting down to hard facts with WB."

"So Tom, what is your game plan?"

"We know that Suarez has contacts on this Island. Interpol has determined that he has couriers running written messages in order to avoid direct verbal or telegraphic communications. We believe they take the instructions from Mexico and Columbia to Canada, Bermuda, Calvert and The Bahamas. They then mail them from "clean" addresses to dummy corporations here, where they are verbally conveyed to the criminals. A Calvert legal firm, Jones & Keller, with an office here in Palm, acts as the control person and members of the law firm are the officers and directors. These corporations have fancy names, but the two most suspected are Palm International Traders Limited, and Island International Finance Limited. We have no legal way to force these corporations to reveal anything to us. We would like to plant an undercover person to befriend an office employee that works there, and has access to the files. From time to time the law firm will advertise for new employees and the reason we came here now is that they have advertised to fill two positions. Ads are running in the Island News Herald as well as in the Times of London. We are hoping that you could arrange for a qualified man or woman to apply. With hard copies in hand we could slam the door shut on the operation."

"That's a pretty tall order my friend," said Bill, "nevertheless, not an impossible task as we have some Scotland Yard people who would likely jump at a chance to get in on the action in this wonderful, sunny place. The Governor has a secure phone line so tomorrow I'll see what he can do."

Bill continued: "You guys can reciprocate by using your skills as scuba divers. You don't need much imagination to think that a couple of couriers could have been victims of a night dive so-called accident. We know couriers are expendable and drug lords have no compassion if they have the slightest feeling of betrayal. What better way to dispose of a couple of employees if they were scuba divers. I'm hoping WB's files will give us a clue about that."

Strong looked around and said, "It's getting late. We still have jet lag and since we go into serious action tomorrow, let's close up for today. Unless we hear from one of you, or you from us, let's meet again at four tomorrow afternoon?"

"That sounds good to me, my friend. We meet again tomorrow," acknowledged Oakley. "Let us know how the food is over there across the road."

"Will do," replied Strong. "Right now we should check out from our cottage at Sandy Shore and bring our stuff over here."

The detectives drove to their unit at Sandy Shore, put their belongings into the Camry, and proceeded to the office to check out. Eisie was at the desk and was surprised to see them. In her alluring sing-song type voice she asked," Are you gentlemen leaving me?"

"I'm afraid we are moving on," said Strong. We have rented *Enchanted*."

"That's a lovely place I hear. Maybe sometime you can show it to me?"

"Well, how can we turn down an invitation like that guv?" asked a smiling Bill Strong. "Can we call you here? Maybe we'll have lunch at Hibiscus and then bring you over for a drink."

"I'd love to do something like that so call sometime for sure. Don't worry about paying now for your cottage. Just sign and we will send the bill to Governor Neily."

"You're too sweet for words," said Strong, "and call me Bill, now that business is over."

Eisie smiled. "Yes, I'll do that."

The men waved a goodbye, and drove off wondering what had just happened. They were sure they would follow up, especially Detective Strong.

Chapter 8 | Investigations Begin

Cole and Strong returned to *Enchanted* and decided to have a swim before taking up the offer of a free meal. The sea was calm and the sun was setting right at water level where the green flash can be seen. They had heard about the green flash, so they immersed themselves to chin depth, kept their eyes on the setting sun, then at the nanosecond when the sun disappeared, the flash occurred.

"Did you see that guv?" Strong said.

"Sure I did. But I also saw the Four Tops in the distance. That place is on my nerves."

"Hey, we'll get around to that place soon enough. Let's get dressed and see what Mr. Webber has for us."

The men dressed in their civvies and headed for the restaurant. They crossed the road, and noticed two vehicles parked in front of the restaurant. They heard a pinball machine banging noisily and loud reggae music coming from somewhere. Once inside they saw four young black men smoking and talking loudly in the small lounge area. There were only two customers in the dining room that could accommodate between fifty and sixty patrons. Webber was in the kitchen preparing a pizza.

Strong approached Webber and said, "Is that for us?" Cole was laughing.

"Not this one," said Webber. "I plan to make a *Super Hibiscus* for you men. Sure glad to see you so you can see first- hand the trash that I have to put up with. Tough to do business with those creeps around but they threatened to bust up my place if I complained to the P.I.Police."

"I'm sure Bill and I can change that," said Curt. "As we eat, fill us in on some details about those guys."

"Will do," replied Gart. "Give me twenty minutes to make you a *Super*"

The Super pizza was served, along with a salad, and a glass of imported Italian red. Cole and Strong were impressed with the food. During the meal Gart sat with them and related what had been happening.

"The four bad actors in the lounge are drug pushers," he said. "Sit here for a while and you'll see other people pop in and out without buying anything from the bar. They come to buy ganja."

"Should be an easy bust for us," claimed Cole. "Who knows whatever else this crowd can lead us to. We'll come back in a few days so they don't get nervous about you talking to a couple of Brits. I'll have a couple of other guys drop in as well. They have lots of experience at busting drug deals. By the way, do those ganja dealers carry any kind of weapon?"

"I've seen a couple of them flashing knives," said Gart. "Don't kid yourselves, this is a rough crowd."

"We'll be careful." Bill said smiling, while thinking, '*Gart has no idea of what we've experienced*'.

The men exchanged pleasantries while they enjoyed a Courvoisier brandy.

"This has been great Gart," exclaimed Curt, "but it's time to go. Do you have the second key?"

"Damn near forgot eh?" Gart reached into his pocket and said, "Here it is." He handed Curt the key.

"Until next time Gart," Bill said. "We're out of here - big day tomorrow."

The two detectives walked across the road to *Enchanted* and were glad to find the place just the way they had left it. It was getting late. Jet lag was becoming a factor, but they still had to organize a plan for the next day.

"One thing you'll have to do, Bill, is find out who cleans this place. We should check with the governor, and with Gart. Sure don't need criminal associates getting free info from our files here. However, I need both of us at WB's headquarters while reviewing the homicide files."

"I can do that after lunch when you assess our findings and start a report," Bill replied.

"Good enough, I'm hitting the sack. See you in the morning," Curt said, as he disappeared into his bedroom.

•   •   •

The morning sun was rising over the beautiful, blue Caribbean Sea, when Curt Cole opened the curtains of his room. A couple walking along the beach were obviously enjoying the stroll. The woman had a nice tan and presented a body ready for The Playboy Mansion. The man was tanned and well- built with no signs that he was eating too many calories. Curt thought: '*How could crime happen in this utopian place? Enough day-dreaming I have lots of work to do.*'

Before Cole jumped into the shower he shouted to Strong, "Hey, Bill, get your ass moving."

He heard his partner reply, "I've already been into the sea, while you were still getting your much needed beauty sleep. I'm ready for action."

Cole hurried and got dressed. Both men wore civilian clothes. The closest place to get something to eat was the Holiday Place Resort. There they enjoyed fresh Island fruit and their customary English tea. Strong noted that the young male waiter was very friendly and spoke without a local accent.

He mentioned it to Cole saying, "I wonder where he came from. Maybe we should find out and see if he can supply any info as our investigation progresses. He must see all kinds of characters - especially the ones with money."

"Not a bad idea, Bill," said Cole. "Add it to your to do list. But today we have to get going. The Police Headquarters is a few miles away. We'll stop at *Enchanted* and call WB."

The detectives called from their house. Audrey answered the call. "Hello, this is Police Headquarters, Audrey speaking."

"Good morning Ms. Black, this is Detective Cole. Is the Commissioner available? Detective Strong and I would like to come by in a few minutes."

"I was expecting your call detective. Commissioner Black has set up a room for you and placed the files there that he thinks you will want to see. I have the key and George will be here if you need his help."

"Great," replied Cole. "By the way, will Detective Spikel be available today?"

"I don't know for sure, sir. He may have to go to Tampa and do something."

"Okay, we should arrive in about fifteen minutes," Cole said in a very pleasant tone.

The detectives packed their tape recorders and note pads, and proceeded to the police station. When they arrived Audrey smiled a famous Island smile, welcomed them and gave them a key. She said," You can just go ahead up the stairs. The key I gave you is for the second door on your left. You'll find an intercom phone in the room, so, if you need anything, just buzz me."

"Will do," Strong said. The two detectives climbed the stairs and found the room. They opened it and were impressed by the good lighting that was protected by heavy screens. The walls were pale green. A picture of HM Queen Elizabeth II hung on the wall beside the door. Furniture consisted of two eight foot long tables, and two folding chairs. On the far side was a three foot high, by two feet wide window, protected by one-inch steel bars. The intercom was on a small table just inside of the entrance door.

Four cardboard boxes, each marked "CONFIDENTIAL" had been placed under the window. Each box had a label designating which event's information was in the box. Strong carried them over to the table while wondering, *'Why were these left over there and not handy to the tables?'*

"What do you want to start with, guv?" said Bill.

"Let's do the scuba diver file. We don't know how long the DEA guys will be here to help us. Put the stuff on the table."

Strong opened the box. He laughed. "I don't know what you were expecting but if this is the whole file on the incident, we aren't going to be solving this case from these few papers."

"What do you mean - explain?"

Strong dumped the contents of the box in front of Cole. Three legal size file folders fell out. One was labelled *Spikel*, one labelled *Samson Black*, and the other *Personal Details*. There appeared to be only a few papers in each file. He said, "Guv, if this is a file, we need to talk to the clowns that are running this place. No wonder no one gets convicted of a homicide here." He opened the file labelled Samson Black. "Let me read this to you. It's headed up *SCUBA ACCIDENT*."

"Black wrote: On the night of June 20, 1989 two scuba divers were reported dead by Amos Delray, the owner of the dive boat Quicksilver. When questioned by me, Officer Samson Black, Delray, said:"

My dive master Delgada reported the deaths. The two men went down too deep and did not decompress when surfacing. There was nothing I could do as we were too far from the hospital's decompression chamber. I called the police station right away. The bodies were recovered and taken away by the police Crime Scene Division. The deceased men were staying at Swim Away Lodge where they had registered for a ten day stay. I was told by the divers, before leaving, that they were experienced deep divers.

Strong continued reading Black's report: *I determined that it was an accident occurring in the normal type of night diving. There was no sign of physical force. There was no indication that the deceased had been using any alcohol or drugs. There was no reason to involve our forensic detective. I am satisfied that Palm Islands Police Department can close this case. The deceased's belongings will be held in our storage facility until next-of-kin instruct us regarding disposal.*

"That's it?" asked Cole.

"You've heard it all, boss."

"What's in the *PERSONAL* file?"

"Looks like immigration forms, one for a Kenneth Dolby and one for a Bruce West; two airplane tickets for a June 29 departure to Miami; some restaurant receipts; thirty dollars of Canadian money; 0ne-hundred and thirty two US dollars; two American passports; and pictures of … are you sitting down… two pictures of *Four Tops*, and a Swim Away Lodge brochure. Oh, and two boarding passes with baggage checks stuck on them."

"So … there are no photos of family, or dive buddies?" Cole queried as he shifted in his chair.

Strong had seen that move before and knew the boss was not happy. He said, "Nope, none."

"What about the *SPIKEL* folder?"

"I see nothing in there. The folder is empty."

"Unplug the intercom, Bill," ordered Cole.

Strong disconnected the device.

"Okay, now we can talk," said Cole. "The Commissioner will have a few questions to answer. Let's look in the other files before we get too upset. We'll need Spikel too. Which file is next?"

"Let's see. This one is also labelled Constable Samson Black: *CANADI-ANS – HOMICIDE,*" Strong said, as he opened the flaps of the cardboard box. "It too has only three file folders labelled; Beach Investigation; Immigration reports; Personal information. Which one do you want first?"

"Try the Personal Info one."

"Looks like we're getting lucky, there are some papers in it."

The papers consisted of two immigration forms, one for Marie LeClerc and one for Gaston Paquette plus a brochure from the Holiday Place Resort; two return air tickets to Miami for June 29; a picture of the man and woman posing with the waiter at the resort; three pictures taken at a gold conference in Vancouver; an address book: three American Express one-hundred dollar travelers' checks; fifty-five P.I. dollars, and forty US dollars. Inside the folder someone had written: '*Could not locate forwarding address.*'

Strong relayed the info to Cole then blurted, "Who the hell operates a homicide investigation and says they can't find a forwarding address!"

Cole shrugged. He was now convinced that this job was going to be very unpleasant. He stared at the table, then at Strong while trying to contain his emotions.

"Look Bill, we have to stay cool for another day or two. Just these two boxes that we've opened are enough to put us on notice that we won't get much, if any, cooperation from this office. What else is in that box?"

Strong opened the *BEACH INVESTIGATION* folder. "Here's a report form, but again, not signed by Spikel. All it says is: '*We questioned three of the Holiday Place Resort staff and none had any information of value. The coroner reported the cause of death to be head trauma caused probably from blows from heavy steel or wooden items. There are no markings on the bodies of either person that would indicate a physical struggle.*'

"Nice work again I see," said Curt. "What's in the immigration folder?"

"Just the boarding passes issued by PalmAir, and Customs Forms."

"What's the date on those, Bill?"

"June 15, 1989."

"And the date of the death?"

"June 28, 1989. Hey, that's one day before the departure date on the airline ticket!"

"Check the tickets in the Scuba file."

Strong reopened the box, took out the file, and looked at the tickets.

"Son-of-a-bitch," he murmured, "June 29, same as the others."

"Okay, we may be getting somewhere", claimed Cole. "Keep calm and let's take a quick look at the other two boxes."

Strong opened the box referencing the death of the two Islanders. He was not surprised to see three files pertaining to that homicide. One labelled Police Report; one labelled Forensic Report; and the other file labelled Personal Information.

"Where do you want to start, Curt?" asked Bill.

"Look in the Police Report file for the date of the accident. Also the names of who was killed. Don't bother reading the report. We can do that later. Time is running out. I want to leave the station before the Commissioner returns. We want to assess this crap before we do any serious questioning."

"Alright, let's see," as he opened the box labelled *RAND & SCOTT*. "One victim was Karl Rand, and the other, Telford Scott. Both bodies were found on June 24, 1989. Both were white males."

"And the other box?" queried Cole.

Strong set aside the other box and opened the one labelled *DEAD CALVERTIANS*. It had only one file and two sheets of paper. One was a report by Samson Black, and the other by the coroner.

"This is stupid," said Bill. "There's a short report, and a picture of the Calvertians' boat. They are listed as Lyron Malik and Dewain Church. Let's see, here it is June 28, 1989, date of coroner's report. It shows deaths happened late on June 27. Want to hear more, boss?"

"No," replied Cole. "Let's get out of this place. Fix the intercom, but leave the boxes where they are. We have to establish a time line, but I'm sure we can agree that there's some connection between the four incidents. What it could be is for us to find out. Won't be easy and I guess we won't be considering this assignment to be a vacation. We'll be looking over our shoulders from now on."

The men turned off the light, locked the door and were about to proceed to the stairway when apparently out of nowhere, George appeared. He walked towards the detectives saying, "Are you leaving already? Did you find the files? Is there anything you need to take with you?"

Cole thought to himself: '*The asshole knows damn well we found the boxes. A blind man could have found them*.' "No problem George. The contents were quite helpful. We left them on the tables and we'll finish up with our inspection before we meet with the Commissioner. Do you know what time he might be available tomorrow?"

"You should check with Audrey. She should know."

"Thanks George." Strong replied, as he hesitated at the top of the stairwell. "I'll do that."

As they stepped out into the reception area Audrey smiled at them from her desk.

"Everything okay?" she asked, while beaming her Palm Island smile. "Do you need me to arrange any appointments?"

'Yeah, the one between you and me,' Strong thought, as his mind wandered from the task at hand. But, quickly clearing his mind he lied, "We'll call you later on that. Right now, we have to make some personal arrangements for our stay." *'Well maybe it's not a lie,'* he thought, *'I still have to find a housekeeper.'*

Chapter 9 | First Report

They found the Camry where they had left it and drove to *Enchanted*. Strong was driving while Cole was thinking about their visit to headquarters.

"We need a time line here, Bill," Curt said. "It's no coincidence that the homicides all took place within the space of one week. The Yard told us that this island might have one case every three years and that was usually the result of a domestic quarrel. They'll sure wake up when we show them what we've got. This is some kind of international gang warfare by the look of it. We must work closely with Governor Neily to keep our info under wraps while we untangle the mess. That's our only secure communication with London. Meanwhile we can use the Commissioner's system for tidbits to keep them happy. I don't trust anyone in that operation – and you my friend – keep your dick in your pants and don't try to get Audrey into bed. I saw you, and her, trading glances."

"Hey now, guv, she could be a good source of info," Bill said, as he kept his eyes focused on the roadway.

"And a good piece too. I know how you work. Find another honey if you need personal attention."

Strong laughed as he drove along thinking, '*the boss knows me well.*' It took only fifteen minutes to get back to *Enchanted*. Across the street Gart was sweeping off his patio. He waved as they drove by.

"I'm going over to see Gart," Bill said. "He may know who we can trust as a housekeeper."

"Don't take all day," Curt replied. "I'm not in a good mood. We need to locate the DEA boys."

"Fine, fine, fine, boss, I'll do my best." Strong trotted off.

Cole now knew that they had been set up to be tested by Commissioner Black. However, Black had no idea who he was dealing with. Cole's many years of experience, and solved cases, made him wary of every supposed cooperative individual. But he thought, *'This is too simple on the surface. Black has to be involved in a cover-up. But is it voluntary or forced?'*

Strong was gone for only five minutes and came back smiling and carrying two White Stripe beers. He shouted as he opened the door, "I brought you a cold one boss, compliments of Gart." Then sitting down he said, "White Stripe is the beer of the people. It's made in Calvert."

"Thanks, I'd prefer a Heineken "*Greenie*" but take the cap off if I'm supposed to drink it! We are on our own until the boys show up after lunch. Get a report pad."

Strong did as ordered and sat down across from Cole.

"Write this down, Bill," Cole ordered.

Strong began writing:

> *"On Tuesday, November 4, 1980 Detective William Strong and I proceeded to the Palm Island Police Headquarters. We were assigned to a room and began our investigation. P.I Police Commissioner Black and P.I. Forensic Detective Spikel were not available. In the room were four boxes. Each box contained information about a different homicide case. The overview of the cases with names of the deceased persons will be sent by telex from P. I. HQ, to International at Scotland Yard. This confidential report is being faxed from the residence of Governor Neily by using his secure line.*
>
> *We have determined the following time line:*

June 20, 1989 – two Americans die by drowning.
June 24, 1989 – two P.I. residents die in car accident.
June 27, 1989 – two Calvertian fishermen are slaughtered.
June 28, 1989 – two Canadian "tourists" are murdered.

There is no forensic evidence provided for any event. The Forensic Detective is as yet unavailable.
We are proceeding on this assignment on the premise that all of the above-mentioned events are related."

"Let's take this down to the Governor's place and fax it now. Then we can have lunch and relax for a few hours before the DEA guys show up," Cole said.

Strong called the Governor, and briefly told him that they were coming to his residence. They decided not to tell him the reason for the visit, other than that Cole wanted to bring him up to date on their activities. Neily said he'd welcome them, and to come right along.

On arrival at the Governor's Residence they saw Neily at his entrance. He smiled and said, "Hello chaps, I've been waiting to hear how you are doing. Looks like you have a new vehicle. The first one didn't last very long. Come on in."

Neily showed the men into his private soundproof office where he had a secure telex, and fax line to London. Cole got out his short report, and read it to Neily. It was obvious from Neily's expression that he was not expecting the news.

"This is serious material," he said to Cole. "I had no idea. The Yard will sure be shocked not only by the acts perpetrated, but also by the skimpy details available to you. Best we fax it right away, and then we'll have a spot of tea."

Cole handed the paper to Neily who immediately faxed it to London.

"Now there's one more thing, Sir. As you know we are working with two DEA agents, and from what we know already our cases may be intertwined. They know that the law firm of Jones and Keller is involved in washing money through dummy corporations. They unfortunately have no way of penetrating that firm's system. J & K have advertised in the Times of London for a legal assistant. We know of a couple of women who have worked on cases with us, and they'd be perfect for the job. One is Darlene Clark, and the other is Jane Butterworth. We would like you to call the Foreign Office, and request them to get the Yard involved to have both ladies apply for the job. There's little doubt in my mind that one or both would get hired. Once we have someone inside I believe we could take down a major international crime operation."

"That's quite a request detective. I think I would need you at my side when the call is made. Let me set something up, and then get in touch with you so they can get the details first hand. Maybe you should have a DEA person here at the time too."

"I believe it's too early for that." replied Cole. "Those guys are undercover right now, and posing as tourists. Bill and I can explain the situation without involving them right now."

"Fine, as you wish," replied the Governor. "I will make sure we have proper privacy when we make the call. When I get back a comment from The Yard I will call you. In case you don't answer I'll leave a message that that I would like to talk to you soon."

"Sounds good to me," Cole replied with a grin, indicating that he knew the Governor was not taking any chances that locals might overhear the call. "As for the tea, Bill and I would like a rain check. We are going to Hibiscus for lunch then relaxing a bit. We are meeting the US agents at four this afternoon."

"Good-o," said Neily, "Just call. Rest assured that you are welcome here anytime. I want to do anything I can to assist you."

"One more question if you don't mind, Sir." Cole asked, "Tell me about Premier Westwood. He's an elected official. Is that correct?"

Neily answered quickly, "The Premier's position is a lifetime office. He was the first person elected when the Foreign Office washed their hands of local politics. At the time, but not anymore, ex-pats could vote. They easily determined that if a local got elected as Premier the whole place could become a dictatorship. Westwood was very popular with all of the ex-pats and some of the brighter Palm Islanders, so he was convinced to run. Even the Queen sent him a request to run for office. Naturally he is very loyal and trustworthy and I'd hate to see him step down."

"So is he Commissioner Black's boss?"

"That he is, but he tries not to interfere unless I ask him to."

"Thanks," Cole said. "From the look of things so far, you may have to ask him to help."

Cole and Strong shook the Governor's hand and he showed them to the door. As they stepped into the Caribbean heat they noticed a person trimming the driveway hedge. He did not appear to have worked very hard because he was not sweating, nor wearing work style clothing. Cole pointed to the workman and turned to Neily, "Does all of your staff dress as well as that worker?" Cole said quietly.

The Governor looked and replied, "He's not on my staff. He must work for the landscape company. I'll check him out and let you know who he is. Meanwhile enjoy your lunch."

Cole took a hard look at the gardener as Strong drove them out of the Governor's yard. "He's not dark enough to be a Calvertian," Cole told Bill. "It will be interesting to hear what Neily reports to us. I wonder if he was trimming the bushes outside of Neily's private office. There were no windows, but who knows what device he may have used to hear sounds through a wall?"

Bill quipped, "We do get paranoid, boss, but let's get something to eat and enjoy the day. I'm thinking about conch fritters right now."

It was almost one o'clock when they sat down to order at the restaurant. Gart's wife welcomed them and took the order for conch fritters and a cold Greenie each. A half an hour later they were back at *Enchanted* where everything looked okay. They quickly changed into their swim suits and proceeded to soak up some sun and scenery. The ocean was only a few yards away so they were able to dip in and out a few times without losing sight of their house. After sun bathing, both men chose to relax on the patio that was shaded by a canvass roof. Cole read a book he had brought with him, and Strong just gazed at the tourists who were strolling along the beach.

About three, Cole, still lounging on the patio, looked up at his partner and said, "Maybe we should call Oakley to make sure they are coming. I'd expect them to be back at their room by now. If not we can leave a message. Give them a call Bill. The Beach Hotel number is by the phone."

"Will do," Strong replied, and rose to make the call. He found the number where Cole had placed it and dialed.

The phone rang three times then Strong heard a female voice say, "Hello - Beach Hotel - this is Greta, how may I help you?"

"I'm trying to reach Mr. Tom Oakley in room 114."

"Yes, one moment please." Greta came back on the line. "There's no answer from room 114. Would you like to leave a message?"

"Yes," replied Strong. "Tell Mr. Oakley that this is Curt, and I'll have cold beer waiting at 4 o'clock."

"I will leave him a message sir. Does he know where to meet you?"

"Yes. We made arrangements yesterday. Maybe you should tell him to call ahead. Thanks, Greta." Strong hung up, his cynical mind thinking, 'Strange she should ask where. It seems like the boss is not the only paranoid person.'

Returning to Cole on the patio, Strong said, "I had to leave a message. I asked the Hotel clerk to also note that Oakley should call ahead."

By four they were relaxed and ready for the meeting with Oakley and Patton, but no phone call and no men. By four-thirty they started to worry.

"I know Americans think the world runs on their time, but unless something has changed we all use the same clock." said Cole. "Who knows, maybe they set their watches when they were in Hawaii."

The two British detectives used the extra time to talk about the information they already knew, and what they felt was being held back. The delay turned out to be helpful, and the two definitely had the same feeling about the P.I. Police Commissioner, and his loyal men and women.

Chapter 10 | Dive Shop Tour

Palm Dive was owned and operated by sixty year old Amos Delray. He was white, having been born in Grand Palm by white immigrants from Canada. At age sixteen he became a seaman. By age thirty he had saved enough money to buy a boat, and he offered dive and fishing trips. It took him five years to build up his business, Palm Dive, to the point where he owned the property and buildings right on the sea shore close to the main harbor. Some locals wondered how he could have taken in enough money to achieve his success, but there was no question that he knew the sea and how to exploit it. The property alone was probably worth three hundred thousand dollars, or more.

Palm Dive was a short five minute drive from The Beach Hotel, so Oakley and Patton decided to visit it first. They arrived without any traffic problem, and parked in a space marked 'Visitor Parking'. No sooner had they parked, than a swarthy looking man approached them. He greeted them. "Hello, welcome to Palm Dive," he said. "Are you divers, or are you looking to do some fishing? I'm Amos Delray. This is my place."

"Boy", Tom said to Willie, "how lucky can we get?" He turned to face Amos saying "We heard you are a hard man to find because you run the big boat yourself and it's always busy. Yes, we are divers and our friend, the owner of Key Largo's, Dive or Die, told us to look you up. Do you know him – Bill Smart?"

"Sure do," replied Amos. "We met when both of us worked for International Shipping out of Miami. If he sent you, you must know something about diving as he wouldn't send me a couple of rookies. C'mon into the shop and we can talk business."

They proceeded into the shop and sat down at a round table. Oakley quizzed him about fees and other costs. Delray offered Oakley a brochure which outlined his services and the cost of each. He had three boats and they covered different dive offerings that were related to the customers' skills and experiences. To dive the wall, the boat Quicksilver had to be used, as that dive was extremely dangerous, and Quicksilver carried the latest prevention and rescue equipment.

The Palm Wall was world renowned as a premier dive spot. It was only a half mile off of the east coast of the Island where the sea bottom dropped straight down about five thousand feet. Divers could descend to around two hundred feet where there was hardly any current, and a person could inspect the coral and strange creatures that inhabited the ocean at that depth. Unfortunately some divers did not ascend slowly enough and had to be rushed to the decompression chamber at the Palm Island Hospital. Over the time space of fifteen years, only two divers had died. The Tourism Department of the Palm Island Government advertised 'The Wall' in their American media commercials, but no mention was ever made of lost divers.

Oakley asked Delray, "May I call you Amos?"

"Of course," Amos replied. "Do you mind if I call you guys Tom and Willie?"

"Sure, we'd like that," said Tom. "We just arrived last night and are driving around to check out the dive operations. Boy this is a first class shop."

"Business is good and getting better all the time. We had a setback a while back when two men died on a night dive. I think they had been drinking or doing drugs in the evening before they went out on Quicksilver. I'm sure you know that's a no-no. I really don't like to talk about it. Would you like to book a trip - say to the sunken ship or Coral Reef?"

"Not today," replied Tom, "but we'll come back when we've had time to check out our options. We'd like to do a night dive so what arrangements would be necessary?"

Amos replied, "Do you want me to arrange for four other divers to go as well. It is expensive to run the 48 foot Quicksilver. I could mark you two down, and call when I know there is another four or more who want to go. Where are you staying?"

"Beach Hotel, room 114, you can leave messages there."

"Do you captain the boat for the dives at night?" asked Oakley.

"Very seldom," Amos said as he pointed to a man on the dock. "Tony Delgada over there is my night dive captain. He has been with me for three years now."

"Okay, good," Oakley said, as he waved at Delgada. Delgada waved back.

"Willie what do you think?" asked Tom.

"I think we were lucky to find Amos here. We can pay whatever it might cost so no need to put us on a list. We will get back to you when we finalize our activities." He lied, saying, "I also think we should get going if we are to do our tour and get back in time to call our wives."

"You see, Amos, my partner keeps track of things and he's right. We'll be off now, and it sure was great to meet you," said Tom.

They shook hands with Amos and he walked with them to their Jeep. Oakley and Patton got into the Jeep and drove off toward the town of South Shore. As they pulled away they felt that Amos' dive business was a first class operation. They had no idea of the information that Cole had garnered during his stop at police HQ.

Oakley was driving and he looked over at Patton while saying, "It's almost lunch time. Maybe we should get a bite to eat here in Kingtown, before moving on to the Clear and Deep operation. It will take us about twenty minutes to get there."

Patton looked at Oakley and said, "We could try 'Mama's' in Kingtown, but I saw an ad for Clear & Deep Dive in the magazine at our resort. It showed a picture of their neat Tiki Bar that is open from noon until eleven at night. The house specialty is their 'Super Grouper Sandwich'. If it is as good as the ad made it look, and if the report is accurate, it should be a mouth- watering experience."

"That would make sense," said Oakley. "Maybe some guests will be there and, we could chum them up, and get the lowdown on the operation before we question the owner. Did the magazine indicate who owns the place?"

"Yes, but I forget. It is something like Biden, or Bister. Don't take that as gospel, Tom."

They passed through Kingtown quite easily as no cruise ships were scheduled for that day. They remembered some of the landscape because they had travelled over it on the way to the Seaview Grill. It seemed that there were a lot of locals walking the roadway, and many did not watch out for the traffic. Oakley swerved to miss an old man and a couple of dogs that were with him. Wild dogs were a nuisance on Palm Island as they roamed everywhere. The Tourism Department was aware of the problem, but had not taken any initiative to deal with it.

"Hope we don't kill someone's pet," said Tom.

"You'll probably get an award if you do," chuckled Willie. "Hey, slow down, I see the sign."

"Good thing you saw it, Willie. I would have gone past the place. My head was back in Palm Dive mode. That Delgada guy, I think I know the name from somewhere."

Oakley wheeled the Jeep into the Clear & Deep property and parked near the Tiki Bar. Several bathing suit clad customers were standing at the bar, and they all looked like tourists. A few had brown tans that indicated they probably had been on the Island for at least a few days.

Willie quickly surveyed the scene and said to Tom, "Hey, do you think those bikinis could be any skimpier? Maybe I should ask one of those ladies?"

"I suggest you just keep our job in mind," replied Tom. "It's not like there's nothing to see in Miami."

"Okay, I'll try, but it's different when you are in a place like this," said Willie. The men walked over to the bar as a few of the patrons looked them over. Tom pulled up a stool as did Patton.

"You guys tourists? Are you divers?" asked one of the men.

"Yes," replied Willie. "We're down here for a week or so. We stay at The Beach Hotel and are checking out the dive ops here on Palm. Do you dive? By the way, my name is Willie, and this is my pal Tom."

"My name is Serge, and these are my friends from Montreal. We have been coming to Deep & Clear for the last three years. Let me buy you two a beer."

"We could go for that, aye, Tom?"

Tom smiled and nodded saying, "Glad to meet you Serge, thanks for the beer."

Then he said, "Willie, order us a couple of those world famous grilled super grouper sandwiches while I chat with Serge."

Willie immediately headed to find a waitress.

Oakley said to Serge, "You must know where the best places are to dive. What can you tell me?"

Serge smiled saying, "Well, I think I've tried them all. I'd suggest you start at the harbor then maybe go to the sunken ship area that is about a quarter mile off shore on the west side. I tried The Wall once and that takes the cake. You just have to be really careful to not go down too far. When you are down there it's silent, and the beauty is so captivating, you just forget where you are. There is hardly any tide or currents. I did a couple of night dives near the harbor, but a night dive at The Wall is too scary for me. Just this year a couple of divers killed themselves trying to night dive The Wall."

"Thanks," Oakley replied. "Maybe we could join your group sometime for a dive. Give me a call at The Beach Hotel if you line one up."

Serge said, "Sure. I'll get your hotel number from our desk clerk. We could be diving tomorrow if the weather cooperates. I hear a Nor'Wester could blow in so how about later today, Tom?"

"'Wish we could but we promised to meet some friends at four. Hopefully there will be another chance before you leave."

Oakley saw Willie approaching from the kitchen area. He was carrying a tray loaded with two big sandwiches, chips, and condiments. He wore a big grin of accomplishment as he walked up to their stools at the bar. He chuckled, "Hey Tom, did I find the place, or did I find the place, partner. Look at the thickness of these filets. Sure beats the reef fish that we are used to!"

"Where in the heck did those come from?" Tom asked.

Willie replied, "The cook told me that there is a big fishing boat named Ocean Princess that arrives every three weeks or so, from Belize. It's a freezer boat, so as soon as the grouper are caught they are filleted and flash frozen right at sea. They catch them in the deep water between here and Belize. The hotel has to buy by the twenty-pound box, as they don't sell any other way. The boat's destination is Tampa. However, there is enough business here to warrant a stop. Also the crew comes ashore to stretch their sea legs and do personal shopping. He told me that they stop over by Rocky Palm, but he doesn't know why. He thinks maybe they dump their offal there. I asked him when he expects another visit and he said there should be another delivery soon. Nice guy. He sure cooked us up a couple of the best."

They enjoyed their sandwiches, and exchanged more pleasantries with the folks from Montreal. Then Tom asked Serge, "What is the owner's name here?"

"Art Bodder," said Serge. "He's a good operator in my opinion. No nonsense at night, even though locals come to the bar here. I hear the South Shore residents are pretty religious and well-mannered. We haven't had a problem in all the times we've come here. You can usually find Art in his office down at the dock."

"Sure appreciate your info, Serge," Tom replied. "Willie and I will mosey down there and try to find him."

"This stop has turned out pretty well, Willie," Tom said, as they walked down the fifty foot slope to the dock. "Nice looking Bertam cruiser over there. That would get you places in a hurry. Neat name eh?" The name, FISH FOR FUN, was painted on the transom. Two heavy duty rods with reels were in place and ready for use.

Willie was in the lead and spotted the sign, OFFICE. He walked up, and rapped a couple of times then heard a deep voice say, "C'mon in, but close the door behind you."

Once inside, Willie and Tom were impressed by the clean and organized interior. Dive and fishing gear were on one side of the room that Tom thought was probably 20 feet long by 25 feet wide. The wall behind him was covered by photos of divers, and fishermen, and women displaying their trophies. Coral, lobster, grouper, snapper and other fish were displayed before the tanned and smiling tourists. Above the photos was a fifteen foot marlin. Art Bodder appeared in almost every snapshot.

The 'voice' was not looking at the doorway when they entered. "Hang with me for a minute or so," said the voice. "I'm trying to make a schedule."

"We can wait," said Tom. "We're just checking."

After a long minute or so the man turned to the agents. "Thanks for waiting," he said. "I'm not getting any younger so I have a one track mind. What's up? How can I help you? My name is Art Bodder and I own this place. I started out with just a dive operation, but now I have fifteen rooms and four vessels not to mention the bar and dining operations. You can build up a business here because you don't pay income taxes."

"Well, we're just a couple of dive fanatics from Florida. My name is Tom and this here is my pal Willie. We drove over from The Beach Hotel because Willie found an article and read about your famous super grouper sandwich. We each just finished eating one and the advertisement was an understatement if anything. Since we are here, tell us what we need to know about how you operate. Like, could just the two of us go out?"

"Oh sure," Art said "if you want to pay the price. To run the vessel costs three hundred dollars which is split among the number of divers on board. We can accommodate eight divers aboard so it's pretty reasonable at just over thirty dollars each. But it's up to you if you guys want to be alone. I don't run the boat anymore but I hire only experience Palm Islanders. They have a fifth sense out there, and I've never had any bad experiences reported. Not like one of my competitors who lost two divers not too long ago."

"What happened?" asked Tom.

"I don't really know for sure, but the two went for a night dive at The Wall. Have you heard or read about The Wall?"

"Yes," replied Tom. "It's one of the reasons we came to Palm to dive. I guess accidents happen no matter how skilled you are."

"I have a friend who is the forensic detective for our police department. He told me that he was directed to simply write a report for the Commissioner without spending any time on what might have caused the two to die. I shouldn't say this, but the police department is run by a Commissioner who doesn't like criticism, and he has relatives working in all departments. My friend and I sometimes take the Bertam out to relax and talk about things. It's the only real way to get any privacy. Don't know why I'm telling this to a couple of strangers, but it's really starting to get to me. Just be careful if you engage any police officers."

Tom raised his eyebrows and replied, "You can count on it, Art. We had some experience with greedy cops on a trip to Mexico. We had to pay three hundred dollars for a speeding fine where there was no speed limit posted! We appreciate the heads-up."

Willie had observed the two men as they talked. He thought '*Art must be sending us a signal. We had better contact Spikel.*' Turning to face Tom, he said, "I don't want to rush you pal, but we are supposed to meet those guys we met yesterday. I wouldn't want to miss out on the free dinner. We still have to go to Lonely Cay unless you want to do it tomorrow."

"You're right Willie," he said then turned to Art saying, "Thanks for your time Art. We will be in touch, so all the best."

They walked back up the slope, waved at Serge, and got into the Jeep. "You drive, Willie, and this time I'll be the guide. Turn right at the road, and it looks like we have about a mile before we turn left on Stillwater Road. We should get to the place called Billy Bob's Dive at around two, or two fifteen. It will have to be a short visit if we are to make it to *Enchanted* by four."

Willie stepped on the accelerator, and hoped there were no more dogs or people to get in their way. His hopes were realized and he made the left turn onto Stillwater Road. The surface was made from crushed coral and shell and the road was barely thirty feet wide, bordered by four foot ditches, and about a two foot shoulder.

"Hang on, boss," Willie shouted over the noise of the Jeep tires. Then he said, "I got the feeling that Art is really on edge about the Commissioner of Police and his hand -picked crew. Did you pick up any vibes?"

"Well, now that you mention it, his demeanor did change when he brought up the issue. Funny how you picked up on that, but it's not the first time you saw the smoke before we got into the fire. And telling us that he and Spikel needed to get out to sea for a private talk definitely points to him testing us, as well as a cry for help. The Brits are going to need to hear the story."

The Jeep careened from side to side as Willie juiced it, and he had to concentrate every minute to keep it on the road at fifty miles an hour. Adding to his concern was the fact that the speed was displayed in metric, plus he also had to drive on the left side of the road. "Damn," Willie cursed. "I wish we hadn't told Strong we'd meet him so early. I don't have his number to contact him. We sure as hell will have a tough time meeting as planned, but such is life."

They discussed some ideas about what they had seen so far that day and it seemed like only a few minutes passed before Willie saw the main road along the other coast, and a weather- beaten wood sign labelled 'Lonely Key Road'. Nailed to the sign post were half a dozen signs pointing westward including one for Billy Bob's Dive.

"Almost there boss," said Willie. "Keep your eyes peeled. If that sign is any indication Billy Bob does not have a degree in marketing."

"Whoa, slow down man. If you want me to see something it's not going to happen at this speed." Willie slowed down to about thirty miles an hour. They noticed that there were many side roads, and driveways, leading to the seaside.

"Crap, boss, this is some kind of a maze. We're losing time. I guess for sure we won't make a four o'clock meeting."

"My guess is that Billy Bob's is at the end of this road," said Tom. "Keep going. It's not more than a mile now."

They proceeded about one mile before Willie said, "Well wadya know, I see the sign and it's a pretty professional one at that." It was carved from wood and pained in blue and yellow with a slogan embossed *WE STRIVE to GIVE the BEST DIVE!*

"Okay. Let's find Billy Bob and get to work," Tom said.

They drove up to a building with an OFFICE sign above the only door. Tom got out. There did not appear to be any activity outside of the building. About forty feet away there was a dock with two boats tied to it and a large thirty-three foot boat moored about one hundred feet away. There was no one working dockside. Tom tried the office door, but it was locked. He looked through the door window and did not see any movement.

Willie had stayed in the Jeep. Tom shouted to him, "Honk the horn. There has to be someone out here." Willie leaned on the horn and it blasted a noise that could be heard a mile away. Not a person or animal stirred. "Lean on it again," Tom shouted. "And stay on it!" Willie did as ordered. The noise was ingratiating in the silence of the environment. "Holy cow, Tom," he shouted, "this should wake up the whole Island!"

Then, just as Tom was about to give up, a man appeared out on the thirty-three footer. He was wearing shorts and nothing else. His hair was tied back and fell to mid-shoulder. He was tanned and bare foot. He shouted, "What the hell are you trying to do? I'm not deaf."

Tom replied loudly, "We want to talk about a dive. Who are you?"

"I'm Billy Bob. Wait until I get ashore. I own this god-forsaken operation."

Tom waved a high sign then turned to wave Willie to get out of the Jeep. Willie did as asked.

"This is not what I expected," he said to Willie. "We could be on a wild goose chase."

"I'm as surprised as you Tom, but from what I read this operation is the oldest one on Palm Island. Perhaps there were some details left out of the story?"

Billy Bob tossed an inflated tender boat into the water and laddered down into it. He paddled to the dock, climbed out, hauled his craft up onto the dock then walked up to meet his intruders. As he approached, Tom walked a few steps forward saying, "Hi! That's a neat looking boat you have. My name is Tom and this here is my buddy Willie. We just arrived here yesterday and wanted to check out the dive operations. We dive over in Key West."

"Well ya probably came a long way for nuttin 'cause this is more of a fishin business than a dive business. I take out divers that have been customers for a long time but no deep divin. I make a better livin fishin. If yuze just want to dive for tourist sites there's more on the udder side of Palm. I'm the best for shallow stuff and picture takin. I can make a lot more money fishin and that's why I bot this here Cape Islander vessel. These are used up in Novy Scoshy, Canader and ther called Cape Islanders." He pointed and said," She's named Nancy Mae, see ther. I was gonna change it to Sweet Sue, but Nancy Mae could be a southern sweetheart, too. She makes haulin in the biggies real easy. I live on 'er. I saw an ad that some guy had a fishin bizznis and wanted to get rid of 'er cheap. He brought it down to Tamper and I sailed er ere. Ya see it's wide and only a few feet draft so makes haulin in them big wahoos and tuna pretty easy. I was raised in Looziana and fished from the time I could walk. When I came ere it was easier to get divers to make a livin, but I only had those two udder boats ya see there. Now I sell all I catch to them big shot restrants fer rilly good cash. I'd do even better if them cheaters from Calvert wud stay home. They come over in ther little boats and take a bunch of our fish. Ha! A couple of them got murdered a few months ago, but I think thet they wer doin more than fishin. Sellin ganja is good business, too, but I don't play that game. I puff it, but fishin's my game. Those scum didn't get murdered 'cause they cot some wahoos. So after all that - whadya want to do?"

"My God, man, what an introduction" exclaimed Tom - right to the point. I like that. Let me ask you this, how about taking us on one of your fishing trips? We can dive on the other side of Palm. How much would it cost us, and when do you fish?"

"I don't do guests very often, but yuze guys look pretty healthy. The odd time I wished I had some muscle on board cuz the big babies are too much for me now. Yuze ever fished deep water? Key West isn't known for the tuna and wahoos. I get deep snapper and grouper, too, and you need muscle to git those suckers into the boat. If yuze are available on Saturday we could go. Really big stuff is swimming out at Rocky Palm right now. How about payin $100 each? If the catch is uge, it's free."

"I'll tell you what Billy Bob," said Tom. "Willie and I fished deep in Columbia and Honduras, so you can bet we are on base. Let's say we will take your offer unless something unexpected happens." He lied again, "We are married and we never know when shit happens. If we can, we'll be here. What time Saturday?"

"Git here by eight. Be ready to fish all day."

"Got it, what a trip it will be. Sure glad we woke you up. Okay, Willie?" Tom said, as he turned to address his buddy.

Willie who had been taking in the conversation, nodded, and smiling said. "Let's do it!"

Billy Bob extended his rough, tanned hand, smiled and said, "Git out of here now and let me git back to doin nuttin. This here Cape Islander is ready for a real catch."

Both men turned and gave Billy Bob a wave. They climbed into the Jeep with Willie once again taking the driver's seat. He glanced at the petrol gauge and turned to Tom saying, "Looks like we are going to need fuel, but we should make it to Kingtown. I'd better not speed or we could run out, before we get to town. That means we won't be at *Enchanted* at four o'clock. We'll be lucky to make it by six. All we need now is a flat tire and we'll really be screwed. That's sure to piss off the Brits."

"Carry on man," said Tom. "Nothing we can do about it. Start the damn engine and get going."

Willie did as ordered and began the drive back to The Beach Hotel.

Chapter 11 | Meet Fingers

By five-thirty Cole was feeling very uneasy. Even the magnificent sunset, visible from the great room, did not calm him down. Again, his years on the force in England had made him into a robot of sorts. There had been instances when meeting plans went awry, and turned out to be new murder cases. It was second nature for him to suspect that the DEA detectives were in some sort of trouble. He paced back and forth several times hardly noticing the beautiful scene developing outside. At five forty-five he sat down at the meeting table and said to Strong, "What do you think? Should we take off and try to find them? We know they were driving a Jeep and we didn't see another Jeep while we were driving."

Strong moved from the kitchen to sit down across from his boss, pulled up a chair and said, "It's not kosher, boss. Those guys are professionals. Something's wrong, but it could be that they stumbled onto a track and had to pursue it. Let's sit tight until six. That's only fifteen minutes and if they don't call, or show up here, I guess we will be out looking for them. I just made a pot of tea, so let me get you a cup."

"Okay, we can wait. Tea sounds good."

Bill poured for both of them. They waited. Their minds recalled instances not too different than what they were now experiencing.

At exactly six o'clock the two men were surprised by the sound of a honking horn in the driveway. Hastily they went to the door, carefully opened it, and saw the Jeep. A mixture of relief and anger raced through Cole as he shouted, "Where the hell have you been. You've worried the crap out of me, and Bill. I hope you have a good explanation."

"Take it easy ole boy," Oakley relied with a jocular tone. "We've been working. You will be glad we took our time, but yes, thanks for your concern. Do you guys want to do business now or should we go to Hibiscus and get something to eat?"

"I'm for that," Strong chimed in. " but you can't show up with us, over there. The owner tells us that some local bad dudes peddle ganja there. He was told that if he complained to the cops they'd bust up the place. You guys could do a sting job while you are incognito. Who knows whatever else they may divulge."

'Wow, man," Tom said, "that could be a real break for us. They have to be getting the weed from some source. Why don't Willie and I go there and get cozy with them?"

"Not yet," Willie interjected. "It's too soon for that. We have to set up a show where we are buying, and Bill and Curt see the hit go down. Willie and I will drop in and maybe we'll be lucky and be able to observe those guys in action. We won't even tell Webber who we are. We can just have a couple of beers. You guys wait here and we'll get the food. We'd better drive over in case the dudes are there now, and it would blow the plan if they see us simply walk over, then back to this place. We can go out of here on the beach side and walk around to our Jeep."

"I agree," said Curt. "It's six-thirty now. Don't be too long, I'm starving."

"Good," replied Oakley. "Just let Willie and I operate. We want to get in as deep as we can with these dealers."

·   ·   ·

Oakley and Patton got up from the table and exited the house on the beach side. They walked around to the Jeep. Patton had the key so he got into the driver's seat and Oakley sat in the passenger seat. Willie started the vehicle and drove around the circular driveway then out onto Bay Road. They drove north about a half mile then pulled into a resident's driveway to get turned around. They proceeded to the Hibiscus parking lot, disembarked and walked into the place.

Webber greeted them saying, "Good evening. Are you here for dinner?"

"No, but we've heard you have great food. We just felt like having a couple of beers. Is the bar open?"

"Sure follow me, I'll tell Watson my bartender to look after you."

They entered the dimly lighted lounge area that was about twenty-five feet wide and thirty-five feet long. There was bench seating around two walls and cocktail tables in front. The far corner had a table and four canvas captain chairs for seating. That corner had no direct lighting, and was obviously set up for secretive meetings. A bar with eight stools separated the sitting area from the kitchen. The ceiling was decorated by real palm branches to give the effect of a thatched hut. Lighting was provided by Malibu lights so the ambience was very touristy.

Webber showed the men into the lounge, and Watson, standing behind the bar, greeted them. Four black men were sitting at the bar so Webber seated the detectives at the corner table. "How's this?" asked Webber.

"That's just great," replied Willie.

"Okay. If you need food, Watson will take your order. Thanks for dropping in." Webber left.

Watson hailed them from the far side of the bar asking, "What will it be?"

"A couple of cold Buds," said Willie. "None of that warm stuff the Brits drink. I can grab them. Don't bother coming around."

As Willie approached the bar one of the black customers greeted him saying, "Wuz up mon. Bin here long?"

"Just yesterday," Willie replied, while paying little attention to the man and taking the cold beers back to the table.

The black man shifted around to face the DEA men and said, "In case you need anything, like to have a good time, you kin find me 'ere. My name is Joey Black, but my handle is Fingers."

"I think I know what you mean." Tom said. "Friends in Miami told me I could buy Jamaican tobacco here. Maybe in a couple of days, but we're concentrating on diving right now. Are you here often?"

"Most evenins," replied Fingers, as he turned back to face the bartender saying, "What time them's wimen comin? I need supply."

"Should be here now," replied the bartender. "That's all I know. Should we go out back and check on them?"

"Me, and you, Watson, let's go."

"Interesting conversation, Willie," murmured Tom, as they watched the two men leave.

Willie nodded and started talking in a louder voice about the dive operations they had visited. He could tell that Fingers' friends were listening, and he suspected they would butt in at some point. He was right.

"You guys want to know the best dive people?" said a voice from the bar stool.

Tom looked to see a stocky man about five- foot ten. "Sure," said Tom. "What can you tell us? Are you a dive hand?"

"I used to be, but Fingers hired me for his business. This is better. More money workin for him." He continued, "Palm Dive be the best. If you go, tell Marco Delgada that Dorman sent ya."

"Will do, man," Tom replied asking, "where's Watson? We could use another Bud."

"He's with Fingers. I can get you a beer," Dorman said, as he walked to the bar flap that covered the entrance from the seating area.

"I guess you guys all help each other?" claimed Willie. "Nice arrangement, I guess it makes things easy for the owner so he can stay in the restaurant."

"We don't give a crap what he does. He should never have bought this place. But we don't steal from him," Dorman chuckled as he delivered the two beers. "You can pay Watson when he gets back."

"Thanks, what can you tell us about Palm Dive," asked Tom? "You said that guy Delgada is the best."

"Not really," replied Dorman, "but, he helps us and, we send him customers."

Tom noticed the clock on the wall behind the bar. He pointed to it while saying to Willie, "We should think about eating. What do you say that we take a pizza and call it a day?"

"I agree," Willie replied. "I'll find the owner and get it ordered."

Willie headed for the dining area as Tom kept Dorman engaged by asking, "So Delgada helps you, and you help him. Sounds like a good way to do business. Is he from here, or is he an import?"

"He's from Belize or Honduras - maybe - Columbia. He came here about three years ago. People like him. He doesn't talk much so he doesn't piss people off, speaks Spanish too."

"I guess we'll be meeting him so thanks for the info Dorman. We'll let you know how we make out. Glad we could have this chat. You Palm Islanders are living up to your friendly label. Are all of you guys Palmanian?"

Dorman looked toward the other men and said, "Ya, we don't mix with them Calvertians. They try to butt in on our business, so we have ways to keep them out."

Tom smiled an acknowledgement and said. "Enough friend, some info we don't need. Glad you seem to like us."

Dorman grinned.

Willie returned and said, "Let's drink up. Pizza should be here in a few minutes. You guys getting along?"

"Real good I'd say," replied Tom. "Dorman here has been filling me in on a few things." Looking toward Dorman he said to Willie, "If we need any help I'm sure he can help us have a good time."

Dorman smiled, and his buddies turned to indicate agreement.

The agents chatted for a bit and then Gart appeared in the doorway to say, "One *Hibiscus Special* ready to go."

"We're out of here," Tom said to the men at the bar. "We'll be back guys." He and Willie walked toward Gart saying, "How much do we owe? Dorman here got us a second Bud. We have American Express Traveler's Checks and US cash."

"I take both, but prefer cash," replied Gart. "It's a total of twenty-three dollars - eight for the beer and fifteen for the pie."

"Here's twenty five," said Tom. "Buy Dorman a beer."

Webber was expressionless while saying, "I hope to see you again."

The two agents left quickly, and jumped into their Jeep. They were backing out when Fingers and Watson appeared in the parking area. They waved goodbye to them and, the two natives waved back.

"This is going a bit too easily, don't you think, Willie?"

"Sure seems so, but no use getting excited until we get all we want out of those guys."

Tom replied as he pulled out onto Bay Road, "You are right. We've never closed an easy case. Hope the Brits haven't died of hunger. Maybe we should have ordered two pies?"

The DEA men retraced their route and drove back to *Enchanted* feeling very good about their visit to Hibiscus.

Cole and Strong were getting hungry but had used the time to assemble information for Oakley and Patton. The skimpy crime files took priority. The fact that Spikel was absent was noted. Further, Cole felt that the DEA agents would be pleased that the plan to plant a secretary in the Jones & Keller law firm was in motion. '*It could have been a more productive day, but some progress was made,*' thought Cole.

They had waited for over an hour when Cole commented, "Do you think the guys are okay? Maybe they are always late to show?"

Pushing back from the table Bill shrugged his shoulders and replied, "Gart told us there are drug pushers using his bar as a 'drug store' so my guess is that Tom and Willie have something going. I'll give them another fifteen minutes to show. We won't starve."

"Speak for yourself, Bill I'm starving," Curt complained, and added, "so tomorrow we are going shopping for groceries."

As Cole shuffled his note papers into a neat file they heard the scrunch of tires on the crushed marl on the driveway. Strong went to the door and carefully peeked out and saw the Jeep. He also smelled the aroma of the pizza. Opening the door fully he hailed a greeting to Patton and Oakley, "Get that pizza in here before Curt dies of hunger!"

Entering the house Tom said loud enough so Curt could hear, "He might die but it won't be from hunger! Look at the size of this pie. It must weigh ten pounds. Where do I set it down?"

"Right over here, in front of me," Cole chimed in. "We can talk business while we're eating."

The three men pulled up chairs and sat at the large table where Cole was waiting. Cole opened the conversation by saying, "I'll start and you guys can interrupt at any time. Then Tom can take over with his report. So – here's some notes to follow." He handed each man a paper. "We had a lousy visit to Police H.Q. Commissioner Black and Detective Spikel were both absent. The files – as you guys can see from my notes - were pretty useless except that what we did glean from them makes us think all eight deaths are related in some way. Perhaps the dead Calvertians are a separate issue but they coincidentally happened within the same time frame. We used the Governor's secure fax to send the details to The Yard. With his cooperation we also sent the request for an agent to infiltrate the law firm. That's about it. What can you tell us, Tom?"

Patton looked up from the note he was reading, finished a bite of pizza, wiped some sauce form his lips, and said, "I can tell you that this is the best damn pizza I have ever tasted."

Cole was not amused, but Oakley and Strong both smiled and nodded their heads.

Tom continued talking and with a more serious tone in his voice said, "Okay. We had a banner day. We hit all three dive operations. Palm Dive is a slick operation that is owned by a man who is well known to our dive guy in Florida, but we left there with the felling that we were missing something. Palm operates the boat that was used on the night the two divers died. The dive master's name is Tony Delgada. We have to check him out with our people in Miami."

"At Clear & Deep Dive we met some friendly tourists from Montreal, and the owner Art Bodder. We were pleased with what we saw but, damn near fell over when Bodder began talking about the how the police act on Palm. Without any prompting, he claimed that Black and most of his crew are crooked except for Spikel and, so much so, that he and Spikel have to go out on a boat to talk privately."

Interrupting Tom, Cole said, "Now things are adding up. Spikel was probably ordered to stay away from Bill and I until the Commissioner could be in the room with all of us. And you mentioned Montreal, that's where two of the murdered victims were from. We should talk to them. Carry on Tom."

Continuing, Tom said, "We went from there, across the Island to Billy Bob's Dive. That was enjoyable, eh, Willie?"

"For damn sure," Willie said chuckling. "We had a hard time finding the place and when we did locate it we couldn't find a living soul. So we made enough noise to stir up an old geezer who lives on a boat that is moored about one hundred feet from the office. He was surprised to see anyone at that time of day, but got into his dingy and came over to talk. Turns out he'd sooner fish than run dive trips so he bought a specially designed fishing boat, from a guy in Canada. He still has a dive business but says fishing is the way to make money. So - are you ready for this? He's taking us out fishing on Saturday."

"Are you sure you can trust the guy?" asked Curt.

"I'm sure, and both of us are going, so our security won't be a problem. Besides we suspect he's a fountain of knowledge and will likely know something about what happened. He had nothing good to say about the dead Calvertians, and he said they were likely doing more than fishing over here in Palm waters. To top it off, we'll be out at Rocky Palm."

"Anything else?"

"Yes, and this is serious," Tom said. "The reason it took us so long to get the pizza is that we met the drug dealers in Gart's lounge. We ordered beer, and one of the Island dudes right away started talking to us. He said his handle is Fingers, and if we are interested he could get us ganja and women. We said we could be interested but not tonight because we just got here and were looking for a place to dive. Fingers left the lounge with the bartender then another guy who was more muscular, but shorter than Fingers, told us that Palm Dive was the place to go. With the meeting going so well, we ordered another beer. The second guy just went behind the bar and got it for us. He said he didn't give a crap about what Gart might say. We continued our questions about Palm Dive and asked if they knew the dive master Delgada. The stocky guy, Dorman, said Delgada was probably from Columbia, Belize or Honduras. Hey, any one of those addresses can qualify him as a suspect, so we are thinking Delgada is likely involved in the drug business."

The room was quiet for some seconds and all heads were turned toward Curt. He looked straight ahead with a gaze that did not see anything in particular. The three waited silently. Finally Cole stood up, then walked a few paces to his left, turned and looked hard at his compatriots, and said, "We are into a rats nest. Unless we identify a couple of locals who can be trusted we are liable to end up as shark bait over at Four Tops. So here's my thoughts - we know Neily, and Premier Westwood are okay. We can trust Spikel, and Bodder. Gart is for sure with us. The taxi man Harris could help. Tom, you and Willie keep on working the dive operations. Try to find out what happens at sea. Ask dive staff questions about different boats that come to Palm and if any of them seem out of place. Ask about the harbor police and the marine division police. Ask about dive accidents. Bill and I will challenge the Police

Commissioner on the poor work his department seems to perform. We will get Spikel aside for interrogation. We will spend some time talking to bankers and storekeepers. This will take a few days and nights. Tomorrow is Friday the 24TH. We should meet again on Sunday, assess our position, and on Tuesday start picking up suspects for questioning. How's that sound?"

"I'll speak for both Willie and me. It sounds like a plan," replied Tom. "*Enchanted* on Sunday it is."

"Okay, get out of here and only call Gart if there's an emergency. Tell him you'd like a white pizza as a signal that you need help, and where to deliver it, that being where you want us to go. We will do the same. We will tune Gart in, and set him up with our phone numbers."

Tom and Willie immediately gathered their papers, stood up, stretched, and Tom said, "Stay safe guys. We are out of here. Shut the lights off in here before you open the door just in case there's a surprise party waiting for us outside."

Bill turned off the lights and opened the door. He indicated '*all clear*' and then Tom and Willie stepped out, got into the Jeep and drove away.

Bill closed the door, put the lights back on, and said to Curt, "Let's have a snort of that *Pirate's Best* rum."

Curt agreed. Immediately Bill got two small glasses and the rum bottle from the kitchen, poured a couple of ounces into each glass, handed one to his partner and said, "Here's to success!"

The men sipped the tasty treat while complimenting themselves on making progress. Once the glasses were empty they both headed for their rooms, not saying a word, except Curt. As he disappeared into his room he said, "Sleep tight mate".

Chapter 12 | The London Interview

The request for the female help, from Governor Neily to the Foreign Office, on Wednesday, November 22nd, received priority and was immediately forwarded to the New Scotland Yard International Division. Superintendent Gordon Trump was surprised by the notice, but glad that Cole's work was progressing quickly. He opened his copy of the LONDON TIMES and eyeballed the classified *Professional Help Wanted* section. He quickly spotted the display sub section *Admin- Clerical* and there was the ad by International Placement Services Ltd. It was split into two sections. The top section outlined *Essential Functions* and the bottom section - *Skills and Abilities*. He had no doubt that Jane Butterworth was the perfect fit for the assignment. Darlene Clark would have been a good candidate, but she was six months pregnant.

Trump knew that Jane was waiting for an assignment while she was assisting in the Financial Frauds Department. He called down to his counterpart, Corey White, in the FFD, and luckily got connected without any wait time. He heard, "Corey White's office, how may I help?"

Trump replied, "I need to talk to Superintendent White right away. This is Trump in International."

"Yes, Sir, I believe he is in his office. Please hold."

In just a matter of seconds Trump was connected and White said, "What's on your mind old man?"

"Never mind the 'old' part mate. I want to relieve you of Jane Butterworth. Detective Chief Superintendent Curt Cole is in Palm Island and hot on the trail of some major crime syndicate - drugs, money laundering, murders, you know, the whole shebang. He needs to plant into a law firm down there, someone that has experience. Jane did this type of work in Bermuda, you might recall."

"I do, I do recall, Gordon. I can get her on the line if it's really important."

"Yes, get her. I'll wait."

Trump waited about five minutes before he heard Jane's voice.

"Hello there matey. What's bothering you? It's your favourite spy talking."

"Yes, you are a favourite, but put the bull crap aside. I need you right away for a job in the Caribbean."

Jane replied, "My bikini is in my purse. Where's my ticket?"

Trump politely ignored the comment and said, "Can you come over to my office right now. It's not good to tie up the phone line. You know what I mean?"

"Sure," she replied. "I'll be there in thirty minutes."

"Great, I can't wait to show you what I've got lined up. Let me talk to Corey again."

Trump waited mere seconds and Corey was on the line saying, "All okay?"

"Yes, and I owe you one. I really need Jane. Bye!"

• • •

Jane Butterworth, age 36, was an Assistant to the Senior Legal Administrator in the London headquarters of New Scotland Yard. She had joined The Yard twelve years ago when she graduated from Oxford with a Master Degree in Legal Financial Business. During that time she had been in the field and on two occasions she had worked undercover. She was an attractive woman five feet eleven inches tall, firm body and, a thirty-six inch chest to boot. Jane turned many male heads whenever she was in a crowd. Unmarried and with no ties to family obligations she could work anywhere, and no one was involved to complain about the hours she put in at her work.

She arrived at Trump's office within the stated thirty minutes. He greeted her then got right down to business. He outlined the request received from Cole and showed her the ad from *THE TIMES*. She knew Cole, and admired his exceptional work. On one occasion she had to work closely with him and conjured up thoughts of being alone with the handsome brute in a secluded rendezvous.

"Looks like my cup of tea," Jane said. "You might recall that I worked with Cole in Liverpool on the 'Crazy Harry' case. What The Yard thought was just a murder event turned out to also be a big money laundering deal out of Belgium."

"Of course I remember," Trump acknowledged. "That's the main reason you are here right now. Cole was assigned along with a partner, Detective William Strong, to investigate some questionable crimes in Palm Islands. Turns out that they hooked up with the U S Drug Enforcement Agency people, and now it looks like they are onto a major money laundering ring run by known drug cartels. People have been murdered, or as the Palm Island police reported, died of unfortunate circumstances. This is not party time in the sun. We need you to infiltrate a law firm that, according to DEA agents, is the front for the whole scheme. This is a very dangerous assignment and I will let you decide now if you think you can handle it." Trump looked at her and he was not smiling as he awaited Jane's answer.

After a few moments Jane said, "You said you need me. I'm all in. I'll be safe because Cole's in charge. Sign me up."

Trump handed her a paper as he posed the question. "Here's the ad from THE TIMES. Do you think you qualify?"

Jane read it carefully and replied, "I think I do. Now let's find out what the placement agency says, assuming the job is still open. Of course I can't call from here so I'll get back to my place and call them. If I get an appointment I will phone you."

"Good plan and here's the number of my private line," Trump said. He continued to praise her as she left his office.

Jane walked briskly to the flat that was only a few blocks away. Arriving there, she made tea for herself before psyching up to call the agency. Finishing her tea, she dialed and a sweet voice quickly answered, asked for the purpose of her call and then said, "One moment please, I will connect you to Mr. Wilcox the interviewer for that position."

Jane heard the buzz then an aristocratic English accent. "Hello, Johnathan Wilcox speaking."

"Thank you for taking my call Mr. Wilcox. My name is Jane Butterworth and I believe I have the qualifications to fill the position in the Caribbean that your firm has advertised in THE TIMES of LONDON. I would like to make an appointment for an interview. The ad mentioned that you require someone immediately. I am single and can begin at any time."

"That's interesting," said Wilcox. "When might you be able to come to my office?"

"I am available almost anytime tomorrow, Thursday, if that suits your schedule."

There were a few moments of silence then Wilcox replied, "I was checking my book and it looks like I could see you between ten and eleven AM. Could you be here at ten?"

"I can do that," Jane replied. "Is there any special documents or other type of information that you would like me to bring along?"

"Yes. I will need a list of references and a certificate of your final academic year. I assume you have a college degree?"

"I have a Masters' Degree in Legal Financial Business from Oxford."

"Marvelous - I look forward to our meeting. Call if you cannot make the appointment, but I'll say bye, and hope all goes well."

Jane smiled to herself and thought, '*Little does Mr. Wilcox know just how qualified I am. I have to ring Trump.*'

She dialed Trump's private line and before it could ring twice he said, "Hello?"

Then he heard, "Hi, It's me, Jane."

"You weren't kidding, Jane, you do work fast. What happened?"

"I'm on for ten tomorrow morning. Are the reference folks set to go? I'm positive they'll be contacted shortly after I get through. I'm meeting their Chief Interviewer a Johnathan Wilcox."

"Yes. Bill Buck at Brightway Engineering Ltd. is tuned up. You know about Brightway?"

"Of course, it's one of the undercover companies that you guys set up. They helped in the Bermuda affair. You'd better tip off SURETY BANK also. Is Walter Beaufort still our plant there?"

"Yes, Walter is still in gear so use him and Bill Buck as references. Use Darlene as a personal reference. I'll tell her the story and to expect a call at her home. If Wilcox needs more references let me know and I'll set them up."

'If it's raining tomorrow I will need a ride. Otherwise I'll walk. Wait for my call. It's time for this girl to relax. Bye for now.'

Just to tune up her knowledge she decided to go to the nearby library and get a book on how to apply for a job. *'Let's not leave any stone unturned'*, she thought. There were many books to choose from so she chose one titled, 'The Interviewer's Bible – How to Ask Tough Questions.' Jane spent the evening studying the book and getting her thoughts together to prepare for the interview. She watched the BBC for a while then climbed into bed about nine PM. At six AM she was wide awake so she got up and started her physical workout before she made her breakfast. After a shower she dressed for the occasion by wearing a tight white blouse that displayed some cleavage of her ample breasts, navy blue slacks, half- heeled black shoes, and small gold earrings. *'Not bad'* she thought, as she looked at herself in the full length hall mirror. She then turned on the TV to waste the hour before leaving for the interview.

When it was time to leave she looked outside and saw the sky was covered with clouds but it was not raining. *'Perfect weather for a walk.'* she mused, as she exited her building and strolled confidently to her meeting place. After entering the five-story office building she checked the list of tenants that was displayed next to the lifts. It showed International Placement Services Ltd. to be in Suite 306. The lobby was empty of people and a lift door was open. Jane entered, pressed 3, and was swiftly taken to the third floor where she noticed the Suite 306 sign to her right. She opened the office door to see a bright reception area that had many photographs hanging on the walls.

A male receptionist looked up, smiled and said, "Hello Ms. Butterworth, you are very punctual. Welcome to International. Mr. Wilcox will see you shortly."

'How efficient', she thought as she proceeded to walk around the room on the shiny solid oak floor. Just as she came upon a photo of the head office of Jones & Keller in Calvert, a door opened, and a smiling man appeared. She guessed that he was about fifty years old. He was wearing a pin-striped, dou-

ble- breasted suit, a crisp white shirt adorned by diamond and gold cuff links, and a silk, navy blue, tie. His patent leather shoes were shined to the glistening stage. He was clean shaven except for a pencil line mustache.

'*Wow, what an awesome creature,*' she thought, as the palms of her hands began to sweat.

"Miss Jane Butterworth?" he queried. "I am your interviewer. My name is Johnathon Wilcox."

"Yes sir." Jane flashed her countryside smile.

"Come right along," he said while still standing in the doorway to his office. "I am pleased that you could see me on such short notice."

Jane entered his office and Wilcox closed the door. The room was quite large. It had the same shiny solid oak floor as she saw in the reception area. The walls were lined with real mahogany wood, and adorned with large paintings depicting scenes of early London. Wilcox's desktop was also appropriately made of solid mahogany. Behind Wilcox there was a small bookcase with what looked like aged collector's books. Jane like what she saw. Wilcox took up his position behind the desk and beckoned for his guest to sit down. She sat down into a leather arm chair directly across from him.

"When you called you told me that you are a single woman, age 36, and educated at Oxford. Upon graduation you worked briefly at a small accounting firm and then went to make a career at Brightway Engineering Limited. Is that correct?"

"Yes, that is correct."

"Fine, I will ring up your references when you leave, so for now I have some basic questions to ask you."

Jane was not nervous, so far so good. She knew in advance what type of questions to expect, as she had memorized many from studying the library book.

Wilcox started by asking, "What are your weaknesses?"

She answered by minimizing shopping as her main weakness, and emphasized her volunteer work of speech training of new immigrants.

Next came, "Why should we hire you?"

Jane summarized by giving a quick review of her success at Brightway stressing the fact that the whole unit threw a going away party for her when she moved on.

Then Wilcox twisted his chair, stood up and said, "Why do you want to work in the Caribbean?"

Jane smiled and replied, "I made up my mind to work outside of the UK while I'm still young. Calvert, or Palm Islands, excites me. Jones & Keller have an international reputation and I can be of value to that firm as an assistant to one of their solicitors involved with construction and development clients. In my humble opinion, there should be much growth in those areas."

Wilcox approached the side of his desk and said, "You are bang to rights in that idea. I am quite impressed. It seems there is little to be gained by asking you more routine questions. As the advertisement indicated, our client wants to hire as quickly as possible. When could you be ready to leave?"

Jane relaxed as the interview was now going swimmingly. She replied, "I could be ready at your command. I have no responsibilities here other than paying rent for my furnished flat. This is Wednesday, November 22nd and I have to give a week's notice if vacating, but, I'm paid up until the 30th. I could leave tomorrow I guess. Then, looking him squarely in the eyes she said, "We haven't talked terms, Mr. Wilcox. Please tell me what money and benefits are offered."

"Of course, of course," said Wilcox. "In that regard I have one last question – do you speak Spanish?"

"Si senior," Jane replied. "I write the language also." She smiled at him.

"Well, I'm cuffed," he said, as he returned the smile. Here's an offer. Fully paid travel to and from the Island, one month leave after one year, a salary of four thousand US dollars per month with a raise to six thousand a month after a three month trial. That is the maximum I am instructed to offer."

"From what I read, four thousand per month will not pay the freight in those islands. I will need at least five thousand. Can you ring your client and request that?"

"I will certainly be calling them, and I expect they will agree to your request once I tell them about your skills and experience. However, if they turn you down I have several other hire possibilities for you. You can bet on that! This interview is over. Can you get home safely?"

"Yes," Jane said. "I do not have far to walk and I love to get the exercise."

"I will see you to the lifts," and he led the way.

As the lift door opened, Wilcox offered his hand and Jane shook it saying, "Hope we have a deal Sir." She stepped into the lift while once again treating him with her charming smile.

•   •   •

Gordon Trump had remained in his office awaiting Jane's call on his private line. He was not disappointed. The telephone rang and he quickly asked, "Yes?"

"Hi, it's me, Jane."

"Is everything okay?"

"Blinding, for sure! Did you set up my references yet? I expect they will be getting a call anytime now."

"All set," claimed Trump. "You must have had a good session?"

"It could not have been better. I'm ready to go," she said.

"Then I'll double check with my contact at Brightway and the Bank and get back."

"No need to confirm with me," Jane said. "I'll know one way or the other when Wilcox – that's the interviewer's name - calls me."

"You are the bee's knees woman! I love how you operate. I'll stand by. Call me here tomorrow."

"I'll call, and you are a great gaffer, Trump." She hung up laughing to herself.

Chapter 13 | Busy Day

Detective Cole could usually put a day's events behind him and sleep soundly at night. That was not the case after yesterday's meeting with his partner and the Drug Enforcement Agents. There were too many loose ends in this investigation and they were only into it for two days. Racing through his brain was the car explosion; the absence of The Commissioner and Spikel; drug pushers across the street; sighting the strange gardener; Jane Butterworth; and to top it off, the fact that eight people were dead. He knew he had to start somewhere and came to the conclusion that he, and Bill, needed to identify who they could trust.

In his mind the first people who would qualify as trustworthy were Governor Neily and Premier Westwood. Next would be Gart at Hibiscus. Harris the taxi driver seemed OK as did Art Bodder. The identity of the DEA men had to be kept secret at least until Jane Butterworth could infiltrate the Jones & Keller law firm. To top it off he had to find out more about Rocky Palm. He hoped Strong was more relaxed and objective. He rolled over to see the digital clock looking at him. *'Damn,'* he thought, *'it's only four. There's no way I'll get back to sleep.'* That's when he heard a dog bark - then a vicious, bone chilling growl. The room was pitch-black except for the digital clock display. *'Something is wrong. Why is the dog upset? Why is a dog even near the house?'* The drapes were closed tightly so he got up and stood still, listening intently. He knew for sure something wasn't right. The barking and growling seemed to intensify. '*I have to look. Did Bill wake up?*' Stealthily he walked into the main room and then into Bill's room. "Bill, are you awake?" he whispered.

He was glad to hear, "Yes. What do you think all the barking is about?"

"I don't know, but I'm going to put on the yard and patio lights. I think we should stay inside until daybreak. We can look for clues then, but surely someone is, or has been, out there."

"I agree boss," whispered Bill as he followed Cole into the main room. "Not much chance that we'll get back to sleep, but let's stay here in the big room. The chesterfields will be okay for now."

The dogs stopped barking when the lights went on. The men lay down and waited for the sun to rise. Silence prevailed.

Strong actually managed to fall asleep about four-thirty, but Cole phased in and out of sleep. At six they got up and pulled open the ocean-side drapes. The rising sun painted many colors on the clouds that once again seemed to originate at Rocky Palm, then spread across the sky. Again Cole got the eerie feeling. Goose bumps made the hair stand up on his muscular arms. Strong noticed Cole's reaction to the view, but he remained silent on the subject, expecting a comment to come from his boss. He was not disappointed as Cole spoke.

"I know you see me reacting to the cloud display. It looks like we might be in for trouble today, my friend. I hate to sound superstitious, but let's get going. Could be trouble waiting outside." As they cautiously stepped outside onto the driveway they noticed a man in the yard next door. He had two dogs on leashes. He waved at the detectives.

Cole returned the wave and then heard the man shout, "Hello, are you my new neighbors? Come on over."

Cole and Strong beckoned acknowledgment and walked across the yard to meet the man. They saw he was wearing shorts and a tee shirt, no shoes, and beamed a wide smile as they approached. His small dog began to bark while the big dog took a defensive stance and began to growl.

"Stop! Down!" the neighbor commanded. Immediately the dogs sat down and were quiet. Then looking at the men he said, "Hi, I'm Phil Russell, are you moving in next door?"

"For a while I guess," Curt replied. "We're pleased to meet you. I'm Curt Cole and this is my friend Bill Strong. We are renting *Enchanted*."

"Sounds good," Phil acknowledged, then pointing to the two dogs, "Meet my security team – Buster" – and he pointed to the small dog, and Baron, my friendly ninety pound Red Doberman. Buster sounds the alarm and Baron enforces the law. Give them a sniff and a pat on the head."

Cole and Strong obeyed the suggestion.

The dogs accepted Phil's hand command and sniffed the two detectives, took a pat on the head and then they lay down. "There - now you're covered by my B&B system. They will be your friends."

Cole smiled and said, "When we heard the barking and growling last night we didn't know what to think other than some animal, or person, was prowling around."

"Well," Phil said, "there have been a fair number of burglaries along this area of the beach. The police never seem to catch anyone – I guess 'never' is not quite right, but I know of a few arrests that just got tossed out in court because of sloppy police reporting. Anyway, I'm from Boston. Are you both Brits?"

"Yes we are," Strong replied. "This sure seems like a nice island."

"I'll be glad to fill you in on some things to see and do and even what not to do. Drop over when you can."

"Thanks, Phil," acknowledged Curt. "Could we drop over on Sunday? We will bring a pizza or two, and cold beer."

"Sure, I love Hibiscus' pizza. Is that what you have in mind? Don't worry about the beer, I have that covered."

"Hibiscus Special is what we'll bring. We've already had two of Gart's specials and like you, we think they are great. I guess you know the owner is our landlord?"

"Yes, nice guy. Too bad he can't get rid of the hoods that use his bar for their drug business."

Curt ignored the comment and said, "See you on Sunday around one o'-clock. Cheers for now!"

•   •   •

The detectives were pleased by the encounter and felt that, regardless of Curt's premonitions the day had started out well. They talked light-heartily as they crossed the yards and entered their house. They were wide awake and ready to get to work, but it was only about 7AM. Curt looked at his watch, scratched his head then looked over at Bill saying, "Let's try the Holiday Place again. Maybe that young waiter will be working and we can size him up as a contact."

"I'm on for that mate. I'll drive."

They arrived without any problem and got seated by an attractive young female hostess. Strong kept his thoughts to himself. The restaurant had only two customers, giving the men a choice of where to sit. They chose a corner table that offered a full view of the room. Their hopes were realized when the waiter appeared and came to their table.

"Hello gentlemen, nice to see you again," he said.

"Glad to see you too," replied Strong. "Call me Bill, and this is my mate, Curt. What's your name?"

"Teddy Moore," the waiter replied. "Call me Ted. What can I get for you to start?"

"We Brits are tea drinkers, but today let's try some *Jamaican Blue Mountain*."

"I'll be right back. Here are menus for you to look at."

"You do the talking Bill," Curt said. "I'll motion to you if I think we are stretching our luck."

Ted returned with the coffee, a cream jug, and a sugar bowl. As he served he asked, "Are you ready to order?"

Strong looked up at Ted, and asked, "Can we ask you some questions? It's not busy in here right now."

"Sure, what do you want to know?"

"Can you sit down for a minute or two?" Ted seemed a bit nervous as he sat down.

"How long have you worked here, Ted? How old are you?" Bill asked.

"I'm twenty-four and I started here in April of this year. Why?"

"We might have something you can do for us," Bill replied. "Where are you from?"

"Canada," Ted answered.

"You must see all kinds of people passing through Palm?"

Ted answered quickly, "All kinds for sure, especially on my night shift in the bar."

Shifting forward and looking for any signal Cole might give, Bill said, "We are from the British Foreign Office and we are detectives. We need a trusted person to tell us of any suspicious people or activities. You see the big time operators here. They are the ones that flash a lot of cash. Palm Island is becoming a criminal haven from what we know. Alternatively, the ring leaders are usually very quiet, but in charge. They like to have sexy women with them. The small time tax dodgers are just usually getting drunk and having a good time. You know what I mean?"

Ted twitched and cleared his throat. "I see them quite often. Why are you telling me all of this?"

Curt raised a hand, and Strong knew to lay back. Curt said, "We are very good at profiling people – like it is a major part of our job. You strike us as a decent person and the right age to fit our requirement. We need your eyes."

"Well I've never been involved in any criminal activity if that's what you mean. I smoke the odd joint, but only on my day off. I try to be sharp and I get really good tips."

"Can we meet with you later today? You must know of a location that is not too busy."

Ted was silent for a few moments. He looked over to notice two customers being seated by the hostess. He looked back directly at Cole and Strong, and addressed Cole. "Holy cow, are you kidding me?"

"No. We are serious."

"Let me take your order, and serve that other table while I think about it."

Cole spoke for Strong, and himself, and ordered two morning specials with poached eggs. In about ten minutes Ted returned with their meals and a pot of fresh coffee. "Here's your tab," he said as he placed the folded paper on the table. He left quickly.

"Boy, what a change of character," Strong quipped.

"No kidding," replied Cole.

When Cole finished eating he picked up the tab and unfolded it. "What's this?" he questioned aloud. Another piece of paper was folded inside. It had writing on it. He silently read it then handed it to Strong. "Take a read, mate. I believe Ted is more than we bargained for."

Strong quietly read the message aloud. Written on the paper was, '*Gentlemen, the walls have ears. Meet me at the North end of Coconut Park at five o'clock.*'

"Well boss, let's go. Nothing should surprise us now."

Cole paid the tab and they walked directly to their car. Strong decided to drive and suggested to Cole that they should drive north to see the area. As it was still early, Cole agreed. They drove past a mixture of old and new houses all of which were on the ocean side of the road. The other side was under-developed except for a large building with a sign at the road that showed PALM WATER PLANT – NO TRESPASSING. The entrance gate was wide open.

"Want to check out the place?" Strong asked.

"Not now, Bill. We'd better turn back and head for the Police Headquarters."

"You are right, mate, and it wouldn't hurt to be early. Remember we were early when we went to the Cricket Club, and that worked out for sure."

The drive took them through Kingtown. The traffic was heavy. At ten minutes to nine they arrived at their destination. They noticed the Commissioner's Land Rover parked next to the entrance. Only one other vehicle was parked on the lot, a blue Ford Taurus with 'POLICE Unit 10' emblazoned on each door and the rear of it. It had mud splashes on the fenders.

Cole said cynically, "I wonder if Samson Black has been out to Stephen Keith's golf course site to get some C-4? I guess we'll find out if we ask him."

They strode smartly to the entrance, and entered the reception area. Audrey was at the desk. She looked nervous. "Good morning, Audrey," Strong said, in his best friendly tone.

Audrey looked up and curtly said, "Have a seat. Commissioner Black is expecting you. I'll ring him now."

The men walked to an area marked VISITORS and sat down. They glanced at each other to indicate that they both caught the tone of Audrey's voice. Strong noticed a newspaper on the small table next to his seat. He picked it up and was surprised at one of the front page bylines that read *Foreign Office Sends Detectives*. He quickly sighted the date as November 20, 1989. '*Good grief,*' he thought, '*the whole population knows we are here.*' Both of their names were in the article. It also contained a statement from Commissioner Black indicating that he had asked for the assistance. Strong handed the paper to Cole while pointing to the byline.

Cole raised an eyebrow, looked up at Strong and said nothing. He read the story, handed the paper to his partner, and indicated for Strong to place it back on the table. With one eye on Audrey he whispered to Strong, "I'll handle this."

Within seconds the receptionist said, "Please proceed to the Commissioner's office. I believe you know how to get there?"

"Thanks, Audrey," Strong replied. "We know the way."

They retraced their steps from the previous meeting, and were careful to not talk. As they completed the climb on the stairway they saw '*Mr. Slim*' standing at the end of the hallway beside Commissioner Black's door. They waved to him and he waved back. "Good morning George," Cole offered.

"Thank you," George replied, and he opened Commissioner Black's door.

Both men entered. '*That's odd*, Cole wondered. *He's friendly and Audrey is not. Last visit was just the opposite. Why?*'

Black approached them at the door and in a friendly tone said, "I'm sorry I had to be away yesterday. I hope you made out okay." Pointing to two chairs to the right of his desk, Black said, "Have a seat — and meet Detective Spikel."

Spikel was sitting at the left side of Black's desk. He stood up to shake hands with the visitors. He said nothing.

The British detectives sat down where Black had indicated.

"Well, fellows, how is your investigation going?"

Cole spoke, "To tell you the truth, not very well. Before we get into the murder cases what did you find out about our car incident?"

"It seems that you were correct about the C-4," Black replied while looking to his left. "Spikel here ran tests on some car fragments and certified the type of explosive material. Knowing that, I drove out to Keith's project and questioned him. Keith showed surprise at my question and told me that all C-4 is secured in a special compartment in his Supervisor's office. He believes that the C-4 used in the incident could not have come from his supply."

"Did you ask him why he's using C-4 instead of dynamite?"

"No, I did not think of that," Black replied.

Strong was quietly keeping an eye on Spikel as that conversation took place. Spikel was stone-faced but shifted noticeably in his chair when he heard Black's comment.

"Were you alone, or did Mr. Spikel go with you?" Cole asked.

"I went with one of my Deputy, Officer Samson Black, the officer who patrols that area."

"Fine, we will want to talk to him as he will likely know what has been happening out there on a daily basis. Looking at Spikel, Cole said, "Do you have anything to add to the comments you've heard?"

Turning his back to the Commissioner Spikel quickly said, "No Sir," as he gave Cole a determined look that without a doubt meant, *'Of course I do!'*

Cole indicated that he got the message by looking directly into Spikel's eyes saying, "Good, if I need more on this for any reason I'll give you, or the Commissioner, a call. Now, Sir, my partner has some questions relating to our last visit. Go ahead, Bill, and I'll take notes."

Strong did not pussy-foot around. He said," We found that the boxes that were left for us did not contain what we would consider adequate investigative evidence. Did you by any chance have a look into those containers before they were placed in the room assigned to us?"

"Well, no I did not. I never looked into those boxes. I simply gave papers and reports to George and told him to box them. Was there something missing?"

"To put it bluntly, sir, forensic reports were missing. Witness interviews were missing. Contact information was missing. We don't want to jump to conclusions but could these boxes have been tampered with?"

Black was visibly shaken by the tone and direct questioning. Cole made a mental note.

"Not a chance," Black replied angrily.

"Whoa, don't get angry," Strong replied. "If the boxes are still in the room, why don't we go have a look right now?"

The Commissioner picked up his phone and punched Audrey's number. Momentarily he spoke into the phone. "Audrey, call George. Tell him to meet us at the interview room." Turning to Strong he said, "Let's go."

George had complied with Black's order and the interview room door was ajar when the four men arrived. *'I bet George was here when Audrey called him,'* Cole thought. He noticed the door was open. "I see the door is open. Where is George?" Cole asked Black.

"Why?"

"You asked him to meet us here, and I would like to talk to him about the boxes."

"Oh, okay. Spikel, can you round up George and bring him here?"

"Certainly Sir," Spikel said. He quickly left the room.

They entered and Strong saw that the boxes were back near the window. He said, "Who would have access to this room Commissioner?"

"Only, George, Spikel and I." Black replied. "Why?"

"Well we left the boxes by the table here because we figured we would be back today to show you what we found."

"Maybe we needed to interview someone, so George had to move them."

Just then Spikel returned with George and before Black could say a word Strong quickly said, "George, did you need this room yesterday, or this morning?"

Before Black could say a word George nervously said, "No, I haven't been here since you left."

"Well, the door was open when we came here a few minutes ago. That means that someone familiar with this room could have come in and compromised the evidence boxes. Right?"

Before George could respond Black said, "That will be all, George. If these men need you I'll let you know. Oh, find us two chairs and bring them in here." Turning to Cole he said, "It's hard to get competent people these days."

Cole did not respond to Black. He said to Strong, "Get those boxes over here where we can let the Commissioner take a look." Strong obeyed the order.

Cole then opened them and began removing the contents. "Help me, Bill," Cole said. The detectives took the boxes and laid the contents out into four piles on the table. Both men noticed that instead of only three file folders for each case there were now four folders. "Excuse me commissioner," Cole said, while giving him the steely eye treatment, "when we were here yesterday there were only three folders in each box. Why do we now have four?"

Black showed no emotion and said," I have no idea. Spikel did you add a folder to each file?"

Spikel calmly said, "This is the first time I've seen the boxes. No, Sir, I did not add anything."

"So be it, let's see what we've got. Start with the scuba divers' file."

Strong said, "I'm the one who examined these contents so let me see what is in them now." He knew, just by looking, which file had been added and he opened it. It contained a four page written report by Spikel that described in detail the steps he had taken regarding the drowning deaths of Dolby and West. Strong then said, "Well it looks like our forensic friend did a very complete investigation." He handed the papers to Cole.

Cole looked at Spikel and asked, "Did you hang onto this report and not give it to the Commissioner? Did you put this file into this box today?"

To the surprise of all, Spikel replied, "Yes. This one is a photocopy. I gave the original to Commissioner Black shortly after I investigated the incident. I took the opportunity to check the boxes after you left yesterday to see if you had removed any documentation. When I saw that my report file was missing, I put the copy in last evening because I knew Commissioner Black would expect it to be there. My report file was missing from all four boxes. I assumed that you had removed the reports and had taken them with you to study my findings."

Black remained silent.

Cole kept his focus on Spikel and said nothing.

Strong knew the routine and he broke the silence. "So, it looks like we should pack up, take the new files and reassess this whole situation. What is the best way to contact you should we need you Detective Spikel?"

Spikel glanced at his boss. He started to talk. "I …" was all he managed to say as Black interrupted saying, "Before we go any further I want you men to take a break. Give me twenty or thirty minutes to find Detective Spikel's original reports. Audrey probably put them in my office somewhere when I was absent."

"Suits me," said Cole. "Detective Strong and I can look at the copies while we wait."

Black motioned to Spikel to follow him. George departed without making any comment.

Cole eased back in his chair, swiveled to face Strong and said, "It just came to mind. Did you buy us the ticket on the Pools like we talked about before we left London?" He was referring to the Littlewoods Football Pools but Strong knew that by changing the subject Cole was really saying, '*I suspect this room is bugged.*'

Strong played along saying, "Yes, guv, I bought the whole season. Tomorrow the teams play the first match-ups. I feel Lady Luck is about to show up and we can find us an island of our own. What do you say we get some air? Who knows how long Black and Spikel might be."

"Righto, good idea," Cole replied. The two Brits then left the interview room and proceeded to the entrance lobby. They noticed that Audrey was not at her desk.

They walked out into the parking area. A soft Caribbean breeze was pampering Cole's face. It felt like a lady's caress. He didn't know why but suddenly he thought of Jane Butterworth. He had come close to getting involved physically when they worked together in Bermuda, but he managed to keep his hands off of her treasures. Now she would be in a much riskier environment and she would be in Calvert while he was in Palm Island. '*I'm losing my mind,*' he thought. '*Why now?*' Luckily Strong spoke and Cole's mind switched back to the task at hand.

"I think Spikel wants to get a message to us, guv. It's not going to happen in that room."

"You are right. I have the same feeling. I'm going to suggest that you go with Commissioner Black to Keith's project while I stay here and interview Spikel. It won't go down too well, but it will call Black's hand."

Strong nodded his approval. He had no doubt that they were being watched, but with the breeze blowing away from the building it would be very difficult for anyone to hear their voices.

"I guess you noticed whose car is parked next to ours?"

"I did. Samson Black's," replied Strong. "And not by chance, I'll bet." Smiling at Cole he said, "We should set a trap for the lad. Next visit let's leave the doors unlocked and the windows down so he can see into the car. I'll plant some phony documents. If he reacts, we will have him in our net. He could tell us a lot to save his own ass."

"Nice thinking, mate, but right now we should get back into the hornet's nest."

Cole and Strong reached the interview room before the other participants. They began to look at the copies of Spikel's reports when the Commissioner and Spikel returned. Cole noticed Audrey walking past the door.

"We took a break to enjoy your sunshine and breezes," Cole said. "Did you find the original reports?"

"No, we did not find them," Black said calmly. "Audrey said that they were in those boxes when you men first came by. Why they are missing is a mystery."

"That kind of puts us on hold I guess," Cole said. "No use tying you up here Commissioner, so why don't we do this? You take Detective Cole out to Keith's project so he can interview Keith regarding the C-4 explosive material. I'll stay here with Detective Spikel and review the photocopies of his reports."

"Right now?" queried Black.

"Yes, it's still early."

"I'm expecting an important phone call at mid-day. I cannot afford to miss it."

"You should be back by then Commissioner, if you leave now. We checked the map of the Island because we thought we'd be making that trip alone. Thirty minutes each way and thirty minutes at the location should give Detective Strong time to do his work if you give Keith a heads-up. You'll be back by eleven-thirty."

Spikel shifted in his chair and faced Black.

To Cole's surprise Black said, "Okay. Let's go Detective Strong."

Strong glanced at Cole and smiled. "Now we are making progress. Let's go, Commissioner."

'This cooperation is not a coincidence,' thought Cole. 'What the hell is going to happen now?'

Black and Strong left the room. Spikel looked at Cole, waiting for him to break the silence. Cole had worked with Interpol agents before, and he knew many of the secret phrases and words used in the subservice environment. Spikel said to Cole, "Are you married?" - meaning, 'we are not alone'.

Cole replied, "Yes." but my wife wants a divorce." - meaning, 'we should get out of here'.

"I guess I shouldn't ask personal questions," Spikel said, "but you seem such a personable person. I don't meet too many top level Detectives like you."

"That's okay, Thanks for the compliment. - meaning 'I get your message.' You seem pretty personable yourself. Are you single?" - meaning 'can I trust anyone but you?'

Spikel replied, "Yes, but I get around." - meaning 'there are people you should meet.'

"Let's get a handle on these reports Detective." - meaning 'I'm ready to move ahead'.

"Sure, let's read them." – meaning 'I'm ready when you are.'

"You know what Detective? I don't really need to take up your time. There's quite a lot to go over. Why don't I study the information and call you back in when I have done that?" Then, switching back to Interpol lingo, Cole said, "Seems like I would be wasting your time as I can crawl though this alone."- meaning 'we can't discuss things here. The place is likely bugged.'

"You have a good idea, Sir. My office and a simple lab are on the first floor behind Audrey's station. Come on down when you are ready." Spikel smiled and left.

Cole took the Spikel photocopies from each box and laid them out on the table. One by one they all seemed to confirm what Constable Black had written to summarize the events. Cole suspected they were phony reports, but he would want them as evidence when going to court. He pretended to study them and make some notes. With time on his hands he wondered about how to kill some time. Then, like a bolt from the blue, he remembered. *'Audrey has a sign-in register. Black is away so now would be a perfect time to take a look at it'.* He picked up his information sheets and proceeded to the reception desk.

Audrey looked somewhat surprised as Cole approached her. "Can I help you," she asked?

"Yes, Audrey. I have a bit of time on my hands so I thought I would ask you for the sign-in registers. I suppose you may have more than one so bring me all that pertain to this year?"

She paled.

Cole pretended to not notice.

"I have orders from Commissioner Black that I cannot let anyone have them," she said.

"I do not doubt that, Audrey, but I have to see them. My authority comes from Governor Neily, and it is a routine part of any investigation such as the one Detective Strong and I are conducting. Please pass them to me."

She was now breaking into a sweat. Her hands were trembling. She tried one more time to stall, hoping her boss would arrive.

"What is your problem, Audrey?"

"Sir, I do not want to disobey Commissioner Black because he will fire me if he finds out that I disobeyed his order. I am a single mother with two children, and I need this secure job."

"I understand. Look, we have at least forty minutes before he returns. I promise that I will finish with the registers before then, and I will not tell that you gave them to me." In a more stern voice Cole said," Please, bring them to me now."

Audrey obeyed. She got up and walked to a closet to her left. She came back with ten registers and placed them on her desk. "These are the 1989 registers, she said, one for each month prior to now." She handed them to Cole.

Cole took them to the small table where he and Strong had sat. He immediately opened the June register and scanned the entries. *'I've hit the jackpot,'* he said to himself. He saw the names of the dead Americans, and the murdered Canadians. He closed the book and started to quickly scan the other months. One name kept showing up several times each month. Cole wrote it down: Winston Jones.

"Audrey," Cole said, "is Winston Jones the lawyer from Calvert?"

Now Audrey knew she had better get on board with Cole. "Yes. He is of Jones & Keller. They have an office here in Palm."

"Thanks."

"Ken Dolby's name shows up quite often, too. Is he a relative or something?"

"I cannot answer that. But I do not believe so."

Cole noted dates and names of other frequent visitors. "I'm finished now so you can put these away Audrey. You have saved me a lot of time. My lips are sealed."

Changing the subject, Cole said, "Detective Spikel invited me to see his lab. Can you buzz him and let him know I'm here?"

She did not reply but buzzed Spikel. "Hello, Detective? Detective Cole is here and would like to visit you."

Turning to Cole she said, "He'll be with you forthwith."

Moments later a door opened directly behind Audrey. Spikel stepped out and waved Cole to come over. As Cole passed Audrey's desk he saw a picture of her and her two children. He made a mental note that he had heard someone tell the truth. Audrey was likely a victim of circumstances.

"You first," Spikel said to Cole.

Cole walked into the room. Spikel followed, turned, and closed the door. Cole noticed that it contained several instruments and two work stations.

There were no pictures or plaques on the walls so it was not, by any means, a comfortable room in which to work. Then without saying a word Spikel handed Cole a paper with these words written on it: '*Contact Art Bodder at Deep & Clear Dive.*'

Cole nodded agreement, and said, "This looks like a pretty good setup that you have here. Is Audrey your secretary, or do you have your own?"

"Yes, Audrey helps me. The Commissioner set it up that way."

Cole glanced at his watch. "Let's get back to the interview room. I went through your photocopies and they appear to tie into the reports written by Detective Samson Black." Then he popped another Interpol phrase. "Is the weather always this nice? - meaning '*Is this good information.*'

Spikel replied, "No it's not always good for sure. I'm sure you've seen that in your travels." - meaning 'No.'

Cole decided for sure he could trust Spikel so he asked, "Does the Palm Island Police Commission have its own legal department? I might have to visit it."

"No, the P.I. Police Department uses Jones and Keller, a Calvert firm with an office here in Palm."

"Good enough. Let's get cracking upstairs."

Cole stood aside as Spikel opened the door. He then stepped out ahead of Spikel and to his surprise Constable Wilbur Black was standing beside Audrey and very close to the forensic Lab door.

Cole greeted Black, who then walked around to the other side of the reception desk.

Black waited for the others to come around then said, "How the job go, mon?"

'*Smart ass.*' thought Cole. '*But best not to rough up the water right now.*' He replied, "We are slowly getting settled in. Commissioner Black has been very cooperative, as has Detective Spikel. Perhaps when my partner and I are ready to visit the crime scenes you can take us around."

"Not likely you people will see anything, and you will be wasting your time and mine, but if the Commissioner gives me an order, I do it."

"As you should," Cole responded. '*He's not only a smart ass, but he's also a dumb ass.*' Cole thought as he nodded to Spikel.

Spikel got the message and said, "We'd better get back to the room and be ready for the Commissioner and Detective Strong." Cole moved to the stairway. They left the reception room without saying anything more to the Constable.

When they arrived at the interview room Cole checked to see if anything was out-of-order. He found no problem.

"Detective, give Audrey a buzz and find out if the Commissioner called, and if he did not, ask her to call Keith's construction site to find out if he and Bill have left." Spikel buzzed Audrey and reported that she had heard from them and expected them to arrive shortly. Cole overheard the news and said to Spikel, "I guess we have a few minutes to get acquainted. Tell me about your time with the RCMP in Canada."

"I spent most of my time in British Columbia because Asian immigrants were flooding in and crime gangs were developing. White collar crime was also blossoming especially in securities fraud. My wife died in 1980, but I have a son and a daughter to be proud of. My son is a software developer, in Toronto. My daughter is a lawyer with the Canadian Department of Justice, in Ottawa. I loved the scenery in BC so I did not move. When this job came up I was ready for a safer environment. I never knew whether a Chinese criminal, or an East Indian criminal, would be waiting to kill me. So here I am. What about you?"

"Well I was born into a police family and both my brother and I ended up chasing money launderers and murderers. I loved the southern part of England, but had to move to London for a spell. I ended up in Liverpool which is a bit of a cesspool of its own. I got some big assignments and fortunately I'm still alive because I'm sure I was born with a sixth sense on how to stay alive. Speaking of Vancouver, I had a big Chinese case that involved a twisted money and securities fraud. Their headquarters was Vancouver. I was called there to give evidence. You probably know of the *Wing Chin* case?"

"Heck that was, and still is, the case of all cases up there. The Crown Prosecutor, Frank Hill, tied up that case so tight that even Chin could not wiggle out of it. Hill then joined a national litigation firm."

Cole smiled and said, "I played only a small part in the case by tracing some of the marked money. It's a small world Herman. I'm glad to know that you aren't a rookie. I look forward to sitting with you and sharing more experiences." Cole then heard voices emanating from the ground floor and gave Spikel the classic, *'That's enough for now'* signal by bending down to re-tie the lace on his left shoe. Spikel acknowledged by shifting in his chair. The voices moved closer. Cole recognized Strong's voice. As Strong and the Commissioner entered the room they were smiling.

"I'm glad that you men are having such a good time," Cole said. "Detective Spikel and I have been reminiscing about old cases we've worked. So what's happening partner?"

"We got to Keith's project without any unusual events. But, as soon as we climbed out of the Land Rover there was a huge blast. The main explosives shed exploded into a million pieces."

"It did? Was anyone injured? Did Keith have any explanation?"

Black answered, "We have no idea what caused it but there sure as hell is no C-4 available now."

Cole looked at Black, "Where was Keith when it happened?"

"He was on his radio phone in his office."

"Did you ask Keith for the phone?" Cole said to Strong.

"Yes boss, but he said he had to keep it because there was no other way to communicate to that site."

"Did you or Commissioner Black suspect that Keith may have destroyed his own building?"

Black answered, "Are you serious Detective Cole? Why would he do such a thing?"

"Because he knew my partner was coming to the site and might find a clue about the stuff that was supposed to blow us up. Attempted murder goes through my mind. But let's change the subject. I think we've heard and seen all there is to be heard or seen, so my partner and I will leave you and Detective Spikel to do what you do best."

Black was speechless. Spikel stayed emotionless.

"Grab these files, Bill, and let's get some lunch," Cole said. "We will be back in touch next week." Cole looked the Commissioner in the eye, shook his hand, and left. Strong followed as they made their way to their car then drove away.

"I have plenty to tell you partner." said Cole. Strong was driving and replied, "I've got some goodies for you too."

"Look," said Cole, "we have to get to Gart and clue him in on what's happening. We can catch a bite there. At this time of day those drug dealers will likely be just waking up somewhere. Listen, here's my short account of what happened while you were away. Spikel is solid. Thank God we both know how to converse in Interpol double-talk. Bottom line, Spikel says that the whole place is bugged, other than the reception area." Reaching into his shirt pocket he pulled out the note given to him by Spikel. "Spikel slipped this to me. It says we are to contact Art Bodder at Clear & Deep Dive. We'll go there after we meet Webber and the kid. I have no idea what to expect at Bodder's place. Also, I made Audrey fork over all of the visitor registers for this year. I made a quick scan and a list, but two names stood out. Ken Dolby signed in about twice a month until he didn't make it from the night dive. Winston Jones the lawyer made at least two visits a month right up until yesterday. Jane Butterworth will be a busy girl when she gets to her new job. I still have to properly compile my findings. Spikel and I exchanged pleasantries and talked a bit about our past activities. Small world, we both played a part in the big 'Wing Chin' case up in Canada. What can you report?"

Detective Strong kept his eyes on the road while replying, "You are not going to like this boss. On our way to Keith's project Black called Keith. Of course I could overhear the conversation, but I guess Black didn't give a damn. I'm sure his ego is bigger than big. He has no conception of where you and I have been, and the bastards that we put away. Anyway, he asked Keith if his foreman was working today and Keith replied that the man was not, and that he had given him the day off. Black commented "that's good, all set?" Then he turned his head to face me, smiled and said, "We're all set. Keith is waiting for us."

I said, "Well I hope so, but wondered '*what the hell*'. We shot the bull for about twenty minutes then Black called Keith again. He simply said, "Strong and I are about five minutes away". He then dialed some numbers but I could not hear his phone make a connection. Remember, he was driving all the while he was doing this. I made a mental note. I don't have to tell you what happened when we got to the project. Turning toward his partner he said, 'Which phone should we investigate, boss?"

Cole coughed nervously. "So you think Black detonated the shed?"

"Could be, and it could be Black's phone that detonated the Taurus explosion. After all, he's the one who doesn't want us here."

"So that's why you were playing along and making light about Keith's phone." Turning to Strong he said with an understanding tone, "Nice work, Bill."

"Thanks, guv."

As usual the traffic was heavy and the men remained silent until they pulled into the Hibiscus parking area. The time was exactly twelve noon and Gart was just opening the door. When he saw the detectives he smiled, and waved for them to come in. The men acknowledged the wave and went directly to the door where Gart was holding it open.

Gart said, "What brings you two here at this time of day? Are you hungry? We have our grouper sandwich special today."

Strong replied, "Hi Gart, that sounds good, but first we have to sit down with you and give you some confidential information. Have you got twenty minutes to spare?"

"I should be okay. What's the news? Come over to the table by the back window and we can talk in private."

They proceeded to the table without saying a word.

There were no customers. Gart's wife was in the kitchen with the cook.

Cole opened the conversation with, "We need your help. What we are about to tell you cannot be shared with anyone, not even your wife."

Gart made a quizzical face and said, "That's a tall order guys. We are a team you should know."

"I understand," Cole said. "What do you think Bill?"

"Two heads might be better than one, guv, so let's get her over here."

Gart look relieved and called across the room to his wife, "Hey, Louisa, can you come here for ten minutes? We need you."

"Should be okay for a few minutes," she replied, as she started toward the three men.

When she sat down Cole asked, "Look Louisa, you know who we are and why we are here."

"Of course I do, detective, and I'm happy as hell to be part of cleaning out the rats' nest."

"We need you and Gart to promise that you will tell not a soul of our plan."

"We promise, they said in unison."

Cole took the lead and quietly, and slowly, said, "The two men that were in your bar last night are DEA agents. One is Tom Oakley, the other is Willie Patton. They are the men who were having beer in your bar and chatting up the druggies. No one but the Governor, Bill, and I, know who they are and why they are on Palm. They cannot be seen with us so we need a conduit to pass information to each other. That's where you folks can help. We trust you."

Gart interrupted, "We hear you detective."

Cole continued, "Okay. We will phone information to you that you will then convey to the agents. They will do likewise. When we phone you we want you to listen carefully but talk like you are taking a reservation for dinner. We, or the agents, will tell you it's a small, medium or large table that we need. You will ask for a phone number. You then must go across the road to Enchanted and call us, or them, to relay the message. I reiterate, the DEA agents must not be revealed. Can you help?"

Gart and Louisa were squirming a bit in their chairs, but looked at each other, then back at Cole.

Gart said, "Okay Louisa?"

"Okay," she replied.

Then it's a go, and here's what we have for you. Next Tuesday evening we plan to arrest the drug dealers in your bar. Oakley and Patton may drop in each evening until then. They will buy a small amount of ganja each night. They want Fingers and his crew to get really comfortable with them. We suspect they offer more than ganja, so on Tuesday night the agents will make a buy of the hard stuff from Fingers. Bill and I will step in to make the arrest. Hopefully you won't have a lot of customers at that time because the event could be nasty. Do you understand?"

"Yes," Louisa replied.

"For sure," Gart replied. "Do you use weapons?"

"Only a slapper, but we've cooled out lots of tough guys with that tool."

"I'm hungry," said Strong. "We have two other meetings lined up so how long do you need to whip up a couple of sandwiches?"

"Ten minutes," replied Louisa. "I'm on it. I'm excited!"

Cole smiled, and stretched as he said, "While we wait Bill, let's take a walk around the property. We won't want any surprises on Tuesday night."

"I'll go with you," Gart said.

"Best you don't, Gart. The less we are seen together the better off likely you will be - anything unusual out there?"

"Not really, just the shed where I store paper goods like cups, take-out trays and the like."

"I guess you keep it locked?"

"All the time." Gart smiled, as if Cole had asked a stupid question.

Cole got up and smiled back, saying, "Let's take a look, partner."

The two detectives walked out through the entrance door then went left to look at the south side of the property. About fifty feet away it bordered a strip of small stores. As they walked to the back they discovered a parking area that had been carved out of the bordering mangrove swamp and filled with shell.

Strong commented, "A person could hide in those mangroves for sure."

Continuing on they saw additional parking spaces, and the shed. It was about fifteen feet from the back entrance to the restaurant. They noticed that it had a cheap lock securing the door.

Strong chuckled and said, "Nothing of value in there I guess. Anyone could pop off that lock without any trouble. I guess it keeps out the honest people."

"Looks okay," Cole said. "Let's get our food and take it home. I should call Governor Neily and ask if he's available."

Gart saw the men as they entered the restaurant and called out, "Food is ready."

Strong replied, "I'm ready too, but we've decided to eat it at home."

"No problem," Gart acknowledged. He called to Louisa, "Box those lunches. The men are taking them out."

"I have one last request," Cole said to Gart. "Make sure on Tuesday night that the back door is securely locked so no one can open it to get in or to get out. If you think you will need supplies from the shed, get them early. One more thing, get a better lock for your shed."

"As ordered," Gart replied. "See you next time. Good luck."

• • •

The detectives arrived at *Enchanted* and found all was in order. They enjoyed their lunches. "Time to call Neily," Cole said. He picked up the phone and dialed. "That's strange – no dial tone. *'What the hell now?'* he thought. He put the receiver back on the stand, picked it up once more and tried again. He heard the dial tone and offered, '*Thank God.*' The Governor answered. Cole acknowledged saying, "Hello, Governor, this is Cole. Are you available? Strong and I would like to visit you now." Cole got an immediate "Yes" and said, "Let's go partner. Neily is waiting for us."

The traffic was not too bad as most of the tourists were on the beach and not touring the Island. Strong was driving and surprised Cole by making a quick left turn into a petrol station. He looked quickly to his righto see a police car driving past. "I watched that car in my mirror," he said. "I'm damn sure it's Constable Black's cruiser. It pulled out from the strip of stores back there beside Hibiscus. I remember seeing the car at Headquarters."

"So the bugger is tailing us. I should have figured as much. Glad you still have your instincts pal. We have about a half a mile to go. I'll watch for him. Drive as slow as you can."

There was no other incident before they reached the Governor's driveway. As they approached the mansion Neily stepped out and waved them in.

"Thank God we can trust someone, eh boss," Strong asked?

Cole grunted his agreement. Strong parked close to the front entrance.

As they approached the Governor, he smiled and said, "I've got some rather good news for you boys. Come right in. Geraldine prepared some tea and a plate of her home-baked cookies for us."

"Well that's a refreshing comment. I wish I could say we have good news for you," Cole replied as and he and Strong were shown in by Neily.

"Oh my, I hope it's not too bad. Have a seat on the chesterfield. I'll sit over here on this side of the coffee table." Neily then poured three cups of Tetley, passed two of them over to the detectives, kept one, before motioning to the guests to help themselves to the cookies. "Let me start by saying it is good to see you here. Premier Westwood and I know that you are in constant danger and we will help you in any way that we can. That said my good news is, I've heard back from London and a Jane Butterworth has been hired by Jones & Keller. Even better, she will be coming directly to work in the Palm office of J&K. She arrives here next Monday."

"That is good news," Cole emphasized. "She is probably our best female operative. How will she communicate with us?"

"She has a friend, a Darlene Clark, who is the intermediary. Do you know her?"

"Yes, a blinding detective, Sir."

Neily continued, "Good. She will get info from Jane, pass it along to her gaffer Corey White, and he will get it to me. How do you want me to relay it to you?"

"I suggest that you call us at *Enchanted*. If I answer, invite us to see you. If you get no answer, say 'Sorry I missed you. I will call back.' We will come here to get all messages."

"I hear you, detective."

"Now," Cole said, "we have a major problem. It seems that Commissioner Black is bent as a nine-bob note, and he runs this Island. He has lied to us a few times and withheld documents. We believe it was him personally who triggered the explosion of our Taurus. We have to get him off of this Island so that I can take command. If we can get our hands on his portable phone I think we could put him behind bars. His second-in-command is Detective Samson Black. I'm not only gobsmacked at this man's arrogance but, also by his stupidity. We can handle him easily if his boss is not around. You see, in that case, I could be in charge, and Bill and I would root out the bad actors. Likely, several members of the force have been afraid to talk about what has gone on here for several years, and they will spill the beans."

Cole shifted forward. "I have a suggestion. Premier Westwood ranks higher than Commissioner Black so he could order him to attend The Commonwealth Police Commissioners' Association's annual meeting in London. Westwood could call UK Police Commissioner Bob Palmer who is the President of the Association. Palmer then would call Black and tell him that he has been nominated to receive the annual award as the best commissioner in the Caribbean group. The event starts next Wednesday the twenty-fifth, which means he'd leave here on Tuesday. We plan to arrest the punk drug dealers at the Hibiscus Restaurant on Tuesday night, and we don't need Black interfering. If necessary, Premier Westwood would order him to go on Tuesday. I cannot stress strongly enough Sir that Black has to be removed."

"My goodness, Detective, I had no idea that Commissioner Black was such a strong arm. He's a bigger crook than I thought it seems. I felt that only outsider cops like you and Detective Strong could get to the bottom of the June deaths. You have uncovered much more corruption than I could ever imagine. Thank goodness the decision was taken by the Foreign Office to assign men of your caliber."

Cole nodded with a determined look. "This is only the start," he said. "We are sure that the deaths reported last June are all homicides. We are arranging to have a private talk with Detective Herman Spikel. He has surreptitiously informed me that he has incriminating evidence. Both he and I have worked with Interpol so we can communicate even though the area may be bugged for sound. Spikel is clean."

"Until we take down Black, You should be very careful, Sir. By the way, did you find out who was trimming your hedges?"

"I must admit that I did not follow your instruction. If I see him again I will promptly contact you."

"Okay, but do not approach him. Just make a note of his appearance, and then call me."

Neily showed relief and said, "Let me try to reach the Premier now. We may get lucky."

Cole and strong helped themselves to cookies. The Governor went into his office to make the call.

"What are you thinking now?" asked Strong.

"I'll make up my mind after we meet with Westwood, Bill."

The Governor returned after several minutes. He was smiling.

"We are in luck. Westy, that's what I call him, is heading here forthwith. I believe I shook him up pretty well with your information. While we wait for him I could show you around the grounds. Would you like to do that?"

Cole and Strong looked at each other for confirmation, rose from their seats, and Strong said, "Lead on, Sir."

The sitting room opened onto the beach patio. It was no ordinary patio. A fifty foot sectional awning stretched the full length of the wall. In the center of the area was a thirty foot by twenty five foot, crystal clear, fresh water pool. Near the corner of the mansion there was a change room and a shower. Two sitting areas, each with lounge chairs, captain's chairs and teal colored umbrellas added to the ambience. The three sides beyond the house were lined with hibiscus bushes bearing several colors of blooms. The hedge hid a wrought iron fence with a gate leading to the beach. Beyond was the sparkling Caribbean Sea.

"This is gorgeous," claimed Cole. *'Oh how I miss my colorful garden back home in Little Harwood'*, he thought.

"Yes, we are spoiled," Neily acknowledged. "Except for trimming these bushes, Geraldine does most of the gardening work. She even has some tomato plants near the side wall bearing lovely tomatoes. A great lady is my Geraldine. Now follow me. We can go out this way." He led them through the gate and onto the beach.

All beaches on Palm Island were for public use. Access by the public was by designated pathways from the road. The area around the mansion was relatively isolated and no beach goers were using it at the time. The soft white sand looked very inviting, but the detectives knew they had better keep their minds on their mission. Neily lead them to a pathway that bordered the building and connected the beach to the driveway. Between the pathway and the mansion there was an eight foot area completely covered with bayonet plants, and it was obvious that no one in their right mind would try to access that side of the building which had several windows.

"Nice security," Cole said, pointing to the area of the bayonets.

"Rightly so, my friend, and I feel quite secure. Those are bedroom windows and we quite often leave them open in order to get the benefit of night breezes. Be careful of the step at the bottom of this pathway. For some reason it is a bit higher than what it appears to be. I was told by the former occupant, Governor Harold Billhouse, that it is an intentional trap to cause intruders to stumble and fall. So far we have had two such occasions. Simple, but effective security, don't you agree?"

"Makes sense to me." Cole grinned.

"Hark, I hear a vehicle," claimed Neily. "The Premier I'll bet."

They quickly stepped along and reached the end of the path. Sure enough, a white Lincoln sedan was approaching. The license plate on the front bore the word 'PREMIER' and the plate on the back bore the marking 'OFFI-CIAL'. The Governor waved at the car to direct the driver to park behind the Camry. He did as directed and the Premier emerged. He strode over to the group who were now standing at the front door and was greeted by Cole who said, "Thanks for getting here so quickly, Sir. Let's go inside and we will top you up. You may be surprised."

"Yes. The Governor sounded a bit vexed when he called. I knew from his tone that we were not going to talk on the telly about anything important. I'm anxious to hear what needs such privacy and immediate attention."

The Governor sat down at one end of the coffee table while the Premier took a chair and pulled it up to the other end. The detectives resumed their position on the chesty.

Cole leaned forward, and with an intense look at the officials he said, "Please do not take what I say as a personal affront. Because the Palm Police Department is sworn to secrecy there is no way that you gentlemen could even dream about the corruption that is prevalent in this country. Now that we understand that we are all starting from scratch we must work together. Detective Strong and I have not completed our investigation, but we know enough about Commissioner Black, and his police force, that I can tell you he is an extremely dangerous person."

Cole then reiterated what he had already told Neily. He finished by saying, "I believe this could be the worst case of corruption and intimidation that I have ever experienced. You can consider your own lives to be in danger. From what I've seen, Black is at the point where he will do whatever it takes to remain in his position. He has buried facts about the deaths that Bill and I were sent here to investigate. We will know more when we follow up on info given to us by Detective Herman Spikel who has stuck his neck out to help us. This man Black has no respect for officers of the Queen. He has likely accommodated international drug lords from the Quintia and Suarez cartels. We have to get him off of the Island so that we can take command of the Palm Islands Police Department. He has a flunky underling that will carry out his every command. I can take care of him, once we are in charge. Further, we think that there are members of the force who would rat on Black if they had the opportunity. So, here's where you come in Mr. Premier. You rank above Black, and in fact you are his boss. Yes, we know everyone thinks your position is of no practical use, but it could be lawfully enforced. Are you with me up until now — any questions? Should I continue?"

"Continue detective," Westwood replied.

"Listen very carefully now. If you suggest to Commissioner Warton Black that he must go to the London conference he will likely balk. However, if you suggest that Detective Samson Black, his chief 'yes man' could take charge for a few days, then there is a good chance he will do as you ask. Once he is on board his flight, you can rescind that order and appoint Detective Spikel. If we are successful with our sting on Tuesday night, I'm convinced that we can get the punks to cough up that they are have been intimidated by the Commissioner. They could not stay in business without paying him off. Spikel will cooperate one hundred percent and he will reveal the real truth about the June homicides. Any questions gentlemen?"

Westwood and Neily looked concerned.

"Why don't I give you five minutes to think about it? In fact, you may come up with a better idea. Bill and I will go to the lanai and leave you two alone."

When they left, Neily was first to comment and said, "Astounding information, Bruce. We are sitting on a powder keg according to what we've heard. Did you have any idea of what the Commissioner has been up to?"

"Not really Dale. I guess we are so involved in our tight little social groups that Black has been slowly pulling the wool over our eyes. You and I are fortunate that London sent us a top level officer. He and his partner haven't wasted any time getting a grip on the situation. I believe we have to buckle up and do whatever they want. My God, can you imagine. Even you, me, and our wives are targets of that power hungry Warton Black."

"Okay, then it's onward, and upward. Risky business but I see no option."

The detectives returned and resumed their places on the chesty. Cole looked at Neily, then at Westwood saying nothing, but his intense stare asked the question. Silence can sometimes be the best conversation. He had played the role more than once.

Neily opened with, "We must do whatever we can. We are with you one hundred percent. We will keep our eyes open now and report anything that seems out of the ordinary. If we see something – anything suspicious - you will hear from us."

Westwood bucked up and commented, "I have never been in a situation like this, but I will do whatever is necessary to make sure Palm Islands have a pristine commercial reputation. That will be my legacy."

"You won't be disappointed, Sir," replied Cole. "Remember, the key element right now is to arrest the drug dealers operating at The Hibiscus Restaurant. And believe me, they are just the tip of the iceberg. For us, these punks and the

Commissioner are just low-hanging fruit. Detective Strong and I are sure that the June murders were ordered by more powerful actors. I stress again that the DEA agents must stay anonymous. They are just tourist divers having a good time. One of them is a forensic expert who needs to be present at the bust to confirm the substance being bought. We'll get those punks. They'll rat on the Commissioner sure as England has a Queen. Once more, any questions?"

"None," replied Neily as he looked to Westwood for affirmation who nodded his agreement.

"Good," Cole said. "I want you to meet the Commissioner early tomorrow. Right now we will call London from here and tell them to set up their end of the plan by calling the President of the Commonwealth Police Commissioners Association. Let's do that now Governor."

"I'm on it. Follow me to the office, Detective."

'*Lady Luck is flying with me today*,' Cole thought. '*These men are in with both feet*'.

Cole called his Commander on Westwood's secure line, outlined the plan and got confirmation that their wheels would be put into motion immediately. The time difference could have been a problem but they knew how to work around it. Cole hung up the phone, looked at the three other men who had proceeded to the office and said, "We're on. All hands are on deck. Thank you, gentlemen, for understanding the severity of our situation. Bill and I must run as we have a meeting arranged with a person who could be a big help to us. We can show ourselves out."

As the detectives got into their Camry, Cole said to Strong, "Well Bill, what do you think? Can we pull off this job?"

Strong started the car, twisted his head toward Cole and replied, "We had better pull it off or a lot of honest folks could end up underground or, undersea – including us!"

"What time is it, guv," asked Strong? "Do you think we will be able to get to Art Bodder after the park?"

"We'll see. It's about four o'clock, so we should make it. I'm anxious to find out what that Teddy kid knows. He's no slouch. Bodder runs a camp so he's likely to be there in the evening."

They drove slowly this time in order to observe if they were being followed. The trip to Coconut Park took about thirty minutes and was uneventful. The park was nothing to write home about but covered at least one hundred acres. It included a cricket pitch and a soccer field. Each had a small spectator stand that could seat maybe one hundred people. Coconut palm trees were everywhere, like it was a plantation at one time. The grass was parched as the dry season had started, but oleander bushes were thriving near the playing fields. Five thatched-roof cabanas were available for picnickers, and to provide protection from sun and rain. A parking area was available away from the coconut trees.

Strong parked the Camry and both men got out to stretch their legs. Their contact, Ted, was not visible, probably because they had arrived a few minutes early. "This isn't the most private place to meet someone," commented Cole. "I hope the kid wasn't setting us up. Let's sit over at that farthest cabana at the North end so we will have a full view of this place. Besides, the kid said we should meet at the North end and it looks like he knew what he was talking about."

"Good thinking, guv. Should I bring the Camry over?"

"No way, it could damage the field. Let's just sit and wait. Sure is hot as hell here. No breeze."

As the detectives watched, six adults and twelve boys got out of three vans. They proceeded to the soccer field and the adults had just began to coach the boys when a scooter with one rider appeared. It drove over the hard surface of the park directly to where the detectives were sitting. At five on the dot, there was Teddy. He parked his scooter beside the cabana, removed his helmet, shook hands with the detectives as he said, "Hi, I'm still a little confused about why we are meeting, but I assume you need some help. I know quite a bit about what goes on here on this Island because people tend to have loose lips when they drink too much. It's your show, ask me what you want."

Cole was blown away by Ted's candor. He turned to Strong and said, "No doubt Ted is exactly the person we need to get info about the high fliers." Turning back to Ted he asked, "Are you sure you can handle our request? Your life won't be worth two pence if the criminals get wind of you doing inside work for us. Usually we would try to plant a trained spy into a resort like Holiday Place. Look at us, Ted, straight in the eye, can you handle the job?"

"I really like this Island. Where I come from we look for opportunities to help people. These Islanders have no idea what is happening politically. Before they know it, this place will be run just like Cuba. Does that answer your question? Oh, and by the way, I have a black belt in judo."

Cole looked astonished by Ted's reply. He adjusted his hat to block out the sun and said, "Detective Strong will be your contact. You will not be seen with the two of us. If you need to contact him urgently, you must call the Hibiscus Restaurant and tell Gart Webber, the owner. Do not tell him why you have called, but just where you are calling from. Bill here will quickly be called by Mr. Webber who will relay the message. Before we part today, you and Bill work out your signals."

"Now Ted, tell us what can about any of the June deaths?"

"Here's what I know. The couple that were from Montreal, were not simply tourists. I served them quite a few times and during their stay they frequently were joined by a lawyer – or whatever they are called here – and they scribbled things on napkins, or our paper place mats that we use for breakfast serving. On two occasions I cleared their table and removed napkins on which they had written names and phone numbers. In addition, I could overhear conversations and pick up the odd word or two. In the evening especially, they would get liquored up and talk more loudly. When they first checked in, in early June, they certainly posed as holiday types. After a week they started getting visits from the lawyer that I mentioned. He was from the firm of Jones & Keller, a prominent firm on Palm. When that person was present, the Montreal couple did a lot of scribbling and writing and voices were subdued. The next thing I can mention is that two American men joined them a few times for dinner. They talked about the stock market and showed them a brochure from a Canadian diamond mining company. On the very last occasion, when they left the table, they shook hands, and all were smiling and complimenting each other. In their enjoyable mood they forgot a brochure so I caught up to them in the lobby and tried to give it to them. They said, "Thanks kid, we don't need that. Just stick it in the trash bin." Because I'm a Canadian I was curious about the company so I kept the brochure and I still have it."

"Cheers for Ted," Cole said to Strong. "He's a real operator."

Looking at Ted, Cole commented, "Look Ted, after all that you've just told us you are shaping up to be a key witness once we get the gang leaders on the stand. You must stay safe. We will follow you to wherever you live so we will know that you got home safely. Hang on tight to those napkins and other material until Detective Strong can safely get them from you. In the meantime, if possible, get the check-in and check-out dates and times of the two from Montreal. We know the two Americans did not stay at the Holiday Place Resort. Oh yes, and if you can get any credit card numbers that will help a lot. Perhaps the Americans picked up one of the tabs?"

"I'll do what I can," replied Ted, "but don't expect any miracles. Right now I'd like detective Strong to give me some sort of code to use when I call Mr. Webber at Hibiscus."

"You just tell Webber your name, and that you want a calzone delivered to your location. Webber will ask for your phone number. That is enough info for me to contact you by phone or in person. Are you okay with that, Ted?"

"I got it. Say no more Detective Strong."

"Good," said Cole. "Let's get our butts in gear. We still have to get to Clear and Deep Dive after we follow you home, Ted."

• • •

The air got hotter as evening approached because there was no breeze at all. The detectives were glad to get into the car and turn on the air conditioner.

Ted lived in a small ground floor condo set back a couple of blocks from the beach. When they arrived, the Detectives did not stop. Ted made no gesture toward them as Strong drove slowly around the circular drive and back out onto the main road. Cole noted Ted's condo number.

The sun was slipping below the tree line and casting heavy shadows. As a precaution, Strong turned on the headlamps. Fortunately, the traffic had thinned out and they reached their destination in good time. As they pulled into the resort they noticed that the Tiki Bar was crowded for happy hour. With so many customers, the parking area was full.

Strong looked at Cole and said, "Where do you want me to go? There's no place to park."

"Stay here at the roadside, we might get lucky. Someone should be leaving soon." No sooner had Cole said that, when a tanned couple in casual attire left the bar and got into a white Toyota. They waved as they drove past the detectives.

"How about that," said Cole, "we got a lucky break. Get this baby parked and let's find Art Bodder."

"More luck boss. It looks like we're right next to the office. Are we on a roll or what? Let's hope Bodder is here and keeps our winning streak alive."

"We'll soon know, Bill."

The office door displayed a sign 'OPEN'. Strong entered first then he stepped aside for Cole to proceed. He said in a loud voice, "Hello, anyone home?"

"I'm in the john," came back a reply from the back of the room. "I'll be right there."

"Take your time," Strong shouted, while smiling at Cole.

A door opened behind the customer counter and a grinning Bodder said, "Hi, you caught me with my pants down! I'm Art Bodder."

Cole chuckled, approached him and offered his hand to greet the man, saying, "I'm Detective Cole. Mr. Bodder, Detective Herman Spikel, a friend of yours, told us to stop by. May I call you Art?"

"Certainly," said Bodder.

"Are we alone?"

"Sure," replied Bodder. "Doesn't happen often, and it may not be this way for long if I don't take down that sign and lock the door. It's a busy place. I'm guessing that you two are the investigators from England – right?"

"Righto Art. Herman told us to look you up asap," replied Cole.

Bodder turned the lock on the door. "My friend Herman has stuck his neck out by doing so but, the man is beside himself because Commissioner Black is really getting out of control. He told me, to tell you, that his evidence pertaining to the June deaths was tampered with. Black ordered him to leave the investigation of the June deaths alone. Herman wants you to know that all of the victims showed head trauma. I guess you know what that means?"

"Sounds like murder to me," Cole replied.

Strong nodded his agreement.

"Yes. So Herman needs to meet privately with you," Bodder continued. "Here's a plan. Because Commissioner Black's people know that Spikel and I go out to sea quite often, we could meet privately out there without attracting any attention. Do you know how to handle a boat? We can't all be seen leaving from my dock at the same time."

"Do you know a taxi driver named Harris," Cole asked?

"Yes. Why?"

"We met this Harris person and we believe he can be trusted. He is also a fisherman and has offered to take us out to Four Tops to fish if we rent a good boat."

"I know the man. He's honest, and a hard worker. I'd trust him. Tell him to come by, and I'll set him up with that twenty-six foot Bertam you see moored outside. Herman said you have rented *Enchanted*. Harris can drive the craft there to pick you up. Herman and I have already arranged to be at sea tomorrow at 9AM, before the wind picks up. I'll tell Harris where to look for us. I'll take that thirty foot Hatteras. Sound good?"

"Perfect, Art. We need all the help that we can get. I guess we should be going now. No use keeping you any longer on this busy night. We will call Harris."

Art shook hands with both of the Brits, put the sign back in place, and opened the door. No more words were exchanged. The detectives had gotten into their vehicle when Strong said, "Maybe we should get a bite to eat here boss. We ought to make ourselves as scarce as possible at Hibiscus so the drug punks don't get nervous and find another hangout."

"Now you're thinking partner, plus this place is where Tom Oakley ate, and rated the food triple 'A'. It wouldn't hurt to chum up some Tiki patrons too. Who knows what surprises they might have in store?"

Strong turned off the car engine and replied, "Let's go, but don't hold your breath!"

The detectives found an empty table for two, pulled up their chairs, and waved for service. The bartender motioned to acknowledge their presence then called over a waitress, and directed her to the table. She appeared to be about thirty-five years old, built like a beauty contestant, and displayed dark black hair, coal black eyes, and olive colored skin. If anymore cleavage showed she might as well have had no top on at all. Standing erectly, she addressed Cole and Strong with a very polite, "Good evening gentlemen. Let me say that I'm honored to serve you. Buzzy, the bartender over there, told me who you are."

Curt and Bill, with raised eyebrows, looked at each other, then they smiled at the waitress. Strong offered his hand, and the waitress shook it while giving him a very warm smile. Bill then quipped, "How long can you stay to chat before we have to order. I'm sure I'm not the first customer to tell you that you are very beautiful."

"Thank you for the compliment. I get a lot of tips by staying in shape and being polite. I'm also a fitness instructor at the Island Fitness Club. My name is Maria. Before I take your order, please know that Buzzy says, "It's on the house."

Cole decided he should calm down Strong's testosterone surge. He said, "We applaud you for staying healthy. My partner is unattached and has a tendency to chat up beautiful women. You should ignore him."

She laughed, but added, "He's okay. Besides, he looks pretty good to me!"

'Oh no,' Cole thought. 'That's all I need. I'd better order.' "Maria," he said, "we are ready to order. How about two orders of the famous grouper sandwich and chips? Bring along two greenies, to wash them down."

Maria cast another, more alluring smile at Strong. Before she left the table, she said," They'll be up right away, sir."

"Is that not the ultimate in sexual tease boss? Sorry, but she got me all worked up. I'll have to find the fitness club – if you ever give me a break."

"Can't blame you Bill, but as you know, we're marked men and there's nothing like a beautiful body to sway a detective to let his emotions rule over his common sense. If we survive long enough to put away all the criminals on this island, then go for it – but don't underestimate that woman."

"Ya, Ya," Strong drawled. "No sense getting killed for a piece of ass. I'll behave. Besides, I have to go to the men's room, and that for sure will kill my animal instinct." He got up and headed for the loo.

Cole observed the room for a few seconds, and noticing that Buzzy was not being slammed, decided to pay him a visit to thank him for the complimentary food and drinks. There was an empty stool at the end of the service bar area, so he parked himself on it and waved to Buzzy who came right over.

"It's sure nice to see some real cops around here, Buzzy claimed. What can I get for you?"

"Oh nothing, I just want to thank you for the goodies and compliment you on the service. That waitress Maria is a standout. Is she single?"

"I think so, but I don't know for sure," Buzzy replied. "On this tax haven island it isn't necessary for me to keep records. I don't do a background check.

The Immigration Department confirms the nationality, and the P.I. Police Commissioner signs off on the background checks. What matters to me is how they look and flirt with the customers. Buzzy was smiling as he got a sign from a waitress. "Hang on while I serve this order. Buzzy prepared two Pina Coladas then returned to chat with Cole. You asked if Maria was single. Well, there is a swarthy, handsome guy who shows up about every three weeks and waits for her to end her shift at midnight. Come to think about it, he is overdue for a visit unless she dumped him."

Cole showed a thoughtful look and asked, "Is she a local?"

"No man, she's an import from Panama. She speaks fluent Spanish."

At that moment Strong returned. Pointing to the table he said, "Hey guv, the food and beer is on the table. Let's get at it."

Cole looked at Strong while saying, "Okay. One second." Then he turned to Buzzy, smiled and said, "Thanks for your time Buzzy. We'll be back."

The detectives took their time eating, but Strong quickly drank his beer in order to get Maria back to the table. She saw him wave, went over, and stood close to him while he finished a bite. Cole, on the other hand, took the opportunity to check her out more closely than before. This time he noticed rather large diamond studs displayed in each ear lobe. *'Must be zircons.'* he thought. *'On second thought, maybe they are real.'*

Strong downed his food, and in order to keep the waitress at tableside before ordering, he told her how great the food was, and about a couple of pubs he liked in Liverpool. Maria persevered then interjected, "Would you men like another cold beer?"

Strong replied, "Yes but just one for me, thanks. My friend here really prefers his beer warm."

She left and then returned with Strong's beer. "Is that it? There is no bill. It's all on the house."

Cole responded. "Yes. We appreciate it Maria. This is for the great service." He subtly handed her a tightly folded ten dollar bill.

"I hope to see you again soon." She smiled and left.

Cole thought, *'You can count on that.'*

The detectives finished their meals and walked straight to their car. As they turned onto the main road to head home Cole said, "You will be seeing more of Maria, Bill. I had a very interesting chat with Buzzy."

While keeping his eyes on the road, Strong quizzed Cole. "Okay, tell me?"

Cole laid out what he knew and the suspicion in his mind. Then said," If she's from Panama and having contact with some swarthy dude on a regular basis wouldn't you be suspicious? Remember Tom telling us about the fishing boat arriving about every three weeks? And how about those ear studs? Those things don't grow on trees. Plus, toss this into the mix, - Commissioner Black decides who can work here and who cannot."

"I can't argue with that, boss. You are usually right. Anyway, we've had a hell of a busy day, and I am looking forward to getting home to relax. God help us if there are a bunch of phone messages, but guess what?"

"Okay, what?" Cole asked.

"I still have to get some groceries. I saw a big store near our edge of town. I think it was called Murphy's Supermarket. It's kind of late, but if the place is open, we're going to stop."

They drove slowly through Kingtown. As they were leaving the main commercial section they saw the supermarket. The lights were on inside, and a flashing red neon sign showed the word 'OPEN'. Strong parked the vehicle and both men went inside to shop.

As they were shopping, Cole commented, "This place is pretty busy for this time of night."

"Hey guv, it's Friday night. Probably it's payday. Anyway, I've got what I need and you seem to have found enough treats to last for a while. Let's move on. You pay while I get the car." Cole dealt with the cashier and within a few minutes they were on their way home.

The rest of the drive to *Enchanted* was uneventful. Both men kept watching for signs of being tailed. Apparently Commissioner Black's people had something better to do. As the detectives approached their destination, Cole said," Hey Bill, "that's Oakley's Jeep over there in the Hibiscus lot. The boys are on the job."

Strong grunted, "Good", while entering the driveway. He parked the Camry close to the front door and they got out. Cole opened the door so Strong, according to their training procedure, could enter first. Once both men were inside they looked over the room and everything seemed to be just as they had left it. The message light on the phone answering machine was not lit, indicating that there were no messages. Strong returned to the Camry to get the groceries and he set them on the kitchen counter. He said, "Take a break boss while I put these things away." He placed the groceries in the fridge and cupboards. "I know we are pretty bushed, but we had better prepare a report about today's activities. If we hit the sack now, then try to write it in the morning, we will likely forget half of the details." Then, sounding upset Strong blurted, "Damn, I almost for got – we have to contact Harris."

Cole said, "You're right, but let's do our report first."

It took them over an hour to complete the task. As Cole tidied up the table he said, "Call Harris now. Let's hope he's available early tomorrow."

Strong dialed the number that Harris had given them. It rang okay. Curt could hear, "Hello. Harris? This is Bill Strong. You drove my partner and me out to Seaview Grill last Tuesday. Remember? Yes, that's me. Sorry to call you late like this. Look, we need your help early tomorrow. Can you go to Clear & Deep to pick up a Bertram that Art Bodder has for us. We told him we'd call you to help us. What time? Say eight or so. You can? Lovely, we need you to collect me, and my partner, at the beach in front of *Enchanted*. Art will tell you where to take us. You're okay with all of that? Wonderful, thanks, and we will make it very worthwhile for you. God bless you too, bye."

Cole smiled and said, "Sounded like we are heading out to sea tomorrow."

"I affirm," replied Strong. "Now let's get some sleep. Don't make a lot of noise if you get up before me. Let's hope the dogs stay quiet, too."

"Don't worry boss, the way I feel, you could be up before me. What a day!"

Then both men, dead tired, disappeared into their bedrooms.

Chapter 14 | Diving, Dope, and Sex

The sun was just over the eastern horizon when Oakley pulled back the drapes that covered his patio doors. He checked his watch. It showed six o'clock on the button. To his surprise he had slept soundly in spite of the previous day's activities. Looking at the morning splendor he thought *'This beats working in some Columbian hell hole.'* He slid his doors open to feel the cool air.

Patton was also awake and his adrenalin had started to flow. He tended to be more edgy than Oakley and it had got him into big trouble a couple of times. It also caused him to toss and turn in his sleep so he was not as sharp of mind the following day. This time however, he felt rested as he opened the drapes covering his patio doors. He relaxed completely when he saw the sun rising and shining on the calm, crystal clear blue sea. Patton shouted across the room, "Hey Tom, are you awake?"

"If I wasn't, I sure would be after hearing you shout. Are you trying to wake up the whole resort?"

Patton ignored the remark. "Why don't we start the day right and take a fast dip in that gorgeous blue sea?"

"Sounds good, but first I'm going to crank up the complimentary coffee pot. Coffee should be ready by the time we come back in."

Oakley put on his swim trunks. He headed to the mini-kitchen, and got the coffee underway.

"I'll be outside," Patton said as he slid open his doors and stepped out onto the patio. The fresh air felt good.

The coffee had started brewing and Tom was ready to join Willie when the phone rang.

"Good Lord, Willie, who would call us at six in the morning?"

"I'll answer it, boss." Patton stepped back into the house and picked up the receiver. Oakley could hear, "Hello? Yes. When? Just hang on for a second." He looked at Tom to say, "It's Palm Dive. They have two slots open for this morning's dive. Leave at ten, back at one."

Tom replied, "Why not, Willie, how much?"

Willie asked, "What's the price? You say thirty dollars each? Okay, we can be there by ten. How many are going? It's eight plus us, or just eight? So it's ten. Stand by."

Looking at Tom again he asked, "Okay?"

"Green light, we're on."

"What's your first name Delgada? 10-4. I'll see you at nine forty-five." Patton hung up the phone. "How convenient, Tom, now we have a chance to check out - get this - Salvador Delgada. Did Amos not say his name is Tony?"

"That's what I heard. It's just one more complication. Let's swim. The coffee is ready now. I'll set it on 'warm'."

They waded into the calm water and bobbed around for a few minutes. They joked about how great the trip was turning out to be. Action was starting to stir as a few folks began to walk along the soft, sandy shore. From the sea, the men were able to see the length of the shoreline and Tom said, "If I wasn't dying for a coffee I'd say we should jog a mile or two along the beach, but, maybe tomorrow."

"Is your memory failing, pal. Tomorrow we are going fishing. Remember?"

"Damn, you are right about that, and we have to get to Billy Bob's real early. Let's get dried off and test the coffee."

They were sitting on the patio enjoying their drinks when Tom said, "We'd better not eat breakfast if we are doing the dive. I packed a few Nutri bars. We can eat a couple of them to keep from starving. Hang tight while I find them." Tom returned with the bars and the coffee pot and as they enjoyed the fare.

They were enjoying their respite as they watched flying terns attack small schools of fish. It also gave them time to review events of the previous evening, and time to plan their next encounter with the drug punks. Willie was listening while scanning the sea for no reason at all. Then, pointing to his right Willie said, "Hey, Tom. See that huge yacht anchored out there about three-hundred yards from shore. It's flying a Canadian flag, and a Panama flag. Doesn't that seem strange to you?"

"I never noticed it, but yes, it is unusual. I've never seen a boat flagged like that. Don't tell me you want to check it out right now."

"No, partner, but I think our dive is out in that area. Maybe we'll get a better look, if it is still sitting there. For now, since we have an hour or so to kill, this could be a good opportunity to check out downtown Kingtown."

Tom looked at Willie and grinned while saying, "Since when did you give up sitting on your ass for doing business?"

Willie laughed. "Screw you." he said. "You know, partner, I'm thinking this sting looks just too easy. Am I missing something?"

"I don't think so," Patton replied, "because the top cop here has an iron grip on this Island. Those punks have to be part of the Commissioner's system. They feel that they can act with impunity – and that becomes our biggest advantage. Also, throw in the fact that the Brits have plenty of experience and it all should go down easily - if we are synchronized."

Willie gave a shrug, and nodded his agreement.

"Look, Willie," Tom said, "let's dress and get going. You never know what we may discover downtown. We'll take our dive gear. Palm Dive is close to the center of town."

Within fifteen minutes they were in the Jeep and on their way to town. The downtown area was small – about three blocks north/south and three blocks east/west. The core of the area had three story buildings on each corner, and every one of them bore the name and logo of an international bank. Located each way along the street were clothing stores, duty-free shops, and one restaurant. The fringe streets were dotted with local food shops, and tourist traps offering souvenirs. Willie parked the Jeep on the fringe area near a straw market. There they chatted with a friendly merchant who informed them that no cruise ships were expected and that the shops would not be busy. Willie thanked the man for the info and bought a straw hat from him. The men started walking toward the business section. Willie took off his baseball cap and replaced it with the straw hat.

"Hey, Tom, do I look like a tourist, or what?"

"You look great, pal. I'll tell anyone who asks that you are a tomato farmer from Florida."

They moved along to the core area where they entered a brightly lit, well designed duty free shop. The sign on the door bore gold colored letters that read, '*Welcome to Treasures Unlimited.*' Inside were six isles of glass display cases. Three of the interior walls were lined with display shelves. Watches bearing every expensive label were displayed. They bore price tags ranging from four hundred dollars to twenty thousand. WATERFORD and SWAROVSKI crystal figurines were in several of the display cases and were priced from fifty to five thousand dollars. LLADRO and INTRADA ITALY porcelain creations were displayed on top of the showcases. Three cases displayed gold, silver and platinum jewelry.

As they moved through the store Willie whispered, "There has to be a million dollars of stuff displayed here."

Tom answered in a low voice, "No kidding!"

At that moment the attendant walked over and welcomed the men. She was a statuesque white woman who appeared to be about sixty years old. "Good morning, gentlemen," she said. She flashed the Palm trademarked smile. "Take your time to look around. I'll be over by the cash register if you need help with anything."

"Thanks, mam," Tom replied.

They spent only a few minutes more in the shop before leaving. The clerk did not look up as they left. Smiling, Tom offered, "She knew there was no use wasting time on us."

"Why do you say that, pal?"

"Ha! She took one look at you with that straw hat on your head, and made up her mind that we couldn't afford the cheapest item in the store."

"Screw you. I like my hat," Willie grunted, "makes me feel like I belong on this Island."

"Yeah, raking the beach, maybe," Tom joked. "Let's walk."

They laughed at each other as they moved along to the core area. Well-dressed people of both sexes and a range of ages were hastily walking into and out of the office buildings, banks and the restaurant.

"Nice looking crowd," Tom noted. "For sure it must take a bunch of help to count all the cash that flows into these banks."

"Yeah.", said Willie, "and then they have to package it up to have it flown to the US. I suppose some of it stays here. These people don't buy the Gucci shoes and Armani suits with sea shells."

They stood in front of the Palm Island Bank & Trust building for several minutes before Patton said, "Let's keep going." About one-hundred feet further down the street they noticed signage that showed, 'THE DIAMOND STORE'. Moving along they stopped to look at the window display. As they gazed at the merchandise on display, a person walked behind them and quickly entered the store. By natural instinct, Oakley looked up and saw the person go directly to someone who appeared to be waiting for him. Tom elbowed Willie to get his attention and said, "I'll swear that is Amos Delray."

"Damn sure looks like him," was the reply. "It's pretty early in the day to be buying jewelry, or whatever. He's peeling off a lot of greenbacks that look like C notes."

Willie nodded his agreement, and sarcastically said, "Looks like Amos did not get rich from operating a small dive operation. We may have stumbled onto something."

At that moment Delray stopped placing cash on the counter, and became vigorously animated. His face was almost into the store clerk's face, and his arms were flailing. He continued for less than a minute, turned to leave, then turned back, shook his fist and started for the door again.

Oakley grabbed his partner by the arm and said, "Turn around, Willie. We don't want Delray to see us here. Let's head back to the Jeep, and figure this out later." They wasted no time and were in their Jeep within a few Minutes.

"Look," Tom said, "it's nine-thirty. Drive around the perimeter of this business area and head to our resort. We want to approach Palm Dive from the right direction." Willie did as suggested and got them there right at nine forty-five.

Delgada saw them drive in. He was on Quicksilver and shouted, "Go to the office, I'll meet you there."

Willie waved an okay, parked the Jeep then said to Tom, "Looks like we're the first ones here."

They entered the office and were surprised to see a group of eight gorgeous women in bikinis. All of them wore caps embroidered with the words, 'GREEN DIVERS – Biloxi MS'. The agents smiled. Willie asked, "Is this PALM DIVE or is this heaven? Can we join the club?"

"No you can't!" shouted a slim blue-eyed blonde. "You can join the party. We're celebrating Karen's divorce." She pointed to a slim, five-foot-ten woman who was wearing a turquoise bikini. "We're all divorced or single so you may see us do some crazy things. Hey, but you two guys don't look like you'll mind our company. In fact, you two are just what we need – something to fight over! I'm Sally."

Tom and Willie laughed. Tom lead off with, "We're from Key West. Nothing surprises us. It looks like we should fit right in – no pun intended."

The ladies laughed. Sally turned to face them and quipped, "This could be one trip to remember. Think they can handle us?"

"Oh yes!" they replied in unison. Sally continued, "How about an introduction?"

"Oh, sorry, we're in shock. I'm Tom, and this is my partner Willie."

The agents then mingled with the divers whom appeared to be in their late twenties and early thirties. All of them were tanned and in perfect physical shape. *'Divorcees', thought Tom. 'Can't be - too good to be true - could be casino staff.'* His instincts were in full bloom. *'Too bad Jane Butterworth isn't here yet, she could pick their brains.'*

Willie worked the group just like he had done many times in Miami's South Beach clubs. Being surrounded by half-naked women, and chatting them up, was not a new experience for him. One of the lovelies, a beauty with coal black eyes started eye dancing with him. He recognized the signal and moved through the group to meet her. She exuded sex, and the vibes went through every molecule in his body. He moved close to her and started with his usual line. "I hope I don't embarrass you, but I caught you looking at me. Did I get the wrong impression? I'd sure like to know you better." He smiled and continued, "Sounds corny, eh, but that's my line."

The woman did not flinch, but smiled in return. It was a signal to Willie that he was on the right track. She said, "I'm Janet, call me Jan. Corny is good.

It's much better than the slimy sweet talk that I get most of the times; turns me off. I felt a thrill as soon as our eyes connected. Maybe after the dive we could do something." She inhaled a bit to accentuate the positive.

Willie opened his eyes wide, grinned and said, "Wow, you don't have to ask me twice. I feel our chemistry, and it's oh … so good; later Jan, for sure."

Out of the corner of his eye, Tom was watching Willie in action. *'What an operator*, he thought, *the guy never ceases to amaze me. I can guess what comes next.'*

At ten on the dot Delgada opened the office door and shouted, "Let's go!"

The group immediately followed him to the boat 'Quicksilver'. It had benches for seating five people on each side. Tom sat closest to the helm. Willie sat next to him on his left side. Janet sat next to Willie. *'I don't know how much of this that I can stand'*, Willie thought, as he glanced to see Jan's cleavage and beautiful legs.

Janet coyly glanced back. Words were not required.

Tom leaned to speak to his partner and said, "This scene doesn't add up. You work the women. I'm going to work on Delgada."

"I hear you, Tom, 10-4."

When all of the divers were seated, Delgada got down from his seat at the helm to address them. "Listen up," he commanded. "Please, place your tanks in front of you, so I can check to be sure they are topped off. You need an hour's supply of air for this dive." He slowly moved along and checked every one. He spoke again. "For those who don't know me, my name is Tony Delgada. Sally here knows who I am. What's this, Sally, your fourth trip?" Sally nodded her agreement. He continued, "We are going to the Blue Reef. The sea and the weather are great so you should have a good dive. The reef is about twenty feet down but in this water it looks more like five. It runs for a quarter of a mile and is two hundred feet wide. Beyond the reef the sea drops straight down for one thousand feet. I'll drop a dive flag marker every forty feet along each side. Raise your hands that you understand." All raised a hand. "Okay, after I drop the markers on both edges of the reef I will come back to the middle of it and anchor the boat. Then pair up and jump in together. Got it?" The passengers nodded to affirm. "Be careful. You can come back on board anytime. Use the ladder on the starboard side. You all have watches so synchronize the time. It is ten-twenty right now. We leave the reef at noon. Now get this straight – his voice rose a couple of decibels – do not swim beyond the flags. Let me hear a loud '*Yes*'!"

The passengers shouted loudly, "Okay, Tony, yes, we hear you!"

Delgada showed no emotion as he returned to his station. He then sounded a load blast from the boat's horn, and out of nowhere a young man appeared on the dock.

Tony shouted, "Cast off Agwe, all clear." The dockhand released the mooring ropes. The screws began to turn and propelled the craft slowly away from the dock.

Tom seized the moment to walk the few feet where there was an empty seat beside the captain. "Can I ride here, Captain?"

"No problem, man," came back the reply.

Tom let a few minutes pass as Delgada was concentrating on maneuvering the boat. Once it was headed it out to sea he asked, "Is our dive spot nearby?"

Delgada stared straight ahead for a few moments as he increased the speed. Turning to face Patton he said, "Pretty close. About a half hour trip but, we won't be going too far from shore. We'll be out about a half a mile and four miles to the west. It's usually a safe place on this side of Palm."

"Sounds good - any sharks in that area?"

"No, the reef fish are too small for their taste. The odd time we see some barracudas. They can be nasty if they get challenged."

The two men were quiet for a while before Tom spoke again. "Do you need help placing the marker flags?"

"Sure, I can use the help. Have you done that before?"

"I've done that many times, Tony. Willie and I often take dive trips. By the way, did Amos ask you to call us for this trip, or did your friend Dorman refer us?"

Delgada turned to face Tom while saying, "Amos asked. He had your info. As for Dorman, he's what you might call an agent of mine. How'd you meet him?"

"We were having a beer at The Hibiscus while waiting for a pizza last night. He was there with a pal called Fingers, and a couple of other guys. We had a nice talk. At least I know where to get me some ganja. Willie and I never know when we might get lucky with the broads, and need some for a party." With a lilt in his voice, continued. "Dive spots usually have more than a few loose women around."

Tony nodded and smiled. The two men had a few minutes of silence. The boat moved along the coastline as Delgada kept his eyes on the sea. Without a prompt he said. "I get a lot of unsolicited offers. Women tourists are an easy mark if you have Jamaican tobacco handy. You puff them into la-la land."

"Yeah, man. Right on," *'Thinking now is the time for the real question,'* Tom stated, "pot is great but snow is the real ticket. Should I ask Dorman if he can find some for us?"

"No need to ask him. I'll make sure he has what you want. How much do you need, and when do you want it?"

"Tuesday evening would be great. We're working on some lovelies at The Beach Hotel. How much will it set us back?"

"Five hundred for each person will get you through a few parties."

"U S bucks I suppose."

"Yes, U S."

"Look, we'll be back at Hibiscus tonight so we'll make arrangements with Dorman. We have plans for tomorrow night, as well as on Sunday and Monday. We plan to be diving at other spots if the weather holds, and we want to check out some clubs at night. I'll say Tuesday evening will be a good time. If we need weed before then we'll just drop by Hibiscus and see Dorman. We'll have the cash to give him on Tuesday."

"No problem, but you'll be dealing with Fingers. He's our leader."

"Great!" Tom replied. "Glad we got hold of you. This visit is shaping up to be one of our best. By the way, Dorman said your first name is Marco, but Amos calls you Tony. We use nicknames a lot in the States. Which one do you want me to use?"

"My first name is Marco, but my second name is Antonio. Tony is easier to use. Call me Tony."

"Okay, Tony it is. Do you miss your homeland? Dorman told me you are from Columbia."

"I miss it, but I make a lot more money here. I don't like Englishmen as they treat us like we're shit. Even the native Palm Islanders are a pain in the ass. Americans and Canadians are okay. Like you and your buddy – you appreciate us little guys."

Tom nodded, then, looked back to see what the loud laughing was about. Willie was entertaining the women by telling them a crazy story that had just enough truth to cover the fictitious parts. His story telling worked well as a cover for their real activities. Resuming his position Tom said, "What do you think Tony? Looks like Willie could get lucky."

"Tom, what I think is for you to get ready to drop the markers." He cut the boat's speed to idle. "When I say, 'drop', toss one in." He then turned and shouted at the guests. "We're here. Stay two by two, and then when I say, 'go', I want pairs of you to go overboard." You divers will be on your own for about an hour. I will cut the engines after I anchor the ship, then you go in the water paired up. The engines will be off until everyone is back on board. Set your watches for eleven-fifteen. That will give us time to get on our way back to the harbor."

After six women were in the water, Willie and Janet were next into the sea. Tom got his tank and gear on, smiled and exclaimed, "Okay Sally. It looks like you are stuck with me!"

"I've been with a lot worse. You won't catch me complaining. C'mon, let's have a look down there." She adjusted her gear to show more of her physique. They held hands and dropped into the sea. Tom's testosterone level was rising as he thought, 'Be careful, man, you're getting horny.'

The underwater scene was spectacular. The perfectly clear water made objects look bigger, and closer, than they really were. The coral waved gently back and forth as the current slowly passed through it. Small multicolored fish darted in and out of crevices, and everywhere Tom looked, schools of fish came and went in waves. He and Sally stayed close together, frequently touching, to indicate to one another, objects they saw. Tom was enjoying the action and he was pretty sure Sally was too. They had been down for about thirty minutes when he suddenly noticed a monster-like thing peering out from a crevice. It was a huge moray eel. Tom grabbed Sally by her ankle and motioned for her to see the dangerous creature. She nodded and pointed to the boat. She quickly swam toward it. Tom wasted no time and followed her. They surfaced close enough to Quicksilver for Tony to hear Tom shout, "There's a huge moray eel down there."

Tony shouted back, "Don't go near it. Warn the others to get over here fast!" He sounded the alarm horn.

Tom and Sally stayed together as they swam to warn the others. They gave them the universal divers' warning signal. Within five minutes they all surfaced near the boat. Tony waved to indicate that he wanted them back onboard and he yelled, "Move it!" They did as ordered. "Look down there," he said, as he started to weigh the anchor. "Sure enough, the eel was at least ten feet long and swimming beneath the boat. The sight of it scared the crap out of the women. Tony got the anchor aweigh and secured it. He looked at the divers and said, "Glad you got on board or that sucker would be eating diver for lunch. I've never seen an eel out here until now. Good thing you spotted it, Tom, before it began to hunt. Eels are one sea creature that I don't trust. They have killed a few swimmers down where I come from in Columbia."

Delgada started the engines and let the boat idle. He said, "I can take you to another dive spot that's in the harbor or we can call it a day. It's your choice, but we have to be docked by noon."

"That's an easy decision," Tom said. "By the time we retrieve the flags, and cruise back, we will almost be out of time." He turned to face Sally. What do you think, babe?"

"I'll speak for my crowd," she replied. "Let's go home. I could use a drink."

A breeze began to put a slight chop on the sea. Two slick cruisers passed Quicksilver. Tom pointed to them as he asked, "I guess those are fishing charters heading out to sea?"

"Ya, I recognize the crew. They go out about ten miles where there is a three mile long reef, and it's very deep on the edge of it. Big fish cruise the edge of it – like marlin, wahoo and tuna. Sometimes fishermen get lucky and a large patch of seaweed – we call it a float – drifts along with the current. Schools of mahi-mahi follow it. They love fresh bait, and with four lines trolling, you can load your boat in an hour. The restaurants buy all the mahi-mahi that they can get."

"That's interesting," Tom said. "Early tomorrow we are going fishing with Billy Bob LaRue. I guess you know him? He needs a couple of strong helpers so Willie and I volunteered. He's going over by Four Tops where he claims there are big tuna and sharks."

"Are you crazy? That BB is a drunken piece of shit. He thinks he can go anywhere with that Canadian boat of his. One of these days he'll learn he can't. On two occasions, since I started working for Amos, a couple of pretty big craft never made it back to our harbor from Four Tops. The crew probably got eaten by sharks. The boats were never recovered. Could be that they got carried away by the Gulf Stream. Amos seems to know something about what might have happened. I can't believe that old bastard BB has been out there and made it back."

"Wow! Now you've got me worried."

"I know they blame stuff on pirate ghosts, but I sure as hell am not going to test the idea. I've overheard Amos talk about a small cay on the far side of the island. He has anchored in it when the sea got too heavy for his boat."

"I guess I'd better ask him."

"Shit Tom! Don't tell him I told you anything about Four Tops. I only know what I overheard. If I wasn't worried about you going out I'd have kept my mouth shut."

"Hey. Sorry I'm so nosey, Tony. I'll keep my mouth shut. Wherever Willie and I go we talk to the locals and their stories are interesting, just like yours. To put Tony at ease Tom turned around to face Willie and said, "You all okay back there?"

Willie responded, "Do I look like I'm suffering?"

"Yes, you do. Your brain must be sore from trying to figure out which of these gorgeous creatures you're going to take to lunch."

"Wrong buddy, it's sore from helping the women chose which one of them you are taking to lunch. Right now Sally is fighting with the rest of her crew."

"Just make sure it's only for lunch, pal. We have a big fishing trip tomorrow. Let's settle on meeting at their hotel. We can plan other activities then."

"Sounds good pal, they are staying at the Holiday Place. I'll ask them to meet us in the in an hour."

As they finished their exchange, Tony maneuvered Quicksilver to the dock. After it was secured, and before the divers disembarked, Tony offered everyone a free beer. That went over with great enthusiasm and the group enjoyed more fun moments. When they finished partying they went to the waiting area beside the office. Sally walked into the office and came back out with Amos. He thanked everyone for going on the trip, then, instructed Tony to drive the women to their hotel as he pointed to the white Ford van parked next to the agent's Jeep. The women piled into the van and Tony drove it away. Amos shook hands with Tom and Willie and said, "I hope you enjoyed our service and I look forward to seeing you again before you leave the Island."

Tom replied, "We sure did, Amos. Tony was a great host and captain. To top it off, it looks like Willie and I will be having company for lunch."

"Good," Amos said with a grin, "Try to behave yourselves."

As they were getting into their Jeep Willie chimed in, "We'll try, but no promises."

They drove straight to The Beach Hotel, changed into their beach attire, and went directly to The Holiday Place Resort. Sally and Jan were waiting for them as planned, and the two couples proceeded to a table on the hotel patio. They spent several minutes having a nice time talking and laughing then all ordered salads and beers. The beer was served quickly. As they waited for the food Sally said, "Amos usually doesn't let me, and my entourage, mix with any men. This is an exception for us to be with two handsome guys."

Willie responded, "I guess he feels we're harmless, and that we'd sooner dive into the sea than other places."

Sally caught the innuendo, grinned and rolled her eyes as she spoke, "My god, if that isn't a sneaky proposition, I don't know what is. What do you think, Janet?"

Jan just smiled back, turned to Willie and gave him the eye chemistry. It caused Willie to shift in his chair. His testosterone started to surge again.

Tom, sensing the friendly rapport asked, "When do you two leave Palm? I can't believe your story about being a group of divorcees. What men in their right minds would dump women as gorgeous as you two?"

The two ladies looked at each other for support. Sally talked. "Here's the truth. We work as Courtesy Girls at the SALEM CASINO in Biloxi. Amos is a friend of the owner Mr. Mancini. About every three months, as a perk, he'll pick several of us to come to Grand Palm in his big yacht. We love it. I guess he's well connected because we never have any problem. The Palm Island immigration officers just smile and ask us to show our driver's licenses. Amos probably keeps them happy."

"Could be," Tom said. "Such a deal; well, Willie and I have been around, and we weren't buying your first story. Now the picture makes sense. By the way, is that his yacht flying the Canadian and Panama flags and moored out from this hotel?"

"That's it, Tom. Great looking ship don't you think? You should see the inside. It's beyond description."

"Wow, if you get a chance, see if you can get us a tour."

"Not a chance, my dear, but I can show you another tour."

Tom had no doubt about what she meant and he glanced skyward. To further acknowledge her remark he scanned her body up and down. She caressed his forearm.

The chatter stopped as the waiter served their salads. He stood beside Tom and said, "My name is Ted. Will there be anything else right now?"

"No. That's all," replied Tom. Then he added - "bring the check to me please."

As they enjoyed the food Willie asked, "Maybe you'd like to join us tonight for a drink or two. We found a quiet little bar down the road at the Hibiscus Restaurant. We could pick you up at seven o'clock and have you back here by nine. I'm sure we'd enjoy hearing more of your escapades."

As Willie talked, Tom was hoping they would say "no", as he feared things were getting too hot, too fast.

Sally looked wistful and replied, "We can't leave the hotel at night so, if and when – I hope when – it would have to be here. We have separate rooms and there's no curfew, eh Janet?"

Janet shifted closer to Willie and leaned close to his ear, "None in my room, number three-one-three."

Willie pushed back from the table, looked back and forth at both women, then said, "I think we can work with that, don't you Tom?"

"Yes and no. We have to get up before daylight tomorrow to go fishing. How about Saturday or Sunday ladies? This evening we could drop by our drug store - he winked at Sally – to get some party supplies."

"If that's the option," Sally replied, as she put on a sad face, "then tomorrow is it. We never know when Amos is going to give the '*all aboard*' signal. The last couple of trips ended on the Sunday."

"I like that option." said Willie. "If we don't drown at sea, we will be ready to be spoiled. Maybe a massage could happen?" he asked Jan.

She held out her hands and said, "With these, you will never forget your treatment. But, hey, yours look like they could make a person feel relaxed and ready too." They both laughed and sealed the deal with a kiss.

"Let me get the bill, and we can all have an afternoon soaking up the sun." Tom waved at Ted who immediately approached the table.

The group was standing. The waiter simply said, "Thanks for coming." He handed the bill to Tom.

The women hugged their escorts with passion. Onlookers enjoyed the sight.

• • •

It was a short ride back to The Beach Hotel, and as they poked along in the heavy afternoon traffic Tom said, "Can you believe what has happened, pal? We may have landed in the middle of the damn cartel. Now we have to figure out how to *not* get laid."

Willie looked at him and said, "You sound like you're over the hill, man. A good operator should be able to get laid and get info on the same date."

"You know better my friend. I hope you are kidding."

Laughing loudly, Willie replied, "I knew I could get a rise out of you. Don't worry. But, you know we still have to hit Hibiscus tonight, so let's just kick back for now. Wake me if I get stuck dreaming about what I'm supposed to miss!"

Chapter 15 | The Premier Takes Charge

The Premier's residence was set well back from the sea. The seaside yard was a vast spread of craggy, black coral with no vegetation. It was about twenty feet above sea level. Westwood had recently had his home built there because when he resided on the main beach section, tourists would wander up to it, thinking it was a small hotel. Now he could watch the sea crashing against the coral barricade and observe the big ocean tankers moving back and forth from South America to Houston. Also, in his planning, he knew this home would be safe from burglars who frequently broke into beach residences. Not even a fool would attempt to walk over the jagged coral in front of his house. The fact that this home was fairly isolated caused him to have a modest villa built on the property for his staff of two - Austin Small, his wife Gela and his two sons. Gela was the Westwood's housekeeper. Austin served as the handyman, and chauffeur. Security was buttressed by two trained German Shepard dogs, one for Small, the other for Westwood.

When Westwood finished meeting with the Governor he was driven directly to his residence. Austin, a native son of the country, noticed that his employer was unusually silent. He and the Premier always chatted about something when only the two of them were in the car. On this trip quiet prevailed. His employer was obviously very concerned about something. When the trip was about to end, Westwood broke the silence by saying, "Sorry to be so quiet Austin, but I got some distressing news back there at Dale's. I'll need you to be available on a moment's notice for the next three days."

"I can do that, sir."

Westwood continued, I must speak to Gloria immediately, and then, I'll bring you up-to-date."

"I understand," Small replied, as he pulled into the Premier's driveway. He parked the Lincoln, got out and opened the back door. Westwood stepped out and said, "I'll see you in a bit, - We may have to drive to Kingtown in an hour or so."

Westwood's dog Kip started to bark when the car stopped. Hearing this, his wife Gloria opened the front door. Kip bounded out, and with his tail wagging furiously, he greeted his master. Bruce patted him on the head and gave a one-word command, "House". The dog turned immediately and led the way to the front door where Gloria was waiting. She hugged her husband, stepped back and said, "You don't look too happy. How was the meeting?"

"The meeting was fine, but the news is not good. Come, he beckoned to her, let's go into the kitchen and sit down. But before we talk I have to call the Police Commissioner."

Gloria pulled up a chair and sat down as her husband went directly to the phone and dialed the Police number. She heard it ring then, "Hello is this Audrey? Yes, this is Premier Westwood. I need to speak to the Commissioner. I have some great news to report. He's there? Put him on."

"One moment please," Audrey replied.

After a pause that seemed like an eternity to Westwood, Commissioner Black said, "Hello Bruce. You have good news?"

"Warton I'm sure glad that I caught you. I have some exciting news to tell you. I am so happy for you. If you are not too busy can I come down now? In an hour is fine, I'll be there at four sharp."

"What's that all about, dear," Gloria asked as Bruce hung up the phone.

He answered, "You know that two detectives are here from England. Well, they have uncovered evidence that Commissioner Black has hidden facts pertaining to those deaths of last June. And, in fact, he is actually running a police state right here. According to the British Detective, Black is a very dangerous man and we should fear for our own safety, and that of the Neily's if we should try to interfere in his operation. The detectives have a plan to take him down. That is why I have to see the Commissioner right away. There is no need for you to worry about things at this moment, but be sure to keep Kip with you at all times."

Gloria, as usual, did not question her husband's advice. She looked at him with a knowing expression and said, "Can I do anything for you before you leave?"

"Thanks, dear, you can call Austin and tell him to pick me up at three-thirty."

As instructed, Austin had the car waiting and they left on time. The drive to Police H.Q. took about thirty minutes during which time Westwood chatted about the weather, and the upcoming cricket match. Upon arrival at H.Q. he instructed Austin to park in one of the spaces marked 'Reserved for Officials'. Austin parked next to the Commissioner's Land Rover. Before they exited the Lincoln, Westwood said to his driver, "Come inside to wait for me. I might need you in there. I also want you to keep track of who enters or leaves the station while I am with Commissioner Black. I'm especially interested to know if Deputy Commissioner Samson Black enters or leaves the building."

"I can do that, Sir." Austin did not ask for any explanation, nor was any offered.

Audrey was at the reception counter when the two men entered the building. She greeted them with a pleasant, "Nice to see you Mr. Premier. It has been quite a while. And Austin, how have you been? And, how is Gela?"

"Nice to see you too, Audrey. The wife is fine."

"I know you want to meet with Commissioner Black, sir. Let me ring him. He has had a busy day."

"Thanks", said Westwood. "I have some really exciting news for him."

She pressed the intercom button and in a moment said, "Yes, sir, I'll tell him you are busy." She looked up to address Westwood and said, "He's just finishing up. Please have a seat for five minutes and George will be down to show you to the Commissioner's office."

"Of course, not a problem," was his reply. '*Busy?*' he thought. '*I'm his boss. Cole is correct, the man has no respect for me.*'

They took a seat, then, the Premier commented, "You've been working here for quite a while, Audrey. It's easy to lose track of time. When did you start?"

She replied, "I started this job in 1976. I guess it's a lifetime thing. I hope it is."

Westwood thought, *'She sure has seen it all, so Cole will be asking her some tough questions.'*

Her intercom buzzed. "Oh, that's him now. She picked up the receiver and Westwood heard, "You are ready? Yes, we will wait for George."

Westwood turned to Austin and quietly said, "Remember what I asked you to do."

"Yes, sir, I do."

Almost immediately George appeared. Westwood was fond of George and thought of him as a friend. He said, "Hello, my friend. How are you?"

"I'm fine, sir. Let me show you up to the office."

They exchanged more pleasantries as they ascended the stairway, and walked the long hallway to Warton Black's office. Westwood's attention was diverted when he passed by a room that had an open door. Two people were sitting across from one another at a table. He could see the person facing the doorway. He recognized Amos Delray. Being suspicious of everything connected to the Commissioner, he thought, *'Interesting, I hope Austin can identify the other person.'*

George tapped twice on the office door then heard, "Come right in." To their surprise the Commissioner stood just inside waiting to greet them.

"How nice, George," Westwood joked, "we have a greeter today."

George smiled and excused himself saying, "I'll be right outside if you need anything."

The commissioner shook the premier's hand and said, "Let's have a chair, Bruce." They sat across from each other. "Tell me about this exciting news."

Westwood smiled and said, "Congratulations, Warton! I've just heard from the Governor. Next week you are to be honored at the annual meeting of The Commonwealth Police Commissioners' Association. You have been chosen to receive the top award as The British Commonwealth Most Outstanding Police Official for 1989." He added, "What a tribute to you, and what great publicity for our country!"

"Me?" Black asked. "I don't usually like surprises, so how did this come about?"

Conjuring up his best ability to lie, Westwood proceeded to deliver fact and fiction. "Every year three officials, one from the UK and two from the Commonwealth countries are chosen. I assume you know that, if you receive their quarterly report. This year the Canadian and the Australian chiefs are on the award committee. They review crime statistics for all of our Commonwealth countries and assess them relative to their locations in the world, plus the force size relative to population served. They do not reveal their winner until a week before the award ceremony.

Black looked puzzled and said, "To say I'm surprised is an understatement because we had those deaths last June. Perhaps the other countries had more incidents."

"Certainly." replied the Premier.

Black queried, "I understand the ceremony is next Thursday in London?"

"That's right. It's a two day event starting on Wednesday morning. We know you'll need a couple of days to get organized with your Deputy Chief, so Governor Neily has booked you on that once-a-week, Tuesday, British Airways direct flight to London. First class, too, I might add!"

"I'm very honored, Bruce, but there's a lot to look after here in Grand Palm right now. New people are trying to get in every day. Calvertians are sneaking in by boat. Financial sharks are coming here in their private planes - and so on. I don't see how I can leave."

Westwood hesitated and showed a furrowed frown. He remained silent and shifted in his chair thinking, '*I have to keep him talking. I have to shut up and wait.*'

Black sensed that Westwood was waiting for more. He got up from his chair, took a step to his right then turned to face his guest. He continued, "Let me think about this," he continued. "What would happen if I did not attend?"

"Oh! The answer is simple. Our country would be extremely embarrassed. And I can't imagine the financial loss. Foreign investors and tourist agents everywhere would get suspicious that something is wrong here. No, you should be happy that you can give great, positive prestige to us. Let's get Samson, your Deputy Chief in here and find out from him how he'd handle the job for the five days that you would be absent. You'll be back here next Saturday."

"You're putting a lot of pressure on me Bruce. I don't like that."

Westwood thought hard. The idea was getting attacked. Then he came up with his ultimate excuse. "Sorry, Warton, but I want you to go. It's for the good of all, especially you. I know you are thinking of running for Chief Executive of our government – what better credential could you hope for? Maybe this opportunity makes it happen sooner."

Warton smiled. "Well, you do have a point my friend. Let's see what the deputy has to say. You are making it very hard for me to say no." He walked to his desk and buzzed Audrey: "Is Samson here today, Audrey? Good, send him right up. Tell George there's no need for Samson to knock, he can just come in." Turning to Westwood he said, "I guess you heard that. He'll be here in a minute or so."

'*Now for some real diplomacy,*' Westwood thought.

It took less than three minutes for Deputy Chief Samson Black to enter the office.

"Have a seat, Samson. The Premier here wants me to go to the UK for a few days to receive a big, prestigious award. I've been selected as the top cop in the Commonwealth for 1989. I'd have to leave on Tuesday and return on Saturday."

"Gosh, almighty, why would you not go? I can handle your job for that short spell. I'd call you if I had to."

Westwood seized upon the chance to chime in. "See, Warton. You've trained him well. Now you have no excuse. He rushed to shake the commissioner's hand. I'm so proud of you Warton. What a great tribute for your many years of service."

Warton stepped back saying, "You are more excited than me, Bruce. I guess I never paid much attention to our relationship. To me you are simply a figurehead even though I know you are my boss, but thank you." Looking at Samson he said, "I'll organize things over this weekend. I may have to call you at home. We'll start early Monday morning and announce to the staff and the officers that you will be fully in charge while I am away. Are you okay with that?"

"I'll be ready, sir. You have earned the honor. Enjoy the limelight."

"That's the plan then, Bruce. I suppose my itinerary is available?"

"Yes. The Governor has been back and forth with the UK officials so he should have it by now. He will be delighted to hear that you will go to show the world how we operate here. I'll stop by his residence, and since we don't want the good news to leak out until Monday, maybe Samson here could follow me to get the itinerary. He can bring it to you on Monday. As far as the flight goes, you know that BA comes in on Monday afternoon then leaves at nine on Tuesday morning. You will be met at Heathrow by some upper rank folks from New Scotland Yard. It should be a trip you'll remember for many years."

"Enough, enough, Bruce, let's get on with it. Can you find your way out, or should I call George to help you?"

"I've been here before, my friend. I'll make it out okay." Westwood left and made his way to the reception area where Austin was waiting. He said, "Let's go Austin. Bye Audrey."

Audrey waved them a good-bye.

No words were spoken before Westwood was in the Lincoln and Austin had started to drive. When they were clear of the parking area the Premier asked, "Austin, did you recognize any people?"

"Yes sir. Shortly after you left with George, Mr. Jones, the lawyer came down the stairway. He seemed very preoccupied. He didn't say a word to Audrey or I. Also, the Deputy Commissioner came in, and said '*hello*' to me. That's all, sir."

"Good work, Austin. Thank you. Please take me to the Governor's residence."

They arrived at Neily's residence without any problem. Westwood did not chat with his driver. The Premier's mind was spinning from the interaction with Warton Black. He also replayed, mentally, the sight of Amos Delray meeting with, who had to be, Winston Jones. It was obvious that they were the people who were tied up with Commissioner Black. Never did Westwood imagine that he would ever be entangled in such dangerous activity. Thoughts ran from fear to joy. '*Could Cole's plan actually work? What if it didn't?*' He felt a bit more relief as they arrived at the Governor's place. As Austin was parking the Lincoln, Bruce could hear Kip barking furiously. Dale appeared in the doorway and waved him on over. Before Westwood reached the doorway Dale said, "Is everything on track? How did it go? I've been worried. Come sit in my office. The London folks are waiting to hear from us."

Westwood felt relieved to be with his friend. He smiled as he sat down, and said, "I outdid myself Dale. What a con artist I've become. It looks like

Black took the bait, hook, line, and sinker. He hesitated at first and made excuses, but for some unknown reason I threw this at him: I told him such an honor would certainly assure him of an election victory when he runs for the office of Chief Executive."

"You bugger, you," Dale said laughingly. "Look, The Yard phoned me back to tell me that before anyone can be arrested in the UK for offences committed in another country an official request must be made to the FCO, Foreign & Commonwealth Office. I immediately prepared a report pointing out Commissioner Black's suspected involvement in eight murders plus his connection to drug cartels, and the threat to the national security of the Palm Islands people. We also need to send an arrest warrant to Yard, Special Forces. I faxed the report about an hour ago. We have to get the warrant right away. I got another phone call to tell me that although it usually takes several days to reach a decision, our situation calls for special attention. The request should be approved before Monday evening."

Westwood replied, "So you have been a busy bee too. Did you get Commissioner Black's itinerary?"

The Governor replied, "I have it right here on the desk. Based upon the assumption that we could pull off this con, The Yard faxed it to me. It's even on the official letterhead of The Commonwealth Police Commissioners' Association. They are sending his airline ticket by courier. I will receive it on Monday. The trap is set, my friend."

"Okay," Bruce replied, "Deputy Samson Black will come by this evening, probably shortly, to pick up the itinerary. When he comes, make a big fuss about this great event. Pump him up. Oh, and tell him about the ticket. Tell him that Detective Cole will drop it off on Monday afternoon. Right now I just want to get home and relax." He got up to leave when, suddenly, he remembered the Amos Delray sighting. "Damn, Dale, I almost forgot. When I arrived at Police headquarters I had to wait several minutes before we met Wharton. Audrey said he was finishing up an important meeting. Well, guess who was there, – Amos Delray and Winston Jones. Up to no good would be my guess. Be sure to get that info to Detective Cole."

"Good Lord, Bruce. You sure walked into the lion's den. Did they see you?"

"No, but the Lincoln parked outside would give us away. I doubt they would worry about me seeing them."

"That's fine old friend. Get on your way. Stay safe." Dale saw his guest to the door and waved as the Lincoln pulled away.

To the surprise of both men, just then, the Deputy Commissioner's cruiser was entering the circular driveway. '*What timing*,' Bruce thought. He did not bother to wave. He was thinking about relaxing with Gloria and sipping Tanqueray gin – their evening ritual. "Let's get home, Austin," he sighed. "It's been a hectic afternoon."

Neily stayed in the doorway and waved for Deputy Black to come over. As they shook hands Neily greeted him with, "Good to see you Samson. How are things down at the station? Great news about our Commissioner's award don't you think!"

"Yes," was the reply, "I'm not surprised, for many years now, he's kept things under control. I came to get his itinerary."

"Step inside for a moment. I have it in my office."

"I can wait here, sir, no problem."

Neily moved quickly and returned with a sealed envelope that he handed to Deputy Black. "Here's what you came for. Looks like a great trip, Samson. The plane ticket will be delivered to me by DHL Courier on Monday. This will be a great opportunity for you to run the show. I have no doubt that you will do fine."

"Thanks, Governor. If I need your help next week I will call you. I have to run now."

Neily watched as Deputy Black exited the driveway. He then stepped back into his home, knelt down, and prayed out loud. "Dear Lord, please guide us and keep the detectives safe as they root out the bad people who are trying to control Palm Islands. You are in charge, Lord, and I believe you will cause justice to prevail. Amen."

He then went to join Geraldine who had prepared martinis. She was awaiting him on the seaside patio.

Chapter 16 | Friday Night

By seven o'clock Patton and Oakley were rested and ready for a meal. They dressed in Bermuda shorts and tailored shirts as they wanted the drug punks to think they had money to blow. Before they drove into the Hibiscus parking area, they drove around the '*Enchanted*' driveway to see if Cole's Camry was in sight. They were surprised that it was not there. They proceeded to the restaurant. Willie parked the Jeep and he commented, "I guess Webber is having a slow night. There are only two cars parked here and I don't see any customers in the dining room. We should make a note, Tom, that one is a beat up Toyota, the other an '89 Explorer. When we get inside, if only the punks are here, at least we can assume that those vehicles belong to them. Let's go. I'm hungry."

Webber noticed the Jeep arrive. He went to the restaurant entrance to greet his guests. He greeted them saying, "Hi. I remember you two. It's great to have you back. Do you want to sit in the dining room or the lounge?"

"We like to be casual, Mr. Webber, and we like your lounge. But make no mistake, we want some grub. Can we eat in there?"

"Sure you can. Watson will look after you. If you need me, just call."

Webber showed them to the corner table in the lounge where they discovered that they were the only guests, other than Fingers and his associates.

"Hey guys, we're back," said Tom. "Glad to see you again. We need a couple of cold Buds, Watson. And bring a menu over. We're hungry." Looking at Fingers, Tom said, "We could use an item from *your* menu also, pal. Have a seat over here. Can I buy you guys a beer?"

Fingers smiled. "Why not, man? Set the boys up Watson." He joined the DEA agents at their table and said, "Delgada tells me you guys were busy today. Pretty nice broads he served up. Are you still working on them?"

Tom chuckled as he replied, "So much for secrecy eh, Fingers?"

Fingers replied, "Not much happens on this Island that I don't know about." He sipped his beer.

Tom looked at Willie and said, "Did you hear that? I'm glad we don't know anything except how to have a good time." Shifting to look at Fingers Tom continued talking. "Speaking of good times, we are going to meet the girls on Tuesday night. Tony told us he'd talk to you about party supplies."

"Yeah, I got the word. You need cash, nothing bigger that twenties. I'll be ready right here about this time, let's see - seven Tuesday."

Dorman piped in, "Did you tell Tony that I sent you?"

"Yep, I sure did."

Fingers leaned over to address Tom and quietly said, "Ignore him. He's dispensable. I call the shots."

"Oh, he doesn't bother us. Tony told us you are in charge. Look, we want to relax tonight because we're going fishing early tomorrow and..."

Before Tom could finish Fingers interrupted, "I know. Tony told me. You had better be careful if you goin' out with that ass hole LaRue. He's bad news, man."

"Not to worry," Tom replied, "two of us and one of him. We'll be okay. Thanks anyway for the heads up. What Willie and I need now, if you have them, are a couple of joints. We are planning a quiet evening and sweet dreams."

"I have what you need. You need thirty dollars. Why don't you order your food while I step out to my Explorer?"

"Good idea. What do you suggest?"

"Ask Watson. I don't eat what Webber makes." Fingers got up and went out.

Willie got up and walked over to talk to Watson. He noticed a bulge in Dorman's left pant pocket. The other two punks said nothing, but Willie took notice of their size. Both men were at about six feet tall and both had very slim bodies and muscular arms. He addressed the bartender. "Well Watson, what's good here other than the pizza?"

"Go for the baked ziti, man. I could eat that stuff every day if Webber would let me."

"Good enough then. Two baked ziti - how about two glasses of Italian red to go with it?"

"Ten minutes for the ziti, the wine I'll bring right away. Is Chianti okay?"

Willie gave the '*green light*' and returned to the table. He sat next to Tom so they could speak quietly. He nudged Tom and said, "Check out Dorman's left pocket."

Tom looked and studied Dorman. He saw the bulge and thought, '*I'd better get a better look*'. Motioning with his hand and simultaneously speaking he said, "Dorman, c'mon over."

Dorman got off of the bar stool and walked over to the table and sat down across from Tom. "Wazz up, man," he said.

"I talked with Tony and he wanted you to know, in so many words, that he likes being your partner." Tom watched Dorman smile. "He said Fingers is your leader, but for sure he has praise for you. I just thought you should know that. We had a really good trip."

"Thanks, man. Nice to know I'm appreciated." They talked about diving and drank their drinks until Dorman turned around on his chair as Watson approached. "I see Watson has your supper so I'll leave."

Watson placed the food on the table and offered this comment, "Enjoy. It will taste even better than it smells!"

As Dorman stood up to leave Tom was inches from the bulge in Dorman's pants. It appeared to outline, without a doubt, a large switchblade knife.

Tom took a chance and said, "In your business, how do you stay safe?"

Dorman reached into his pocket and pulled out a folded eight-inch switchblade knife. He flipped it open to show it off. He grinned. "This works for me," he said.

"No doubt, nice tool for sure," Tom replied. Then looking at Willie, and in order to sound stupid he said, "Hey, Willie, maybe we should borrow that for our fishing trip."

"Fat chance of that eh, Dorman?" Willie said, as they all laughed.

Dorman was still next to the table when Fingers returned and walked over to the table. His six-foot-four muscular body was very imposing when viewed from any angle, but especially from the agent's sitting position. Tom and Willie continued eating, hoping that Fingers would start a conversation. They knew from experience that it was best if the other person spoke first. And they sure did not like the surly expression on Fingers' face. He looked at Dorman and, angrily said, "What the hell are you doing over here. Get your ass over where I told you to sit!"

Dorman did as ordered.

That interlude gave Tom a chance to open with, "I guess I'm to blame, man. He's the guy who told us to dive with Delgada at Palm Dive so we asked him to join us so we could thank him – why not?"

"I'll decide later, why not. You have to understand that his brain is not too sharp. He could be talking to a DEA agent or a British cop and not have a clue. I don't tolerate a loose tongue."

"I can understand where you're coming from." Then to change the subject Tom said, 'Willie, give Fingers the cash."

Willie took a roll of twenties from his pocket, peeled off two of them. He said, "I know you said fifteen bucks each for a joint, but here's forty bucks. I only carry 'Jacksons'." He hoped Fingers would be impressed and also, distracted. His plan worked and Fingers took the money. Two joints were placed on the table.

"I like how you guys do business. You'll need fifty of those Jacksons' on Tuesday."

Willie carried on, "We can get cash from two or three banks so we don't have to answer a bunch of questions about who we are and what we do. For God's sake, it costs three-hundred or more just to buy dinner on some of the islands we've visited for diving."

Fingers had calmed down and before he left the divers he said, "I'm here every night after seven so come by any evening if you need more supplies. I don't keep the good stuff handy and only deliver when I get an order. Tuesday I'll be ready."

Tom acknowledged the comment with, "Glad we found you. We'll see you on Tuesday at seven or maybe a bit after." Willie managed to contain his glee.

They ate every morsel of the ziti, finished their wine and asked for the check.

Watson said, "I have it here. Hibiscus policy is to not add a gratuity to the bill. Customers can pay what they think the service is worth. Looks like you owe forty-two bucks."

Willie peeled off three more twenties and said, "This should do it. Everything was great."

The agents took their pot and smiled at the punks. "Thanks again guys. We're off to dreamland."

When they were on their way in the Jeep, Tom laughed and said, "What the hell just happened? Can we take down those guys that easily, Willie?"

"Tom, when I saw the size of Dorman's blade I decided the Brits had better be extra careful. You and I should expect the unexpected too. There's no easy take down that I've heard of. Let's get back to our shack. Hope we don't get stopped by some cop and get arrested for having pot."

"You're right, but we will warn Cole. Let's get home and get some sleep."

"Look, I know we have to get some sleep but we'd better get some grub and drinks for our fishing trip. Not likely there'll be anyplace to buy it before sunrise."

You can bet your pretty ass on that," said Willie. "I saw a place near our hotel that might be open – Carl's Treats. We can put stuff in the fridge in our room. Let's give it a shot."

Carl's Treat's was less than a quarter of a mile from the Hotel. As they drove up to it they smiled because a neon sign displayed 'OPEN'. They walked in to see an empty room except for a man who greeted them as he scraped a grill. He talked as he worked, saying, "I'm the owner. Be with you in a second. Have a seat."

Patton said, "Take your time. We need four sandwiches and six drinks to take on a fishing trip early tomorrow morning."

"No problem. There, finally finished. I had a block buster crowd tonight. Customers were packed in like never before. The word is out about my mouth-watering chicken and juicy burgers. It's a mad house in here on Friday evenings." As he talked he walked over to a switch near the door and shut off the sign. "There now," he said as he went to greet the men holding out his hand to shake Tom's, and Willie's. "Four sandwiches; I can offer ham, beef or cheese. You name it!"

"Ham should travel best," replied Tom. "Do you have beer and some sodas?"

"No beer, just 7-UP and Coca-Cola."

"Alright, six Cokes. We are probably better off without the beer. So, four ham sandwiches, and six Cokes to go. What do I owe?"

"It's sixteen for the food, plus eighteen for the sodas – thirty-four all together." It took no time at all for the owner to whip up the ham sandwiches. He put everything into a couple of bags and handed them to Willie.

"Here's forty bucks", Tom said. "We appreciate the fact that you stayed open."

"Have a great trip. If you catch some wahoos or tuna, bring them to me. I'll buy them from your captain. Sunday is fish day at Carl's Treats. By the way, you may have guessed, my name is Carl."

Willie replied as they went toward the door, "You're on, Carl, see ya!"

Then they drove the short distance to their room. It was untouched. Tom said, "Okay, partner, let's finally get some sleep. You pack the fridge. I'll see you at five AM."

Chapter 17 | Privacy at Sea

Cole was accustomed to expect the unexpected when planning to arrest suspects. Each event had had its own peculiarities, and none of them went exactly as planned. For some unknown reason this case was far different than prior ones. He had never had to work without an honest police department. As he lay in bed this Friday night his mind was churning. The lack of secure communication support which necessitated engaging complete strangers bothered him more than anything. Having to go out to sea in order to talk openly with Detective Spikel gave a different twist to this case. Adding to his racing assumptions, the fact that he had to count on Teddy Moore and the Webbers to do undercover work, led him to think up several crazy scenarios. '*What if*' situations were racing in and out of his mind; he tried to stop tossing and turning. His biggest worries were: '*What if Spikel gets suspected by Commissioner Black and he wipes him out? Or what if Spikel can't meet at sea? Or even a way out thought that Black could call London and get suspicious of the con.*' Usually Cole could disperse his worries by having thoughts of his boyhood days when lots of happy events took place. Thinking about fishing with his father calmed his mind. Finally, as he stared blindly at the ceiling, he resorted to his ultimate fall back motivation, he prayed: "Heavenly Father, I ask for protection for Detective

Spikel. He is a warrior for your cause and he dearly wants to rid this Island of those who intend to oppress the citizens of Palm Islands. AMEN." It was three AM before Cole dozed off to sleep.

Detective Strong got up from his sleep to have a bathroom break and heard Cole mumbling to himself, but knew there was nothing he could say to relieve him of his insomnia. Strong had never been completely in charge of an operation and simply followed the plan set forth by his superiors. In most cases the unexpected did happen. When it did he simply followed new commands that were issued. When cases were reviewed, several of his commanders jokingly related to him, their restless *'what ifs'*. He returned to his bed thinking, *'I sure hope those ominous clouds don't greet us in the morning.'* He too, found himself with a small case of insomnia. It took some time for him to go to sleep.

• • •

Despite the fact that a sound sleep had escaped them, both men got up daybreak. They immediately took a wake up dip in the perfectly calm sea. The swim left them completely refreshed and ready to tackle the problems that might lie ahead. Strong toasted some English muffins while Cole prepared tea and got out the raspberry preserves. Their shopping trip was paying off already. They sat on the patio to enjoy their tasty fare and sip their tea.

No mention was made of the activities that lay ahead until Strong opened with, "Well guv, I notice those nasty looking clouds are nowhere to be seen. Can you believe I laid awake last night thinking about them?"

"Yes, I notice. Thank God they are not here today. Did you really worry?"

"Sure as I sit here, I did. And look at that sea. It's flat as glass. Let's hope it stays that way."

"Don't count on it Bill. It seems that every morning we've seen this sight. Remember we are on the lee side of the Island."

"Right, boss, but surely we'll be back here before the wind picks up. Besides we know a Bertram can take just about anything the sea has to offer."

They were quiet as they watched the beach come alive. The sun moved higher into the clear sky. Beach walkers were few and far between, and they seemed more interested in watching the birds scramble to and fro than anything on the land side of the beach. The beachcombers seemed to enjoy just getting their feet wet in the calm water. The men had about one hour to kill as they waited for Harris to show up. Bill amused himself watching the action. Curt was busy writing.

"What are you writing guv?" Curiosity overcame his common sense that it might be none of his business.

"Oh, just getting a note off to my wife. If I post it today it can go out on the Tuesday BA flight and Vickie will get it probably on Thursday. I miss the kids, Little Harwood and Vickie."

"I don't blame you for that. This assignment is becoming very complicated and who knows how long we'll have to stay here."

Curt smiled, put down his pen then said, "Bang on, partner. Look, I'm going to clean up our dishes and put things away. Give me a shout if you see the Bertram."

He was still in the kitchen when he heard, "I see a cruiser headed this way. My guess is that it's a good two miles away, but moving faster than hell." Within three minutes Bill shouted again, "It's him boss. It sure looks like the Bertram we saw at Bodder's place."

Cole finished his chores, grabbed a shirt and a note pad and joined Strong to watch the boat knife across the calm sea. "Crimey, Bill, that sucker must be pushing thirty-five knots."

"Yeah, guv – nice, I hope the sea stays calm. Fast trip if it does."

The boat slowed to a crawl as Harris maneuvered it to the anchor buoy just off of the beach, and cut the engines to idle. *Enchanted*, and most large residences had anchor buoys although many kept their large craft anchored in a protected sound on the south side of the island. Harris used a telescoping gaff hook to capture the buoy, then pulled the craft close enough for him to attach a rope to it. Finally, he waved to the detectives while dropping a small raft into the water. He climbed into it and paddled it to the beach. The detectives went to the water's edge, and climbed into the raft. Cole greeted Harris who had remained silent while he was working.

"Good morning, Harris," Cole said, stepping aboard. "We really appreciate your help."

He replied, "It be an honor that I help men like you. You take many chances to help us."

"We've never seen a situation like this, my friend."

"Sir," Harris said as he paddled to the Bertram, "Plenty, plenty bad."

They boarded the Bertram and hauled the dingy on to the deck where it was secured by special tie-downs. Harris quickly released the buoy rope then turned to face his passengers to say, "This is fastest boat on this Island, so please be seat while I drive. It got two 150 horsepower engines. I tell you, this my baby, this Bertram. We go now to near Four Tops to meet Mr. Bodder." He engaged the engines and slowly turned the craft seaward. "We go full speed on the flat sea so you must hang on." The men did as told and within seconds Harris had the craft practically flying across the calm water.

• • •

That same morning, the DEA agents rose before daylight. Patton made some coffee and they sat to reflect on the events of the past few days. Patton and Oakley had worked as a team for twelve years and their assignments had always been to new locations so that their anonymity did not get compromised. But, never had they accidentally turned up clues as they did on this job. Oakley broke the silence saying, "You know, Willie, there's something strange about this case. Everywhere we turn we come across some person or fact that ties into our job. We're just putting in time taking down the ganja dealers who we stumbled on to, and for Pete's sake, we run into a bevy of women who are here for more than just a good time. Now we go fishing with a stranger and who knows what the heck we'll find next."

"I was thinking the same thing, Tom. This Billy Bob is probably loaded with info too, but we better expect some embellishments. After all, fishermen are known to exaggerate from time to time. I hope we catch some big fish, and I'm sure we will, but we will likely get our limit of local events from Billy Bob. Then turning to face the ocean he said, "Dawn is breaking pal, we'd better get on the move. I'll get the grub and drinks. You check how we leave this place so we'll know if we've had visitors during our absence."

• • •

Within a few minutes they were in the Jeep and on their way to Billy Bob's location. The traffic was very light and they made the trip without any problem.

On arrival at their destination they were surprised to see Billy Bob standing by his office door. Willie parked the Jeep near the office and they were greeted with a loud, "I like people who do what they say. Howr ya doin guys. Were gonna git the big babies today. Perfect sky. Perfect sea. Let's git at em." He led the way to the dingy and all three got in for the short paddle to the Nancy Mae.

"This boat sure looks different from down here beside her, Billy Bob. Now I see how she's made to take a choppy sea because of that big bow. Let's go and have some fun."

They scrambled up the portable ladder and into the boat. Billy Bob said, "Sit yer asses down and let's get out to sea." This Nancy Mae is only thirty-five feet long but she's a wide bugger. 200 horses drive er so she can push water no matter what. Listen tuh this," and he started the diesel motor. "Ain't that a purrty sound? Eere we go. We git outa this cove and move along the coast a bit then point to the Rocky where we'll drop the lines. On the way across I sometime snag a shark, so why not try, eh? This aint a speed boat, jist a friggin work horse. Trollin' speed is good enough."

The agents were enjoying the chatter from the Captain. The fresh air felt really good. Tom thought, '*is this real?*' "Hey Captain," Tom shouted, just say when you want us to drop those lines. We've had lots of experience. No need for you to come back here to help us. By the way, will we have competition out near Rocky Palm?"

"Nah, the locals are scared. Some Calvert bastards try it sometimes. Sometimes I see the big friggin refrigerater boat."

"You mean the one that sells grouper?"

"Ya. She's out ere parked in the cove lots of times. I'm not stupid. She's haulin' more than fish. I think them murdered Calvertians maybe got too close for comfort. Jist sayin, ya know. I pretend I don't see nuttin an keep my mouth shut. Palm is so corrupt ya have to tink of what yer goin to say or the big Black ull ave yuh fed to the sharks."

"If you mean Police Commissioner Black, we've been warned, don't cross his path."

"Okay, yuze guys, time tuh peel some line. That there pail's got some bait and yuze said yuze know what to do. Git at it, three lines."

Tom got the bait pail and Willie took one rod from its holder. "What's the bait?" Tom asked.

"I brought some yellow tail, and parts of a cuda. Use the cuda fer shark."

Willie baited the rod and handed it to Tom to release line. Then he repeated the action for the other two lines. They let out about one hundred feet of line from two of the rods, and only fifty feet from the other.

"Yuze know what yer doin fer sure," BB claimed. "Most tourist tink the line should all be way the hell back bout three hundred. Sharks come cuz the boat stirs em up. T'day we cud be lucky cuz them fish like the calm sea."

They watched the lines for five minutes when Tom felt comfortable asking BB more questions. "You have me wondering, Captain. That fishing boat, does it stay there long? Willie and I never have had experience fishing in waters that may have drug dealers in action."

"Never seen it stay mor'n three days. I see em burnin stuff. Don't know what, but sure makes some weird smoke an lots of it. It drifts tward Palm an people tink it a cloud made by ghosts. Like I say before, none of my bizznis. Probably garbage wit sometin that causes the color, like cood be bodies fur all I know. Them crooks av tuh get rid of ther enemies, somewhere, somehow." He chuckled as he said, "Maybe sharks dunt like Columbian dead meat!"

"Hey, you're scaring the crap out of us. You are one tough hombre. That's quite a story eh Willie?"

"Yeah, man. We thought we'd seen and heard it all. This story takes the cake." Turning to BB he said, "You aren't putting us on are you?"

"Hell no, but I don't say nuttin unless I'm ask. Look, see that move out there - we goin to have a shark soon."

Both men looked and noticed nothing. The ship left a trail of turbulence for a short distance but because of its configuration the movement was not too bad.

"You have better eyes than ours you old bugger. We just see the swell from the boat," said Tom.

No sooner had he spoken than one line went tight. "Fish on, Billy Bob shouted!"

Tom grabbed the pole. The reel screamed as line was peeled. "Get me a harness, Willie. This aint no baby shark or whatever it is." He adjusted the tension on the reel and the line started to slacken. "Hurry man," Tom said. "The sucker is starting to dive."

Willie put the harness on Tom. "That's no shark, Tom," Willie shouted. "That bugger has to be a tuna. Reel the slack before it turns and snaps the line." The fish took the slack and Tom released more line. "Son of a bitch BB you didn't say there were tuna out here."

"Never got one 'ere before, cause they usually swim closer to the Island. Yuze guys sure know what ure doin. I'll try to keep the boat eded away. There's eight hundred feet of line on that there reel, so ure gona to be fightin for a while."

Tom had fought tuna before. '*This one is something else*' he thought. Willie quickly reeled in the other two lines, got a towel and soaked it with ice water from the cooler, then wiped Tom's neck and arms. BB smiled as he saw they were pros and he would be cashing in on some big meat.

"Do you want me to take over," Willie asked Tom.

"Not yet. I think I can handle the bugger. But stand by, watch where the line is going in case it dives under the boat."

Twenty minutes passed when finally they got a look at the fish. Billie Bob was concentrating on slowly steering the boat out of the fish's track. He was first to see it as it surfaced about forty feet away on Tom's side. "Holy cow, I see the monster! U better let Willie take over. It gotta be over a undred pounds. He's gonna fight for at least another twenty minute. Ule not 'ave enough strength tu land the sucker."

Tom's arms were on fire, and sure enough, BB was right. The fish began another dive. Tom hung on as the reel screamed again. "Okay Willie, get set to take this rod."

Willie adjusted his harness and Tom passed the rod to him. The fight was on again. Willie shouted, "Man, I don't know how you hung on this long." He felt the fish try to shake loose. Tug, tug, tug on the line. Finally the line went slack again. Willie reeled like crazy to keep it taunt and up came the biggest tuna they had ever seen. It swam beside the boat.

"Stay wit it, Willie," shouted BB, as he slowly increased the speed. I'll have to drag the bugger 'til e goes belly up an as no strength. It's gonna take the tree of us tu get it on board. We'll lasso it and gaff it too. I'll say when. Keep the line tight 'til I say wer ready."

Even though the fish was dying, it kept trying to shake the big hook out of its mouth. Willie was getting sore arms as he kept towing the monster. Finally it rolled over and gave up. Billie Bob put the craft into idle. He went to the stern and pulled off some rope that was wound on a winch. The end had a slip knot. "Take this rope, Tom. I gonna get that gaff there an use it tu slip the rope over the back end of that fish an pull it up by its tail. Watch out as u tightens it, that bugger aint dead yet. I'm gonna gaff him too. Willie can loosen the line an wer ready tu wind that baby out of the water. We bring it tu the back and haul it over the stern. Ready? Let's go. Tank the Lord for this calm sea or we'd be screwed." He then carefully slipped the noose over the tail of the fish and pulled it tight. He deftly sank the big gaff into the fish and instantly gave the order for Tom to crank the winch. The fish resisted for only a second then gave up as the men did their job. Only when the huge tuna was lying in the bottom of the Nancy Mae did they realize that they probably had a record catch.

"Begeezus, guys, that's a month's wurt of fishin' lying there," exclaimed BB. "Uze are the best crew I ever ad!"

Tom and Willie were smiling as they high-fived themselves and stood back while BB secured the fish. "Heck BB, we're just getting started. Take us where the big ones are."

Billie Bob faced the guys and, with a big smile, said, "If uze guys keep this up ule sink the boat. Let's look for some wahoo tu top off this trip." He revved up the engine and steered toward Rocky Palm. As the craft was about a quarter mile off the shore of the island, he said, "Looks like we got company. See der in dat cay entrance. It's dat der friggin boat from Columbia. It don't usually come on weekend. We'll make a couple of passes and maybe get lucky, but I don't stick around when I see that sucker. Toss in the lines. Use the yellow tails for bait this time."

Tom said, "You seem pretty nervous Captain. Do you know something you aren't telling us?"

"I do, an I'm not sayin."

"Okay, none of our business. We're just a nosey couple of guys. Once on a dive we did down in Honduras we stumbled upon a sex traffic deal going on at sea. We had pulled into a cove something like that place and almost got shot. We were told to scram and keep our mouths shut. When we got back to the States we reported it to a friend who worked for the drug enforcement people. Kind of scary but we felt maybe it might do some good. From your action, I feel that boat could be doing something illegal. We could report it next week when we get home to Florida. I know there's no use reporting it to the Palm cops. From what we've heard, they are likely involved."

"Jist let sleepin' dogs lie. I dun't need anyting tu happen. They aint botherin me if I dunt botherin them."

"Fine, Captain, let's catch some fish."

"Good, git them thar lines in the water, only two lines this time. I gotta keep an eye on that ship."

The agents followed his instructions and settled into their chairs. In the distance they noticed birds that appeared to be cormorants circling in the sky to their east. They knew that usually it was a sign that schools of smaller fish were being attacked by larger ones. The big fish tear through a large school, eating some and wounding many. The wounded ones would end up on the surface of the sea and be easy prey for the large birds.

"Hey, BB," Tom shouted. "Look over there to the East – birds."

BB waved acknowledgement and slowly steered the boat eastward and away from the Island. "Not often that many," he said. "Could be plenty of wahoos an' cudas there. Use two hunred feet of line now an I'll circle the site."

Tom and Willie were hungry and thirsty after fighting the huge tuna so they grabbed their grub and a drink. It took them only five minutes to eat their sandwiches and wash them down. Willie shouted. "We're ready, BB."

The water was not rippling where the birds were circling. Billie Bob got out his binoculars to try to make out what was happening. The birds were circling but not diving. He thought he saw shark fins breaking the calm water. The engines were set to idle and an eerie feeling came over the captain. He was silent as he tried to focus on an object about a hundred yards away. "Holy shit uze guys. I pretty sure I see a body. C'mere, Tom, take a look."

Tom set his rod in the holder and quickly moved up into the cabin. BB handed him the binoculars and said, "Look under the birds. See it?"

"I see something? If it's a body why don't the sharks take it apart?"

"They don't eat rotten flesh, jist rotten fish."

"Crap Willie", Tom said. "Take a look."

Willie moved up and peered through the binoculars. "Put the boat in gear, BB, we'd better see what it is. If it's a body, we may have to tow it to shore. I hope it's a bag of garbage."

"We're gitin outa here. I don't give a damn what it is. It 'aint something the sharks or the birds want. Jist a big problem for Billy Bob is what it is. Reel up them lines. Sorry, boys, but the Captain dunt want no trouble."

"Hey, Cap, you got to report the damn thing," said Willie.

"No friggin' way, buddy. It's probably some sorry dude that the Palm Police Commissioner or his drug cartel friends wiped out. If I drag it in I'll be sure as hell charged wit a murder. Or maybe somebody fell overboard on a holiday cruise. I don't care. We're goin' ome straight away."

Tom looked at Willie and indicated '*keep quiet*'.

Tom, not wanting to blow their cover as DEA reps, said, "Wow, Billie Bob, I don't blame you if the cops are *that* corrupt. We sure don't want to get tagged with a murder either. Let's move."

•   •   •

On the West side of Rocky Palm the Bertram had covered the course and Harris had slowed the boat to a mere crawl. It was about a quarter of a mile offshore and the detectives could see the very uninviting terrain. Cole said to Strong, "This Island looks like it is covered with lava. I'm going to research it when we get back to England."

"Don't you think Neily would know?" Bill replied.

"You're probably right. I'll ask him." Facing Harris he said, "Look Harris, if we have an hour or so to kill why don't you take us to the East side of Rocky?"

"No mon. We not go there. We know pirates are on that side. They kill people and steal boat."

"Are you serious? These are Palm Islands' waters. The Marine Police should prevent that. Even the Royal Navy could legally go there."

"Mr. Curt, you not understand. We do what Commissioner Black orders us, or bad things can happen."

Cole turned to his partner with a bewildered look. "I knew we'd run into a bad situation over here from the first time I saw those strange clouds. We'll have to figure out a plan to deal with what Harris just told us."

"No doubt, I'm as surprised as you are by Harris' comment. How the hell did this colony get to this stage?"

"It's simple, Bill. London has ignored this place and would still be looking the other way if eight murders had not stirred up Neily and motivated him to call for help. By doing that he likely thought he was doing Black a favor. Now he knows the truth."

Turning back to face Harris, Cole said, "I get the message Harris. Bill and I will deal with the problem. You are a smart man and you are helping to clean out Black's rats nest. We'll make sure you get credit when we've done our job."

Harris nodded and smiled. "We are at the meeting spot now so we drift a bit until Mr. Bodder show up."

Cole got out his note pad to record the details of what he had just heard. Strong was admiring the seascape as the sun slowly rose above Rocky Palm. The calm sea and the sunrise made an incredibly beautiful scene. '*What a beautiful sight*' he thought before his mind switched to reality and steered his thinking to, '*We may not get off of this case alive. So many things can go wrong before we close down Black's operation and deal with the drug cartels.*' He snapped out of his thoughts when Harris announced, "I see the Hatteras. Look like it anyway. Hope so. It about two mile away."

The boat was closing the distance quite quickly when Cole asked, "Is that them?"

"Yes sir. We go close to shore now to anchor. You take dingy to their boat, I stay on Bertram."

As the boat approached, Cole saw Spikel gesturing for them to come over. Harris dropped the dingy over the stern and the two men got in and paddled to Bodder's craft. They tossed a rope up to Spikel and he secured the dingy to the Hatteras before putting a ladder in place so the men could climb aboard.

"Welcome," Bodder said. Then turning to Detective Spikel he said, "Toss the dingy rope to Harris, we are taking off from here. I have no idea if Black's marine crew will be cruising out here today. We'll leave Harris to fish this area and we will cruise and fish about two miles away. Actually I'll be fishing, you'll be talking. If I get lucky I'll call for help."

The Hatteras had a large cabin so the three detectives decided to meet in there. Cole opened the conversation by asking Detective Spikel, "What held you up, Herman?"

"Commissioner Black decided to call me in to meet with him and Samson, the Deputy Commissioner. He is going to London for three or four days and he wanted me to know, in no uncertain terms, that Samson Black would be in charge. He expects me to fully obey whatever Samson commands. I complimented him on getting the award and affirmed that I understood why Samson would be in charge. We then covered a few loose details – oh – and Audrey was there, too."

"Good," Cole replied, "so let's get down to business. We were sent here to try to solve some accidental deaths. Bill and I now know there's more to those events than the Police Commissioner wants us to know. You claim that you investigated and that your reports have been withheld from us. What can you report? I'm going to write while you talk. Herman, bring us up to date on what we *don't* know."

"First," Herman replied, "Commissioner Sylvester Black, in conjunction with the Jones & Keller law firm, has created a base from which the big Mexican and Central American drug cartels can operate. He has put the fear of god into members of the police force. I'm surprised that I'm still alive. The other trusted operatives in his command get paid to keep quiet – and I'm not talking peanuts. The balance, about fifteen constables just live in fear. No one has the nerve to reveal anything. Those June deaths, well, murders is a more accurate term, were all related to a huge movement of drugs and diamonds, as well as a stock promotion. I reported the deaths as 'suspicious murders'. Here are copies of my original reports." He handed Cole a file folder. "You'll see that I reported that six victims had their skulls cracked. The two Calvertians actually had their throats slit before being hacked."

"So what happened to the bodies, a cracked skull or a slit throat should be obvious?"

"We don't have a morgue here like most places, so dead bodies get cremated as quickly as possible. The ashes are put into metal containers and are shipped to whoever claims them. It helps to quickly bury the forensic evidence."

"Is the morgue or crematory a government operation?" Cole asked.

"No, it is owned and operated by the Commissioner's second cousin Homer Black."

"That son-of-a-bitch Commissioner, the man's an animal."

"Yes, sir, and it gets more interesting. The tentacles stretch from here to Calvert, Vancouver, Toronto and Tampa. There's a connection to Biloxi, too. That big yacht registered as DIAMOND QUEEN, and moored out from Holiday Place Resort, is from there. Get this. It was here in June when the murders happened. The Palm Marine Unit made several trips to it then, and the same thing is happening now." Herman paused and looked at the Brits.

Cole prompted him. "Go on. I'm a fast writer. What do you know about the punks that deal drugs at the Hibiscus Restaurant?"

"They are Commissioner Sylvester Black's private team of local enforcers. They intimidate whomever Black suspects might be his enemy. They usually take their victims to that cliff where the local men had their so-called car crash. They rope them and perch them on the edge to get them to behave. I believe that the two who were killed probably stumbled onto the big deal and tried to pry some hush money out of that lawyer Winston Jones or Commissioner Black. The gang has a leader who goes by the name of Fingers. He oversees the local drug operation that sells heroin and ganja. There's a woman involved, too. She's a fitness instructor at the Palm Fitness Club and she deals with pharma drugs, and not the hard ones. She has a male associate, but I don't know exactly where he fits in."

"No damn wonder you can't do your job. Well, this operation is going down, and you are going to retire with honors. I'll see to that. Now tell me, is there any police staff that you can trust or are they all scared to do, or say, anything?"

"Yes, Sir," Herman replied. "Most of the people talk to me when they feel it is safe for them to do so. In my opinion, those who are related to Commissioner Black or the Keith clan cannot be trusted, so count on fifteen we can trust, out of twenty."

"Does that mean Audrey and George are Okay?"

"Both of them live in fear, Detective Cole. Given the chance, I'll bet they will fill a book with incriminating evidence against the six. If it weren't for Art, here," Spikel said, "I probably would have given up. He's the only contact that I can trust right now, and I surely need a shoulder to cry on."

"Okay, I've heard enough for now. Stay the course Herman. On Tuesday, you, not Deputy Samson Black will take over the Police Department under the direction of The Premier. Bill and I have a plan but my head is spinning right now." Looking at Strong he said, "We may have to rethink things."

Strong nodded but said nothing. Then Cole stepped from the cabin and said to Bodder, "Times up. Let's not press our luck. Find Harris so we can do some fishing. Hopefully we will put the Commissioner's troops, if they get nosey, on to a dead end track."

Pointing, Bodder said, "I see the Bertram down the coast about two miles. My bet is that Harris will have caught a couple of wahoos already. He's the best fisherman that I know. It's like he was born to fish."

Art put the Hatteras into gear, throttled up, and said, "Look at the sea, we have some ground swells now and I see a breeze starting up. We have about a half an hour before we should head to port. Those swells tell me that there's a big storm out in the Caribbean somewhere and we never know if it's destined to come here. Even the weather forecasters get it wrong many times, so I simply give nature its respect. You'll have to be extra careful when you transfer from here onto the Bertram."

Harris had been approaching with full throttle and the swells were obvious when the craft sliced through them. Cole said, "I see what you mean by swells. Maybe we should just call it a day and if Harris has been fishing, like you say, Art, he probably caught one or two keepers."

Art kept his boat at crawl speed so he could maneuver it close to the Bertram while Harris had his craft in idle. The Brits made the transfer without a problem, and before pulling away from the Hatteras, Harris held up a huge sixty pound wahoo. Art waved and shouted, "Great fish, Harris. You are the best. Run your flag up and tell the nosey folks that you got a big one. See you at the dock later after you drop off your guests."

Cole complimented Harris on his catch and tossed in a comment, "Looks like we both had a good fishing trip. We landed a ton of information and you landed a good day's pay!"

Harris smiled, but kept his eyes on the sea as it continued to produce bigger swells and the wind became somewhat stronger. "We 'ave big storm come. Monday be rough."

• • •

It was noon hour by the time they disembarked at '*Enchanted* '. They quickly showered and shaved.

"Damn I'm hungry Bill," Cole said, as he emerged from his room.

"You're always hungry, guv. What else is new?" claimed Strong.

Curt laughed.

"I know exactly where to go. Follow me, boss, we're going to Gart's."

"No argument here. We'll have to tell Gart to get in touch with Patton. We may have to plan something different if we want to pull down this whole criminal operation. For sure we will need help from Her Majesty's Navy."

Strong agreed, saying, "By the way, our American friends are supposed to be on a fishing trip today. I guess we better just wait to hear from them."

•   •   •

At the time Cole was taking a shower, Patton and Oakley were disembarking from the Nancy Mae. They had helped BB get the huge tuna onto the dock and had mentioned that Carl's Treats needed some fish. Billy Bob said he'd look after that request, and with a sincere look, asked the men to never mention the floating body. Patton was in no rush to get going. He thought perhaps he could drag more info out of the Captain. "Say Billy Bob I want to thank you again for taking us onboard. Too bad we have to leave in a few days. You know where we are staying. Please call if anything comes up that you want to talk about. We have friends in Florida who are connected to law enforcement and who knows what they may be working on these days. Your life isn't going to get any easier as long as this Island is run as a criminal haven."

"Tanks, guys, I'm glad I met yuze. If you wunt tuh dive before yuze go, just call. It be free."

"Okay, see ya, we're out of here." Turning to Patton he said, "What a picture, Tom, that monster tuna, and Billy Bob standing over it with his huge knife. We won't forget this experience anytime soon."

Willie put the petal to the metal and the Jeep blazed along. He felt confident now about staying out of the ditch because it was his third run over the narrow, bumpy coral road. Both men were anxious to get back, relax and have a swim. They knew that Sally and Jan would be looking forward to an evening of romance and maybe they could dance the night way in the hotel lounge. When they reached their hotel Patton said, "It's nearly two o'clock. I say we kick back for a couple hours before we get into any heavy planning. We have to call Cole sometime and fill him in. He's likely got info we could use. Too much, too fast, is what's happening. I'll call him at five."

Cole and Strong were almost out their door when the phone started to ring. "I'll get it", Strong said as he rushed across the room to pick up the receiver. Cautiously he inquired, "Hello, this is Detective Bill Strong." He was taken aback when he heard, "Hello, this Harris. I at Mr. Bodder place. He say to tell you that big, Cigarette31, speed boat at his dock. He say Detectives should see it. Maybe I pick you up?"

"Hang on for a minute, Harris." He turned to Cole and relayed the message.

Cole nodded okay, and said, "Tell him we will be at the Hibiscus Restaurant."

Getting back to Harris, Strong said, "Okay, Harris. Pick us up at the Hibiscus. Twenty minutes? Make it thirty. Fine, we will be ready."

They walked over to Hibiscus. Fingers and his gang were not there. Quite a few customers appeared to be enjoying themselves. Gart and Louisa were both busy in the kitchen when Gart looked up and saw his tenants, waved at them to be seated, and by holding up five fingers indicated that he would be with them shortly. The men headed for an open table by the front windows.

"Nice to see our landlord doing some business," Cole commented.

"Bang on, boss. It's the old story - if the food is good, people will find you."

Gart finished what he was doing and approached the detectives. In a normal tone he greeted them, then, almost whispering, he said, "I heard from Teddy Moore this morning. He needs to meet with you ASAP."

Cole winked an okay then asked "Can you get us two subs to go, no anchovies?"

"Hot or cold, Gart replied?"

"Cold is best. We may have to take them with us. Harris is on his way to pick us up."

"I'm on it. Ten inch '*Gart's Greatest*' coming up."

The subs were truly great. Strong washed his down with a Greenie, Cole had a warm Guinness. Strong wiped his mouth and said, "You know, guv, something new turns up every time we feel we can take a bit of a break and get time to think."

Cole replied, "That's because this Island is rotten to the core. It's hard to believe Spikel hasn't been eliminated. There's Harris pulling in now so Bill, go meet him. I'll be right out." He waved for Gart to come over. Cole met him half-way. "We're on our way, Gart. Thanks for the quick service. The subs were excellent. You know where to send the bill. Look, we have to talk to our DEA friends. If they call you, tell them to call me."

When both men were in Harris' air conditioned car, he said, "If you are too cold, let me know. Most American tourists like it this way."

Strong answered, "You can warm it up a bit, my friend. Tell us about the boat."

"She be a new Cigarette31 that came in just after I get back wit the Bertram."

Cole took over the conversation and said, "I didn't know they made 31's. The legendary Don Aranow designed the Cigarette31 and as far as we know he was murdered by the Mexican Medellin Cartel. The Columbians ran several Cigarettes, but they got word that Aranow was designing a faster boat for the U S Coast Guard so they wiped him out in 1987. Patton will know. Probably Art might know also. When we get to Bodder's you talk to him, Bill, and I'll see what I can get out of Buzzy at the bar."

• • •

They arrived at Clear & Deep Dive and Harris pointed to the boat that was attracting quite a few lookers. "That boat," said Harris, "was here last June, but docked at Amos' place. Something bad go on maybe. I park now to wait. Mr. Bodder has 'CLOSED' sign on door but not closed. He say you walk in."

"I've never seen a Cigarette 31 up close," Cole commented. "It's quite a picture."

"Sure is guv. I'm headed for the office. I see Buzzy is at the bar but the dark-haired waitress is missing."

"Yes, she's conspicuous by her absence."

The detectives separated and went to their destinations. Cole did not engage Buzzy until he was sure Strong got into Bodder's office. Buzzy smiled and waved at Curt and Curt waved back with a, *'come over here'* gesture. Buzzy came immediately and his countenance indicated a degree of fear. "I said we'd be back," Cole said to him. "You look worried, what's on your mind?"

"Well, that big boat pulled in about noon hour and two guys got out. One was the dude that I saw before with Maria, my waitress. The other guy was slim, about fifty maybe, long blondish hair, about six feet, wearing Gucci deck shoes, a navy blue shirt and khaki slacks. They did business down at the office. They left with the Deputy Commissioner. I don't know what they told Art, but right away he got Harris to call you."

"Was Maria working?"

"No, she called in about eleven and said something came up so I should not expect her."

"Did she sound okay?"

"Yes."

"Have you seen this craft before?"

"No, but Harris says it's the same one that was over at Delray's last June."

"Alright, I'm going to join Bill," Cole stated. "Keep your eyes open for activity at that boat. There's something very big happening. We were filled in earlier and some huge shit is going to hit the wall very, very soon. Call me if Maria shows up."

Cole proceeded to the office and walked in. Art and Bill were waiting for him. "Here's what Buzzy knows," Curt said as he took a chair and sat next to Bill. "The dude that hustles Maria was on the boat. Maria was supposed to work today, but called in to say she would not. No excuse given. What can you report?"

"I'll let Art speak," said Strong.

"Look, Detective," said Bodder, "that Cigarette31 has the colors of the Medellin drug cartel. I asked the Captain why he came to my dock and he said there's a big storm coming and Delray's place is not secure. I did not think it would be wise to boss him around and better if I get what info I could for you. I asked if he was entering a race in the Caribbean and he replied, 'Yes, I race the US Coast Guard.' I asked how long he might be staying and he said, 'As long as it takes.' I recognized the man that was with him. He's hooked into Maria somehow and he flies around the Islands."

"Did you get the registration on the boat," Cole asked? "Did he give you his name?"

"No, but these boats have a date plate on the stern to show when the craft was launched. No need for numbers because only a couple of them are produced each year and they are all customized in one way or another. This one shows March 1989. It can travel at 90 mph or 80 knots on a calm sea. Even the U S Coast Guard does not have a craft that fast. I hear that even Donzi speed boats are a bit slower. As for his name, I don't care as long as I have the boat and the plate has not been removed. On Palm we don't ask too many personal questions."

"Do you have a camera handy?" Cole asked Art.

"Sure, I keep a Polaroid here for my guests to use."

"Does it print a date automatically?"

"Yes. Do you want some pictures of the boat?"

"Yes. And enough background to show that it's at your dock, plus a picture of the ID plate. Three will be enough. Get Harris to pose by the craft and then give one pic to him. Make the event look like Harris wanted a souvenir. Keep the other two and post them up on your wall with the other tourist pics. Do it now. Bill and I will get something to drink at the bar. Tell Harris to put his picture in his car. We will try to make everything look normal like any other tourist event. One last request, I'd like Buzzy and you, Art, to make a record of who comes and goes. That could be great evidence if we live long enough to see these people in court."

"We can do that."

"Fine, we will get seated. We'll call Harris over to explain the plan. Wait about fifteen minutes before taking the pictures. Once we know Harris has his picture we will be on our way."

The Detectives filled in Buzzy, and Harris, with the details. The picture taking went well and they got back on the road. Harris, being no fool, waited until no one could see him before he handed Cole the picture. They arrived at *Enchanted* without incident, paid Harris while thanking him, jumped into the Camry and drove directly to Holiday Place Resort.

Once inside the lobby of the resort, they could see that a flight had probably just come in because many suitcases and gear bags were stacked against a wall. The new guests were waiting to check into their rooms. In the meantime, they were milling about in the pool area and drinking complimentary cocktails. With so many people in the area it worked in the detectives' favor, and they did not attract any unwanted attention. They headed straight for the restaurant area and asked the hostess if Teddy was working. She replied that he was and sat them at a table in his station. In a few minutes Ted appeared and came straight over to the detectives' table.

"Hi, gentlemen, it's nice to see you back again. Can I get you a drink for starters?"

In a voice loud enough for the hostess to hear, Strong replied, "We were hoping that you'd be working today. You are the best waiter we've come across on Palm Island. Yes, you can get us a couple of cups of Tetley tea."

"Coming right up, sir, here's a menu for you to look at. Be sure to look at the specials on the insert. There's also a sheet you can take home in case you want to order ahead sometime."

Cole watched the hostess as Strong opened the menu and took out the insert. "The kid has balls guv. This paper has a lot of details that we asked him to get for us."

"Quick, put it away, Bill. The hostess is headed over here."

Bill quickly put it into his pocket before the hostess could see it. She came next to Cole and said, "Is Ted looking after you okay?"

"Very well ma'am. He's really a treat to deal with. This is our third time here and although the food and ambience is great, he's one of the best waiters we've ever come across in our travels. He's got such a great attitude. I'll bet a lot of your customers ask to be seated in his station."

"Oh yes! We have some high rollers who come here a couple of times a year and they love the kid. He's fast and accurate and always smiles. By the way, I'm Sheila. Let me know when you are coming and I'll make sure you get seated in Teddy's station. Enjoy your tea. I'll get you some complimentary cookies. I recognize you from the newspaper article. I wish you a lot of success." She left as Ted approached with the tea.

As Ted served the tea, Cole said to him, "What's up with Sheila the hostess?"

"She and I are buddies. She's the one who got the info you asked for. It's on that paper that you stuffed into your pocket. Here's the brochure and place mats that I kept for you."

"Good work, Ted. Now, heads up, there's another big deal being set up. You are sure to see some loud-mouthed big shots soon. Let us know if they show up. Stay safe, kid. We have to keep going."

Ted smiled as the detectives put some money on the table. They finished their tea and got up and left the room. Cole motioned for Strong to go ahead and said, "We'd better get home and figure out a plan. We have a lot of balls in the air and I'm not sure we can cope with the situation. We may have the cart before the horse. I'm ready for a swim and a drink of that Palm Island rum. Then we have to bear down and figure out the logistics of what we've set in motion. We really need to talk to Patton and Oakley."

At five o'clock the phone rang. Strong rushed from the patio to get it and was delighted to hear Oakley's voice. "We were hoping you'd call, Tom. We have a ton of information to share with you. We have to take another look at how we can take down Palm's den of thieves. Can you come by now?"

"Sorry, Bill, but Willie and I stumbled – or should I say – dove into a nest of women whom we suspect are tied into the drug cartel operation. We're supposed to meet two of them right about now at their hotel. Why don't we walk down the beach to your place early tomorrow morning about eight? I don't think that should make anyone suspicious."

"I hear you. Good idea. We'll have coffee and make some toast. This won't be any celebration. We may be planning our own wake."

"Fear not, man," Tom said, "we can pull in reinforcements overnight, if need be. Relax, get your facts together and enjoy the evening. See ya."

Strong turned to Cole and said, "I guess you heard that conversation."

"Yes, but those guys are in for a major surprise. Let's relax."

●　　●　　●

On Saturday nights the clubs, restaurants and bars were always busy because tourists flocked in on weekends and locals were out mixing with the crowds. Saturday, November 25, was no different. When Patton and Oakley arrived at the Holiday Place Resort they were lucky to get a place to park their Jeep. Upon entering the large lobby they enquired as to where the house phones were located, found them and Willie dialed three-one-three. Before it could ring a second time he recognized Janet's voice answering with a simple, quiet 'Hello'. He replied "Hi Jan, this is Willie. Tom and I are in the lobby."

"Sally and I are both here in my room. We were waiting for your call. Do you want to come up or should we meet you down there?"

"If you are ready, why not meet us down here and we can go to 'Starfish', the main dinner restaurant. Or if you prefer we can go there after we have a drink in The Quiet Oasis Lounge."

Jan's sexy reply was, "We'd love to go to the lounge. They have a piano player there. We heard that he can really set up a romantic mood."

Willie felt shivers as she spoke. He quietly replied, "You leave me no alternative. I got your vibes. You sound so sexy on the phone. See you in a few minutes." He knew from experience that the women like to talk sexy and really liked to get a sexy reply.

Turning to Tom he said, "Look partner, I just lost my self-control. I don't know about you and Sally, but Jan and I are going check out her bed. I just hope she isn't a con."

"I heard your plan buddy, but take it easy. You know these quick decisions can get you into trouble. Your problem is that you fall in love at first sight. Let's see if we can get a better handle on whom these women are before we jump into bed with them."

The elevator doors opened. Tom and Willie were speechless as the women walked toward them. Both wore sleeveless lace Bodycon cocktail dresses that had see-through halter tops. Sally's darted sleeveless bodice was secured by a band of pink pearls. Her dress was coral pink and it highlighted her blonde shoulder-length hair which had just enough curl to make her look like a Hollywood star. Janet's dress was just as stunning. It was a light sage color with an open bodice and sheer cap sleeves. Her coal black hair and ruby red lipstick were a breathtaking sight. Their skirts were a floral lace over stretchy jersey knit that ended about seven inches above the knee. The finishing touch was their beautiful ankle strap shoes. Sally' shoes complemented her dress. They were rose gold color creations with four inch stiletto heels. Jan had a more traditional sandal type shoe that matched the color of her dress.

Without anyone saying a word the women took the few steps to reach the men and then gave them a full body press embrace. The men were trained to expect the unexpected, but never had they conjured up what had just taken place. As Sally released her hold on Tom she tossed her head just enough for her hair to brush across his face. Janet released Willie then took his hand to lightly stoke her silky hair.

Tom broke the silence. "You ladies look simply ravishing. We thought you were awesome in your bikinis, but tonight you are gorgeous beyond words. What did we do to deserve this?"

Sally spoke. "Let's get a table in the lounge and we'll tell you. Right, Jan?"

Jan replied as she squeezed Willie's hand, "Let's go."

Heads were turning as the two couples walked hand-in-hand. The lounge had rose colored lighting that gave a wholesome hue to the patrons. It had a small dance area and seating for about 40 people and the piano music did set a romantic ambience as strains of "Memories" wafted through the room. They chose a circular bench type plush seating that also had a high plush back. Immediately the ladies pulled the men to kiss them with passion. The men did not resist as they stroked the backs and necks of their dates. The waitress, seeing from a distance what was happening, gave the couples a few minutes to settle in before going to the table and taking their order for four manhattans. They were no sooner on the table when the piano player, Roger Bench, took a break and went over to greet the four patrons. Willie was under no illusion and knew that their visitor just wanted to have a close look at the women's breasts. Bench asked if he could play a request so Tom suggested 'Moon River'. Bench played it beautifully giving Tom, who was anxious to hold his woman closer, a reason to ask her to dance. Willie grabbed the opportunity to ask Jan, and she was ready for the action.

When they got back to their seats Tom said, "Okay tell us why you chose to date us. You ladies could have the pick of any crop."

Sally spoke. "We are usually with some rich guys who are cheating on their wives or girlfriends. Mancini wants to get the '*goods*' on them and coerce them to cough up hush money. We are trained to turn men on. There's never any sex involved but lots of pictures and quite often we wear wires to record conversations. You can get the picture. Now you brutes show up and are fresh meat for Jan and me. You and Willie are good looking, muscular, great personalities and appear to be young enough to have the stamina for great sex – and that's the story. We may be out of practice but I'm sure we will do a good job. So why don't we go to our rooms and do what we all are craving for, then come back here and order something light to eat and dance the night away?"

"I'm so turned on I think I'm going to explode," Tom said.

Sally stroked his leg while whispering, "Hey, not here. Let's go and explode together." Jan and Willie laughed and Jan said excitedly, "I'm for that! She took Willie's hand and pulled him from his seat."

Tom said, "How about we come back here at nine, spend an hour together and plan another date."

The hour of passion passed quickly and the two couples recovered from climaxing with barely enough energy left for more romance downstairs. At nine, as planned, they went to the lounge and romanced for an hour as the piano player catered to their requests. As Sally snuggled against Tom and stroked his neck she whispered, "Will we see you guys again?"

"I would bet on it if I were you. When Willie and I get back to the States we could call you at the Casino. Is there any special number to call? Heck we don't even know your last names."

"Mancini doesn't let us give out a last name. But none of the girls' first names are the same. If we work for him we get paid well but we don't ever leave. We can't. Well that's not quite right, we are threatened to be beaten and disfigured by his mob if he ever hears that we have said what goes on in his world."

Willie was listening to the conversation as Jan caressed his arm. He looked into her eyes and said, "I heard what Sally just told Tom. Look at me, honey. I'm overboard for you and I want our relationship to last. When I get back I will make sure we meet again. I have friends who are just as tough as Mancini's goons."

"No, sweetheart", she replied. "Please don't make trouble. But I crave to be with you again. You can call me in a week or so and I will have worked out a plan, trust me."

Willie looked at Tom and said, "We have some work to do if we care about these women, and I for one, do."

"Look Willie, I'm on board." Then speaking so both ladies could hear Tom said, "Let's end this evening now. Maybe we'll be together again before we leave Palm or maybe we won't. But we have associates who would put their lives on the line for us and they have taken down bigger operators than Mancini. Carry on as usual. Don't talk about this evening if you can avoid it. Don't worry. We have never met two such intelligent, beautiful, compassionate women and we do not intend to lose you."

Both Sally and Jan broke into tears. "We love you two, we don't want to lose you. Sally sobbed."

"Cheer up. Let's go now before we all start to cry," Tom said. "We'd better go out alone or we're likely to create a scene."

With that, they hugged, and then the men left. On the drive back to their hotel it took a few minutes before Tom said, "What a damned mess. Those women are slaves. I'm sure Mancini is part of the Magdalena cartel. We need that yacht seized. How the hell did this job blow into a world class operation? Our asses won't be worth five cents if we don't pull this off right."

Willie wasn't smiling when he said, "There's some blood going to get spilled, Tom. We can do it boss. HQ told us they could rush help, and for sure we are going to need it. After we meet the Brits in the morning, all of us will know what to do. But let's spend the night savoring tonight's experience, and remember, you said that I shouldn't fall in love at first sight. Ha! Eat your words lover-man. He parked the Jeep and when they entered their room everything checked out okay.

Tom said, "I'm still in shock. Let's get some sleep."

"G'night Tom," Willie said.

"Same pal," Tom replied.

Chapter 18 | Sunday November 26

Cole was awakened by a flock of screeching birds searching the beach for food. They run up and down the beach when the sea starts to get a bit rough. The backwash provides food for the fish. His clock showed 7:15. He got up and opened the drapes. Overnight the weather changed. Small waves had developed from an impending storm. *'Good thing we met with Spikel when we did.'* he thought. Feeling refreshed he remained out of bed and went to the kitchen to make coffee. As it perked, the aroma drifted throughout the house and caused Strong to crawl out of his bed. Cole had opened the drapes and was gazing at the waves washing upon the beach. He did not hear his partner approaching. "Coffee smells great guv!" Strong startled Cole.

"Damn you Bill, are you trying to give me a heart attack?"

"Take it easy boss," Strong said. "Don't be so jumpy."

"You're right partner. I have a hundred thoughts rolling around in my head. I tried not to wake you but it seems the coffee did the job. Anyway we have to sit down and get a plan together. There's no way we can clean out the rat's nest by ourselves. We need Spikel to guarantee us some support from the honest cops on the force. The DEA guys mentioned reinforcements. Maybe we could get The Yard to put a few of our people on the flight tomorrow."

Strong listened. He said, "That's a possibility, but right now, let's wait for Patton and Oakley. Once the four of get our facts together we should be able to figure it out." He stepped outside, looked around and commented, "I guess the sea is not too bad. That yacht is still anchored out there."

"You're right." Cole agreed. "I'm so concentrated on what we've found so far I didn't notice. For sure we should keep an eye on it. There's no practical reason for it to stay there with a storm on the way. I see all the resident boats have left their anchorages."

"My brain seldom works better than yours, guv, but you know we are supposed to meet with our next door neighbor Phil. He seemed to be wired in to what's happening around here. I'll bet he's kept an eye on that ship."

Cole smiled and replied, "Mark one up for Bill. I hope Patton and Oakley show up soon. I don't usually drink coffee but this Green Mountain brand is good. You can watch for our visitors. I'm going to have another cup then brew another pot. Do you want a refill?"

"Sure." Strong said.

The breeze felt good as they sat on the lanai and drank their coffee. They observed only one person trudging along the beach which was starting to get covered with seaweed. Finally, they saw two people coming toward them.

"I guess that's our guys, Bill," Cole remarked. "Can you believe it, this is the first time they've been on time."

"Well, guv, on a case like this, the ducks are not exactly lined up in a row."

The detectives stood up to welcome Patton and Oakley. Tom said, "We've had one hell of a time since we saw you last. Where's the coffee?"

"Follow me," replied Strong. "Do you want toast now?"

"Sure. Make some for Willie too."

Strong and Oakley talked in the kitchen while Cole and Patton conversed on the lanai. Strong made enough toast for the four of them. He poured two cups of coffee for the visitors.

"Okay, guys," Strong said. "Let's sit at the table and talk while we eat. Anyone who wants another coffee can go get it himself."

Cole closed the sliding doors. They all took a seat at the big table.

"Let me talk first," Cole said. "Then Tom can report. Once we have a handle on the whole ball of wax, we will get down to the details of the arrests." Cole told them about their experiences and how it seemed that clues about the murders kept popping up everywhere. He finished by saying, "This is the first case I've ever managed where the usual help, the local police force will not work with us. We probably need more trained personnel. What can you tell us Tom?"

Tom looked around the table before opening with, "I'm not surprised. We've had the very same experience where each time we go somewhere we get clues. He proceeded to tell them how the pretense that he and Willie are divers was working perfectly. "There's no doubt that Palm is the center for a huge drug operation. We are going to need help from the U S Coast Guard and the British Navy. We think Amos Delray is involved, as is the diamond merchant downtown. We, by chance, saw him passing a pile of cash in the store. And by chance, we met some beautiful women from Biloxi, and now we are sure the yacht, that you see anchored out from this shore, plays a key role in the scheme. Complicated eh?"

"Thanks Tom," Cole said. "We'd better get our heads in gear. This will be no picnic. I'm going to make notes. If you want more coffee, get it now. We need to concentrate. If anyone has a suggestion, lay it on. Nothing can sound too crazy. And we'll need a plan 'B' too. So let's start with the easy stuff. How many men will we need to arrest the drug operators across the road at Hibiscus?

Tom replied, "From what we've seen there's likely to be two big body-guards plus Fingers and his lackey, Dorman. They are armed with switchblades and maybe more. I wouldn't expect them to cooperate. We could let the body-guards run, and round them up later. I doubt that they would stay to defend Fingers. There will be four of us so unless they have guns we should be okay."

"Got it," Cole said. "Alright then, let's talk about the Police Station and the Marine Division. There must be a ton of culpable people to round up. Spikel will likely need help. He has to arrest the Deputy Commissioner Samson Black, Constable Wilbur Black, and Audrey the receptionist. Other constables are involved, but we can deal with them once we have the place secured. We damn sure want the visitors' logs." Turning to address Strong, he asked, "What is your impression of George, Bill? Westwood told me he really knows the man, thinks he's honest, and has stayed because he is afraid for his life if he leaves."

Strong replied, "He seemed quite friendly when we met on our second visit. If Spikel says he's okay, I would count on him to help us. He probably has access to the Commissioner's Office, too. It would have to be locked up first thing."

Oakley butted in, "Can you get some officers over here to help? There's still time to get them on the BA flight."

Cole spoke, "Looks like we'll have to arrange it, but we have to deal with three more locations. Amos Delray has to be arrested and, from what you suspect, there's plenty to be uncovered at The Diamond Store. Teddy Moore, the waiter at Holiday Place, supplied details of a diamond mine in Canada that appears to be supplying big quantities to it. It looks like the store is the key laundering site." Handing him the paper and brochure that Ted supplied, Cole said, "These are credit card numbers of the murdered Americans for you to check out, Tom. This is the PR brochure of that Canadian company Blue Lake Diamonds Ltd. I can check on that one with a lawyer friend in Vancouver."

"Tom, your guys will have to deal with the refrigerated fishing boat, the Cigarette boat and the yacht from Biloxi. Damn near forgot that I have a picture of that sucker. Look at the plate on the stern. You can identify the owner by that plate. Have your HQ check it out."

Oakley replied, "Good work, will do, and yes, that's going to involve some FBI guys and our Coast Guard. This is obviously a huge operation and charges will likely be made under the RICO law. Willie and I will get busy and contact our bosses. This rough weather could work in our favor because the fishing boat will have to stay out at the Four Tops cay, the yacht will have to go over to the lee side of the Island, and the Cigarette won't be able to handle the sea. Our Coast Guard vessels that patrol the waters out here can handle just about any weather. The Guard will have to get official authority to patrol and make arrests in Palm Waters. You will have to get that done for us, Curt."

Curt answered quickly, "Affirmed. I'll get that today. The Governor will have to get those orders sent from the Foreign Office to your people in Miami. Also, The Governor needs to get us an order from the Chief Magistrate for us to search The Diamond Store. By eight tomorrow morning I should have the orders approved. Tom, call us tomorrow at ten, okay?"

"Will do," Tom replied.

"Man," said Patton, "this is like planning for war. I'm a forensic expert, but I've never sat in on anything like this meeting."

Cole looked at him and said, "We aren't finished yet. We still have to deal with the core of this rotten apple, the Jones & Keller law firm. We have Jane Butterworth, our special op girl arriving on BA tomorrow afternoon. Winston Jones will be meeting her at the airport when she gets off the flight. I think we should leave Jones alone. He will be running in circles trying to cover his tracks once he hears we have taken over the police headquarters. I'll wager that he will put his new employee to work immediately as he tries to destroy evidence. Even if he takes off for Calvert we can round him up later because we will be loaded with evidence, to say nothing about having a key witness to explain his activities."

"You're calling the shots, Curt," Tom replied. "You have my agreement."

"Let's stand up and take a break guys," Curt said. "Then we'll go over this one more time."

They got up from the table. Strong walked over to open the sliding doors. The wind was noticeable but not angry, as the fresh sea air blew into the house. Tom and Curt went outside onto the lanai. They noticed that DIAMOND QUEEN was still moored out from the Holiday Place Hotel. The sea did not seem to affect it. Bill and Willie chose to go for more coffee. It was nine-thirty before Curt decided it was time to reconvene. They went over the plan and were satisfied that they could get the job done. As they arose from the table, Tom said: "When you see Gart, tell him who we are so he will recognize us. He has seen us, but he probably thinks we are hooked up with Fingers' crowd."

"Good thinking Tom," Curt replied. "We have to pick up a couple of pizzas to take next door. We can tell him then. If by six we don't have the signed order from the Chief Magistrate I'll make sure Gart lets you know."

As the DEA agents turned to walk down the beach, Cole looked both of them in the eye, and said, "We WILL make this happen guys! See you later."

Strong commented, "Those guys know what they're doing. They must be top agents in their unit to be able to call in help at a moment's notice."

"No doubt about that, Bill."

The detectives relaxed and read some complimentary magazines that Gart had placed in the house. About eleven-thirty Cole said, "I'm calling Gart now. Will two pizzas be enough?"

Strong replied, "Sounds okay to me. Give him a call. I'll drop over to get them and take them to Phil's – meet you there."

Cole placed the order. Gart said it would be ready shortly. Cole then said, "Let's go. I'll see you at Phil's."

As Cole approached their neighbor's house Phil's dogs sounded the alarm. Phil quieted the dogs before stepping out to greet his guest. "I was hoping you guys would make it over. I have some interesting news for you. By the way, where's the pizza. Where's Bill? I've got the beer."

Cole shook Phil's hand and said, "I've been looking forward to this, and don't worry. Bill is picking up the pizzas at Hibiscus."

"Sounds great, c'mon in, Curt. Can I get you a beer?"

"I don't usually drink cold beer but I'll take a cold Greenie if you have one. Actually it goes really well with pizza, but, otherwise I drink warm Guinness. And what is the news you have for us?"

"Sit over on the couch by the coffee table, Curt, while I get a beer for you. When Bill comes I'll get into that." He went to his entertainment bar fridge and came back with the cold one.

"Nice place you have here, Phil," said Curt.

"It's not what you might call humble, but why should it be?" Phil said. Smiling he added, "I like it. There's just me and my dogs, and whomever I want to invite in. I have a cleaning lady and she'll cook if I want her to. I do most of the work outside, although I have an islander who rakes my beach every day."

"I could be jealous Phil, but my wife Vickie and I have exactly what we like over in England. It's a four bedroom Tudor style home with lovely gardens. We've been there for twenty years now. Our two kids are away at Oxford, but live with us during semester breaks. When I tell her about this place she may want to think about an alternative." He smiled at Phil, and continued, "Or maybe I won't tell her what a great place you have here."

"Look," Phil said, "When you get through with your business here, ask her to come over and the two of you stay here for a while. Heck, I'll bet the weather in November isn't all that great where you live. Or, go home and come back."

"I just might do that, friend, if I'm still alive. In my job, one never knows."

• • •

At that moment Baron and Buster sounded the alarm once more. Phil went to the door, looked through the peep hole and saw Bill. He quieted down the dogs before opening up the door to greet Strong. "Boy, those pizzas smell great. I thought I was only a little bit hungry but the aroma has got my stomach growling! Get in here, man, and let's get at em."

Strong sat them on the large circular table that was the centerpiece of a dining area in the great room. He commented, "I thought there was supposed to be cold beer in this place today. Are you hiding it, Phil?"

Phil, smiling as usual, said, "At your service, cold one coming up, smart ass." Then as he got the beer and sat down, "I guess you detectives have been busy, but so have I. I've been watching that big yacht out in front of the hotel. Yesterday morning a Cigarette31 showed up and a guy with long blonde hair got out and boarded the yacht. Soon, thereafter, the P.I. Marine Police boat tied up alongside and a man who looked like the Police Commissioner boarded. I have forty strength binoculars that I use for close up views of the beach traffic and I was busy checking out females when the yacht activity caught my eye. Both of the visiting parties left about an hour after they arrived. I was having lunch when I saw the Police craft return to the yacht, so I watched. Many boxes were taken from the Police boat and put aboard the yacht. We all know that the Commissioner is as crooked as a pretzel. I can only guess, but those boxes probably had drugs. I can't think of anything else. Surely it was not a grocery run."

Cole interjected with, "Did cops unload the P I Craft?"

"No. Two big black guys whom I've seen hanging around Hibiscus were doing the work."

Cole looked at Strong and said, "Our neighbor is a pretty good detective, Bill."

"Certainly seems so, guv. We may have to subpoena him as a key witness when we get to court." Looking at Phil, he continued, "What about it Phil?"

"I have no problem with that. If you two can stop the corruption here, and need help, count me in. I know property values. They'll tank, including mine if Commissioner Black's op is not taken down. Hell, if he gets in charge he'll probably confiscated whatever us foreign residents own."

· · ·

"In that case, Phil, we could use your help," said Cole. He told Phil of the plan for Tuesday night, then, "There's a chance the dudes will bolt toward this beach. Could you sit outside, with your dog Baron when we raid Hibiscus? Could Baron attack one of the crooks?"

"Baron can take down bigger guys than I've seen at Hibiscus. If I tell him to attack, you would not want to be his prey. He's a retired K9."

"That's what we want," Cole said. "If you have to use force we can absolve you. We don't give a crap about how much force you use. If it happens, be aware that the guy will likely have a knife. Break his hand with a baseball bat if you have to."

Phil smiled, as usual, and said, "I'm a former Seal Team Marine so don't worry about me, and as a matter of fact, I do have a baseball bat."

Cole looked at Phil with an amazed look. "I'm speechless, Phil. You *are* the real thing. Look now, we may or may not, talk again before Tuesday night. If you need us, stick a note on the door and we'll come to your place. Just write, 'Call Phil'."

"Fine," Phil said. "And look, if you've got a few more minutes, why don't I give you a run down on some of the coercion activities I know about?"

Strong accepted. "We're all ears, friend."

Phil told of several instances.

"Good info, Phil. I don't want to rush away, and I really want to hear more, but we must see the Governor today. We're on our way. Secrecy is paramount Phil. You know the story. Wish us luck."

When they got back to *Enchanted*, Cole said to his partner, "Are you okay with what just happened?"

Strong replied, "We need all the help we can get. Hell, if we can't trust a U S marine we are in deeper shit than I thought. Sure, I think we got lucky again."

"Good," Cole said, "so let's call the Governor right now. He has some work to do."

•   •   •

Governor Neily was just returning from brunch at the Holiday Place when the phone rang. He was glad to hear from Cole and told him to come right over. When the detectives arrived, and told him what they needed, Neily said,

"I'll call Chief Magistrate Clyde Curry right now. Hope he's available." Luck was on their side again. Curry said he was available, and that the three of them should come to his place straight away. His residence was only a quarter of a mile away and they wasted no time getting there. They took two cars, as Cole suspected he and Strong would leave on their own.

Curry and Neily were very close friends. Neily treated Curry, who was twenty years the younger, and single, like a son. He knew he could get him to do almost anything if it was of utmost importance. He introduced the detectives and proceeded right away to tell Curry details of the planned arrests.

Curry's face lit up with a smile. He said, "Oh how I look forward to seeing those losers in the courtroom. You can have whatever you need from me, my friend. Let me get busy and prepare your documents. I will take about fifteen minutes. Let me mark this down - you need search warrants pertaining to Palm Dive, The Diamond Store, Police Headquarters, and one for the arrest of Deputy Commissioner Black. The authorization to let the U S Coast guard operate in our waters will have to come from Premier Westwood. Why don't you call him from here while I get busy with the warrants? His number is on the index file beside the phone."

They were directed to Curry's den. Neily called Premier Westwood. More luck, as the Premier answered. "Sorry to bother you on a Sunday my friend," said Neily. "I'm with Cole and Strong over at Clyde Curry's residence. We need you right away. Can you come by?"

"God, you sound stressed out!"

"I'm fine, but the roof is caving in on the crime operation. We have a real timing problem that only you can solve," said Neily.

"In that case I guess I can forego the bridge party. Gloria won't be too happy, but when I tell her why, she'll be okay, I hope. I'll likely make it to Curry's within thirty minutes. Bye!"

Westwood called his driver and told him to come right away. Austin complied. After an apology from his boss for the hurried task, he got instructions where to go. "That should take us about twenty minutes, Sir." They arrived on time and Austin asked, "Should I wait for you to leave?"

"Yes, please do. I have no idea where we might need to go from here."

Neily was waiting by the door for the Premier to arrive. When he saw the Lincoln he stepped outside to greet his friend by saying, "Thanks for getting here quickly, Bruce. Our detectives are ready to arrest some suspects, but need reinforcements. Only you can authorize what's needed. Come in."

"I imagine there's a master plan now," Westwood stated.

"Yes, but I'll let Detective Cole do the talking. They're waiting in my office. Follow me."

Cole got up to greet The Premier.

Westwood said, "You look pretty serious, detective. Tell me what I can do to help."

Cole replied, "I believe you have the authority to let the U S Coast Guard operate within Palm's 12 mile limit. Is that correct?"

"That is correct, unless the Royal Navy is operating nearby. I will have to check it out."

"I understand," Cole replied. "Can you possibly do it today?"

"Well, this is Sunday and all that, but I suppose someone would be available in the Defense Department. What's the message?"

Cole then explained the fishing boat operation and the Rocky Palm activity. He also described the search warrants that Chief Magistrate Curry had issued, and finally their planned arrests on Tuesday night.

Westwood listened intently then offered his comment. "I never thought this could happen here in Palm Islands. I'll get onto your request as soon as I get home. I'll leave now."

The Governor interjected, "Do you want me alongside when you call the UK? There could be some new law or other problem that would fall into my bailiwick."

"Excellent thought my friend. Come along in about thirty minutes and I should be ready to make the call."

"I'll see you then," said the Governor.

Westwood excused himself. Cole suggested that he and Strong get on their way but added, "Bill and I have to call The Yard to fill them in and request additional force. Governor, could you contact me when you get back to your residence? I should use your phone to make my call."

"Whatever you need, detective, we are all in this together now." said Neily.

The Chief Magistrate showed his visitors to the door. He assured Cole that he could call anytime, day or night.

Tom Oakley and Willie Patton could feel their anxiety as the sting deadline approached. They knew from experience that there was always some surprise, and usually it was not a good one. The fact that they now had a time constraint simply added to their pressure. Oakley looked at his partner and said, "What do you think of the situation, Willie?"

He answered, "Off the top of my head I think this a far bigger deal than we expected, but those Brits are no slouches. That Cole is a tough, experienced bugger, and he knows this is no cakewalk. I'll bet they're getting stuff together for us right now and, since you asked, I say you should get on the phone and update our boss, Marcel Savage."

"Yeah, he's the top dog, and he has never tried to second guess my decisions. His last comment to me was, "Call anytime, day or night". He'll have to line up help from both the FBI, and the Coast Guard. No time like the present. Bring the phone over here Willie."

Marcel Savage, DEA Southeastern Region Director, knew that the case might get complicated and had given Oakley his emergency phone number. Tom dialed it. After only two rings he heard, "That you, Oakley?"

"Yes it is, sir," replied Tom. "Sorry to disturb you on Sunday, but we're ready to act and need your help right now. In a nut shell, by Tuesday, we need at least four FBI agents, and the Coast Guard. Let me read you our plan. When he finished reading, he said, "The Brits are preparing authority for U S operatives to work in Palms' jurisdiction. I will have them in hand by five today. I can have them faxed to you from the Governor's office by Detective Cole if you give me your fax number."

"Wait a minute and I'll get it." Savage returned then said, "Fax '335-333-5555', you'd think I'd remember it eh? Got it?"

"I got it, sir."

Savage continued. "Sounds like a utopia for criminals. I never would have suspected something as elaborate as a crooked Police Chief and a citizenry living in fear. It's tyranny, and by the sound of it, you and Patton have stumbled onto the Magdelina operation. You did say that the Cigarette31 bears Magdelina colors didn't you?"

"Yes, sir, due to the weather it is sitting right here in Palm. We could easily seize it, but we'll need the Coast Guard right away."

Savage asked several more questions before saying, "I'll contact Miami

FBI, and the Coast Guard there. I've dealt with their top ranking people before and there's no doubt they will jump onto this. I'll get on it right away. There's no time to waste." Excitedly he said, "Man, Oakley, we have a chance to shut down the entire east coast Magdalena operation. I want you to call me at nine tonight."

"10-4. In the meantime Patton and I are going to check for sure that the Belize fishing boat will be out at Rocky Palm Tuesday night. If you don't hear from us to the contrary, you know the target is as planned. If you don't have any more questions, I'll hang up."

Savage replied, "Talk later. Bye."

Tom turned to Willie. "It looks like full steam ahead. Savage wields a big stick so we can be sure our help will be on its way. For now, let's get over to Clear & Deep and talk to Bodder's cook about the boat. We could have a drink, too, if you're up for one. Then, later, let's run out to the Seaview Grill to take a break."

Willie smiled, "I'm on. I'm wondering if the beautiful Maria will be serving at the Tiki."

"Good point. But from what I've seen lately, what she will be serving is time in prison. You can hold her hands as you cuff her."

"Enough, partner, can I help it if I have testosterone buildup? Let's move on."

When they arrived at the dive resort it was busy as usual. Buzzy was serving at the Tiki Bar, but Maria was not to be seen. The agents were about to step out of their Jeep just as a police cruiser pulled into the driveway. "We've got company, Willie. Sit tight," Oakley said. "The cop doesn't know us so let's go straight to the bar. We will be facing Buzzy and can ask him who the cop is."

They took two stools at the end of the bar, and when Buzzy had finished serving a waitress, he came over to take their order. "What will it be, guys?" he asked. "Nice to see you back."

"Two Buds, thanks," Tom answered. "By the way, I see you have a visitor. Does he come here often?"

"No. He's probably here to check on that Cigarette31. In fact, cops haven't been around our place for several weeks." Buzzy left to get the beer.

As the beer was served Willie asked, "Can I have a word with your cook? And by the way, is your waitress, Maria, working today?"

"Yes and no." came the answer. "By the way, that is no flunky cop, it's the Deputy Commissioner. Something's up."

Willie went to find the cook. Tom stayed at the bar to observe the crowd. It was only a minute or so before the cop left Bodder's office and went directly to the boat. He boarded it, disappeared for a couple of minutes then reappeared. He was carrying a leather briefcase. '*Cole will sure like to hear about this*', he reasoned. He knew he could not approach Bodder, because he'd have to expose his DEA connection. But he sure was curious.

Willie seemed to be taking longer than expected and that started to worry him. As Tom was finishing his beer Willie appeared and headed straight to the bar. "You took your time pal, what happened?"

"The cook got edgy when I asked him about the next delivery. He wasn't exactly friendly, but, as far as he knows, the fishing boat will be here on Wednesday. I stayed to make light conversation and he came around pretty well. He wondered about the twenty pound boxes as he usually gets frozen trout and meat products in ten pound boxes. I asked if he was ever invited on board and he said, 'never'. I told him we'd like the experience, if he could arrange it. He said 'forget it'."

Tom, feeling less worried said, "You sure know how to talk people up. Let's get out of here."

They settled their tab and thanked Buzzy. When they got on the road, Tom told his partner about the scene he had witnessed. Willie was driving and commented, "I guess Cole will have to call Bodder once we tell him the story. The plot continues to thicken."

The Seaview Grill had a nice crowd in the dining area. The agents managed to find a table where they could have a little bit of privacy. Kenneth the waiter recognized them and waved. Tom beckoned him over and he did so.

"Hello gentlemen," Kenneth said. "I remember you from the other morning. How is your holiday?"

"It's going great," Tom replied. "Thanks for asking." Tom lied, "We came back because your service was so good and we thought you might be able to tell us a bit about the history of this place. On a dive we made, a guy said that the owner died, but many folks thought it likely wasn't from an accident."

Kenneth looked surprised. "I've always really wondered how Mr. Scott died. The news reported it was from natural causes, but Mrs. Scott told me he had a cracked skull. I really don't want to talk about it. What would you like to order? Here's the menu and the 'specials menu' is on the wall by the entrance."

"Thanks Kenneth," Willie said. "Give us a minute or so. In the meantime bring each of us a Greenie and a Palm patty."

"Coming up," the waiter said. "I'll be right back."

Tom looked at Willie and scratched his brow. "Will it ever stop, he asked? Everywhere we turn there's someone getting killed. Natural causes my ass. Add one more to Cole's list."

The agents enjoyed their late lunch. They chatted as they drove back to The Beach Hotel.

"It's five o'clock Willie," Tom said. "We should get over to the Hibiscus and talk to Gart. Hopefully Fingers and his team won't be there this early. You drive, Willie."

"No rest for the wicked eh?" said Willie.

When they arrived at the restaurant there were no cars in the customer parking area. Tom parked very close to the entrance and they walked in. "Hello, anyone here?" shouted Tom.

Immediately a voice replied, "I'll be right with you. Have a seat."

The agents sat close to the kitchen entrance thinking that it would make it easy for Gart to attend to his business and still deal with them. Gart stepped out from the kitchen, smiled, and said, "I just got off of the phone with Detective Cole. He told me who you are and that he's bringing me some papers to give to you. He's running a bit late and you should wait for him to arrive. He will meet me in the kitchen and will not let on that he knows you. But he said that he has what you need."

"Sounds good, Gart, but there's a slight change of plans. Please call the Governor's residence and ask him to have Cole fax those papers directly to this number." He handed Gart a slip of paper with his boss' name and fax number, 335-333-5555. My superior's name is Marcel Savage. He is putting assets in place and will get them into action once he has the documents. Get Cole to call me at The Beach Hotel at nine tonight. I will be waiting for his call. "

"Will do, guys," Gart replied.

"Great, Gart. Call me at room 114 at The Beach Hotel after you instruct Cole. We should be there to take the call, but if not, don't leave a message. We really appreciate you taking the risk of getting involved with us."

"Thanks. Do you want any food to take with you now, maybe a quick ham sandwich to go?"

"Sure," Tom replied. "One other thing, Gart, is King a trained guard dog?"

"He was trained by the best in Canada. If I give him the command he will kill his prey if I don't tell him to stop. King is ninety pounds of muscle and teeth."

"Good," Tom said, "we might need his help on Tuesday night."

"I'm counting on that," said Gart. "I'd love to see King tackle Fingers."

Tom smiled and said, "That would be a scene for sure. Right now though, we'd better get our asses out of here before Fingers' punks arrive."

The agents took their grub and returned to their room. They anxiously waited to hear if Cole got their message, and had completed faxing the documents to Savage.

As soon as Oakley & Patton had left, Gart called Governor Neily, and relayed the message.

• • •

Premier Westwood hastily prepared the letter of authority to send to London. Governor Neily looked it over and agreed that it was sufficient. Both men proceeded to the Governor's residence in the Premier's Lincoln. During the trip they talked about the upcoming action and agreed that it was a huge gamble. Westwood asked Neily, "Dale, did you ever expect that your request for Scotland Yard assistance would lead to such a major development?"

"Not at all, Bruce, but luckily we got, probably, the best detective in the UK. Cole can get the job done. I have no doubt about that. He'll get all the help he needs. We just have to hope the weather doesn't get too nasty. Don't forget that we have to call him when we get to your place, Dale."

Neily nodded affirmative.

Westwood spoke to Austin saying, "When we get to the Governor's, I want you to stay in the car and wait for me. If you see any unusual activity while I'm inside I want you to honk on the horn three times. The Governor said that there was a strange person supposedly trimming bushes when he met with the detectives a few days ago. It could have been one of Commissioner Black's people."

"I will do that, sir."

Austin drove them to the front entrance and then parked the Lincoln in a designated area that had a shade cover. Upon entering the residence Dale's wife greeted them. The Governor politely acknowledged her. Both men went into Dale's office and Neily called Cole. Neily told him about the info he had received from Gart. Cole said he and Strong would be over straightaway.

When the detectives arrived, the Governor showed them into his office and he gave Cole the information relayed by Gart.

"I'll deal with that after I call Trump," Cole said. Cole immediately dialed Gordon Trump at The Yard. He was surprised when it was Trump who answered, and said, "G'day mate, I thought you'd be calling."

Cole replied, "You mean good evening, Gordon. It's darned near eleven at your end."

"Don't worry about it Curt. You and Strong have stirred up a hornets nest, and this whole office is on standby. Bring me up to date."

"We're here with Governor Neily and Premier Westwood who has authority to permit American assets to help us. The Yanks want to confirm the authority with you, so expect a call from them. I'm faxing the Premier's written direction to you as soon as we finish this call. The DEA agents, Patton and Oakley, have been in contact with their superior, Marcel Savage the DEA Southeastern Region Director, and he is requesting FBI and U S Coast Guard help. What have you got for us?"

Trump responded. "Here's the way we see things. There is a drug cartel to be busted and an Island crime syndicate to be closed down. We should leave the action at sea to the U S Coast Guard. They will decide if a seal team is needed. Our objective is to take over the Police Department, execute search warrants to arrest the onshore drug operators and the accomplices to the eight murders. I have our Taylor team ready to go. Remember them?"

"Yes, the best team in our business. They pose as the Taylor family on vacation. Larry is the father, Eve is his wife, Andrew is Larry's' grown son, and Jackie is his wife."

"That's correct. They will arrive tomorrow, Monday, on the same BA flight that Jane Butterworth is taking. I've instructed them to rent a vehicle and proceed to The Beach Hotel. They will act like a family on vacation at the hotel. They are to have meals delivered to their rooms and not leave the premises unless you tell them otherwise. Be careful to not use their proper names before you are all in action. Now, we know that the drug bust has to happen before arrests are attempted anywhere else. Seven PM on Tuesday has to be synchronized. Here's what I suggest. Are you ready?"

"Yes," Cole replied. "I have a pen and paper."

"Okay, here's the list, in point form."

Larry and Eve work with Spikel, and you, at Police Headquarters.

Detective Strong is to assist agents Oakley and Patton at Hibiscus.

Andrew should take Jackie and raid The Diamond Store. If that place is closed before seven, have the Governor or the Premier, call the store early Tuesday and tell the owner that there's a wealthy couple on Palm who are friends of his. Say they would like to buy some diamonds as an investment, and they can be at the store at seven PM, and they must leave at daybreak on Wednesday.

"Should I repeat?" Trump asked.

Cole finished writing then said, "No, I have it. But we need one more officer to secure Palm Dive. I'm sure there's a load of evidence there regarding the dead divers. Homer Black's crematory is another spot we must raid. Send two more men if you can get them here. If not we will take our chances that Bill can do the dive place with Oakley, once we have the Hibiscus raid completed. Homer Black can wait until Wednesday. He won't have anywhere to hide."

"Sorry Curt," Trump answered "there's no way I can get even one person on that BA flight. They bumped two reservations to make room for our Taylor family. I know you'll find a way to get the job done."

Trump continued, "Listen now. There is a Royal Navy training operation in progress off the coast of Honduras that we are routing to Palm, but they can't arrive until Wednesday. They will have marines available to secure whatever place you use to confine your prisoners. From what you have told me there is a series of interview rooms on the second floor. Use them to hold your prisoners until the marines can put them on board their ship for interrogation. How many prisoners do you think you will have to deal with, Curt?"

"It could be as many as fifteen. We can handle it, based on what you have told me. Don't forget the DEA is sending assets too, but their prisoners will likely be held on the Coast Guard boats. I'll sort that out with them tomorrow.

I have to fax Savage right now, so make sure that the Foreign Office does their part. If anything changes, fax or call Governor Neily. That's it. Bill and I are ready to relax for once. Oh, I forgot to mention Jane Butterworth. Is she up to scratch on the plan?"

Trump hesitated for a moment then said, "Damn, she's not. I'll get on to it first thing tomorrow even if I have to drive her to Heathrow."

"Look, Gordon, she has to be sure to ignore the people that she'll recognize. Tell her to go with her employer when she arrives, but to not leave the Island. If her boss, Jones, wants to make a run for it she has to make herself disappear and contact the Governor's office. Make sure she has the number. We don't care if Jones runs, but Bill and I think he will stay to dispose of evidence. We'll get him in due course. Jane's safety comes first. The same thing goes for The Governor who is standing right here nodding his head. He understands. And finally, we will fax the arrest warrant for your men to take Commissioner Black into custody. Let's hope that the Nor'Wester blows itself out by Tuesday. That's one element we can't control."

"I'm with you Curt. God bless." Trump ended the call.

As the documents were being faxed to London and Miami they heard honking. "My goodness, exclaimed the Premier, that's my driver honking. Something is happening. I'll take a look." He went to the door and looked through the peep hole. He saw nothing unusual so he stepped out onto the porch. When Austin saw him he got out of the Lincoln and went to his boss.

Austin said excitedly, "A police cruiser came and drove up beside the Camry. The officer got out and tried to open the driver's door. He tried another, but it didn't open either. He got out a pad and wrote something and then he drove away. He did not see me because of the dark windows on the Lincoln."

Westwood remained calm. He said, "Fine Austin, you did well to stay out of sight. I won't be much longer. Remain in the car and stay vigilant." Westwood reentered the house and told the group what he had heard.

Cole spoke. "Very interesting, Sir, I'd like to talk to your driver before we leave. I think we are finished Governor. Detective Strong and I will remain in our house after we get there. First we will talk to Gart at the Hibiscus. We will be available for any call after seven. The men exchanged compliments about their successful afternoon. The detectives left.

Cole walked over to the Lincoln where he talked to Austin. "Was it a patrol car that you saw or the Deputy's car?" he asked.

"It had no special markings." Austin replied. "The Officer was about six feet tall."

"Thank you, Austin," Cole replied. "We'll work with that."

Strong unlocked the Camry after checking around the car for anything unusual. Finding nothing, he drove it over close to the Lincoln. Cole got in. "What do you think guv?"

"I think they got word of this meeting somehow. Probably they took a chance that we might have left some papers or other clues laying on the seat. Too bad we didn't set up some phony docs. When we get home we should talk to our neighbor and ask if they came by *Enchanted*. Let's get to Gart and find out what he knows."

• • •

The Hibiscus had a few customers and Gart was busy talking to them. He motioned to Cole that he saw him, and the detectives took a seat near the window. Gart did not rush to greet them. After he took an order to the kitchen, he returned and went casually to Cole's table. In a voice loud enough for other patrons to hear he said, "Well, how are my tenants getting along? Mind if I sit down to chat?"

"Sounds good, Gart, have a seat. Then Cole lied. "Bill and I want to talk to you about the place. I made a list of what we need over there at *Enchanted*," Cole said as he winked. "But I don't have it here. The main item is that we need maid service and wanted you to recommend a trustworthy person.

"Sure, I'll set something up."

"Also, Gart, we were to meet a couple of guys here and talk about diving, but we are a bit late."

"I did have a couple of guests who came in earlier. They were from The Beach Hotel. They did mention something about meeting someone, and told me "If some guys come in asking for us tell them arrangements have been made, and to call us at the hotel at nine."

"That's them I guess," Cole said. "No problem, thanks for the message, Gart." Turning to Strong he asked, "What do you think partner, had enough pizza? Maybe we should just relax and have dinner."

Strong answered, "Right on, guv. Do you have grouper on the menu tonight, Gart?"

"No, I don't. I have some fresh wahoo though, and my specialty is Turtle Steak Picatta."

"Really," Strong spoke up, "no grouper? Over at Art Bodder's Tiki Bar I had a great sandwich. He gets his supply from a refrigerated ship out of Belize.

"Good for him, my friend. I hope he doesn't get the wrong box. I got one six months ago that had twenty, one pound packages of white stuff. I returned it before the ship left and the Captain of the boat came to me, called me into a room, tossed me into a chair, stared down and said, "This mistake never happened. Do you understand?" He pulled a gun and waved it in my face. "If your Commissioner of Police gets wind of the mistake, you can be sure he will make you have an accident. Now, get the hell off of my ship."

"Holly shit, guv." Bill whispered. "Here we go again. We step into it everywhere we turn." Looking at Gart he asked, "What else can you tell us Gart?"

"I can't say for sure, but a lot of those boxes were being loaded onto one of Harold Keith's refrigerated trucks. Whether it went to his warehouse or onto one of his brother's ships, I can't tell you."

Cole chipped in with, "I'm no genius, but we know Commissioner Black and the Keith family are tight. We are going to need another search warrant or two. You are more of a help than you'll ever guess, Gart. That being said, I'm still hungry and your turtle steak dish sounds interesting."

"You can't tell it from veal. Louisa prepares it with a side of rice and green beans."

"Okay, we are both on for the experience, and pick us a bottle of wine that goes well with it."

Cole then looked at Strong. "It's six-thirty. Hope we get out of here before Fingers and his boys show up."

Twenty minutes later Gart served the meals. It was perfect. When they had finished eating Cole called Gart back over to the table to compliment him. "We can't finish the wine Gart," he said, "so keep it for us 'til next time. We want to run before Fingers shows up. The less they see of us at this place the better. We're out of here and going home."

They drove down the street for a quarter of a mile to be sure the police were not tracking them. They noticed nothing out of the ordinary until they got out of the Camry. "Look at those footprints, Bill. They weren't here this afternoon. Let's drop in on Phil right now, he may know something."

As they approached their neighbor's house Phil's dogs started barking. Strong knocked and shouted loud enough that Phil would hear. "It's Cole and Strong, Phil. Call off the dogs."

The barking stopped and Phil shouted, "The door is unlocked, c'mon in."

They entered. The dogs remained calm.

"Have a seat, guys. I guess you noticed how strong the wind is blowing. Did you look out at the sea?"

"Yes. Why?" Strong asked.

"Don't panic, but the waves are crashing and rolling almost up to our lanais. It happens every time we have a big Nor'Wester. It's scary, but no problem when you get used to them. I thought I should warn you."

"I appreciate that," said Cole. "Tell me, did that yacht move?"

"Oh, yeah, it left around two. It's likely in the lee on the other side of the Island. What is really important is that you had a visit from the police. I recognized the constable, Wilbur Black, one of the Commissioner's pawns. I have no idea what he was looking for, but he went to the lanai side and the front door."

Cole looked at Strong and commented, "That accounts for the footprints we saw over at our place. It was probably him who was snooping around at the Governor's property too." Turning to face Phil he said, "Thanks, Phil. I'm sure he wasn't stopping by for a drink. If you see him again, be sure to call and leave me a message." Being sarcastic he continued," Nice time we're having on this friendly island! Seriously, Phil, we've had a busy day. This whole Island will be turned upside down on Tuesday night. We've arranged search warrants for several spots. Extra officers are flying in from London, and the DEA is teaming up with the U S Coast Guard. By Wednesday night the Royal Navy will be helping us as well. Your job is to have Baron on guard."

"Don't worry about that, he'd love to get some action. We'll be watching." As Phil walked over to his fridge he asked, "How about a cold beer? I'm having one."

"Thanks, but Bill and I will take a rain check. We are expecting a call. We had better get over to our place. I'm sure glad we came over to check with you."

• • •

The wind was blowing furiously as they crossed the yards to get home. Sporadically, moonlight would shine through the storm clouds and light up the sea. It was nothing but white water as far as the eye could see. Close to shore they saw what Phil had referred to, as waves crashed onto the beach and rolled up toward the buildings, stopping just short of lapping onto the lanai. Cole shouted to Strong, "We'd better pray that this storm blows itself out by Tuesday evening!"

Bill nodded to agree. "We should call Bodder, or Harris. They will know, and don't forget we have to call Oakley at nine."

When they entered *Enchanted* the place appeared to be as they left it earlier. Just to be sure, the detectives checked their rooms and the drawers in their bureaus. They found nothing out of place.

"I'm going to call Harris right now," Strong said. "Maybe we should ask him if he's free on Tuesday night. He could drive Larry and Jackie to The Diamond Store. "You're right, Bill. Call him."

Strong dialed and heard, "This is a recording. Leave a message and I will call you."

"Crap, I guess he's working. I'm sure we'll hear from him. It's almost nine anyway, and we have to call Oakley, so let's do that right now." Cole nodded. Strong dialed then he handed the phone to Cole.

Oakley answered quickly and after a few words of 'BS', he said, "Let's have it Curt. Are we organized?" Cole went over the plan in detail. Oakley asked only a few questions then said, "I can't wait for the action, man."

Cole ignored the comment and carried on. "We have some real hot information for you and your DEA friends. Gart told us this evening that for sure the grouper fishing boat, or boats, are carrying cocaine. He had a firsthand experience looking into the barrel of a 45 Colt. Get him to fill you in tomorrow. No sense you, and us, taking a chance on being seen together. Oh yeah, we had a cop snooping around, so keep your eyes open. Is everything on track at your end?"

"My boss is in action. He has four agents ready to fly in here. They arrive about eight Tuesday morning on a Lear35 run by charter operator CaribFly.

They will be posing as divers and friends of mine. I have to book them into our hotel. I will get a call tomorrow morning, and if anything changes I'll tell Gart and get him to get the info to you."

"Ten-four, my friend," Cole said. "Let's get ready for action. Bye."

Strong had been listening and said to Cole, "I heard you mention the Keith operation. We don't have a search warrant for that raid."

"Damn it, you are right Bill. So many balls are in the air. I'm glad you are keeping track. I'll have to get it tomorrow from the AG. Right now I'm heading for the bed."

Chapter 19 | Jane Goes to Palm Island

Jane Butterworth decided to wear the same outfit that she wore for the interview with Johnathon Wilcox at International Placement Services. She knew she could turn every head in a crowd just by walking erectly. Stretching a wee bit from time to time didn't hurt either. But her main prey was Winston Jones, her new boss. She had tidied up her flat, and was ready to go early Monday morning, when she received a call from Gordon Trump. He briefly described the plan to carry out the raids and that she must not leave the Island. She made some notes and suggested that he should drive her to Heathrow so they could talk. He was in favor of that idea and arranged a time to pick her up. She had time to call her pregnant friend Darlene, and they cemented their plan of action.

"Well here I go Lord," she said out loud. "It's all in your hands. Truth shall prevail." That said, she had about 30 minutes before Trump would arrive, so she turned on the telly to watch the BBC news channel. "Good grief," she exclaimed aloud, as she saw shots of police surrounding Heathrow. *'That's all we need'*, she thought, *'a big delay at the airport.'* The announcer reported that a suspected terrorist was loose on the grounds and flights would be delayed. She looked at the clock and knew Trump would be down at the street in a few minutes. She turned off the telly, got her things and left.

She was right. Trump drove up in a plain car, flashed the headlamps to get her attention, and then got out to assist her with her luggage. She immediately said, "I just watched some action going on at Heathrow, boss. Is it going to mess up our plan?"

"I hope not, Jane. I've been staying on top of it and my assistant says they have the suspect cornered outside of the Terminal, but they don't know yet if he's got explosives. Orders are to take him out. Since that's the case, the delay should not be a problem." Changing the subject he said, "By the look of you, you are sure ready for Palm Island. You look like a runway model, not a New Scotland Yard detective."

"Hey, I'm supposed to be a secretary impressing her boss, not a detective."

He smiled then went into his 'Yard' mode. He said, "Jane, what was supposed to be a simple mission, has developed into a major criminal operation. Damn good thing I assigned it to Cole."

"The bigger, the better; I'm ready, willing, and able, boss, and chomping at the bit. A little nervous, but that usually happens before most of my missions. Knowing Curt Cole is in charge gives me a thrill because he's all business at crunch time. Will he be contacting me when I get settled?"

"Yes, when he's ready," he replied. "You contact him only if you need him. If you cannot locate him, call the Governor or go to the Hibiscus Restaurant that is operated by a supporter of ours, Gart Webber. He or his wife Louisa will help you. We don't know where you are going to stay, so call Darlene on the premise that you want her to know that you arrived safely. Give her your location and a phone number. Tell her how excited you are about your new job. She will call us and we will relay the info to Cole, via the Governor. When you have the evidence that is needed by the DEA guys, then you call Curt for sure. By then the dirty Palm cops should be out of the way. The Jones & Keller firm will be trying to destroy evidence so you have to get to a safe place as quickly as you can. The Hibiscus Restaurant is your best bet. At seven Tuesday evening our teams will be executing arrests at several places."

"Good, sir, I'll do that. Tell Darlene to expect my call."

The drive to Heathrow was slow because of the police action there. When they got to the first police roadblock Trump identified himself. He was told that the terror suspect had been shot dead. The crime scene was still active, but that he could proceed. The officer realized who Trump was, and radioed ahead so they could clear all checkpoints. "So this is it, Jane," Trump said, as he parked to let her out of the car. "Remember, the Taylor family will be in there but steer away from them."

"Don't worry boss, just be ready to act if I need you." She proceeded to the check-in area.

The flight was scheduled to depart at 9:50 but when Jane checked the monitor inside the terminal she saw it would not leave until 10:50. It would arrive in Grand Palm at 16:30 Palm time. There were quite a few armed security personnel visible to the public, due to the ongoing terrorist investigation. Security inspection went smoothly nevertheless, and she was in the boarding area with an hour to spare. Looking around, she did not see any members of the Taylor family, and she began to get worried. She used up some time by going to the news stand and buying The Times. Returning to the boarding area she could not find a seat so she walked aimlessly around the area.

Suddenly she heard, "Don't turn around." She stopped. Passing her was the Taylor group. *'Thank God they made it in time'* she said to herself. As instructed by Trump she ignored the Taylors and waited for the boarding announcement.

Fortunately she had a window seat in a forward section of the big 747 aircraft and boarded after the Taylor family. They were seated in the rear section. As she settled in, the passengers assigned to the two seats beside her, a middle-aged couple, sat down and the man took the seat next to her. It was obvious to Jane that he liked what he saw as he shuffled into his seat. He took as much time as he could to look at his attractive seatmate. She made things easy for him by stretching a couple of times and then introduced herself. "My name is Jane. Hope we have a smooth ride."

"I'm Spencer, Spencer Orr, and this is my wife Kris," he said, as he leaned back so Jane could see her. "Just call me Spence." Kris smiled. He continued, "This is our fifth trip to Grand Palm, how about you?"

"First time," Jane replied. "I have been hired by a law firm there. I'm excited about that."

"Very nice, which firm hired you?"

"Jones and Keller, have you've heard of them?"

"For sure I have. They are out of Calvert. I used them once for a property deal, but they charged me way too much, so I don't use them now. I never felt quite right during that deal. They had a lot of Spanish speaking clients and they seemed to get priority. It took over a year to finalize my land purchase. They wanted me to hold it in a company that they would administer, but I told lawyer Jones that I'm wasn't trying to hide the ownership, and I wanted it in my personal name. I guess he was trying to get an annual fee out of me. Anyway, I hope you enjoy your work. Trust me if you think of changing your job sometime. I have good connections with the two biggest international financial firms operating there."

"Wow," Jane exclaimed, as she twisted her torso for him to have a better view. "What do you do – if it's okay to ask?"

"I'm a financial advisor to several of the big hedge funds that have been set up as Palm companies. I make sure they are investing properly and not skirting any SEC or other laws pertaining to their charters. Operating out of a tax haven is trickier that most folks realize."

"I'll keep you in mind, Spencer. It looks like we are ready to take off. I'm going to catch up on some sleep that I lost last night." She gave him one more chance to look her over as she closed her eyes and stretched back against her seat back. Before she dozed off, she had time to reflect on what she had just heard. *'If I survive this mission I just might like a job with Spencer's operation. Should be interesting work and something I'm good at.'*

Jane awoke an hour later and decided to read The Times. Spencer Orr was not paying any attention to her as he appeared to be engrossed in reading papers that he had removed from his expensive looking valise. His wife was reading a book, and appeared to be in her own space. It wasn't long before the beverage service started. The flight attendant interrupted everyone's concentration, and Spencer turned to Jane as she was asked for her order. She requested tea. Spencer passed it over to her saying, "This flight has very good service. How was your nap?"

Jane smiled, and replied, "Well to tell you the truth, I dreamed about what you had said. You see, I have a BA degree from Oxford, plus a Master's Degree in Legal Financial Business. If the job with Jones & Keller doesn't work out, I'd like to contact you."

Orr reached into his valise and picked out a business card. "Here, hang on to this," he said as he passed it to her. "It has both my UK and Palm addresses, as well as my telephone numbers. You never know what the future holds."

'That's the understatement of the year' she thought. 'I might not even be alive a couple of days from now.' "Thanks, Spencer," Jane said, as she leaned forward to place the card into her purse. I'll be sure to keep it handy. From what you've told me, my new employer may not be completely on the up-and-up."

Spencer smiled.

Jane changed the subject, by offering him her copy of The Times. "Would you like to read the Times? I've finished reading it."

"Sure, thanks. I guess it won't be long before food is served."

He was correct. Food service started almost as soon as his words were spoken. After they ate, they snoozed off and on. Between naps, they chatted during the rest of the flight. The captain announced the landing instructions as the huge aircraft descended and circled to the west side of the Island. Jane could see the turbulent ocean below. She nudged Spencer and said, " Look down there at the sea, it's practically white. The waves are huge."

Spencer rose from his seat and leaned over her to get a look. His leg touched Jane's as he pressed forward and said, "I heard there's a Nor'Wester. It sure looks like it." He pressed a little harder against her as he described what that meant. Finally, he settled back into his seat as the landing decent began.

'Too bad he's married,' Jane thought. 'I could use more of that! I'll bet he could too.' Her though didn't last but for a moment as the aircraft touched down and reality set in. The huge machine taxied to the gate as she looked out of the window to see that even paradise can have crappy weather. There was no sunshine, and workers on the ground were obviously straining against a heavy wind. She turned to face Spencer and said, "Is this weather going to last long?"

Spencer replied, "Not likely. By tomorrow Grand Palm Island could be a tourist's dream, come true. Let's hope so."

Jane smiled a 'thank you' and got ready to disembark. 'Time for business, Jane', she said in her mind. 'I hope Cole and Strong are safe.'

Chapter 20 | Monday - Getting Set For Action

The British detectives were up and ready for action very early. Cole had received the call from Oakley at nine Sunday night. He was waiting for another call to affirm that everything was on tap as planned. Shortly after eight the call came. Oakley reported that all DEA and U S Coast Guard assets were ready for their assignments. Cole then asked, "What are you plans for today?"

Oakley said, "Willie and I plan to visit a couple of banks to get cash for tomorrow night's buy from Fingers. We want to also take another look at Amos Delray's place, as well as check out the fitness center where the lovely Maria said she worked. Other than that, we plan to lay low. What about you and Bill?"

"I'm not quite sure yet, Tom. We will visit Commissioner Black, and deliver his airline ticket. We plan to go to The Holiday Place Resort for lunch to check with our man Ted. Maybe you should try to be there too, just in case we want to point out some suspects that Ted identifies. We don't have to actually sit together, as we can pass information via Sheila the hostess, or Ted himself. The way things are developing, by Wednesday we could have a whole new list of criminals to arrest. Also, by then, you won't have to be anonymous. After lunch we want to be at the airport to see if Jane Butterworth is met by her new boss, or someone else. Maybe, if you are out there, you could follow lawyer Jones and Jane, and then let us know if she was taken to his office, or to some other place. What do you think?"

"I like it Curt. I just had another thought. Willie and I should get properly dressed and visit The Diamond Store to get a read on the owner. So, we will get into gear and see you at lunch. Be careful! I'll see you later." Tom ended the call.

Strong made a fresh pot of coffee while Curt was on the call to Oakley. The aroma was too much for Cole to stand, so he poured himself a cup before sitting on the chesterfield to begin talking. "Here's an idea Bill. Tell me if it's too crazy. I dreamed about this all night. We have to drop off the Commissioner's airline ticket this afternoon. Why don't we embellish the scene and ask Black for a souvenir picture of the three of us as I hand him the ticket. We can tell him that we have almost completed our assignment, and on Wednesday we are going to Miami for a couple of day's R & R before heading back to England. We will ask him to set up a meeting with the Deputy Commissioner, and the whole complement of constables and staff, for seven Tuesday evening. It will be a celebration party to honour the Commissioner. As a special compliment we will hand the Deputy Commissioner our report. The big, fictitious, announcement will be that we have found everything to be in order, and wish to thank everyone as we hand over our report. I'll suggest that we have food and drinks available for the farewell party. I'll bet they will fall for the ruse."

"From what we've seen of these criminals so far, Curt, I'm pretty sure we can pull it off. The Commissioner has proven to be arrogant enough. Pumping up his ego one more time should work."

Cole continued, "If we can get them all in one place, we can arrest the two top dogs. We'll tell them the Commissioner has been arrested in the UK, and that anyone who wishes to cooperate with us could get absolution from being arrested. I'd be surprised if they don't cheer."

"Sherlock Holmes would be proud of your scheming mind, guv! We can do it!" exclaimed Strong.

"I thought you might like it, Bill. Give it more thought. For now, why don't we go into town and take a look at The Diamond Store? If we are sending Larry and Eve to that location we have to give them an idea of what to expect."

Strong smiled. "You think of everything Curt. Let's look respectable and go!"

As Cole and Strong drove into town they could see the huge waves breaking against the shoreline. Salt water spray, blown high by wind gusts, sprinkled onto the windshield of the Camry and had to be washed off by the windshield washer and wipers. Although the sea was still churning, the waves were noticeably smaller than what was the scene on Sunday evening. The town was not very busy because cruise ships had to relocate to the lee side of the island, keeping their passengers from getting to town before noon.

"Looks like we picked a good time to hit the downtown," Cole said. "The storm has kept the tourist traffic down to practically nothing. I can park right in front of The Diamond Store."

"That might not be a good idea, guv. We should park a block or so away just in case one of Commissioner Black's people should see the car and wonder why we are diamond shopping."

"Damn, Bill, you are awake today for sure. I'll park around the corner near a restaurant. We can use the exercise anyway."

The detectives walked past several shops that were open. Unlike the retail clothing and duty free shops, The Diamond Store doors were locked. There was a small sign above a button that read 'Press Button for Service'. Cole pressed the button, and waited for over a minute. He pressed it a second time before a well-dressed man appeared. He unlocked the doors and welcomed the two detectives. He was smiling, as he said in a Canadian sounding voice, "Good morning gentlemen. Are you in a hurry? I'm just finishing up some paperwork in my office. You are welcome to look around. I'll be about five minutes."

"That's okay by us," Strong said. "We've heard that you have a very nice shop so we just wanted to have a look and maybe buy something not too expensive. Can I ask you your name?"

"Of course you can, sir. I'm Lawrence Jones. I'm the manager and part owner. I'll be glad to help when I return." He locked the door and walked back toward his office.

Cole and Strong moved slowly to the showcase that was farthest from Jones' office where Cole turned to Bill and said in a very low voice, "Can this Jones possibly be linked to the Jones law firm?"

"Nothing can surprise me now, guv. Time will tell, but if I had to guess, I'd say, 'yes'."

The manager returned and said, "Thanks for waiting. What can I show you?"

Cole spoke, "We don't really know much about diamonds. We are primarily 'gold bugs'. Is there a difference in quality depending on where the diamonds are mined?"

"Very much so, sir," Jones replied. Recent discoveries in Canada have caused turmoil in the diamond trade. We buy in bulk and we have found the diamonds from a mine in British Columbia to grade much higher that any shipment we formerly purchased from South Africa. Consequently we offer only stones from Blue Lake Diamonds Ltd. in Canada. Would you like to see some of them? I keep a few South African stones here so clients can see the difference. Come this way, and I'll show you."

Cole looked at Strong and grinned.

Jones walked ahead along a narrow hallway that was about ten feet long. He punched in a code to open a door to his right.

Cole noted that the hallway ended at a blank wall.

"This is very kind of you to take time with us," Strong said.

"I like to make sure my customers know what they are getting," replied Jones. He led them through another door into a brightly lit room. Have a seat he told his guests, as he sat across from them at his desk, and reached down to open a drawer. He took out a velvet covered tray that had six diamonds on it. "See these," he said, as he pointed to the three on the left of the tray. "They are from South African mines. Those, he said pointing to the ones on the right, are from Blue Lake."

"My goodness," exclaimed Cole, "what a difference. Let me ask you. Do you ship abroad or only sell to tourists like us."

"Oh yes. I have a large foreign clientele. I keep a good supply in the wall safe that you see to my right."

"Well, look, Mr. Jones, we shouldn't take much more of your time. Can you show me something in the five hundred dollar range that I could take to my wife?"

"Yes. Let's go back out to the showroom."

In the showroom, Jones showed the men a few pieces of jewelry, and Cole singled out a bracelet, then he said, "Can you put this piece aside until tomorrow, sir?"

"Of course, I'll be happy to do that. When can you come by?"

Cole turned to Strong and asked, "What time tomorrow do you think we'll get finished with our contractor, Bill."

Strong replied instantly, "Well, he's bringing the decorator and the painter to meet with us. We are going to the other side of the Island with a realtor, and she said we'd be several hours over there. To be safe I'd say we could be here around seven tomorrow evening. Since it's for your daughter I guess you want her to see it, Curt. Aren't Eve and her husband Larry coming in on Palm Air late this afternoon? Maybe we could all come back tonight."

"Not a chance, Bill," Cole commented, carrying on the charade. "but maybe tomorrow, because, she will be going straight to the celebration party. Who knows when that will end?"

Lawrence Jones was listening to the detectives' conversation, and with a chuckle he said, "If you can make it by seven tomorrow, that's okay. I'll be working in the back anyway as I have a big order to ship to the Sultan of Broania."

Offering his serious look, Cole said, "That will be great. Many, many thanks, Mr. Jones. I really appreciate it. So, Bill, we should run."

Strong agreed and they shook hands all around. The detectives left the store, straining to keep straight faces until they rounded the street corner and got into the Camry. "Now that was one of our better acts, guv. However, we'd better get to a phone real quick, and tell Trump that we have a new plan for searching The Diamond Store."

"Right on Bill, we have time to go to Governor Neily's place and use his phone before we hit The Holiday Place for lunch."

The Governor was home, and greeted the detectives with his usual British flare. They went straight into Neily's office and called Trump. He agreed with the new plan, and once again wished them a safe, successful operation. Wanting to avoid calls to Oakley, Cole took time to write a note for him about the change in plans. As he was writing, he got a thought that he should contact Detective Spikel, so he wrote another for Oakley to drop off to Bodder at Clear & Deep. The note to Bodder was, '*Art, ask Spikel to visit Gart at Hibiscus. Tell him, if any plans do change, to have Gart relay the message to me.*'

When Cole was finished writing Governor Neily said, "Here's the airplane ticket for Commissioner Black. No doubt he will be expecting you. Why not call him and set up your meeting?"

"Right on, Sir," Cole replied.

He dialed the Police number and Audrey answered. They agreed that two-thirty would be a good time to meet, and she would arrange it with the Commissioner. Cole requested that he would like to get a picture of the three of them, so a camera should be available.

Cole then thanked the Governor for his cooperation. The two detectives proceeded to have lunch at The Holiday Place.

As they approached the restaurant, they were pleased to see that Sheila was on duty. She acknowledged them, and showed them to a table that was not in a busy section. She said, "Will one menu be okay for the two of you?"

Strong answered, "Yes that will be fine."

"Ted is on a break right now. I will let him know he is to be your server. Can I get you a drink, some water perhaps," she asked.

"Sounds good," Strong replied.

While they waited to be served they took note of four men seated across the room who were deeply engaged in a lively discussion. They were dressed in business suits, white shirts and wearing expensive looking ties. Cole in his usual cynical tone said, "I wonder if we will be meeting those gentlemen before we finish this case. Who wears five-hundred dollar suits in a beach restaurant?"

Bill grinned at him and said, "Guv, your instincts are rarely wrong. Ted, I see him now, he'll fill us in I'll bet."

Ted approached the table in a professional manner and greeted the detectives. He served them their water and quietly said, "Two of those men over there are from Vancouver, and two came in from Toronto. They arrived last Saturday. I wasn't working yesterday and when I came in this morning they were in here having coffee with Amos Delray, and Jones the lawyer. I did not serve their table. Give me your order and I'll place it, then I'll go by their table to bus it. I'll try to catch what they are arguing about."

"Bring two orders of fish and chips along with two greenies," Cole said.

Ted walked to the kitchen and entered the order. He reappeared shortly, and approached the table in question. He removed some dirty cups as he moved around, slowly placing them on a tray stand as he stayed within earshot of the customers. He then went back to the table with clean ashtrays and efficiently removed the dirty ones. All the while, the men paid no attention to him. They kept a heated argument going, using four letter words and naming people. Ted heard, '*Commissioner Black*', '*Samson*', '*Blue Lake Diamonds*', Delray, and, '*fishing boat*'. Returning to the kitchen he wrote a short summary of what he had just heard, picked up the orders of fish and chips, for Cole's table. As he placed the meals on the table he left his note under Cole's plate and said, "Enjoy your meal, I'll bring you the desert menu when you finish what I've brought."

"I don't often eat desert at this time of day, but bring me the menu anyway. I might see something interesting," Cole said.

"You can count on that, sir," replied Ted.

Cole took the note from under his plate and set it aside until the two detectives had eaten their meals. Before Ted returned Cole looked at the paper, raised his eyebrows while looking at Strong who was leaning forward to hear Cole comment. "It sure looks like all the bees have come to the hive. If Ted's note means anything, I've no doubt those guys are arguing about the deal that we are about to bust. You and I just seem to step into the pile of shit, everywhere we go on this Island. There could be a replay of the June murders because I'm betting that group is being screwed by Delray and his crowd, and are ranting about their treatment. I can hardly wait for desert."

Strong commented by saying, "If you are right, guv, we have to save their asses somehow." Looking away from Cole he nodded his head in the direction of the kitchen to indicate he saw Ted coming.

Ted kept his professional posture, and told a concocted a story to mask the real intent of what he knew. He said, "We have a special desert for you. It combines flavors from Canada and Florida. When the chef mixes them with Palm Island ingredients they usually work good together, but they sometimes get destroyed. I believe what was served over at the other table was not what was expected. I think they know the chef sometimes gets very angry at customers who don't like what he serves up. In your case, Sheila herself made sure that you would enjoy your servings, and she made a thank you card for being such frequent customers." Ted place the card on the table beside Cole's serving, then said, "I will be back shortly in case you want something else."

"One moment Ted," Strong said. "Did you serve this same desert last June?"

"Yes sir, but we haven't served it since then, until today. The flavors don't last long, it seems, so we have to wait until a new shipment arrives, and it did arrive last Saturday."

"I'd be interested in how long the chef thinks the new batch will last. I just tasted what you served and it is very interesting – almost too good to be true."

"Oh, it's true," Ted replied. "But let me find out how long he expects to be able to use what we have. I'll be right back." Suddenly Ted said, "Hey, I see the two men I served the other day at lunch time. They just walked in. They had a couple of fabulous looking women with them on Saturday. Should I bring the check now?"

"We know those guys, Ted. Yes, bring the check," Cole said. "Add two more Greenies. We aren't in any hurry to leave. Besides we are enjoying watching the four men over there. Then quietly he said to Ted, "Can you get their names for me?"

Ted just nodded and did not reply. When he returned with the beer he slipped Cole a note with the names he had requested.

"Thanks, Ted, great service as usual," Cole acknowledged. "We may be back tomorrow for more good service."

Ted said, "Thank you." He stayed calm, and proceeded to serve another table.

Both detectives turned their attention to the DEA agent's table. Strong had been watching the action there. He said to Cole, "Oakley nodded to me to indicate that he saw us. He also cranked his head toward the table where the four men were arguing, as if to ask, '*Who are those guys?*' Sheila gave them our notes while you were focused on Ted. Do you think we should send them another note?"

"Good idea, Bill. Write it out on a napkin. Give it to Sheila when we check out. Those four men are going to be witnesses, only if we keep them alive. Add to the note that we need to meet at our place very early tomorrow morning to discuss how we should handle those four guys."

Strong complied. He and Cole went to pay their bill, and gave the note to Sheila. They were walking to their car when they saw Harris pull up in front of the entrance and let two passengers out. One they recognized as Maria, the other, a male, looked like the man that Buzzy had described as her friend. Harris began to drive away, so Cole ran toward his car and waved for him to stop. Harris pulled over and stopped, rolled down his window, and said to Cole, "No talk right now. I call you." Cole nodded. Harris drove away.

Cole looked perturbed. Strong said, "Here we go again. Looks like Harris has been hired by some of the cartel crowd. Let's go back in. I have a hunch that Maria, and her friend joined the four guys who were arguing."

Cole agreed. They walked directly to take a quick look into the dining area. Strong had guessed correctly. Six were now at the table and talking quietly. Cole said, "I've seen this action before. Maria has brought new info to the table to cool those guys down. The con is on. I think someone here might have called her to say those four guys were arguing too loudly. We'd better tip off Sheila and Ted, that there's a cartel plant in here."

They waved for Sheila to come to her station and she came immediately. "Sheila," Cole said, "just in case someone gets nosey and wonders why we popped back in, mark us down in the reservation book for seven tomorrow evening, but the real reason we came back is to tell you we suspect there's a mole in here working for the bad guys. Tell Ted right away, and both of you be really careful."

"I'll tell Ted," she said. "Look, one of the two men over there saw you and told me he wants to meet you in the Men's Room. Good thing you returned. I'll tell him now."

• • •

After receiving the call from Marcel Savage, Oakley and Patton started out their day by dropping into Carl's Treats for breakfast. Carl recognized them and greeted them with a handshake and a smile. He said, "Nice to see you guys again. Thanks for telling Billy Bob that I needed some fish. He told me the story about how you guys helped him get the monster tuna into the boat, so now I've got my freezer full. Thanks to both of you. Let me treat you to breakfast. What will it be?"

Oakley responded. "That's a great offer Carl, but you don't have to do that."

"I want to, and I'm going to, so order up."

"In that case," Oakley replied, "ham and eggs and wheat toast for me. What about you Willie?"

"Thanks for the treat, Carl, I'll have the same," Willie answered.

As they were eating they discussed their next moves. They had to get cash for Tuesday night, and decided that while they were in Kingtown to surveille

The Diamond Store. After that, they could drop by Palm Dive on their way to have lunch at Holiday Place Resort. They enjoyed the breakfast, got coffees to go, and thanked Carl. They could see the ocean on the drive into Kingtown, and they noticed that the waves, although still very large, were not as angry as they had been on Sunday. They parked their Jeep near the Palm Bank & Trust building where they had a good view of The Diamond Store. As they drank their coffees, a police car pulled up in front of it. To their surprise, two civilians got out. One they recognized as Amos Delray, the other had long blonde hair. Delray was carrying a valise. Neither Patton, nor Oakley, could see into the store, and for sure they didn't want the police officer to see them, so they stayed in the Jeep. About ten minutes later Delray and the other man came out of the store, got into the police cruiser and left.

"Let's follow them," Oakley stated. "We have time, it's only ten." Patton complied. The police cruiser drove straight to the station and all three men got out and proceeded to walk in. "I wonder, Willie, if Cole knows who the blonde guy is. Amos certainly isn't buying diamonds. In this weather he isn't getting any cash from the dive operation. He has to be showing the blonde guy how they work. "

"You can bet on that," Willie answered. "Look, we had better get our banking done. We'll still have time to go by Amos' Palm Dive. I'll go to the Palm Bank & Trust, and you go to the Royal International across the street."

Tom agreed. They had American Express checks to convert to cash, and they anticipated no trouble at either bank in getting the $US twenty dollar bills. They met back in the Jeep where Tom said, "I met the manager, Don Sasko, in there. He asked if I wanted to open an account and, if so, he'd be happy to accommodate me. I told him I might return to talk about it, but had to rush to meet you. We should meet with him if we get time after the raids."

"My bank wasn't as friendly, Tom. The teller called the manager over to quiz me about why I wanted the twenties. I told him it's easier to use cash than the traveler's checks, and besides, some places wanted to screw me for a conversion fee. He bought the idea, but did not seem happy to part with the bills. Anyway, let's head out to Delray's op. I'm curious to see if the 'Quicksilver' is there. Our new team members will want to know for sure."

The drive was pleasant. The sun had broken through the clouds, giving the sea a whole new character. The white water topping off the waves was beautiful to watch. When they arrived at Palm Dive they noticed a Ford truck, and a white van parked next to the office. "Looks like he might be here," Tom commented. "Maybe not though, as the last time we saw him, he was being chauffeured by the cops. Park beside that Ford Ranger, and I'll jump out and see if he's here." Tom tried the office door but it was locked. Then he saw movement inside. Amos appeared at the door, opened it and greeted Tom.

"Hey, it's nice to see you again. C'mon in. Is your dive buddy with you?"

Tom answered, "Yeah, he's in the Jeep. I'll get him. Willie," Tom shouted, "Amos is here."

Willie stepped out of the Jeep and replied loudly, "Great." He went to the office.

Tom opened the conversation by asking, "Where's the *Quicksilver*, Amos?"

"Oh, we had to take it over to the lee side because of this major Nor'Wester. It looks like we'll have her back here by tomorrow. Are you interested in going out again?"

"Yes," Tom said, we are thinking about a night dive. Do you have any divers lined up that we could join?"

"Not before Thursday night, guys. I have a dive scheduled at eight tomorrow night, weather permitting. There's only four men going, but they don't want company. They are paying the whole fee. I'm sorry. They are well heeled, I guess, two from Vancouver, and two from Toronto, Canada. Then on Wednesday I've scheduled Quicksilver for quarterly maintenance, and that's why Thursday would be the soonest you could go, assuming four more divers show up. The boat will be spic and span and in top mechanical condition."

"Damn, Willie," Tom said "should we stay over just in case?"

"I told you Tom I can't. You know that."

Amos was amused by the two men trying to sort out their travel plans. He said, "Wish I could accommodate you, but the people who have booked *Quicksilver* are adamant about going alone. And, in fact, they insisted on me going as Captain. They have the bucks so why not, man?"

"I understand," Tom said. "We like this Island, so you'll be seeing more of us. I guess we should get on our way, Willie, and let Amos attend to his business." Turning to Amos and offering a handshake, he said, "Thanks for your time. By the way Amos, we heard that there's a great fitness club here on Palm. Is it far from here?"

"Hell, no, guys. Go east about a half a mile and turn left on Juniper Drive. You'll see the sign, PALM FITTNESS CLUB, about one hundred yards on your right. It's a good idea to stay in shape if you do night diving."

"Thanks again, Amos," Tom said. "We'll see you soon."

Back in the Jeep, Willie took the wheel. Patton looked at him and said, "My God, are you thinking what I'm thinking? Amos just told us in so many words that four unsuspecting souls are about to die at sea. He's a ruthless bastard, Willie. Spic and span eh, no blood stains anywhere."

"Yes, I caught the story. I wonder if Detective Cole knows about the guys from Canada. We should cross paths with him and Strong at lunch. Somehow we have to get the message to them."

The men easily found the fitness place entered the Club. There were only three people working out. The agents could not see Maria. They approached the check-in counter and were greeted by a young woman who claimed to be the manager. Patton said to her, "Hello, we came by because one of your instructors told us about this facility. We met her at Clear & Deep Dive. Is she here today?"

The manager replied, "Hi! I'm Molly. Thanks for coming by. If you mean Maria Solarno, she doesn't work here anymore. She called in yesterday to say she was leaving us and returning to her home in Panama. We will miss her. She has a good-looking male friend who showed up from time to time, and she indicated that he's Panamanian. They are going to get married. Can I help you myself?"

Tom spoke. "We are in a bit of a hurry. Can we have a raincheck? We will be coming to Palm more often in the future."

Willie thought, '*He shoots BS more than me!*'

"Here's a brochure", Molly said. "Sorry you have to run. I'll see you soon I hope."

The agents smiled, shook her hand, and said, "Sounds good!"

They proceeded to The Holiday Place Resort. When they drove into the parking area, Oakley noticed the Camry. He told Willie to hurry. He said, "That's the Brits' car. Let's move our butts, man. Maybe I can get a meeting set up in the Men's Room.

· · ·

Cole had received the message from Sheila, and he went directly to the men's room. Strong stayed outside in case someone might interrupt the meeting. Oakley walked by, and acknowledged Strong by winking. Inside Oakley wasted no time, and told Cole about the blonde guy he saw going into The Diamond Store as well as the action planned by Amos. He further added, "The name of that good looking broad that was waitressing at Bodder's Tiki bar is Maria Solarno. She's headed for Panama with her grease ball lover who is Panamanian. I'll bet she'll be transporting more diamonds than the ones we saw her wearing. I'll have her checked out by Interpol. We'll have to nab her tomorrow. If she gets away from Palm we'll never see her again."

Cole got that awesome, fierce look in his eyes, and even Oakley felt a little uneasy. Cole told Oakley that the blonde guy owns the Cigarette31, and his suspicion about the four loudmouths getting screwed by the cartel. They agreed that the story fit with what Tom had learned at Palm Dive. The meeting ended with Tom agreeing to meet at six Tuesday morning at *Enchanted.*

· · ·

"We have to watch the time, guv," Strong said. "Two-thirty is our meeting with Black. Let's be a bit early, and make it look like we've got lots of time. We can chat with Audrey and get a feel of how friendly she is, or is not."

Cole looked at his watch before he replied. "It's two already. I like your suggestion, mate. The more casual we appear to be, the better."

They drove directly to Police Headquarters. The Commissioner's Land Rover was parked there, as well as the Deputy Commissioner's cruiser. As Strong parked the Camry, Cole commented, "Looks like both ring leaders are here. I've got the plane ticket so let's get busy."

Audrey was at the reception desk. She greeted the detectives with a real smile. "Good afternoon gentlemen, great news about the Commissioner. You are a bit early, but he could be free to see you right now. Let me try to get him."

"Thank you my dear," Strong replied. "I'm glad to see you looking so happy today."

Audrey smiled then picked up the phone.

They heard Audrey say, "Yes, sir, I'll send them right along." Turning to the detectives she said, "He's waiting for you, so go right on up to his office."

Cole and Strong proceeded up the stairway and saw George standing near the Commissioner's office. As they approached him he smiled, motioned for them to come over. When they got there he offered them a handshake. He said, "This is exciting. We are happy to see the Commissioner go to London."

Cole answered, "We are too, George. I guess the Deputy Commissioner is up to keeping things running smoothly while he's away?"

"You've nothing to worry about, sir. Audrey and I are up to the task too. If we can help you just let one of us know. Here, let me open the door for you."

George entered first, and said, "Detectives Cole, and Strong, are here for their appointment."

Commissioner Black was seated at his desk, and as he arose to address the detectives he sounded friendly, saying, "Welcome gentlemen, how is your investigation proceeding?"

"We are pleased, Commissioner," Cole replied. "We will have this wrapped up by tomorrow. But first, here are your tickets to London, and return. Enjoy the first class service. Bill and I only get to see first class when we fly. But if someone deserves it, you sure do." He handed him the ticket folder.

"Thank you Detective, and thank the Premier, and the Governor, as I feel they must have had a hand in making this trip, and the award, possible."

"Yes they did, Commissioner. And they asked me to wish you a pleasant experience. To answer your first question, sir, we are now writing up our report. We have one small area to finish up, but we don't anticipate finding any new facts. With that in mind, Detective Strong and I would like to treat all of your people to a 'get together' tomorrow evening, as we hand a copy of our report to the Deputy Commissioner. We usually thank folks before we leave a case. For your information, Bill and I will be leaving on Thursday to spend some R & R time in Miami."

"Well, that's an unexpected treat, detective. Let me call in Deputy Black. I'm quite sure he will jump at the opportunity to hold such a meeting." He went to his desk and buzzed Audrey. The intercom sound was open, so all could hear him say, "Audrey, please tell Samson we would like to see him in my office right away."

She answered, "He's standing right here, Commissioner, and he heard what you said. He will be right up. And, sir, I'll give him the camera so George can take a photo of the occasion."

As they waited they talked about the Nor'Wester.

The Commissioner, trying to be humorous, said, "How are you enjoying the blow job? We Palm Islanders like it."

Strong smiled and answered in a matter of fact tone, "I don't mind it, but I'm sure your tourists are a bit ticked off."

"Yes," came the answer, "but things will be back to normal by tomorrow."

Cole could hardly contain himself while thinking, '*not if we have our way, you arrogant, despicable bastard*'.

Deputy Commissioner Samson Black walked straight in. He asked, "What do you need, sir?"

"Well, it would be appropriate if you could say hello to our guests."

"My apology, gentlemen, but this storm has caused me to shuffle some staff, and my mind is a bit preoccupied."

Cole looked at him and said, "We understand. Things don't always go as planned, especially in our business."

They all chucked at the comment, then The Commissioner told his deputy about the Wednesday evening event. "Can you get everyone together for the presentation?"

"I sure hope so, sir," the deputy answered. "Just think, we both get a presentation this week. I'll put George in charge and he can work with Audrey to make it happen. I'm sure crime can stop for an hour or so while we celebrate. And, showing the Polaroid camera given to him by Audrey, he said, "Let's get George in here to get a picture."

The deputy stepped out of the office and found George nearby. "Come, George," the deputy ordered, "I need you to take a picture."

George complied and took four shots of the four men with their arms locked in a celebration pose. Cole thought, '*How the hell did we pull off this stunt? Puffery gets the job done!*'

Cole said, "Thanks for the souvenir Commissioner. We'll take some pictures for your memoirs tomorrow evening. Detective Strong and I will count on being here at seven to celebrate. Get some food and drinks, Deputy, and hand me the bill tomorrow night. Happy times are here again! So, men, Bill and I will get out of your way and get our report together. We may, or may not, go to the airport later and watch the big BA plane come in. Ever since I was a kid I've liked to watch the airplanes. Anyway, we are very close to completing our mission. Thanks for everything."

Cole and Strong let themselves out, and walked straight to their car.

• • •

The airport was crowded with people waiting for the big British Airways plane to arrive. Cole and Strong could have used their authority to get a tarmac-side view, but chose to stay back and observe the crowd. Right on the revised arrival time, the public address system blared, '*British Airways fight now on approach.*' Moments later the huge aircraft glided onto the runway, tires squealed, and a roar sounded as the engines were set in reverse. It looked like the plane would travel right into the sea at the end of the runway, but it slowed to a crawl, turned, and started to move slowly toward the terminal. The crowd cheered.

Cole experienced a surge of nationalistic pride as he observed the aircraft was powered by huge Rolls-Royce engines, and it displayed the British flag. He turned to Strong and said, "Well, Bill, the fuse has been lit. There's the baby that will take the Commissioner away tomorrow morning. Hard to believe what has gone on in the short time we've been here. Clue after clue, everywhere we turned – another clue. But now comes the hard part."

Strong had a serious look on his face as he replied, "There's so many actors in this mission that I can't believe we are still alive. So yes, guv, let's get the ball over the line, and finish the game."

Passengers had started filtering through, and getting rides or hailing taxis. Suddenly the Commissioner's Land Rover appeared. It stopped in the 'RESERVED' area where passengers exit the terminal. Black stepped out of the passenger side, and lawyer Jones, stepped out from a rear door. They proceeded into the terminal. The driver remained, and kept the engine running.

"I wonder what that's all about, Bill?"

"It could be a welcoming committee for Jane, guv. I guess we'd better hang around and see what happens. You told the commissioner that we might be here, so let's watch."

The crowd was thinning out which gave the detectives a better view of the arriving passengers. Twenty minutes after the plane landed, they recognized Larry, and Eve, of the Taylor family. They stood in a shaded area and refused several offers from taxi drivers. Cole made eye contact with Larry to assure him that he was there if needed. Larry smiled and nodded to acknowledge.

The Commissioner and the lawyer finally appeared, accompanied by Jane Butterworth. Jones was carrying Jane's suitcase. Black was talking to her as they walked to the Land Rover. Jones opened the back passenger door and beckoned for Jane to get in. He then put her suitcase into the boot, and he entered the other rear door to sit beside Jane. The Commissioner stepped up into the front passenger seat. They drove off in the direction of Kingtown.

"Look!" said Strong. "That's Oakley's Jeep. Where in the hell were they hiding? Oakley said he'd tail Jones and Jane, and he is."

"Sure enough, I'm surprised that they're on time! Now we can concentrate on the Taylors, and make sure they get to The Beach Hotel."

Andrew and Jackie finally appeared. They joined Larry and Eve as they packed into a Toyota van. They showed no indication that they recognized Cole, or Strong.

"So far, so good Bill," Cole said.

"One more night until the Commissioner actually gets on that plane at nine tomorrow morning. Let's hope he doesn't get sick and can't go."

"Sick, I doubt it," Cole responded. "Even if he gets sick, that pompous bugger is in with both feet. Of course you and I will be back out here at the airport to see him leave. Right now, though, we'd better tail that Toyota. If all goes well we can go to somewhere simple, like Carl's Treats, and get something light to eat. Get in, I'll drive."

• • •

The Toyota van went directly to The Beach Hotel. Cole and Strong watched from the parking area until the Taylor family disappeared into the hotel. Strong commented, "Looks like things are on track, guv. I hope they like their adjoining rooms. Sure is plenty of room for a party if we get through this mess alive."

Cole nodded, and replied, "Let's get some food."

They proceeded to Carl's Treats and sat at a window table. Before they had a chance to order Cole noticed a police cruiser enter the parking area. It pulled into the space next to the Camry. The officer driving the cruiser got out, and walked around the detectives' car. He then got back into his vehicle, and while Cole observed, he began talking on his radio. A couple of minutes later he drove away.

"That was pretty obvious, Bill," Cole said. "That's the same asshole that drove us home from the Cricket Club. Remember him, Wilbur Black?"

"Sure, I remember him. What do you think it's all about?"

"He knew damn well that I could see him. He's delivering a warning of some sort. Do you think he followed us from the airport? Could be he put two and two together and watched us follow that van. Maybe he saw us leave when its passengers were dropped off?"

"Could be," replied Strong. "We let our guard down by not looking for a tail."

Carl, the owner, had been watching the detectives and approached the table. "Hello," he said. "I'm Carl. I recognize you two gentlemen. You are the outsider cops I read about in the paper. I'm happy that you're here to investigate crime on this island, and I'm honored to have you visit my restaurant. In case you don't know, that officer who was snooping around your car is a leech. His name is Wilbur Black. He's one of Commissioner Black's flunkies. He comes in here like he owns the place, and never pays for anything. He probably took off when he saw you, afraid to try his usual intimidation routine. Look, I'd like to treat you to dinner. And, if I can help you in any way, let me know."

"What a pleasant surprise," Cole replied. "I'm Detective Curt Cole," and nodding towards Strong, "this is my partner Detective Bill Strong. It's not ethical for us to accept the dinner treat, but we sure appreciate the offer. However, you certainly *can* help us right now. It's urgent that we contact some folks who just checked into The Beach Hotel. Could you phone there, and say you wish to talk to Larry Taylor of London, England? Tell the operator who you are, and if questioned, say that there is an order ready to be delivered. As soon as you get connected to the room, hand me the phone."

"I will gladly do that. I know the number. Come over behind the counter."

Cole followed Carl who placed the call. He heard the operator say to Carl, "Yes. One moment please." Then, when it started to ring, Carl handed the phone to Cole.

Cole heard Larry say quizzically, "Hello?"

"Don't talk detective. It's Curt Cole. You may be getting a visit from a Palm Island police constable. Warn the others. If he comes, don't panic. He's several bricks short of a load, but quite snarky. He tailed us and you folks from the airport, and saw us while we watched you go into the hotel. I feel he suspects a connection, so this is a heads up. We are down the street at a place called Carl's Treats Restaurant. The owner's name is Carl, and he is pure. I will leave instructions with him for you, so plan to walk here to have breakfast at nine to get them. Bye."

Turning to Carl he said, "Hope you don't mind being involved, and I thank you for what you just did."

"My pleasure, detective, and I'll watch for them in the morning. Now, what can I get you to eat? I serve world famous fish and chips, tuna today, and that's not an exaggeration. It comes with fresh rolls and slaw. Want to try it?"

"Hey, Bill, did you hear that? Let's try it."

"I'm all for it, guv, if I don't starve to death first."

"Give me ten minutes. Have some pretzels to chew on," Carl said. He handed them a bowl full. I'll get you a couple of Cokes to wash them down. I don't serve beer." Ten minutes later Carl served the meal.

The detectives enjoyed the fare and when Cole finished eating he motioned to Carl to come to the table. He addressed Carl, saying, "You weren't kidding, Carl. You serve awesome food. How much do we owe you?"

"Twenty dollars, Palm. Or twenty-five U S dollars will do it."

Strong handed the money to Carl. Cole then said, "I will be back in the morning with a note to hand to the older man. His name is Larry and there will be another man, and two ladies with him."

"I can handle it," replied Carl. "Don't worry about a thing."

"Okay, my friend, I'll try. It's time to get home and get organized."

They left the restaurant, and Strong drove home. Before turning in to *Enchanted's* driveway they looked at Gart's place and saw Fingers' vehicle. That prompted Strong's emotions to surface. He said, "Enjoy your last night of freedom, Fingers, you slimy bastard."

Cole looked at his partner and said, "Don't take anything for granted, Bill. In the past, our raids were successful, but they never went off without some kind of a glitch. From what Oakley has told us, I do agree with your description of Fingers. Right now, let's get in and get settled for tonight."

They entered the house and once again everything looked just as it was when they left. Cole got a pad of paper and wrote instructions for the Taylor group. At that point it dawned on him that there was no message from Harris. He called Strong, who was already in his bedroom, to come over.

"What's the matter, guv?" Strong asked.

"We didn't hear from Harris. Call Gart. Find out if he knows anything about Harris."

Strong called, Gart answered, and Strong said, "Hey, Gart, this is Bill Strong. Have you heard anything from Harris, our taxi man?"

"Yes. He told me that you should call him at nine tonight."

"Thanks, Gart, bye."

Cole looked at Strong and said, "You are in charge. It's eight already and I'm still writing up our day's activities. Ask Harris to be here tomorrow morning at eight forty-five.

Strong decided to open the sliding doors to find out how strong the wind was blowing. He felt the cool trade winds and not the ferocious Nor'Wester gusts. He raised his voice and said to Cole, "Blimey, guv, the wind has almost died down. I'm going to sit out here on the lanai."

Cole acknowledged by saying, "I'll be out shortly. How about getting us a snort of *Pirates' Best*? I'll join you in a few minutes."

"Good idea, guv."

Strong got a couple of small glasses and poured the rum. Cole joined him and they started to relax as they sipped the drinks. At nine Strong called Harris. The phone rang twice before Harris answered and said in a low voice, "Hello?"

Strong noted the low voice. He said, "This is Detective Strong. Are you okay? Can you talk? Just say 'yes' or 'no'."

"Yes, sir," replied Harris. "I okay. I been driving bad people. I must see you tomorrow."

"Good. Come here to Enchanted at eight forty-five tomorrow morning, and drive us to Carl's Treats."

"I do that, sir. Bye."

"Well Bill, not much more we can do tonight but pray. I can do it now or you can offer your own request to our Lord."

Strong replied, "Go ahead, guv, I know that when two or more get together to praise the Lord and ask for protection, He hears our prayer."

Cole kneeled, and asked for protection for each person involved in arresting the criminals. He also prayed that the Lord would give Bill, and himself, the wisdom to conduct a successful operation. When he rose up he said, "Let's get some rest, we won't be getting any tomorrow."

They headed for their rooms feeling secure in God's hands.

· · ·

Patton and Oakley followed the Land Rover from the airport, and watched it drive into Paradise Suites, a condo complex next to The Beach Hotel. The three passengers got out. Jones carried Jane's suitcase from the vehicle, then they walked inside. Oakley said, "Holy cow, this is convenient. Let's just park at our place, where we can observe without them getting suspicious."

After parking next door they waited for over thirty minutes in the Jeep before the men appeared again, but without Jane. They were smiling and talking. The Land Rover pulled up, they got in and left.

"Not much more we can do now," Tom said, "except report to Cole in the morning. Let's get settled for the night. Tomorrow will be a killer."

"I like your sense of humor, Tom, or was that just a slip of the tongue!"

"Maybe so, but could be a fact, too. Anyway, we'd better get to our room and get some rest. We still have to make a room reservation for the gang that's arriving early tomorrow, so let's stop at the front desk and set that up. Then we'd better get to our room and get some rest."

At the reservation desk they had no problem booking two adjoining rooms. The male clerk was happy to make the reservation in Oakley's name, but pointed out that his friends would have to register under their own names when they checked in on Tuesday. Tom agreed to the terms. He asked the clerk if there was a pizza restaurant nearby. He was told that Hibiscus Restaurant had the best pizza on the Island, and if they wished, he would order one to be delivered. Tom said, "We'd like that. Can you bring it to our room when it gets here?"

"Yes, I will arrange that," the clerk said. "It should be here within thirty minutes."

"Good, only pepperoni," Tom said. "We'll head for our room now."

In the room they each got a beer from the mini fridge. Tom was gazing out at the ocean when he started to think about Sally. He turned to look at Willie and said, "You know, Willie, we haven't even mentioned Sally and Jan since we left them the other night. Looking at the ocean triggered my thoughts. God only knows where they might be now. I wish this mission was over and we could chase them down in Biloxi."

Willie looked up at Tom and replied, "I'm with you on that, pal, but no use fretting over them right now. If we never see them again, I hope we do, we won't ever forget them. Let's keep focused on the plans for tomorrow."

The phone rang. It was the desk clerk calling to say he was on his way with the pizza. Tom answered the door when the knock came, thanked the clerk, and tipped him. The men enjoyed the pizza, had another beer, chatted a bit about clues, then they called it a day.

Chapter 21 | Tuesday – Making It Happen

Cole and Strong arose at daybreak after an unsettling night because their minds kept churning with 'what ifs'. Cole made coffee and toast, while Strong got ready for the day. They both had opened their drapes to look out at the sea, and were comforted by the fact that the wind was blowing offshore. Only ground swells were rolling in onto their beach. As a precaution, they decided to not open the drapes that enclosed the main room. Instead they sat outside on the lanai to wait for Patton and Oakley to show up. Their conversation focused on events that had transpired since they had arrived on the Island. Cole finished his toast then went to the kitchen to get a second cup of coffee for each of them. Strong stayed put to watch for the DEA agents. They finished their coffee, and Cole suggested that Strong should prepare another pot just in case their visitors would like a drink. It was almost six when Oakley and Patton did arrive. They were glad to get a cup of coffee.

The four men gathered around the big table in the main room. As a precaution, Strong had closed the drapes in his room, and in Cole's bedroom. Cole took the lead, and said to Patton, "Regardless of how this day turns out, I want you to know that Bill and I feel that we are fortunate that you and Willie have teamed up with us. I felt every day that we were all pulling in the same direction, and we fully trusted each other. Now comes the nut cutting. The first thing we have to do is synchronize our watches. Right now, set your watches at exactly fifteen minutes after six. As soon as you meet the new agents, be sure to synchronize with them."

Cole continued, "We now know that the woman, Maria Solarno, is probably a key figure in the cartel operation. The guy that she is with could be calling the shots. We want them both before they get a chance to leave the Island. My guess is that they live on the DIAMOND QUEEN when it is here, but on the other hand, Maria has a residence, and they may be shacked up at her place. Harris will know her address. I'll get it from him and give it to Gart, so check with him, Tom. If my gut feel is right, they should be at the airport this morning to watch the Commissioner leave. I would like you, Tom, or you, Willie, to tail them until you can assign one of your new guys to do it. Her associate came here on the Cigarette31 and my guess is that they will both try to leave on it. The boat never left Bodder's dock, and that could work in our favor. You guys could seize the boat, and capture the blonde guy along with the other two all in one fell swoop. Can you arrange it Tom?"

Tom smiled, and said, "I have four top agents arriving at seven. Until they are here and ready to relieve us, Willie, or I, will follow them. I hope you are right. I'd love to be the one to seize that boat. Interpol is checking out the broad, and will try to ID her associate and the boat owner also. Interpol will report to Savage, and at noon I will be calling him. Whatever I find out, if I can't find you, I will tell to Gart. You can check with him."

"Good," Cole said, "so the rest of our plans stay intact. Is there any more questions or comments?"

Patton replied, "Yes. It looks like Jane Butterworth is residing at Paradise Condos. That's where she was dropped off by Jones and Black."

Cole replied, "Thanks, Tom. Bill and I will take it from here. Anymore comments from anyone?"

Patton got up from his chair. "Which of us is going to protect the four Canadians and take them into custody? Maybe we could nab them at Palm Dive, although they might be dead by then."

Cole replied, "I forgot about them, Tom. They are part of the drug operation so you get to do it. I believe they will be alive when they get to Amos' place. From what you have told me, his office could be a meeting place to do their deal, whatever it is. He could kill them there and dispose of the bodies at sea. Who knows? Stay on their tails."

"Fine," Patton replied. "I'll have enough help. I can station two men early enough to watch them. It doesn't get dark until seven now, so hopefully we don't have to act before then, Curt."

"Look Tom, it's now six forty-five, and you guys have better beat it if you are to meet your people at seven. I think Harris has new info for us because he has been driving some of the cartel operatives. I'm anxious to hear what he has to say. Take care."

Exactly as planned, Harris arrived at eight forty-five. Cole was watching and immediately stepped outside to get Harris' attention. Strong finished tidying up inside and heard Cole call his name. Both men greeted Harris as they got into his car.

Harris said, "I park here a bit. I must tell you the woman and man you saw get from my car yesterday are criminals. I hear words like 'stupid Canadians, they be dead by Tuesday night'. I hear about diamonds and cash and a deal. I hear Commissioner Black needs more. I hear woman call the man, Moses Alvarez. He said, 'We go to Panama soon'. "She kiss him. Detective. They very bad people."

"Are you driving them today, Cole asked?"

"Yes. I go for them at ten today. They pay lots." He smiled.

Cole said, "Start driving. We must be at Carl's Treats at eight. Now, listen to me. Those criminals will probably want you killed by tonight. You must bring your wife and kids to *Enchanted*! Wait, a better idea is to bring them next door, to my neighbor Phil's. They will be safer there. We can tell Phil that they are coming. Tonight we need you to drive some of our detectives. This evening, the woman Maria, and her man, will likely want to go to a restaurant and expect you to wait. Tell them you wish to be home by six tonight for a special supper. If they give you an argument, tell them you can be at their service by seven. Then, drive to Phil's as fast as you can.

"I follow your orders, sir. I not scared."

"Okay, here we are. I'll run into the restaurant. You and Detective Strong wait in the car."

Cole went into the restaurant. The Taylor group was there. Cole showed no indication that he recognized them, and they simply looked up as they would if any customer came in. Cole greeted Carl. He gave him the instructions for Larry.

Carl grinned and said, "Thanks for the recipe. I can prepare it, but you'll have to let me know in advance when you wish to have the meal."

"Probably on Thursday if that's okay, I'll be busy as hell until then."

Larry and his group overheard the comment by Cole, and they immediately dove into their food in order to keep from laughing.

Carl said, "I'll make a reservation for you."

Cole turned and left without any more conversation.

Larry, sitting at his table, looked up and said to Carl, "Is that a British meal you have to prepare? Can I look at the recipe and maybe we will come along on Thursday."

"Sure," Carl said. He handed the paper to Larry.

He saw, '*Be ready to go at six. Be in the lobby.*' "Thanks," Larry said, as he handed the paper back to Carl. "I don't know which part of England enjoys that recipe, but it's not my taste."

"To each his own," Carl replied. "That man is a Scotland Yard detective so whatever pleases him, pleases me."

The Taylor family did not discuss Cole's message while they finished their meals, but as they walked back to their hotel Larry told his associates what it said.

Andrew commented, "Cole knows every trick in the book. I can hardly wait until we get to meet him at later. I guess we just play our role as tourists until then."

Larry agreed. When they reached the hotel, and were still able to talk securely, he said, "We must remember to stay within eye range of each other all day. Any conversations with strangers must only relate to the weather, or to Palm Island attractions. Be extra careful to use only our Taylor first names, not our real ones, when talking to each other. It's easy to slip up." He heard the others say, "Yes, guv, we hear you." They headed for their rooms.

•   •   •

Cole got back into the taxi and asked Harris if he knew where the woman Maria has a residence. Harris answered, "Yes. Two house this side of Clear & Deep. It brown wit white shutters on windows."

"Got that Bill?" Cole asked.

"Yes sir. I'll take the info to Gart while you talk to Phil."

"Harris," Cole commanded, "drive directly to Phil's house."

When they arrived, Strong walked over to Hibiscus, and Cole went quickly to rap on Phil's door. The dogs made their usual racket until Phil ordered them to be quiet. After looking through the peep hole he opened his door. "Hey. What's up detective?" he asked.

"We need your help, Phil." Pointing to the taxi he continued, "Harris, our trusted driver, has been driving two of our suspects for two days now. They have loose lips, and Harris has heard some scary details of what they plan to do. He will be driving them again today until he drops them somewhere this evening. I'm sure that he or his family could be killed when the suspects have no more use for Harris. They can't be so stupid as to talk with Harris listening, and hearing about their plans. He heard them talk about having Canadians killed, and about a deal to be pulled off tomorrow. They must plan to eliminate him. I want him to bring his wife and two kids here. I need you to protect them." Cole then took a couple of minutes to go over new developments.

Phil replied, "I told you, whatever it takes, count me in. Sure, bring them over."

Cole motioned for Harris to come to meet Phil who greeted him. "I'll look after your family, Harris. Thank you for helping us rid this country of the scum that has taken over here."

Harris said, "God bless you, Mr. Phil. I return soon."

Chapter 22: Commissioner Departs, Agents Arrive

Strong returned from Hibiscus and joined Cole who addressed Phil, saying, "This is going to be a hectic day." He Looked at his watch and said to Cole, "We'd better get to the airport, guv. It's eight-thirty already."

They shook Phil's hand, ran across the yards, and took off in the Camry. When they got to the airport they saw that passengers were already boarding the plane. Cole said, "I don't see the Land Rover or any of Commissioner Black's flunkies. He may want to make a big scene as he departs. I wouldn't be surprised if the plane leaves late. I don't see Maria, either."

Looking over Cole's shoulder Strong chuckled, and said, "Look, here comes the show now."

The Land Rover, and two cruisers, pulled up in front of the terminal. Four officers got out of the cruisers and cleared a path through the waiting people. The Commissioner fully dressed in his ceremonial attire, disembarked from the Land Rover and strode to the boarding area, bypassing the security check. At the top of the boarding ramp he turned, and gave a presidential type wave to the crowd before he disappeared into the aircraft. The police officers returned to their cruisers then pulled ahead of the Land Rover as they all drove away.

Strong said, "It looks like he's gone, guv."

Cole replied, "When I see that baby take off, then and only then, will we know for sure."

Their hopes were soon realized as the boarding ramp was moved away, and the big airplane's engines started to whine. The aircraft slowly made its way out to the take-off runway. It stopped with its head to the wind before the pilots revved up the engines, released the brakes, sped down the runway, and became airborne.

"Well," Cole said, as he smiled at his partner, "pride cometh before the fall. Commissioner Black won't know what hit him when he steps off of that plane."

Strong returned the smile. "I have to hand it to you, guv. Only you could think up a scheme like this and make it work."

"Thanks, Bill, but we'd better track down the AG to get a warrant for the raid on Keith's, Palm Shipping warehouse. We may have to get the Governor involved. Let's go."

• • •

Patton and Oakley were anxious to meet their new support team at the airport. They parked the Jeep in the airport short term parking area, and walked to the observation area that bordered the tarmac. At seven on the dot, a Lear35 came screaming in. It taxied to the area reserved for private security and customs clearance. An officer walked out to the aircraft. He walked up the plane's extended steps and into the Lear. Within five minutes he reappeared and he was followed by the four undercover DEA agents, and the crew of three.

Oakley waved at the men and agent Ian waved back. "Damn, Willie, did you see what I saw? They were cleared like royalty."

"I saw it, and I can guess why – payola. Anyway let's greet them, and make sure they get checked in okay."

Patton and Oakley made their way to the arrivals area where Oakley shook agent Ian's hand, while Patton did likewise with Lou, Juan, and Carla. In case the Palm police might be suspicious, Tom Oakley talked loudly that he was excited to see his friends, and anticipated that they would have a great time diving. He decided that Ian should ride with him in the Jeep. The others, including Willie hailed a taxi van.

As he drove, Tom said, "Ian, we can talk here, but not everywhere. How the heck did you guys get cleared so fast?"

Ian replied," The airline is a CIA operation, and our pilot has been here several times. Savage handpicked the flight crew. The person who cleared us is one of the corrupt officials and we were told before we left to lay five hundred dollars cash on him. These guys on Palm are well known to our bosses, but they've never had an opportunity to pin them down until now. Thanks to the Brits we can get the job done."

"Willie was right on then, because he commented that there had to be payola involved. And on the subject of the Brits, Detective Cole and Detective Strong can match anything I've experienced before. They seem to find clues even when they aren't looking for them. It's uncanny."

Ian grinned. "I'm anxious to meet them, and to get to know Cole."

The Beach Hotel was not busy when the group arrived to check in. They registered in their phony names that showed on their passports created for the mission. Oakley and Patton went with them to agent Ian's room, where immediately Oakley convened a meeting. He opened by saying, "Call me Tom. You can unpack later. Get a juice from the fridge, if you want one. I'll tell you what our assignments are and then you can ask questions. I have a map of the Island and one of Kingtown. Our strike points are circled. Look at the map as I speak."

Ian piped up, "We can drink later. Get on with it."

"Okay, make notes," Oakley said. "It's almost noon now and at seven tonight we will be taking down suspects in several locations. I believe you were told about that. We have to synchronize our watches. Willie and I did it with the Brits this morning so in twenty seconds I'll say the time." He hesitated then said, "It's exactly seven-forty." The agents set their watches and listened. "Now hear this," Tom said. "It's very important. In this country when people are arrested they must be given a verbal notice called, 'Right to Silence'. Don't screw this up. Listen closely. It goes like this. *'You do not have to say anything, but it may harm your defense if you do not mention when questioned something which you later rely on in court. Anything you do say may be given in evidence.'* Write it down. Memorize it and also carry it with you." He quoted again as the agents wrote. "Now, guys, he said while pointing to the map, "here is Police Headquarters. Detective Cole has conned the whole P I force to attend a celebration party at which time he and his officers will arrest the Deputy Commissioner and several others. Before the news of that action can hit the street, Willie and I will take down the local drug dealer and his strong arm enforcers at the Hibiscus Restaurant." He pointed to the location on the map. "We will need one of you to assist us, so by seven I want you, Lou, to be outside. British Detective Strong will be with you. The 'buy' will be done in the lounge. The owner, Gart Webber, is working with us. There will be shit flying as we attempt to physically take them down. The leader is called Fingers, and he has hands almost as big as his head, plus he's six foot two at least, and built like a boxer. He won't go down without a fight. His main accomplice is about five ten and built like the stump of an oak tree. Both carry switchblades. Each time Willie and I dealt with them there were two more big guys who never said a word. I think they are Fingers' body guards."

"Next there are two Panamanians, a woman and a man, whom we must arrest before they get a chance to leave Palm. I should be tailing them right now, but I know they have hired a taxi driven by a man who is working undercover for us. I want you, Carla, to rent a car at the concierge desk downstairs. I will meet you here in an hour, and you will follow me until we locate the two suspects. That gives you time to unpack and get a bite to eat.

"Ian, you and Juan will partner with Willie this afternoon. There are four Canadians who will likely be murdered this evening if we don't get them out of harm's way. They are checked in at the Holiday Place Resort. I believe they are stock brokers who have been making illegal trades on the Toronto Stock Exchange and on the NASDAQ, and piecing off the Police Commissioner. They buy on Toronto using dummy Palm corporations to pump up the price. They sell on the NASDAQ with proceeds going to Panama corporations owned by the cartel mob. Sometimes they simply bring share certificates that are in street form to Palm. As far as we know, they deliver them to the Jones & Keller law firm. J & K sets up brokerage accounts here and in Panama where the shares are sold into the market. The proceeds are turned into US cash at a local bank, no questions asked. At my request, the Brits have planted a female detective inside J & K. She will try to determine exactly what happens, who is involved, and bring evidence to us."

Oakley paused, took a breath, and continued. "The four Canadians probably have no idea that the Magdalena cartel simply murders peons like them when a big deal is going down. Eight people were murdered last June as far as we can tell. We want to offer the four Canadians some kind of leniency if they cooperate as witnesses. I suggest that you rent a car, Willie, and go to the Holiday Beach Resort for lunch. We have two undercover people there, a waiter, Ted, and the hostess, Sheila. Somehow you guys have to coral the four, and hide them until we nail their suspected assassins after seven tonight. Take their passports. I will have Detective Cole get one of his men to relieve Willie this evening, after he confirms the substance we buy from Fingers. When we have the situation under control at Hibiscus, we must rush to Palm Dive where the owner is expecting to see the four Canadians. I don't know if the owner, Amos Delray, is expecting them to be dead or alive. You can bet that if we don't save them, they will be shark bait by midnight. If all goes well tonight, at two AM we will converge on the Palm Shipping Limited's warehouses. We could get lucky and seize a major load of cocaine."

Looking at Carla, Tom said, "You are in charge of commandeering the cartel's Cigarette31 speed boat that is docked at Clear and Deep Dive. The owner of the business, Art Bodder, is working with us. This could be the most dangerous play of all because the boat owner is a top tier member of the cartel. He will likely carry a weapon. Willie and I believe that the man and woman whom you will be tailing today are planning to flee to Panama on that boat. Guns aren't allowed on this Island but they too could be armed. We may have weapons after Cole closes down the Police Station."

Carla smiled and said, "Let me show you something boss." She went to her duffle bag and pulled out a 45 caliber Beretta. Sporting a perky grin, she said, "Gun fight at the old coral, Palm version. When you lay enough payola on a pompous customs officer, you can get away with almost anything."

"Son-of-a-bitch, I'll be damned!" Tom exclaimed.

Willie spoke up, "Way to go Carla!"

Ian chimed in, "If you're finished talking Tom, we'd like to give you and Willie your presents." He opened his luggage and handed them each a 45. "You know, boss, this is a lawless place right now so why should we be the only law abiding fools?"

Patton and Oakley grinned from ear to ear. Tom said, "You guys have balls. You could be behind bars. What a surprise! Thanks, we'll probably need these. Now, if you are all tuned in, I'm getting out of here. I'll leave the map for you guys to study." Looking at Carla, Tom said, "Be ready in an hour." As he was leaving at the doorway he thought, *'Savage sent me the best of the best.'*

· · ·

Oakley had a hunch that Maria and Alvarez would be at either The Diamond Store, or at her residence. Carla followed him in a rented Plymouth. The two agents killed some time at Carl's Treats before heading into Kingtown where Oakley was hoping to spot Harris' taxi. They parked and waited for a while but had no luck in spotting Harris. Tom then decided to drive towards Clear and Deep Dive when he suddenly spotted Harris driving the two suspects toward town. "That's them," he blurted aloud to himself. He made a quick U turn and was able to keep his suspects within eyesight. Carla was able to follow at a distance. The taxi pulled up in front of the Palm Bank & Trust building where Maria and Alvarez got out. They walked into the building. Oakley drove a bit further, parked, jumped out of the Jeep, and ran back towards Carla's car. She stopped, opened her window, and said "Is that them?"

Tom answered, 'It's them. You're on your own now. As long as you have Harris's taxi in sight, you should be okay. I'm heading for Clear and Deep Dive to tell Art Bodder that you are in charge of making sure those two, and the boat doesn't get away. Good luck."

Carla gave a 'thumbs up'.

Tom arrived at Clear and Deep, and waved 'Hi!' to Buzzy, as he drove past the Tiki bar to Bodder's office. While he was driving to see Art, he remembered that the Coast Guard would need Art's VHF marine radio frequency. Tom walked right into Art's office. Art was there and he listened to Tom describe what was about to happen. Tom then said, "You are our link to the Coast Guard's operation, Art, so they will need your VHF frequency. I'll be talking to my boss shortly, and I'll pass it along."

Art said, "Here it is," as he wrote '157.06 VHF mobile band'. He handed the paper to Tom. He assured Tom that he was in tune with the plan, and that the Cigarette31 would not get away from his dock because he had boxed it in by mooring the Hatteras in front of it and the Bertram at the stern. Tom thanked him and returned to his hotel to make the noon phone call to his boss.

Chapter 23 | DEA Final Arrangements

DEA Director Marcel Savage was waiting for Oakley's call. When it came he wasted no time getting down to business, saying, "The Miami Coast Guard has assigned two Cutter Class ships. They are one-hundred and ten feet long. One is USCGC Bradenton. It will conduct the DIAMOND QUEEN raid. The other ship is USCGC Venice. It will commandeer the Belize fishing craft at Rocky Palm. Both have a complement of marines. Each of them will arrive at their targets at seven PM. Do you have the VHF radio band?"

"Yes, boss. It is 157.06 at Clear and Deep Dive. Art Bodder is owner and he has been a big asset for us."

Savage acknowledged the info and continued, "Interpol has identified the female suspect as Maria Solarno, a Panamanian citizen. She is wanted here in The States on a RICO charge for money laundering. She should have been picked up in Miami a year ago, but our boys screwed up and she disappeared. We want her. Next, the man with her is Moses Alvarez, another Panamanian. He runs the cocaine traffic into Miami and Biloxi for the cartel. We let him loose to lead us to the king pin of the cartel and it looks like we got lucky. The Cigarette31 belongs to the blonde guy, Romeo Balluchi. He works for Carlos Guintia, head of the Mexican arm of the Magdalena cartel. Balluchi is linked to some mass killings in Belize that the CIA knows about. Balluchi is usually carrying a weapon, and Alvarez could also be armed. That's why I sent the heaters for you and Patton. Tom, we are hoping to seize the Belize fishing boat, so we can get the hard evidence to the cartel killings. Informants told us that cartel victims are loaded onto the refrigerated fishing boat and disposed of at sea. If we can seize the DIAMOND QUEEN, the speed boat and the fishing boat, you guys will be famous."

Oakley said, "Hey I forgot something. On the DIAMOND QUEEN, there are eight beautiful women, two of which Patton and I have feelings for, if you know what I mean."

"Fine, Tom. As I said, The USCGC Bradenton is in charge, and the plan is to escort the DIAMOND QUEEN to Biloxi. Marines have been ordered to board her and contain the crew and passengers while in route. Why are the women there?"

"They are de facto slaves of Mancini's. He uses them as spies. He does not even allow them to be addressed by any name other than the one he gives to each of them. They are not criminals, so take it easy on them. The two whom we have met are Sally and Janet, and I want them unharmed. Pass the word. Okay? And you can be damn sure Mancini's people will be armed. "

"I hear you," Savage replied. "I'll get on it right now. Call me at midnight if you can. Let's get it done. Bye."

As Oakley hung up he checked the time, and stared blankly out to the sea. He thought, *'It's almost one, six more hours to go. I'd better find Cole. He may have heard from Jane Butterworth.'* He headed for Hibiscus to query Gart Webber.

Chapter 24 | Jane Goes To Work

Jane Butterworth was jetlagged and by the time she unpacked her luggage Monday evening, she did not even feel like eating a meal. She found some cheese and crackers in the mini fridge, so she settled on having that along with a Greenie. She then called her contact, Darlene, in London, and reported on her day's activities and where she was staying. She crawled into bed and it felt good at first, but she tossed and turned all night as she fought a five hour time change. Thoughts about her new assignment also caused her restlessness. To unwind she went out onto her balcony where she listened to birds. She watched the sunrise. It was good therapy. While she showered and prepped her body and hair, she let her imagination run wild. She was under no illusion about how dangerous it would be to deal with a high profile drug operation. A smile crossed her face, as a fleeting thought of working with Curt Cole popped into her mind. She thought, *'If only he wasn't married'*. She was ready for Winston Jones when he called from the hotel lobby at eight. "I'll be right down, sir," she said. "I can't wait to get to work."

Jones was impressed as Jane strode across the lobby to meet him. Dressed in a crisp white blouse that revealed a teasing amount of cleavage, a tight navy blue skirt that highlighted her perfect buttocks, and four inch heels, she watched Jones try to not melt at the sight. "I'm ready, sir. I hope you can spend some time to get me oriented."

"Yes, Jane, I plan on doing that. I must say that you look very professional. I hope my secretary, Leona, doesn't get jealous. I'll interrupt your orientation for a bit as I want to see the Commissioner depart at nine for London."

Jane thought, '*It's time to soften this guy up*', and commented, "It is very exciting for him to be honored by the CPCA. I hope I can get to know him when he returns. Will he be away for long?"

Jones replied, "Not long, in a few days he will be back on the job. I can show you around the Island after work on Wednesday if you would like. Maybe you can find a place to live. We could have dinner and talk business."

Jane thought, '*Where have I heard that line before.*' and replied, "I really don't know for sure. I've never had an invitation from my employer. Is it proper to do so here in Palm Island?"

Jones sort of grunted and said, "Commissioner Black and I decide what is what on this Island. Think it over and let me know later. I'm not hitting on you, but I do want you to feel like you are part of my team. You are my first employee from the UK. Naturally, any locals that I have hired were familiar with the place." As they drove into Kingtown, Jane kept the conversation alive and Jones appeared to be under her control. She asked questions about the law firm, how they communicate with foreigners, and various office routines. Jones seemed to be getting very comfortable, knowing he had hired a competent assistant. Jones had a reserved parking space in the covered section of the Palm Bank & Trust parking area, and as he drove into it he said, "It's time to get to work, Jane, our office is on the top floor and you will have a good view of the town from your work station. Follow me."

Outside of Jones' office she saw name plates of over a thousand different corporations and trusts. She commented on it and Jones said, "We manage several thousand corporations and trusts. Most of them are set up to avoid tax laws. Some do international business by having products shipped here for packaging. They get then reshipped at huge markups. Jewelry items and diamonds are perfect items for that arrangement."

They entered the office and Jane was introduced to Leona. Jones suggested that Leona get Jane started right away dealing with the filing of corporate information. Leona agreed, then added, "You had better get going, sir. The plane leaves in thirty minutes. I'll get Jane set up."

As Jones left, he said, "I'll be back by ten, Leona. Alvarez will be here for a meeting."

After a few minutes of pleasant talk, Leona took Jane into a room that had no windows. "Everything we do in here is highly confidential my dear," she said to Jane. "This room contains our clients' corporate records and trust documents. Mr. Jones and I are the officers and directors of every corporation and trust that we manage. Each month we have to put bank statements into those files. Once a year, for each entity, we write up minutes of the shareholders' meeting and directors' meeting. I want you to start by filing the October bank statements. I will be busy in my office preparing packages to be used tomorrow to ship diamonds to clients in Asia and Central America. Call me if you need me." She pointed to a pile of papers and said, "Those are the bank statements. Organize the ones with names alphabetically, and the numbered companies by lowest to highest. That will make it easy for you to find the appropriate file in those cabinets over by the wall safe."

"I'm on it, Leona," Jane said. "I'll call if I need you."

· · ·

Harris followed instructions given to him by Detective Cole. Fortunately, he went directly home to pick up his wife and family because his phone rang just as he entered his house. The call was from Maria Solarno asking him to pick up her and Alvarez at her residence. He asked if she would require his service all day. She affirmed that she wished to do so. He said he would be there at ten and thanked her for calling. He had a brief conversation with his wife and boys about what might happen, and that Detective Cole ordered him to take them to Phil's house where they would be safe. They obeyed him without any argument. When they arrived at Phil's he graciously received them and introduced his dogs.

"Get going, Harris." Phil ordered. "Be careful and be sure to call me if you need help. I know how to contact Detective Cole."

Harris looked at his watch and said, "I pick up those bad people now, Mr. Phil. They hire me for the day so I listen, and I call you if I hear plans. Thank you." He hugged his wife and boys and went to pick up his passengers.

He drove into Maria Solarno's driveway, and within a minute, she, and Alvarez, exited the house and climbed into the car. They greeted Harris. "Take us to The Palm Bank & Trust," Maria instructed.

"Yes, mam," Harris replied.

"We then go to the Palm Shipping office," Alvarez said.

"Yes, sir," Harris replied.

Talking to Maria, Alvarez said, "He said he has fifty boxes ready to go?"

"That's right, fifty, Mo, with twenty pounds of glory in each one. We'll be rich. Our end will be one million dollars. But it gets better. Tomorrow the fishermen bring another fifty boxes. They'd be here now if that storm had not screwed things up. Romeo Balluchi may decide to go tonight anyway depending on what he finds out about the diamonds. He and Amos Delray are likely checking things out right now. We have to get out of here quickly and there's nothing like the Cigarette31 for that. "

"This is no kid's game we are playing, Mo replied. I can't believe how Sylvester Black has taken over this Island. Even those outsider Brits have found nothing and they are leaving this week, according to Black. No wonder he is being awarded as a top cop. Crime doesn't get exposed here. Give me a squeeze babe." Maria squeezed more than his hand. Mo smiled.

Harris kept his eyes strictly on the road, but his ears were tuned into the back seat conversation. He never even looked into the rear view mirror for fear that his passengers might think he was spying on them. He found a place to park directly in front of the bank and said, "How long do you think you might be sir? I might have to move the car."

Mo replied, "Maybe an hour upstairs at Jones & Keller law firm, then another hour at The Diamond Store before you take us to the Palm Shipping office. We will call you just after twelve noon. Do not take any other passengers because we want instant response from you."

"I do that, sir. Call at my home if you need me sooner. I be near The Diamond Store by noon hour."

As they left the taxi Alvarez said to Maria, "Jones should have the orders ready to mail. He said he was hiring an assistant to facilitate our business."

They entered the bank building and took the elevator to the third floor. Jones had returned from the airport and greeted the visitors when they walked into the office. He showed them into the conference room, and then went to get Jane. He told Jane, as she worked filing the bank statements, to stop what she was doing, and join him in the conference room where he would introduce her as his new assistant. Jane joined Jones. They got to the conference room where Jones had her sit beside him. She had no idea that the people across from her at the table were cartel kingpins. Alvarez sized her up and down like most men would do, especially as she bent over to sit down and displayed her treasure chest. Jane ignored his action, while Maria glanced in his direction with a sour look. Alvarez asked Jane about her credentials then said to Jones, "Looks like you did well, Winston. Not often you can find beauty and brains in the same package."

Maria shifted to look at him, scowled, and commented, "We came here to work, Mo, enough of your stupid comments."

Winston, sensing that the two could go off the rails, said, "That will be all for now Jane. I just wanted you to meet these important people. They have over fifty corporations and trusts with our firm. You will see them as you file. They all have the numbers 468 in their corporate names. You may go now."

Jane rose, once again exposing her cleavage. Before exiting the room she said, "I am very happy to have met you. I hope I can be of service to you." She thought and smiled inwardly, *'I wonder how Alvarez will take that comment?'*

Returning to her job she was now very curious about the Alvarez accounts. She began looking through the pile of bank statements for those with 468 in the name. She had no problem finding the first one and it showed a very low balance. The only entry shown was a small interest credit for the month. Several more revealed the same lack of activity, but then she struck pay dirt. *'Oh my god,'* she gasped quietly, as she read the statement. It displayed several large transactions and a balance of $21,508,110.56. The corporate name was International Traders Limited (468). Moving to the file cabinets she pulled out the drawer lettered, 'I – It'. The file was near the front. She removed the sheet labelled "Shareholders' Register". Three names were listed: Moses Alvarez, Amos Delray, and Romeo Balluchi. She had to make a split-second decision. She removed the sheet, folded it, and stuffed it into her panties. She then closed the file cabinet. Jane returned to the pile of bank statements, took the incriminating one and folded it one into a small square. She put it in her bra and under her left breast. She worked furiously to get all of the bank statements into alphabetical files and began filing. *'I'm sure I got what the DEA wants,'* she thought. *'God only know what else I could find but I'm sure to have company shortly.'* No sooner did she think someone would come to check on her, than Leona stepped into the room.

"How's it going, Jane," Leona asked.

"I got the statements sorted A to Z and numerically, and now I'm putting them into their proper files. This is a big job. How often does it have to be done? Did you have to do it?"

"Yes, it's a pain in the ass, but Winston pays well. Come to my office when you finish. Winston is still with those two. If he needs you I will let you know. Have fun."

Jane looked at her watch and noted the time. She decided to slow down her filing until Winston called for her because she didn't want to be questioned by Leona. She was sure that she could handle Winston and she knew she had to get a break away from him somehow. At eleven her boss came into the file room.

"Are you nearly finished filing," he said.

"Hi, almost done," she replied.

"Good. Sorry to put you onto such a mundane job, but there's a lot happening today. We have to prepare packages to ship to Alvarez's customer in Broania. He's gone to get the diamonds that he sells. You and I can do it after lunch. Right now I want you to review some finance documents that pertain to a new warehouse to be constructed by Palm Shipping Ltd. Come to my private office when you finish filing."

Jane finished her job and as she passed the reception desk she told Leona that Mr. Jones wanted her to go into his office. Leona pointed. Jane rapped on Jones's door and heard, "Come right in". She was surprised to see a fairly large room with a desk, an executive chair, and three twelve by four folding tables.

Jones said, "How do you like my fancy office?"

Jane did not take the bait and replied, "I've seen worse."

"I hope you didn't think I was serious. My real office is over in Calvert and I'll likely take you there tomorrow or Thursday. We use this room to handle the diamond shipments that I referred to earlier. I have another problem I would like you to work on, however. Harold Keith is in charge of the warehouse and his brother Donald handles the shipping line at Palm Shipping Ltd.

Handing papers to Jane he continued, Harold signed this contract, but Donald wants to amend it to have more refrigerated space. The contractor says he wants a lot more money because the changes will take time and prevent him from booking more jobs. Commissioner Black is related to the contractor and will intervene on behalf of him if necessary. We are looking to collect some big fees if we can somehow drag this dispute out for a while, so I want you to write up a conciliation program that the Commissioner can use. As I've told you, the Commissioner and I are a team and we want to get as much money out of those wealthy Keith brothers as we can. Can you handle it?"

"Can I go back to my room to review what you've got? I don't see where I can concentrate in this environment. I worked a deal similar to this in England, and you are correct, a lot of fee money can be made by dragging things out."

Jones smiled and replied, "Johnathon Wilcox told me he was sending me a winner. I'll have to bonus him. These three files are pretty bulky, but all of the details are contained in them. Do you wish to leave now? We could stop for a bite to eat?"

Jane played the game. "It's almost noon," she said. "Yes. I could use something light like a fish sandwich."

"I know a place and it's close to your condo. It's called Hibiscus. We will go there. Here's a valise for you to carry the files."

"Nice," Jane said. "Thanks." 'How convenient' she thought. 'If only I can get alone with Mr. Webber I can pass the documents to him. God is definitely in our camp'.

Leona looked up and raised her eyebrows as Jane and Winston passed by her desk. She seemed upset.

They arrived at The Hibiscus Restaurant and were greeted by Gart. He shook hands with his guests and said, "Nice to see you again, sir. Would you like that table in the corner?"

"Yes, Gart, meet my new assistant Ms. Butterworth. We will need a little privacy while we discuss business. That table is perfect."

Gart showed them to the table where they sat opposite each other. He served them each with water and took the order for fish sandwiches. Gart explained that he could not offer grouper due to the storm. They settled on fresh snapper that local fishermen provided. Jane made sure that Jones could admire her breasts as she leaned forward to take her seat, and each time she spoke to him.

Cole had dropped off Detective Strong at *Enchanted* and instructed him to check things out at Phil's. He went over to Hibiscus to see Gart Webber. He walked to the restaurant then went straight to talk to Gart who was at his cash register. He did not see Jane and Jones at the corner table. Immediately Jane recognized Cole and said to her boss, "Sir, please excuse me. I think I should go to the ladies' room before the food is served. Would you please excuse me?"

Jones rose, as a gentleman should, and replied, "Good Idea, and I think I'll freshen up too."

The movement caught Cole's attention and he could not believe his eyes. Jane was walking slightly behind jones and she winked at Cole. She moved her lips without making a sound. The detective new the signal and whispered to Gart, "That woman is Jane Butterworth, our spy. She wants to tell me something. And isn't that lawyer Jones with her?"

Gart confirmed it was Jones, and asked, "What should I do?"

"Look, the man usually takes less time in the loo than the woman. Seat me at that table in the far corner. Jones will get back to his table before the woman does. Go to the ladies room door and when she exits, ask her what she wants to tell me. She knows you are helping us."

Before Jones appeared, Gart seated Cole at the farthest table from Jones' and said, "Keep your back to Jones' table. I'll get Louisa to serve you. I'll meet Jane."

When Jones returned to his table, Louisa informed Cole.

"Good," Cole said, "go over there and talk to him. Keep him busy. Louisa did as requested and started small talk with Jane's boss. He was relaxed. A few minutes passed before Jane returned, then Louisa excused herself. Gart had met Jane when she left the washroom, and she gave him the documents. Gart went directly to the kitchen, got the meals for Jane and Jones, and served them. He went back into the kitchen. Gart placed the documents inside of a desert menu. Louisa had made a salad for Cole, that Gart served, and he also laid the desert menu on the table saying, "This is our desert menu. Be sure to look it over."

Cole waited until Jones and Jane left the restaurant before opening the menu. He smiled as he looked at what Jane had stolen, and thought, *'I knew*

Jane was a good detective, but wait until I tell Trump what she has done. This is amazing.' Unable to contain his excitement he called Gart over and shared the story. "I can't thank you enough, Gart, for helping us. When this night is over, you will be able to run your business without any intimidation."

"Those are sweet words, detective. I know you'll take down those SOBs. I want to see them squirm."

"I have to run now," Curt said, "but what a break that I should have dropped in. Tell Oakley or Patton to call me around three. Let them know that Jane has already got evidence for him."

Detective Cole left the restaurant, and went to get Strong at Phil's. He and Strong strode quickly over to *Enchanted* where the Camry was parked. "You drive, Bill. Time is running out. Drive directly to Governor Neily's residence while I tell you what just happened over at Hibiscus." Cole reported, Strong listened, grinned, and simply said, "Wow!" Cole continued, "I have to phone Trump to report Jane's success, and also call the Chief Magistrate to get a warrant ready for the search of Palm Shipping's office and warehouses."

Governor Neily was not surprised to see the detectives. He knew that the detectives would have to communicate with The Yard each day. He ushered them into his office where Cole used the private line to inform Trump about Jane's success. Trump reported that he had heard from Darlene and that Jane was checked into suite 222, at Paradise Suites. Next he called Clyde Curry, and requested a search warrant for the raid on Palm Shipping. Curry told Cole to come by his office straightaway to pick it up, which he did. As they drove back to *Enchanted*, Cole kept thinking about Tuesday evening, and wondering if Lady Luck would stay with them. Out loud he thanked God for His blessings, and asked Him to prevail with more blessings during the upcoming raids. Strong kept looking in his rear view mirrors for anyone who might be tailing them, but he saw nothing suspicious.

Chapter 25 | Surveilling the Canadians

After discussing Oakley's instructions and reviewing the map, Willie, Ian and Juan ordered room service. They needed to formulate a strategy. After exchanging stories about some of their similar missions, they agreed that the best option would be to tail the Canadians until they became threatened. That way they could likely capture the assailant before any murder took place. They drove to the Holiday Place Resort and proceeded to the dining room reception desk. Sheila was not at her station, but they noticed Ted, waiting on a group of six women. Patton took a second look and was relieved to see that it was not the women that worked for Mancini. As Ted left the table he noticed the three agents waiting to enter the room. He recognized Willie and walked over to greet them.

"Nice to see you again, sir," Ted said. "Sheila is taking a break. I can seat you over at the side where it is more private if you wish to talk business. Are you expecting anyone else, or is it just the three of you?"

Willie replied, "Nice to see you again too, Ted. Meet my friends Juan and Ian. We all work for the same company. Sure, that table over there looks fine." When they were out of earshot of other customers Willie got close to Ted and whispered, "We need to follow the four Canadians that you served the other day. Can you, or Sheila, tell us where they might be?"

"I can't right now, but I'll let Sheila know. She can make inquiries that I cannot."

"Alright, Ted, bring us three iced teas and we will wait."

They were served by Ted. Shortly thereafter Sheila came to the table. She said, "I see you've brought some friends today." Looking at Juan and Ian, she continued, "My name is Sheila and I guess Mr. Patton has told you that I am the hostess here. I'll bring menus and give you a few minutes to decide." She left for about five minutes and returned with the menus. Then, turning to Patton, she said, "I know you will find something interesting in there." She returned to the hostess station.

Willie said, "Juan sit on this side. I need my back to the wall." When he changed seats, he opened his menu to find a note from Sheila. She wrote, '*The mole in here is watching. He is the Spanish looking waiter. The 4 Canadians went out about 11- still registered.*' He slowly folded the note and placed it in his shirt pocket. In a low voice he said to his partners, "The Spanish waiter is a spy. Our targets are not here. We'll wait."

They enjoyed lunch and passed the time talking about football. All of them had played college ball and purposely laughed at each other's stories, knowing that it would cause the Spanish waiter to come near to the table. That gave the agents a chance to get a good look at the man as he pretended to be uninterested. It was almost two o'clock when Sheila returned to the table on the pretense that they should leave so the room could be set for dinner.

She said, "They're back. Delray dropped them off."

"Okay, call Juan in room 215 at The Beach Hotel if you see them leaving. Tell Ted the same thing."

Sheila nodded.

Willie made small talk, and asked for the check. He paid it, and they all went to the men's room for privacy. Willie said, "Things are shaping up. If Delray dropped them off you can bet that he will pick them up later for the slaughter."

Juan agreed saying, "We should go back to the hotel. Ted or Sheila will phone us if those dudes leave before evening. My guess is that Delray will pick them up just before dark and take them to his place, drug them, and put them on the boat before he kills them. We will need our weapons anyway."

"Let's get out of here, men," Willie said. "Sure is good to work with guys who know the score. We can stop for a beer at Hibiscus. You can case the place and meet Webber. Then I think we should rest a bit because we won't be hitting the sack this evening."

Gart Webber greeted the three agents when they arrived and reassured Willie that he was ready for the forthcoming raid. The beer was 'on the house'.

When they got back to their hotel Willie said, "From now on the Canadians are your problem. I'll see you later."

At the request of the DEA agents Sheila stayed alert, watching for movement of the Canadians. She stepped into the kitchen to get some napkins, and stopped in her tracks as she saw the Spanish waiter on the phone. Slipping behind a rack of dishes she heard him say, "Constable Black, there are people tailing the Canadians. Yes. How many? I don't know. Three I think. Sheila? I don't know. Yes, come here and talk to Sheila."

When the waiter turned to talk to the chef, Sheila slipped out and made her way to a lobby phone and dialed Juan. It rang four times. She was getting very nervous. On the fifth ring Juan said. "Hello. Who's calling?"

"It's Sheila from the Holiday resort. The Spaniard has called the police about you guys." She hung up.

He turned to Ian and said, "We have a problem. We have to get our asses to the Holiday Place Resort. Bring your weapon. We may not be coming back before the action starts."

They flagged a taxi and rushed to the Hotel. They saw the police cruiser and when they went inside the cop was talking to both Sheila and the Spanish waiter. Juan and Ian went on the offensive and stood at the hostess station where they were visible to the Spaniard and the cop. The waiter motioned to Sheila that she had customers so she went to seat them.

"Hello again, Sheila," Juan said. "We got thirsty. Can you serve us here?"

"No, not here at this time of day. The Quiet Oasis Lounge is open. Quietly she said, "That is Constable Wilbur Black," as she nodded her head toward Black.

Hearing the name Black put Juan on full alert. He warned Ian, as they went into the lounge. They ordered two 'Buds' and started chatting about diving. Five minutes later the Constable walked over to their table. "Good afternoon", he said. I'm checking IDs today. Don't be offended but I'll have to see your ID. It's a routine police procedure here in the Palm Islands."

"Sounds to me like a sensible thing to do," Juan said, as he and Ian rustled through their pockets to find their Florida Driver's licenses and their immigration slips. "They make movies about tax havens like this, here are our IDs. We were supposed to be on a night dive this evening, but it has been booked by some other dudes. I guess we will get out Thursday night. Have you got any touristy advice for us?"

Constable Black looked at the IDs and handed them back. He said, "I hope you enjoy Grand Palm." He walked straight out through the hotel lobby.

Juan said, "That seemed to work out okay. It's getting late. I think we should just hang out here."

Ian replied, "I agree but we are going to need a car. I'll go rent one at the Budget desk in the lobby. You can watch the elevators while I do it."

Juan enjoyed watching the hotel guests coming and going, especially the bikini clad women. One man went by dressed in business attire. Almost immediately Ted came up to Juan and whispered, "That's Delray". Ted left.

Ian returned and said, "We have wheels."

Juan replied, "And we have action. Delray just went into the elevator."

Chapter 26 | Jane Runs

Lawyer Jones dropped off Jane and told her, "I will be in the office at three. Is that enough time for you to prepare something?"

"Sounds okay, sir," she replied. "I might have to call you once I go through the documents. Do you have a business card on you?"

"Sure." He reached into his pocket and retrieved his wallet, then handed Jane his card. "If I'm not in, Leona will know how to contact me."

Jane thanked him for the lunch and once again gave him a chance to look over her physical assets as she got out of his car. "I should finish this project in a couple of hours. Do you want me to call Leona for you to pick me up?"

"No, Jane," he said. "We both will be very busy today, so just take a taxi."

"Righto sir, I'll see you later." Jane was grateful for the break.

• • •

Jane studied the documents that Jones had handed to her. She had no problem putting together a hypothetical solution to the Keith brothers' problem. It was almost four o'clock when she called for a taxi and was driven to the Palm Bank & Trust building. She took the elevator to the law office and entered it without knocking. She was surprised that Leona was not at her desk, but she heard arguing. Leona and Jones were in his office shouting her name and cursing the number '486'. A sixth sense told her *'this is not right. Get out!'* She made a quick decision to not take the elevator, but ran down the stairway exit. On the street she hailed a taxi. She got in quickly, and said, "Hibiscus Restaurant, please." Her heart stopped pounding when she arrived at the restaurant and saw Gart. Gart looked surprised. He asked, "Jane, what's up?"

"I think the woman who works for Jones is on to me, Gart. Just a sixth sense I get based on experience. She was not at her desk when I entered the law office half an hour ago. I heard loud voices coming from a side office and my name was being shouted at Jones. I have to contact Detective Cole."

"Relax, you're okay here. Sit down. I'll call to find out if he's across the road at Enchanted. Here, have a drink." Gart offered a glass of ice water then dialed. Cole answered. Gart said, "Detective, Jane Butterworth just came in here in a panic. I'm sending her over to you." He listened to Cole. "No I'm not kidding. She'll be right over." Getting back to Jane, Gart smiled, hoping to relax her, and said, "You're in luck. He's stays right across the street and he's expecting you. I can't leave this place, but, he pointed, the house is behind that big hedge over there."

"Thank you so much, Gart. And good luck tonight. I'm aware of the plans." Jane crossed the street and ran to the house. She was getting even more nervous as her dream of working with Cole was about to come true.

Cole was waiting in the open doorway, and when he saw her he waved for her to come along. Once inside he smiled, looked her in the eye, and said, "You sure don't look like any underground spy that I've ever worked with. Don't take this compliment for more that I mean it, but you look like a million quid! Sit down and tell me what's happened."

Jane had butterflies in her stomach, but they dissipated as she told her story to Cole.

He listened intently. "You did an amazing job, Jane. Time is running out, so I'll take you to your hotel. I want you to get some of your things, but do not check out. You'll move into Enchanted here for a couple of nights. As you can see, there are two empty bedrooms. I can use an extra hand for tonight's raids. In fact, you can work with the DEA agent Carla who is tailing Solarno and Alvarez right now. They will likely beat it to Art Bodder's marina where they expect to flee in a speed boat moored there."

"Whatever you wish, sir. It will be a pleasure to the put cuffs on them, especially the woman."

Cole drove to Paradise Suites as Jane kept looking for anyone following. When they got there an empty police cruiser was already parked outside of the entrance way. Recognizing it as Constable Black's vehicle, Cole drove into the Beach Hotel next door, parked, and ordered Jane to crouch down and stay in the car. He then went to room 114 and knocked. Oakley answered, "I've been looking for you."

Cole said, "Hang on, Tom." He turned and walked quickly to his car. There he signaled Jane to follow him. Oakley was waiting and ushered them in. He locked his door, and asked, "Okay, what's the score?"

"Meet my agent, Jane Butterworth, Tom. She has to lay low until we go into action tonight. Jane, this is DEA agent Tom Oakley. Tom, there's a police cruiser next door and I believe the cops are already trying to find Jane. She needs some things from her room, so I'm going outside to watch. I'll be back when the cop leaves."

"I'm with you, Curt," Tom replied. "Go do your thing, we'll be okay." Looking at Jane he said, "What happened?" Jane gave him a quick rundown. "Woman, you are something else! Now we have real evidence, and tomorrow, or Thursday, we will raid Jones & Keller to shut them down. The DEA is grateful, believe me."

"I appreciate that," Jane said, "but we have to finish the job of cleaning out Palm's rat nest. I'm ready for the next hit. It's an honor to be working with top pros."

They chatted for about ten minutes before Cole rapped on the door and Tom let him in. Cole said, "C'mon Jane, the coast is clear. "Let's get your stuff and take it to Enchanted."

Jane went up to her suite, collected her uniform, lingerie, and some toiletries then was back downstairs in five minutes. As Cole led the way she got into the back seat of the Camry, and at Cole's insistence, stayed down on the floor. They reached Enchanted , and he told Jane to remain down. He said, "I'm going next door. The owner there is working with us. I'll be right back."

Cole ran across the yard to Phil's and pounded on the boor. Phil's dogs were barking like crazy as Cole shouted "Hurry Phil, I need you, it's Curt."

The barking stopped. Phil stepped outside, and said, "My God, man, what's happening?"

I have in my car one of my agents who is was working undercover. I don't want to take a chance on her being seen, but I want her positioned at Art Bodder's Marina. If I stay here at your place can you take her? The cops would spot me, and likely want to ask me questions."

"Anything you want."

"Good, tell Bodder who she is and that I want her to assist the DEA agent named Carla. Keep her out of sight until you get to Art's. She can fill you in on everything during the drive. Her name is Jane. Tell her to take her uniform and to put it on once she's there."

"Okay, first, c'mon in to meet Harris' family. I'll get my keys and Baron then we'll go. No one approaches my vehicle when Baron is in it."

Phil took a couple of minutes to introduce the family to Curt, then loaded Baron into the front seat of his Jeep, and drove into Curt's driveway. He got out and said, "Jane, I'm Curt's neighbor. Get into my Jeep and stay down in the back. I'm taking you to Art Bodder's Marina where you will meet a cohort named Carla. I'll grab your things. Curt wants you to dress for action when you get there."

They quickly looked at each other as Phil grabbed her belongings, gave instruction to Baron, and drove away. About a half mile into the trip he noticed a police cruiser driving in the opposite direction and told Jane about it. Quickly he said, "It went straight on, Jane. We're okay." He then told her a bit about himself and what had been going on in Grand Palm since Commissioner Black took over the police force. Meanwhile, Cole phoned Bodder from Phil's and gave him a heads-up about Jane coming there. Art said he understood the plan, but had not seen DEA agent Carla yet.

Phil drove straight to Art's office door and took Jane's belongings into Art's shop. Art motioned for Phil to put the items near the washroom behind his desk. Then Art said, "Get her in here. From what I've heard, the woman is tougher than nails. I'm dying to meet here."

"Me too," Phil said, "so far I've been talking to my back seat." He went to the Jeep, let Baron jump down, and told Jane, to go into the office. He finally got a good look at the woman and felt that old sexy feeling. He said, "I heard you were tough Jane, but I sure didn't think you would look like a runway model."

"Thanks, Phil," she said, while smiling and looking him up and down. "And I didn't know you were a cover model for GQ. If we live through this action maybe we can get together and talk careers."

Art piped up, "Enough small talk, Jane, Cole wants you to uniform up right away. He thinks Carla's suspects will be coming here before much longer. Use this bathroom." Looking at Phil he said, "Thanks for helping us, we should get to know each other better. I could take you out on the Hatteras for a day."

"That's a very kind offer, Art, and that's a deal. I'll run now. Baron and I expect to be busy tonight. Cole has a lot to do too. Bye."

Bodder's phone rang again. It was Cole. "What is your radio frequency Art? Can you communicate with the U S Coast Guard on it?"

"Yes I do, and I gave the info to Oakley. I won't leave the office until you tell me to, so Coast Guard can call anytime to communicate."

"Thanks, Art. We could not pull off this job without you. I'm calling Tom Oakley right now to give him some info. You'll likely hear from him. Bye."

Chapter 27 | Taylor Family Gets Ready

The Taylor group spent time on the beach enjoying the sea which had quieted down. They stayed to themselves, getting Island information from brochures that were in a rack near their hotel entrance. A visit from the police, that Cole had warned them about, did not materialize. At five-thirty they put on their official T-shirts emblazoned on the back with the words POLICE OFFICER. To conceal them they wore Caribbean tourist type shirts.

Cole was still at Phil's when he took the opportunity to call Larry. They confirmed jointly that Harris would pick them up shortly after six and take them into Kingtown. Larry and Eve were to walk about town until seven and then go into action at The Diamond Store. Andrew and Jackie were to stroll the streets near the police station then enter it at seven-ten. By then Cole would have dropped his message bomb on the party.

Chapter 28 | Alvarez & Maria at Palm Shipping

Harris was parked near The Diamond Store at noon, when Solarno and Alvarez emerged smiling. Harris honked to get their attention. They waved for him to drive over. They did not say anything to Harris when they got into his cab, so Harris asked, "Palm Shipping, sir?"

Alvarez answered, "Yes."

Harris began driving and listening to his passengers talk about diamonds.

"Do you think we can go tonight, dear?" Maria said.

He replied, "We'll be out of here by eight o'clock. Romeo said he'd be at the boat."

She continued, "Donald Keith should have the diamonds. It's his fault if he did not deliver the coke to Miami."

Harris was nervous but kept quiet until they arrived. He said, "Do you want me to wait?"

Alvarez replied sharply, "Of course I do, you dumb ass. Do you think we want to walk back?"

Harris ignored the comment. "I will wait here, sir," he said.

• • •

Palm Shipping Limited was situated on five acres of flat, open land. The main warehouse was eight thousand square feet and housed the administration offices and Donald Keith's private office. A six thousand square foot refrigerated storage building was located about forty feet away. It contained Harold Keith's office. Both buildings had loading ramps that would accommodate large trucks. Security cameras were located on all four corners of both buildings.

Solarno and Alvarez were expected, and Keith's secretary announced their arrival. Donald Keith came from his office and greeted the visitors, saying, "It's good to see you again, Moses. And Maria, how have you been keeping?"

"It's always good to see you too Donald." Maria said. "I've tried to stay out of trouble. I'm well."

Donald showed them into his office, closed the door and said, "Have a seat." He went to his desk and sat down. He did not continue with pleasantries, but got to the point. "I know you came for the diamonds, but I have not yet gotten the last shipment on its way to Miami. Most of it is still in the warehouse if you want to see it. As you probably know, I put thirty boxes on the DIAMOND QUEEN for drop off in Biloxi. I have that payment here for you." He handed a small velvet bag to Moses who passed it to Maria. "Jones certified the value as three million dollars, and the paper is in the bag. Seventy boxes are still here and I'll ship them to Miami on Friday along with the hundred that will arrive tomorrow on the Belize boat."

Alvarez stood up, visibly upset. He said in a menacing tone, "You are not making me happy. I don't trust you. Show us the stuff in the warehouse."

"We'll have to go next door. That warehouse has a climate controlled room that only Harold and I can access. Follow me." Harris watched as the three people walked to the warehouse and entered it.

Harold Keith was surprised to see his visitors and said to his brother, "What's happening Donald? He did not address the other two.

"Mo and Maria want to see the Belize cargo."

"No problem," Harold replied. He led them almost to the back of the building, punched a code into the electronic lock, and opened the door to a separate room. "There are seventy boxes, Mo. Count them."

Alvarez did exactly as suggested and then said, "Open that one," as he pointed to one that was in the middle of a stack.

"Why, that one?" Harold asked. "I'll grab one off of the top."

"No, do as I ask," Alvarez ordered, in a stern tone.

Harold looked at Donald and said, "Get me that knife over there while I take down this pile." Harold started to lift the boxes as Alvarez watched him.

Donald had retrieved a two edged knife with a ten inch blade. As he poised to stab Alvarez, Maria screamed, "Mo, duck!' Alvarez went down and as he did he pulled his 38 Berretta, rolled once and rose while firing two shots into Donald. Donald dropped to his knees while holding his stomach.

Harold dropped to help his brother. Alvarez looked at him. "You punks think you can screw with the Magdalena Cartel. This is a lesson. Get your shit of a brother out of here. I'll be at Jones' at seven tonight and I want diamonds. You bastards laid off that coke somewhere for cash. Get your ass down to Jones' diamond store. I know he has plenty. You have the cash somewhere, and I don't give a shit where. Just take it to Jones and get my diamonds ready for me. C'mon. Maria."

They walked quickly, got into Harris' waiting cab where Alvarez said, "Back to The Diamond Store, driver." Looking at Maria, he blurted, "That bastard would have killed us both if you had not yelled. Sons of bitches, I'm not through with them yet. I'll give them until seven to come clean and deliver."

Maria replied, "We could go to a nice restaurant near The Diamond Store and relax after you do business with Lawrence Jones. He'll need some time to get our package together. What do you think?"

Alvarez had cooled down a bit and suggested that they go to Maria's house to relax. She liked that idea. She said to Harris, "Take us back to my house, driver."

Harris did as ordered. At Maria's house he asked if he should wait. Maria told him to take time off and return about five-thirty. Harris drove straight to Phil's house to check on his family. He was surprised to see Detective Cole answer the door. Cole said, "This is a surprise. Get in here, Harris. I sure did not expect to see you before six. Are you okay?"

"Yes, sir, I take a break now. I have news." Harris' boys came running when they heard his voice. He hugged them and said, "Not now boys. I must talk to Detective Cole." The boys obeyed. His wife stepped in to give him a hug, then left.

"Sir," he began, "I just dropped the people at her house. I go there again at five-thirty. Today I hear lots, even gun."

"Come," Cole beckoned to him, "we'll sit in the kitchen, Harris."

He told Cole the conversations he had heard, and he believed Alvarez had shot someone at Palm Shipping. Cole thought, '*one of the Keith brothers must have taken a bullet. It could screw up our plan for tonight*'. Cole made notes and when they stopped talking he offered Harris a drink and called for his wife to make a sandwich for her husband. When Harris finished eating, Cole said, "I think you should go now, Harris. The cops are snooping around and it's best that they don't find you here. Hang around Solarno's area. Be at the Beach Hotel at six." Harris left. Cole anxiously waited for Phil to return.

When Phil returned he commented to Cole about his attractive detective. "I thought you might notice that," Cole said. "Meanwhile, I've got work to do. Thanks for helping me and good luck tonight." Phil showed him to the door and said, "Semper fi!" Cole saluted him and left. It was almost show time and Cole wondered about the four Canadians, and exactly how they fit into the scheme.

Chapter 29 | Canadians Cooperate

DEA agents Ian and Juan waited patiently in The Quiet Oasis lounge for Amos Delray to appear. Both men had experience in surveillance, had checked the hotel, and knew Delray could not exit the hotel without using the lobby, even if he took a stairway exit. At about five-thirty their suspect stepped out of an elevator accompanied by one of the Canadians, Mike Crawford. Sheila had provided the names of the four Canadians when she pointed them out earlier. Delray and Crawford talked for a minute before Delray left. Ian and Juan moved fast. Before Crawford could get an elevator, Ian stepped in front of the man and Juan stood behind him. Ian said, "Excuse me, sir." He showed his DEA badge. "Please come with us quietly for your own safety."

The suspect looked around for a chance to escape, saw Juan, and said, "What the hell is going on?"

Ian told him quietly, "You, sir, will likely be murdered if you do not listen to me and my partner. Come over to the lounge with us where we can talk." The Canadian paled, and followed instructions. The agents sat the man between them and said, "We have knowledge of who you and your friends are. You have broken securities laws, but that is an offense you can litigate. Being murdered does not offer that option. Listen to me. Don't speak, and don't do anything stupid. The man who just left you is a dangerous criminal. Last June he was involved in murdering two people who were also stock brokers."

Crawford squirmed.

Juan took over the conversation. "Tell me if you are planning to meet Amos Delray just before seven tonight?"

"How do you know that?" the man foolishly asked.

"We know plenty," Juan replied. "Get this straight. Right now we are putting you under arrest and you have this option. Cooperate and avoid USA RICO charges, or don't cooperate, still be under arrest, and probably never see Canada again. RICO charges usually mean long prison sentences." The three remained silent. The agents watched the Canadian start to sweat. Juan continued, "We want Delray, more than we want you. He's involved not only in your stock washing scheme, but he's also a big league drug cartel kingpin. Do I have to tell you more?"

Crawford nervously took a drink of water before saying, "Tell me what I have to do."

Ian took over and said, "It looks like you understand, but one more piece of information. We carry guns and we have used them before." Ian looked fiercely into Crawford's eyes. "Okay now, tell us when Delray is coming back."

"He's not coming back. He's sending a van to pick us up at six-thirty."

"Where are you going?"

'There's a meeting at his office at seven."

"Why?"

"To get our money. We brought him some share certificates."

"How much?" Ian asked.

"Five hundred thousand, that's one twenty five each."

"Has he already got the certs?"

"Yes, he just picked them up."

Ian looked at Juan and said, "Here's my plan, tell me what you think. You, Mike, have a chance to save your life and the lives of your crooked friends. I want you to stall that van. Do not let it leave here until seven-thirty. That gives our team more time to converge on the place. Turning to Juan he said, "If we can get Delray before he does something with those certs we will have him stone cold. Mike and his pals can identify the proof. We can bring Mike's crew back here for the night and they can leave in the morning on the direct flight to Canada on the Sun Airways charter. We will keep them under our guard until they leave. What do you think?"

Juan said, "I like it. What about you Mike?"

"I don't have any choice, but here's what I ask. Come to our suite right now and lay it out for my pals."

Juan stood up, left some money on the table, and led the way to the elevator. He said, "Sorry, Mike, but you have to walk between us."

Mike cooperated and when they arrived at the suite Mike opened the door and announced, "Hey, guys, I've brought company." The three men were watching the six o'clock news and turned to see the DEA agents. Mike said, "Keep cool you guys. These are US Drug Enforcement Agents. They are chasing Delray and if we cooperate we should be still alive tomorrow. If not, Delray will murder us tonight. Shut off the TV, don't get up, and listen to agent Ian."

Ian explained what would happen if they should fall into Amos Delray's hands. He also scared the crap out of them when he outlined a RICO arrest. He finished by saying, "Take your choice. Right now you are all under arrest and I will read you your Right to Silence? That's it. Delray has a plan for your silence, but that one doesn't give you a chance in court."

Both agents showed their weapons. Juan motioning with his said, "Oh yeah, I sometimes have to enforce silence with this."

Mike walked over to join the other Canadians, looked at them and said, "I told these agents we would cooperate. Do you all agree?" Almost in unison they voiced their agreement.

Juan said, "I thought you might prefer our plan. Stay cool and we can keep you alive and give you a chance to plead before a judge in Canada. Make damn sure that the van does not leave here before seven-thirty. And one more word of warning. That Spanish waiter in the dining room is a cartel spy. Do not go there this evening. Use room service. We'll see you at Palm Dive tonight."

Juan and Ian left the hotel in a hurry and drove to the Hibiscus Restaurant. They knew if they got the news to Gart he could relay it to Oakley. Gart understood and said to not worry, he'd tell their boss as soon as he arrived.

Chapter 30 | The Hibiscus Raid

Oakley and Patton entered the Hibiscus Restaurant at six forty-five, wearing DEA T-shirts underneath their colorful, tourist type, garb. Gart immediately relayed the message that agent Ian had given him about the planned raid at Palm Dive. Detective Strong and agent Lou stayed behind the hedge across the road waiting to see Fingers and Dorman arrive. Four customers were in the dining room. Gart moved near to them hoping that they would not get injured in the sting action. Watson, the bartender, greeted Oakley and asked, "Same thing, guys?"

Tom answered, "Sounds good, my friend." This time they did not sit at the corner table. They chose the table closest to the exit of the lounge. As the bartender was serving the beers, the two large black men that Oakley had previously seen entered the lounge and sat in the same place as before. They did not order anything and they did not say a word.

Oakley and Patton ignored the visitors and chatted about the storm. Tom worked in a comment to Willie, "They're casing the joint because the real stuff is coming."

At seven o'clock Fingers and Dorman appeared, walked straight to Oakley and said, "Who has the money?"

"Right here," Willie said, "as he pulled out a wad of twenties. Count it."

Fingers gave a hand signal to Dorman who sat down and counted the $1,000. "After making five piles of $200 each, he told Fingers, "It's all here." He handed it to Fingers who put it into his pocket. Willie said, "I want to see what we're buying." Fingers handed two small packages to him. "It's real, but check it if you want." Willie opened one package, wetted his finger, sniffed the white stuff and rolled some between two fingers. Looking at Tom, he smiled and said, "Let the party begin."

●   ●   ●

Tom stood up, looked Fingers in the eye, and said, "Sir, you are under arrest. Please place your hands behind your back." He began quoting The Right to Silence.

"Fuck you, asshole! I'm protected by Black!"

Tom kept reading. Fingers kept ranting. Willie tried to cuff Fingers when the two bodyguards stepped forward. One black guy tried to get behind Willie who picked up a chair and hit him. The attacker didn't flinch, and instead he struck Willie knocking him down. Strong and Lou had come as planned and Strong raced into the lounge. He tackled the man. Both fell to the floor. Willie got free, rose to his feet, pulled out his Beretta, and shot the attacker in the leg. The second big guy got past Patton and was running for the door when Gart yelled, "King, attack!" The huge Doberman had been lying close to Gart in the dining room. King got to his feet, took two long strides then the ninety pound ferocious animal jumped onto the black man's back, and sank his fangs into the man's neck. The man screamed as he went down with the dog on his back. Blood was squirting. The man lay motionless but alive. Gart called off the dog then grabbed a tablecloth to wrap around the wounds.

Agent Lou ran inside, cuffed the fugitive's hands and tied his ankles to-gether, before reading him his Right to Silence. Dorman started to run. Strong caught him in the doorway, swung his flapper, and flattened him with a direct hit to his temple. The customers screamed and fled.

Fingers did not cooperate. He suddenly elbowed Patton in the neck and landed a blow to his abdomen. Patton reeled backwards. Fingers swung his legs up and over the bar counter and ran into the kitchen to escape. Gart had locked the back door, but Fingers thrust his two hundred and thirty pound body against it, and it crashed open. Fingers ran across Bay Road to get to the beach. Phil was on guard, and as Fingers ran between *Enchanted* and his home, he gave the command. "Baron, kill!" The K9 trained animal tore across the yard. It was dark and Fingers did not see the animal until it grabbed him by the arm and wrestled him to the ground. Phil ran over with his baseball bat and smashed Fingers' left knee. He screamed in pain, but Phil wasn't finished. He called off the dog and pounded Fingers across the back of his head. He lay unconscious.

Lou had heard the screaming and ran across to Phil to help tie up the suspect. "Is he dead?" Lou asked.

"Hell no," Phil replied, "but when he wakes up he'll be in no shape to take off. He'll die behind bars I hope."

The dog remained in guard position and Phil gave him a treat reward. "Back, Baron," Phil commanded and the dog walked to Phil's side. "Good, Baron." Phil complimented his K9 pet.

"I'm DEA agent, Lou, Phil. Nice work. No sense tying his ankles, he's not about to run anywhere now." He took Fingers' arms and tied them behind his back. Fingers started to moan so Lou read him his Right to Silence. "It looks like we've got all four of the bastards, Phil. But the night is young."

Chapter 31 | The Police Station Raid

The festivities were well under way at police headquarters when Detective Cole arrived just before seven. Audrey was at her reception desk. She greeted Cole with, "The party has started, sir. We've set up in the training hall. You can go through that door beside my closet and I'm sure you'll have no problem, just head for the noise."

Cole smiled and said, "I met a couple of folks from the office back home, and asked them to the party. His name is Andrew Taylor, and his wife is Jackie. They should be here in a few minutes. Can you wait until they arrive and show them where to go?"

"Oh sure," Audrey replied. "I'll lock up after they get here."

Cole entered the party room and spotted Spikel serving at the bar. He shook hands with folks as he moved through the crowd. Deputy Commissioner Samson Black spotted Cole and walked over to meet him. Constable Wilbur Black made no move to come toward him so Cole made a mental note of which officer was chatting with the constable. *'Bed fellows?'* Cole thought. He reached the bar and Spikel said, "Nice of you to throw us a party, Detective. What can I get you to drink?"

"I'm OK for now, Herman."

"I got George to setup a small stage with chairs over by the door. If you are ready to make your presentation I'll get everyone in place."

"I'm ready now," Cole replied.

Spikel banged on the rim of an empty glass. Heads turned toward him and he invited The Deputy Commissioner to join Cole on the stage. As The Deputy walked over, Spikel asked everyone else to take a seat. George approached and said, "Audrey is not here. Should I call her?"

Spikel looked toward Cole and got the answer, "Let's proceed. We don't need Audrey right now." Facing George, Spikel said, "I guess you heard the answer. Have a seat beside me."

Cole stood up, looked back and forth across the assembled audience, and began, "I was sent here to Palm to assist in the investigation of deaths that occurred last June. I, and my partner Detective Bill Strong, are both seasoned detectives and not easily fooled by unexpected circumstances." He watched Samson Black and Wilbur Black shift in their chairs. "We had been here only a couple of days when we came to the conclusion that your Commissioner of Police was not forthcoming and was, in fact, lying to us." Sweat began to appear on Samson's brow. "Thankfully, we were able to identify certain individuals who wanted to tell us truthful facts. Bill and I know from experience, that many of you would have liked to help us but have been coerced by Commissioner Black. I'm happy to announce that the coercion ends this minute!" A resounding cheer erupted and officers were slapping and handshaking. "Please sit down until I finish."

Cole continued, "As I speak, Commissioner Sylvester Black is in the custody of New Scotland Yard. He will be returning, in custody, to face charges." Another raucous cheer went up. "I am now arresting you, Deputy Commissioner Samson Black, as an accomplice to the murders of last June." The crowd was stunned and remained silent. Looking at Spikel he said, "You, officer Spikel, are by my decree, now the Acting Commissioner of Police for the Palm Islands. Please read Samson Black his Right to Silence and secure the prisoner." Samson Black offered no resistance and said nothing. Looking across the crowd Cole pointed and said, "Constable Wilbur Black, you are under arrest also. You can come forth or I can go over there and read you your Right to Silence." He did not move. "Cole said, "I need two officers to bring Wilbur Black to this stage and secure him." Several officers got up to obey the order.

Cole pointed to two of them and said, "You two please bring him here." The two saluted Cole and did as asked. He then directed Spikel to take the suspects and lock them in one of the rooms upstairs. Spikel picked two officers to help him and they left.

"Now," he said to the remaining staff, "you should know that four more detectives from England are working with me, and there are also six DEA agents on the Island who are going to end the drug trafficking here. Over the next few days, each one of you will be interrogated by these agents and I expect you to answer any questions with full cooperation." Heads nodded and the officers talked quietly amongst themselves.

Turning to George he said, "Premier Westwood told me you are to be trusted. Is that correct?"

"One-hundred percent correct, sir."

"Okay, there should be two agents in the waiting area whose assignment was to arrest Audrey. Get them and bring them here."

Turning back to face the audience he said, "My team and the DEA team are arresting many suspects tonight. The empty rooms upstairs are where we will hold the arrested felons. I need two volunteers to guard each office until we run them through the court." Everyone put a hand up. "I suspected most of you would be happy to help and be able to freely conduct yourselves as loyal officers. Here's what I need. Would the captain and the first mate of the Marine Patrol step forward please?" Two officers came forward. Cole looked at them with his official stare and said, "I want you to be at your boat and ready to act if you get a radio command from Art Bodder on VHF 157.06. Be aware that two Cutter Class Coast Guard ships are working with us tonight. You will likely be asked to assist in the commandeering of the DIAMOND QUEEN. Go now. They smiled and waved to their fellow officers as they left the room.

Next, Cole assigned four men and a female officer to guard the prisoners. The five volunteers stepped forward. "And further," he said, "I need two cruisers and four officers to go to the Hibiscus Restaurant where, by now, our men should have taken four prisoners. Joey Fingers Black will not be dealing drugs to your kids and the tourists anymore. He and his crew will have been treated to some severe correctional messages by now and they will regret for a long time meeting with two tough, seasoned DEA detectives and my Detective Strong." Four volunteers were picked and they left the party immediately.

George returned with Audrey and both Taylors. Cole said to Audrey, "I believe you are implicated in the crime syndicate run by Commissioner Black. If you will cooperate fully with me, I will see that the court is lenient and you can likely stay out of prison. Right now I'm placing you under house arrest." He spoke Audrey her Right to Silence. When Cole had completed the statement he looked at her warmly and said, "Think of your two children. Will you help us?"

Audrey had started to sob, wiped her tears on her sleeve and replied, "I had no choice, sir. I was threatened almost daily by that man Sylvester Black. I will do whatever I have to. Trust me."

"Fine, I believe you. Can you get home safely or do you want an officer to take you home? I want you back here at your job tomorrow morning"

"No. I have a car. I promise to be here tomorrow morning."

"Before you leave, Audrey, I want you to show Detectives Andrew, and Jackie, where the visitor journals are kept." Turning to Andrew he said, "Bring them here to me. You, George, stay with me. We are going to search the Commissioner's office." There were only six unassigned officers, all anxious to play their role to rid Palm of Sylvester Black's corruption. Cole said to them, "I know you want to help, so," he pointed, "you two handle the phones and the reception area," Pointing again, "You, and you I want on the street in front of The Diamond Store." One male officer and a female officer remained to be assigned. Cole instructed them. "You two proceed immediately to Palm Dive." They saluted and departed. Turning again to George he said, "Quite a party we've had George. Let's go into Black's office and find his phone."

George smiled while he replied, "I think everyone enjoyed the party except Samson and Wilbur. You are going to find lots of evidence in the office because Black has a file cabinet that no one, but no one, has ever looked into. Not even the Deputy Commissioner."

They went to former Commissioner Black's office where Cole decided he should call Gart at Hibiscus. On the phone he heard Gart say, "I'm sorry, but we are closed tonight." Before Gart could hang up Cole blurted, "Gart, wait! It's Detective Cole!"

"Oh my God, am I glad to hear from you. We got them all, detective. Two are in bad condition and the officers that you sent here have taken all of them away. Patton, agent Lou, and Oakley have left for Palm Dive. Detective Strong is still here."

"Good, let me talk to Bill." He heard his partner say, "You there, guv?" Cole answered, "Yes and I'm in the former commissioner's office and sitting in his chair. George is with me."

"Well, well what a difference a day makes. I got bruised, but you don't want to see Fingers and his crew. To say they are wounded is putting it mildly. What do you want me to do?"

"Come here to the station. We have to plan our raid on Palm Shipping. Harris reported hearing gunshots there this afternoon and sounds like it's now a crime scene."

"Okay, guv. I'll leave now. Here's Gart."

Gart said, "Louisa and I want to thank you for taking down those thugs. You have no idea how close we have come to losing this place. Now we can look forward to good times. Thank you, thank you."

"All in a day's work Gart. If all goes well, we'll be celebrating with you to-morrow night. Bye."

George had been trying to open Black's personal file cabinet while Cole was on the phone. None of the keys worked. When Cole finished his call he tried Sylvester Black's desk drawer. It opened easily. Cole shuffled some objects around in the drawer but there were no keys and no portable phone. "This doesn't add up," he said to George. "Help me lift this drawer out of the desk."

The two men removed the drawer and they saw something strange. "Look George," Cole said in an excited voice, "this thing is twice as deep as a normal center drawer on any desk that I've ever seen. It must come apart somehow." They examined the drawer closely and finally found a small hinge. "This damn thing opens sideways," he exclaimed to George. "Hold the top part while I try this hinge."

"Holy smokes," George said, "you've found the motherlode."

A false bottom revealed a mobile phone, an address book, a 45mm Glock pistol, a key, and a hammer. "Wait until Spikel sees this stuff, George! We have to bag it in those clear envelopes that I see over there. Be careful to not get your prints on the evidence. This is the evidence we need to put Black away forever. Try the key on that file cabinet."

George put the key into the cabinet lock. It fit, and he was able to pull open a drawer. George started flipping the file folder tabs, while saying, "There's probably enough in here to identify all the criminals that the Commissioner ever did business with."

"Leave it be, George. Get Spikel in here. Cover for him, while we look at some of the documents. I want to phone Art Bodder to check what's happening out there."

Chapter 32 | Harris In Action

Harris sensed the danger that he was in, so he prayed continually while driving. He asked God to protect his family, and all of the men and women who were working to make Palm Islands a safe country in which to live. When he neared Maria's residence he shifted his focus and stayed alert. He parked at the end of Maria's driveway. At four-thirty she and Alvarez stepped out of the house and waved for Harris to come closer. As they got into his cab Maria appeared relaxed, saying, "Take us to The Diamond Store."

Harris looked into his rear-view mirror. He shifted sideways to see his passengers and said, "Very good Miss Maria." He saw that the two passengers were not sitting close to each other, nor were they holding hands. He wondered, *'Is she is his next victim.*

He heard Alvarez say, "When I talked to Balluchi just now he said he has a car. He will pick us up so we can all go to together to collect the payment. I told him we will be having dinner at The Cricket Club. He agreed to meet us there. He wants to be sure I get what we want from those Keith bastards. If they don't deliver, he wants them dead. He will be at the boat by eight."

Maria nodded and said, "I don't care who gets killed as long as we get our cut."

Harris could not believe what he was hearing. He parked near The Diamond Store. Only Alvarez got out. Maria said, "I'll stay here Harris. Mo will be in there for just a few minutes. Stay parked right here." Alvarez entered the store and Harris could see through the window that the owner was talking to him. He spent less than five minutes in the store and got back into the cab. Maria said, "The Cricket Club, Harris. And we won't need your service tonight. Tell me how much I owe when we get there."

"Yes mam." Harris pulled away from the curb.

Alvarez said to Maria, "Lawrence Jones says he heard from Harold Keith. Keith said his brother had an accident but they have the cash and he will pick up twenty million worth of stones at six o'clock. Lawrence says he'll have them ready for us at seven."

Harris pulled up to the Cricket Club entrance. "It was a pleasure to serve you Miss Maria. I charge one hundred Palm dollars per day, so it's two hundred that you owe me."

She handed him three hundred and said, "Thank you." She and Alvarez entered the Club. Harris breathed a sigh of relief, and drove straight to Phil's.

Chapter 33 | Carla Takes Over

Thirty-five year old DEA Agent Carla Zado had volunteered at age twenty to serve as an intelligence officer in the United States Army. As a daughter of an air force captain she had lived in three countries and became fluent in French and Italian. Wanderlust, and dangerous living, was in her blood. After her tour in the Vietnam War, Carla was a prime person to become a CIA agent. The five foot eleven woman had stayed in shape physically by training to achieve a black belt status in combat judo. She had also won several awards as a marksman. More than once she used her language and judo skills when working undercover in places like Montreal, Canada, and Buffalo, New York. She left the CIA because she was offered a higher rank and more money by the Drug Enforcement Agency. She had never been assigned to a Caribbean mission before. When chosen to work with Tom Oakley she jumped at the opportunity.

After Oakley left her on her own to follow Solarno and Alvarez she had no problem in being discreet. As Oakley had suggested, she kept Harris's cab in sight. When Harris left the suspects at the Palm Island Bank and Trust, then disappeared for an hour, she remained on her watch. Then she followed them out to Palm Shipping and observed from a nearby grocery store parking area. She did not hear the gun shots. When Harris drove away, Carla was able to follow behind another vehicle until Harris dropped his passengers off at Maria's house. At that point she parked just out of sight of Maria's house. She began to worry as time was slipping by and Harris seemed to be taking too much time if, in fact, he was going to return. When he drove into Maria's driveway at four-thirty she smiled at herself for being uptight. As Harris progressed toward the Cricket Club, she almost lost track of his vehicle in the heavy traffic, but she was able to park and watch her suspects enter the Cricket Club. She saw Harris take money from Maria. Carla had no doubt that he would not be returning. *'I'm on my own now, for sure.'* she thought.

While waiting, Carla checked her weapon and psyched herself up for whatever danger lay ahead. At six-forty Maria, Alvarez, and Balluchi came out of the Club and got into a Ford Taurus. Balluchi drove the car. Carla followed at a short distance until they reached the Palm Shipping site. Carla drove past the site then came back. The Taurus was empty. She assumed that they had all gone into the office.

Harold Keith was waiting for Alvarez and Maria to arrive, but he was surprised to see Balluchi. He said nothing. Reaching into his desk drawer he pulled out a plain cloth sack about twelve inches wide by ten inches long. It was secured by a drawstring. Keith set it on the desk and said, "Twenty million worth of stones. Sorry about the screw up. Lawrence Jones' certificate is in the bag."

Balluchi said, "I guarantee no more screw ups. Count on it. You are a bunch of amateurs." He pulled out a 45mm Glock and fired two shots into each of Alvarez, Solarno and Keith. The soft-nosed bullets splattered blood and flesh everywhere. He took the sack of diamonds and casually walked to his car, and drove away.

Carla heard the shots. She saw Balluchi exit the building alone. There was no doubt in her mind the Magdalena Cartel had eliminated more victims. She knew she had to take down the blond haired Balluchi by shooting him because cartel mobsters never surrender. Balluchi drove, breaking all speed limits, to Clear and Deep. He pulled in and noticed that his Cigarette31 was boxed in by two big boats. He drove his car up to Bodder's door and burst in waving his weapon. He said, "Who wants to die? Get those fucking boats away from my boat – NOW!"

Bodder said quietly, "Let's not do anything stupid, man." He said to Jane, "Here's the key to the Bertram, I'll move the Hatteras."

Carla had parked at the top of the driveway. She had just stepped out of her vehicle when she saw Art and Jane being forced at gunpoint. There were several customers at the Tiki Bar who scrambled away. Buzzy ducked behind the counter. Carla silently approached to within forty feet of Balluchi who was standing still, gun drawn, watching Jane and Art board the boats. He did not see Carla. He was not expecting anyone to have a gun on Grand Palm. Carla took aim, and shot Balluchi in his hand. His weapon flew onto the dock. Jane was quick and grabbed the man and put him in a sleep hold. He fell to the dock holding the diamonds in his other hand. Jane grabbed the bag. She gasped when she looked inside. She said, "This sack is full of diamonds." She turned to face Carla, and said, "You must be Carla. What a shot! Agent Oakley told us to expect you. Where are Solarno and Alvarez?"

Carla replied, "I think they've been murdered. I followed them to the Palm Shipping office and watched them go in with this guy, but I heard shots, and they never came out. This guy came out alone. At the DEA we know how the Magdalena Cartel works."

Art went to get a rope and shouted at Buzzy to bring some towels. Buzzy tied Balluchi's legs while Art wrapped towels around the damaged hand. They tied his good hand behind his back and looped the rope back around his neck. Finally they tied him securely to a light standard.

Carla said, "I guess this guy is my problem. Let him suffer a bit before I take him to HQ. Oakley can deal with him there."

Jane said, "Maybe I should go with you. But first, let's have a drink and watch him squirm. The bugger has watched plenty of others squirm."

"I like your attitude Jane. I haven't worked with a Brit before." Carla, trying to be funny and said, "Jolly good, mate!" Jane and Art laughed. The pressure was off.

Art stood up when he heard a voice on his marine radio. "Excuse me girls. Buzzy, buy the women a drink. They should celebrate. Oh, hand me that sack Jane, I'll put it in the safe."

The women enjoyed talking with Buzzy. When they finished their drinks Carla drove down to the dock where Buzzy helped the women put Balluchi into the back seat of the vehicle. They saw that Art was busy so they waved to him, and blew him a kiss, as they left.

Chapter 34 | The DIAMOND QUEEN Raid

Art's radio was blaring, '*P I Marine to Bodder; P I Marine to Bodder. Do you copy?*' Art answered, "I copy, P I Marine. This is Bodder. Go ahead."

Art heard, "DIAMOND QUEEN has launched auxiliary craft. Coast Guard Cutter Bradenton at target, we will challenge small craft, alert Bradenton."

"Will do, P I Marine, be careful. Suspects will be armed."

Art immediately radioed USCGC Bradenton. The ship's Captain confirmed that marines had boarded the target, but he was unaware of the small vessel launch. He reported gunfire aboard the DIAMOND QUEEN but no details. He asked that P I Marine capture its target.

Art called P I Marine and relayed the order.

P. I. Marine Captain, Marcus John, confirmed with Bodder. They began chasing the target. The small craft was powered by one 75HP Mercury outboard motor. It was no match for the 150HP diesel engine that powered the Palm Police boat. It quickly caught up to the small craft, and turned on its spotlights. Immediately gunfire came from the fleeing craft. Captain John thought about crashing the craft, but instead he ordered his second officer Roland Quick to return fire. He used a 75MM turret gun that ripped holes in the target and it began to sink. The two occupants raised their hands and cried for help. Officer Quick then threw two life savers to them and they were hauled into the police boat. The Captain placed them under arrest and read them their Right to Silence. Officer Quick bound their hands and feet and asked them their names. They remained silent. Quick searched their pockets and found ID. "Sir," he said to his superior officer, "we've got Mancini."

The captain smiled and said, "Well I'll be damned. Wait until the detectives hear this!" He radioed Bodder to say they had Mancini and one bodyguard and were on their way to HQ with their captives. Art congratulated Captain John.

Bodder called Cole who could not believe their success. Next he radioed the news to the Bradenton. The Bradenton Captain was pleased when Bodder told him that Mancini was in the custody of the P I Police. The Captain of the Bradenton reported to Bodder that his team of marines had taken control of the DIAMOND QUEEN after a fierce gunfight. One marine had been wounded and four suspects killed. They had found eight women hiding in Mancini's stateroom, none had been injured. He asked Bodder if he had heard from USCGC Venice. Art told him to stand by and he would attempt to reach the Venice. Bodder then radioed, "This is Bodder do you read me Venice? Come in cutter Venice."

The answer came, 'Venice reads you Bodder, over.'

Bodder replied, "Have you reached your target? What is your status?"

'Venice here, target is under control. No injuries to Venice team. One of target crew shot dead, and three injured. We will bring fishing boat to Grand Palm at daylight. Fifteen bodies in boat's freezer.'

"10-4 Venice, we will inform Detective Cole and agent Oakley." He added, "Cutter Bradenton has requested that you make contact."

Art called Cole at police headquarters and relayed the information. Cole told him Oakley was not there as he was involved in the raid at Palm Dive.

Chapter 35 | The PALM DIVE Raid

DEA agents Ian and Juan left Hibiscus and drove to surveil Palm Dive. They noted that the boat Quicksilver was moored close to the office. Delray's vehicle was parked on the opposite side of the lot, away from the office. The van was parked next to the office. They decide that they could trust the Canadians to execute the plan, so it would be best for them to keep the van in sight and if it left Palm Dive they could follow it, or perhaps cause some kind of delay. At ten minutes to seven a man came out of the office and got into the driver's side of the van. As it pulled out onto Bay Road the agents followed it until it reached The Holiday Place Resort at exactly at seven o'clock. Juan said to Ian, "Let me get out and you stay here. I'll get a good look at that guy and wait inside until the Canadians appear. If need be I can start a ruckus and get a few minutes delay."

Ian replied, "I'll back into that space near the door. Good luck."

Juan watched the driver of the van pick up the courtesy phone and dial. Then he started arguing and was noticeably upset. After a few minutes he went to a pay phone and called someone and talked for about a minute. Juan assumed that he called Delray. Then the man went to the elevator area at which time Juan said to himself, '*This doesn't look good. I'd better find out where he's going'*. Juan got to the elevator just as the door was closing but managed to have it retreat. The suspect had punched floor 3 and now Juan was sure there would be action. He casually bumped into the man and said, "Oh, I'm sorry. I was thinking about something. Floor 3? Good, that's where I'm headed." When he bumped the man he felt a weapon tucked into the back of his pants. Both men got off and Juan stalled for a moment looking confused. He walked and stopped at the suite across the hall from the Canadians' room. The van driver ignored Juan, knocked on the door while reaching behind and pulling out his gun. Juan stepped behind him with his Berretta in hand, jammed it into the suspect's back, and said, "Drop that gun or I'll drop you. I know who you are and I'll kill you right here. Drop it!" On the second command the van driver dropped his weapon, whirled around and took a swipe at Juan. Juan kicked him in the nuts and when he folded down, judo chopped him. The blow flattened the driver and he was out cold. Juan knocked on the door and Mike opened it. "Pull this body inside Mike. He came here to shoot you and your friends. Hurry, we have to gag him and tie him up. Get his keys. We'll leave him here. Get a couple of belts." Pointing at the others, he said," Don't just sit there. Get your asses over here and help Mike. Tie him up and gag him. We have to get to Delray's. I'll drive the van."

They did as ordered then hustled to the elevator and out into the van. Ian was watching and could not believe his eyes. Juan waved him to start the car and follow. In the van he said to the Canadians, "When we get to Delray's stay in the van. If we are lucky he will come out to find out what caused the delay. By then there will be more of us agents and detectives. We want Delray alive and we want the boat. I'm not sure Delray is smart enough to stay alive. He will be desperate. He doesn't know that all of his criminal friends are either dead, wounded, or behind bars. Just stay put in this van."

Mike responded, "We hear you."

Juan parked the van just out of sight of Delray's office. Ian parked on the shoulder of the road until he saw Oakley's Jeep approaching. He jumped out of his car and flagged down Oakley, told him what had happened, and that Juan was driving the van. He said to Oakley, "When you have everyone in position, wave. Juan will drive the van to the office but wait until Delray comes out. Curiosity always kills the cat."

Oakley was amazed at what the two agents had planned and told Patton and Lou to get positioned on the right side of the office. He would cover the left side. Ian was to guard against anyone coming, or going, to the property. They did not know that Cole had dispatched P I officers to the place. Those officers arrived within minutes and Ian directed them to stay on the road with him.

Oakley, Patton and Lou sneaked into position. Oakley waved to Juan to proceed. He drove the van to the building, and parked about eight feet from the office door. He honked the van horn. Delray took the bait and came out to the van. Oakley approached from one side and Patton from the other. Lou ran into the office, weapon in hand and confronted the other person. Delray pulled a gun and shot at Patton hitting him with one shot to his leg. Oakley blasted three shots into Delray causing him to go down firing wildly. One shot grazed Oakley as Delray emptied his magazine. Juan jumped out of the van. He held Delray who was bleeding profusely. Oakley shouted to Ian, "Get the cops to call a medic." The two P I Police heard him. One of them called for help, while the other took first aid supplies from the trunk of his vehicle and ran to assist Patton. Willie said, "I'm okay. We can't let Delray die. Treat him and stop his bleeding." The P I officer did as ordered. Oakley too was bleeding, but his adrenalin was flowing fast as he ran to help Lou who held his hostage at gunpoint. "Well, if it isn't Mr. Delgada," he said. "Put your hands behind your back my friend. You are under arrest." Tie him up Lou while I read him his Right to Silence. Don't get any funny ideas, Tony. This place is swarming with cops."

Oakley then went back outside and ordered the Canadians to get out of the van and look at Delray. He asked, "Is this the person who orchestrates the stock trading schemes?"

Mike replied, "That's him." The others affirmed.

"Okay, get back in the van. We are going to Police Headquarters and I want a written statement from each of you. Then you will be put under guard at the hotel until I can get all of you out of Palm on a direct flight to Canada.

A medic arrived in a hospital EMS van. He looked at Delray who was in agonizing pain. The medic said, "He has to go to the hospital if you want him to live. I'll give him a shot of morphine and put him out for now. Here, he said, as he approached Oakley, bandage in hand, let me fix that wound of yours." Oakley cooperated.

Patton spoke up, "Hey, what about my leg?"

The medic looked at it and said, "You'd better get to the hospital. I'll give you a shot to kill the pain, that's a serious wound. You can come with me."

Oakley thanked the medic. Pointing to the P I Officer he said, "You go with the medic. I'll trust you to guard this scum."

"Do not worry, sir," he replied. "It will be a pleasure to keep him alive and see him squirm in the courthouse."

Oakley decided that the Quicksilver wasn't going anywhere, but Delray's office had to be searched. The share certificates had to be there, somewhere. He called to Mike, "Mike, bring your guys in here. We have to find the share certificates. We'll likely find a stash of cash too. They were tearing the office apart when Oakley saw something interesting. There was a ten foot plastic marlin hanging on the wall above Delray's desk. Oakley thought, *'Why is that fish hung so low compared to the other trophy specimens?'* He called for Mike to come over and help him bring down the marlin. He was not surprised to see a portion of the wall side had been removed and a sliding door cabinet inserted. He slid the door open. There were share certificates and several stacks of U S one-hundred dollar bills. He removed the certificates and showed them to Mike.

"That's them," Mike said. "Let me see if they are all there." He looked at each one and said, "Yes they are all registered to Bay Street Securities, Ltd., and signed off into street form. Anyone can to take these to a broker here and get value for them. I brought them here."

Oakley looked at Mike. In a friendly tone he said, "I hope you get a lenient judge in Canada. Get your lawyer to call me and I'll swear to how you and your friends cooperated with me. Bring me that duffle bag that's over there. Put the cash and the certs in it for me. My head is starting to ache. Call that P I Officer up at the road and tell him to come here."

The officer came when Mike summoned him. Oakley said, "I'm putting you in charge of this site. This is now a crime scene so tape it off. Call Detective Cole at headquarters for assistance. There should be some officers available."

"Yes, sir, you can count on me," the officer replied.

Juan was helping search the office and Cole said to him, "Load up the van and take the four down to headquarters. When they've signed their statements take them back to their hotel."

Looking at Mike, Oakley asked, "Do we have to guard you guys or can we trust you to stay put at the hotel? Don't let on that anything unusual has happened. Stay on the premises until I arrange a flight."

Mike replied, "As you say Mr. Oakley. We owe our lives to you and your men."

"Let's go then Juan. I'll meet you at HQ."

Chapter 36 | The DIAMOND STORE Raid

Events were happening fast and Cole tried to monitor them as he got calls from the field. It was almost eight o'clock. He had not heard from Detectives Larry and Eve. He was about to send Andrew to find out what was wrong when the two detectives walked into the Commissioner's office. They brought in Lawrence Jones wearing handcuffs, his head bowed down. Cole walked over to him and said, "According to the visitor registers you've been here before. Take a good look now because you won't be seeing this office again. Those bracelets you are wearing aren't diamonds but they are worth much more in our business." He turned to Andrew and said, "Find a room for him with some of the other scum while Larry fills me in on his raid." Cole turned to his detectives. "Have a seat you two. Fill me in on what happened."

Larry told Cole, "At seven, as planned, I rapped on the door of the store. Jones opened it and let us in, locked it, and showed us to the display case where you had seen the bracelet. I played my role, as did Eve. After handling the item, I asked to see some raw diamonds suitable for an investment portfolio. Jones led us to his office and commented that his stock was low because one of his important customers had bought most of his inventory, just a few hours prior. I complimented him, and asked how do you handle that much cash?"

"He said, 'Do you know in Palm there is a law about asking personal questions?' I told him I knew that, but as a Scotland Yard detective, I am required to ask. He squirmed, then pointed and said, 'I keep it overnight in my safe over there and ship it out by private jet the next day.' I said, 'you are under arrest, Mr. Jones, for knowingly assisting the Magdalena Cartel.' I read him his Right to Silence and he started to sob. I said, 'Cheer up, you are still alive. Some of your associates are dead.'

"We took him without a scuffle. I instructed the two P I officers that you dispatched to us, to guard the place until they got further orders from you."

Bloody nice work, Larry," Cole said. Unless I'm mistaken there should be twenty million dollars in that safe. Add that to the millions worth of diamonds that Jane and Carla scored by taking down Balluchi and we can likely pay for this trip!"

Larry laughed. "It's the best haul that I've ever been on in my twenty years on the force."

Cole continued to tell him about the other raids. He finished by saying," We are going to have one bloody great party when this job is wrapped up. You and Eve can go now, and get some rest. I'll call Trump and tell him we are all in one piece. I'm sure Governor Neily is on pins and needles as well as Premier Westwood so I will fill them in on the details too."

Larry grinned and said," I hope there are no worms in the woodwork. Good night guv."

"Damn you, Larry. Now you've got me worried. Get out of here my friend."

Chapter 37 | Winding Down

While Cole waited for Detective Strong to arrive he talked to Trump on the phone. The Superintendent offered praise for the whole team. Next, he looked through the file cabinet drawer which held a treasure trove of evidence. George kept busy by bagging the physical evidence recovered from Black's desk drawer. Bill Strong arrived at the Police Headquarters and he was greeted by the constable at the reception desk. The officer said, "Thank you, sir, for setting us free from Sylvester Black's control. You men are real heroes."

Strong thanked him for the compliment and before he went up the stairs to Black's former office, Carla and Jane walked in. Jane hailed him saying, "Detective, what a timely meeting. We have Balluchi in Carla's car. Can you assign someone to take him to the hospital and guard him?"

Strong hesitated a moment before saying, "You have Balluchi?"

Carla answered, "Yes. I shot him in the hand before Jane put him to sleep. If you want him in front of a judge he'd better get to a doctor real quick."

Strong gave an order to the Sargent on the desk. "Call Detective Cole, let me talk to him." The Sargent complied, reached Cole and handed the phone to Strong. Strong said, "We have a problem down here, guv. Jane and agent Carla brought us a wounded Balluchi. He needs a doctor. Can you assign someone to take him to the hospital and guard him?"

"You will have to go, Bill. Tell agent Carla to guard him. Send Jane up here. I'll wait until you get back."

"I'm on it, guv. See you in a bit." Turning to Carla and Jane, he said, "Me and you, Carla, have to deliver Balluchi. You will guard him until Oakley sends one of his team. Jane, go upstairs to the far end where Cole is waiting for you."

As she walked down the hallway she saluted the men and women who were guarding prisoners being held in the interview rooms. She did not knock, but just let herself into the office. Cole was on the phone to Trump, again, reporting the capture of Balluchi. He waved acknowledgement to Jane. She went over to George, shook his hand, introduced herself, and then took a seat beside the big desk.

Cole finished talking to Trump and said, "Well, Jane, things could be worse. I'm ready to wrap up for tonight, but we'll wait for Bill. I might as well use this break to call Governor Neily and the Premier. Make yourself at home. George will get you a drink if you want one. George, show her our collection of evidence."

He called the Governor first, and then the Premier. Both had been waiting anxiously. Cole told them of the success and they both heaped praise on him. Cole asked that they contain the praise and to stand by on Wednesday when he'd likely need some political help. When he ended the call Jane said, "You know sir, this night is one for the record book. I think it will go down in Yard history as Cole's War."

"Everyone played a starring role, Jane, and none better than you." Turning to George he said. You can call it a night George. Just hand the evidence to Jane." George handed her a box he had found into which he had put the items.

Before George left the office Strong walked in. He reported, "Balluchi will live to sing. I didn't know Carla was a marksman. She's quite the woman."

Jane said, "I sense a touch of international affection, Bill."

He showed a silly grin, but kept silent. He thought, *'She's too perceptive. But she's right damn it.'*

"Let's get out of here," Cole said, as he rose up out of the big chair. "Jane is our house guest, Bill, so we had better be on our best behavior."

On the way home they stopped at Carl's Treats to get some take-home food. Strong talked all the way, telling Cole of the events that happened during the arrests at Hibiscus. Cole said he was too worn out to give Bill a rundown, but he'd go over the story in the morning. When Cole drove into the driveway, Phil's dogs started to bark. Phil figured it was the detectives arriving home. He stepped out and shouted across the yard, "Is everything okay?"

Cole replied, "Just fine, Phil. Thanks for tonight. Jane is with us. I'll catch you up tomorrow."

"Can I join you?" Phil shouted.

Cole caught on right away and said, "Why not, come over about eight."

The detectives enjoyed their food and the men poured themselves a stiff drink of Pirates' Best. Jane had a beer. They finished their drinks. Cole and Strong had a second one, but Jane opted out. They talked quietly about the past day, as they finally relaxed. Jane was first to bow out saying, "This has to be my proudest day. Working with the best of the best is what agents like me wish for. I'm glad I didn't let you down. Nighty, night. It's time for some beauty sleep."

Both men said, "Good night, Jane."

Within fifteen minutes Cole and Strong were in their beds, too.

Chapter 38 | The Morning After

Wednesday morning was made in heaven. The sea was calm, and the birds were having a great time chasing around on the soft sand looking for whatever birds look for. The sky was clear as crystal with not a cloud to be seen. The morning sun had begun to rise above the trees to the East so daylight prevailed without direct rays from the sun.

Phil Russell was an early riser. He liked to walk his dogs along the beach when it was cool in the morning. He had walked about a mile to the South and was returning when he saw Jane sitting on the lanai at *Enchanted*. During the night he thought often about the woman who had not only a beautiful face, a physically perfect body, but grit and intelligence. Now there she was, enjoying the same ambience as he. She was wearing shorts and her police T-shirt. Her beautiful blonde hair looked so very soft draped over each shoulder. Her long shapely legs were stretched out leaving no doubt that she was enthralled by the moment. Phil could not pass up the opportunity to walk up to her and have a closer look.

Jane, her eyes closed, was daydreaming about working with Cole when Phil said quietly, "Hi Jane."

She opened her eyes, expecting to see Cole or Strong. What she saw was a six foot two, tanned, handsome man with two dogs. Phil was wearing only a pair of shorts so nothing was left to her imagination. "Oh, my goodness, How nice it is to see you. I heard that you had some real action here last night."

"Hope I'm not bothering you, Jane. It is such a perfect morning, don't you think? Yes, action for sure. Baron and I loved it. Fingers, Black's local enforcer and drug king, is in the hospital with a sore head and a busted knee. How did you do?"

"Well," Jane replied, "the cigarette31 is still at Bodder's. The owner is missing one hand because DEA agent Carla blew it off while he was pointing his Glock at Art and me. I got to put him to sleep. He's in the hospital under guard."

Cole was about to call home when he heard the voices. Strong heard them also so both men went out to see who was talking. They both smiled when they saw Phil hitting on Jane. Cole said, "Sorry to interrupt, Phil. Sounds like you are getting to know Jane. Tough operator, she is. Be careful."

"Just my type, Curt, hope you leave her behind when you leave."

Jane laughed. "I'm not sure they could get along without me, Phil."

Strong loved the back and forth, jumped into the conversation, and said, "That's an understatement, Jane. We'd need at least three to replace you!"

Phil liked how the scene was developing and said, "I'll take the dogs home and come back. Maybe I can take all of you to the Holiday Place for breakfast?"

"I'm not turning down an invitation like that," Jane said. "I'll be ready in twenty minutes."

Cole looked at Strong and said, "You know, Bill, we'd better keep an eye on our girl."

Bill answered, "Yes, guv. Strange things can happen on an island such as Palm. Twenty minutes it is."

It was seven when the group entered the Holiday Place restaurant. They were pleased to see Ted who came over to greet them. He was introduced to Jane. He recognized Phil but had never been introduced. Phil said, "I heard that you have been a huge help to these detectives. I'm honored to meet you. I'm Phil."

Ted replied, "Just a small cog in a good machine, sir. I heard on the radio this morning that you did a real job on Fingers. They expect him to be in the hospital for at least a week."

"I could have done more, Ted, but these folks need him to sing. I should have let my dog work him over a bit more. Anyway, let's order."

Ted said, "The breakfast buffet is now set up over there – he pointed – why don't you check it out while I get the coffee?"

"Sounds good to me," Jane commented. She rose and the others followed her.

The meal went well and after an hour Cole looked at his watch and said, "I wouldn't mind going now. I want to call home and let my wife know that I'm still alive."

"No problem," Phil replied. "I'll meet you in the lot. I have to pay."

For the short ride home Jane sat in the front next to Phil. Cole and Strong watched the two get friendly and there was no doubt about the chemistry that was brewing. When Phil parked Cole thanked him and said, "After I call my wife, Bill and I have to head over to Governor Neily's place. You can hang out with Phil, Jane, if you want to. I won't need you until after lunch"

Neither Jane, nor Phil was under any illusion about what Cole was inferring. Jane replied, "Okay cupid, I'll be ready at one o'clock." Phil was smiling.

• • •

Cole wasted no time getting to the phone and dialing home. He figured Vickie would be waiting for a call, and she was. He was relieved to make contact, and his wife was relieved to hear his voice. They chatted for about thirty minutes before Cole told her he had to run. She always understood what a hectic life her husband lived while on a mission. She never complained. She knew Cole loved her dearly and he showed it in many ways when he was not on an assignment.

Strong waited on the lanai during the call and picked up sounds of laughter coming from Phil's house. He mulled the thought of calling Eisie at Sandy Shores. Maybe there could be a foursome. When Cole came out to talk to him Strong said, "Guv, do you think I could take a break tomorrow? I'm thinking of inviting that Sandy Shores desk clerk, Eisie, over for a drink. Perhaps we could arrange a little partying with the two folks that you just shot with your cupid's arrow."

Cole smiled and said, "I promised that you could if we got through working. I won't need you tomorrow so go ahead. I'll be tied up all day tomorrow at the Chief Magistrate's office arranging court dates. I'll be with Oakley."

"Thanks guv, I'll give it a try. I'll call from Police HQ."

"We'd better get going, Bill. I'm sure Oakley will be there to help us sort things out. Besides, we have the Coast Guard Cutter Venice bringing in the Belize boat. And also, we have to make arrangements with Royal Navy ship that's bringing us some help."

Chapter 39: Searching The Belize Boat

When Cole and Strong entered HQ, a smiling Audrey greeted them. Two officers were getting ready to leave and they walked over to thank Cole. He smiled at them and said, "Now, let me see you do the job you've been trained to do. Both officers saluted Cole and offered a crisp, "Yes, Sir!"

They walked along the hallway to Black's former office and received more smiles and congratulations from the guards. Cole did not bother to rap on the door when he entered. Herman Spikel was there sorting through the 'private' file. George was assisting him. Oakley was at the big desk.

Cole said, "Good morning, gentlemen. Tell me, are things under control? Did any of our captives die or do anything stupid? Looks like you have a new boss, Herman!"

Oakley laughed and said, "I love your British sense of humor. I just thought I should make sure this chair was safe for you to use."

Spikel interrupted. "All is going well except for Mancini. He wants a lawyer. I told him to get in line. He's threatening everyone if he gets sent down the river. I spiked his beverage to cool him off."

"Please, I don't need to hear that part, Herman. But obviously you are in charge, and the force likes how you operate. I have to call the Governor and the Premier. I'll need them with me tomorrow at the Chief Magistrates' office."

Strong decided to chat with George. Perhaps he knew Eisie, and what type of woman she is. George said simply, "You could do a lot worse."

Cole made his calls to Governor Neily and Premier Westwood. He asked them to be available at the Chief Magistrate's office on Thursday. They both agreed to be there at ten Thursday morning.

Cole wanted to do some searching in the files, but opted to go down to the harbor and be available when the fishing boat arrived. He asked Spikel to call the P I Marine Captain and to tell him to set up communications with the British navy ship. He and Strong then drove to the harbor. Oakley followed in his Jeep. The Belize vessel had arrived minutes prior and the Cutter Captain was coming ashore. Cole approached him, identified himself, then introduced Oakley and Strong. The Captain said, "I'm pleased that you are here. My name is Bob Fortune. By all reports that I have received, you men have had your hands full. I'm glad to be of service to you and help to stop the drug trafficking on our east coast. Follow me.

They stepped aboard the Belize boat and received a salute from the marines. Captain Fortune asked one of them to show them the freezer compartment. The detectives thought that they had prepared themselves for the worst, but when they saw dead women and children who had been frozen to death, they could not look for more than a minute. Oakley exclaimed, "Those dirty bastards! We should throw Balluchi in here to freeze. The son-of-a-bitch is taking up room in the hospital instead."

Captain Fortune said, "Easy detective, maybe this refrigerated compartment will easy your feelings." He opened a door and said "Step inside and look at those boxes. One-hundred cases of cocaine - two thousand pounds. That should make you feel that your efforts have been worthwhile."

"My God," Oakley exclaimed. "We've finally broken the back of the Carlos Guintia operation." Turning to Captain Fortune he said, "This isn't even half of what we've recovered. We are talking well over two hundred million dollars of cocaine, cash and other assets. Sir, I want to thank you and your crew for a job well done."

"Glad to be of service. We will remain in port awaiting orders from Miami."

Chapter 40 | Final Planning

Oakley made a quick visit to the hospital to check on Patton. He was relieved to hear that the gunshot wound did not damage any bone or arteries. The head nurse assured him that his partner would be released on Thursday.

Detectives Cole, and Strong, went directly to Spikel's new office at Police Headquarters. Spikel was filled in on what they saw on the Belize boat. Cole then ordered George to bring the big whiteboard from the training room up to the office. Spikel helped him.

Cole sat at the big desk, and said, "We are going to lay out assignments. Oakley's team and ours want to get out of Palm, asap. Come hell or high water, Bill and I, will be on that direct flight to Heathrow next Tuesday. List the names on the left, Bill." Strong listed their team first, then Oakley's. Cole continued, "Bill and I will interview each officer on the force. Acting Commissioner Spikel will assist us. As we clear each one, that person will be made available to the teams. The British Navy is providing thirty guards so that our P I force can operate again. The Frigate will be stationed here until I am satisfied, then it can leave."

"Now, let's start with Larry of the Taylor group. He will take two P I officers and interrogate, arrest if deemed necessary, the people at Customs."

"Oakley, who do you want to deal with Immigration?"

Oakley replied, "Agent Ian can handle that. He's the one who passed the bribe."

And so it went, each agent was assigned a role and was expected to be available in court as each criminal appeared before the Judge.

Oakley questioned the honesty and impartiality of the two Palm Island Judges. Cole said, "Good point Tom. I will clear that possibility with the Governor and the Premier tomorrow. If need be we can import impartial judges from The Cayman Islands or Bermuda."

The meeting was adjourned for lunch. Several assignments remained to be allocated.

•   •   •

When the men returned, Cole was pleased to see Jane waiting for them. He did not comment on her visit to Phil's house. He was all business. "Jane, we are assigning jobs to each agent for follow-up. We don't have a warrant to go into Jones & Keller. Call the Chief Magistrate right now from Audrey's station. She has his phone number. Tell him I asked you to call, and that we need a warrant right away. I'm sure he will agree. Get an officer to drive you there and come back here. You and I will raid their office later today."

"Righto, sir," she replied. Jane thought, '*This is surely my lucky day. Start out with a handsome brute like Phil, then get to work beside my hero Cole.*' She was walking on air.

By three o'clock all of the assignments had been allocated. Oakley had made arrangements with his people to convene at the Beach Hotel at four. He told them to enjoy the beach until then. Strong followed up with the Taylor Family, and arranged a meeting for six o'clock. That gave him time to drop into Sandy Shores. Eisie was there and lit up like a lightbulb when she saw her visitor. Strong said, "Guess what Eisie, I'm ready to ask you for a date. I've been busy as you may have heard on the radio."

"Oh, I'm so happy you're alright. I don't know why, but you have been on my mind ever since you checked out from here."

"I'd like to pick you up on Friday and take you to *Enchanted* where we could be together for a while. Then I'd like you to meet our neighbor Phil, and our undercover agent, well she was undercover, agent Jane Butterworth. The four of us could go for dinner at The Hibiscus Restaurant before heading out to dance somewhere."

Without hesitation but showing her teasing smile, she replied, "We could do that and much more. Can you pick me up here at three? I'd love to have a swim first if that's okay."

Strong was churning inside. "That's more than okay. You're getting me all excited."

Eisie leaned toward him. She pulled the neck of her blouse down slightly to show a good portion of her two lovely brown breasts. "That's what I'm trying to do." She laughed. "These are for you."

Strong was melting, but reality set in. "I have to get going. I can't stand any more of that or I'll be jumping over the counter and I'll get arrested. I'm glad I stopped by." He winked, and said, "If my next meeting goes as well as this one, I'll be one lucky cop!" He couldn't wait to start the next meeting and come back down to earth.

Chapter 41| Arresting Jones

About three-thirty Jane returned to HQ with the warrant in hand. Cole asked her, "Jane, what might happen over there?"

"I'd be surprised if anyone is there, but if Winston Jones is there I'm sure he'll be waiting with some bodyguards. Did anyone check if there's a flight to Calvert today?"

"Damn you're good, Jane. No. Study the whiteboard while I check with Audrey." Audrey told Cole that there were flights to Calvert on Monday, Wednesday and Friday and she had often booked tickets for Jones on Islands Airways' five PM flight.

"Jane, we have to run. There's a flight at five. We still have time to get him if he's trying to escape."

They drove, siren blaring, to the airport and rushed into the passenger boarding area. They looked at the assembled passengers but did not see Jones. They were about to give up on finding him when the ticket agent announced, *'The Islands Airways flight to Calvert is now ready for boarding. Please proceed to the airplane.'* Jane suspected that Jones might be waiting in the men's room until the last minute. She said, "Detective, maybe you should check the washroom. I'll keep watching here."

Cole again thought, '*Damn it, she's smart!*' He went quickly to check and just as he entered the 'IN' side, Jones walked out of the 'EXIT' side. Jane saw Jones and he saw Jane. He tried to run past her, but she was too quick, and too strong. She tackled him. He rolled over and as Jane stooped to hit him he slugged her with his valise that weighed twenty pounds. It had brass corners and one of them caught Jane just above her right eye. Blood started flowing. Cole had come back into the waiting area and saw the scuffle. He ran to Jane's defense, took out his slapper, and whacked the fleeing Jones on the back of his head. The fugitive went down screaming. Cole whacked him a second time on his wrist and he screamed, "*Stop! Stop!*" as the valise came loose. He lay still. Jane was determined to cuff the man in spite of the blood that was blurring her vision. Cole lifted Jones to his feet, administered his Right to Silence, and told him to sit down and not to move. He looked at Jane, "You are a tough cookie. Here, let me see that wound." Jane couldn't believe what was happening as Cole took her head and held it in both hands. His face was only a couple of inches from hers. She was oblivious to the wound as she thought, '*If you only knew boss, what I'm thinking now.*' Cole took out his handkerchief and held it over the wound. He said, "It doesn't look too bad Jane. Hold the hankie and bring the valise. I'll take Jones." They arrived at the Station, and booked Jones. Jane's head was throbbing a bit and she said, "We still should go to his office. I'd like to book his secretary before she destroys any evidence."

Cole replied, "Okay, if you think you are up to it. There's first aid stuff here. I'll get Audrey to fix you up."

Audrey was happy to help and she bandaged Jane's wound.

Chapter 42 | Leona's Surprise

When they arrived at the Palm Bank & Trust building they decided that Jane should take the elevator and Cole would go up the stairway. They converged outside of the Jones & Keller office. Jane tried to open the door but it appeared to be locked. Cole said loudly, "Police! Open up!" To their surprise Leona opened the door. She said, "I thought you'd never come. I'm afraid to leave. Jones threatened to have me killed if I talked to you before he got to Calvert."

Jane was stunned. She said, "Leona, are you another victim of the cartel?"

"Yes."

Jane turned to Cole and said, "She sure had me fooled guv."

Cole replied, "When so many people on this Island have been living in fear, you can't take a person at face value." To Leona he said, "We have to take you in for interrogation. I'm sure you'll be home tonight. Tell us, did Jones destroy much evidence?"

Yes, he had me here until late last night shredding things. But I hid what you will need to lock him up. Come over here."

They walked into the women's washroom and Leona said, "I was able to put these boxes in here before he got back from the airport yesterday morning. As soon as I saw Jane I knew she was no ordinary chick secretary, and that the noose was tightening around Winston's neck. Praise God for keeping the man out of this washroom. The pompous creep should have known better that to hire someone from London."

"Look," Cole said, "call Police Headquarters. I have to get someone to tape this crime scene and put a secure lock on the door." Leona dialed and handed the phone to Cole. He heard Audrey answer. He asked for Spikel, got him and gave him instructions. Spikel said he would personally handle the job and bring another officer to help. He'd be there in ten minutes.

"We can go shortly," Cole told the women. "Detective Spikel is on his way here." He spent the wait time interrogating Leona. Jane watched and listened, learning how the top cop did his job. She had never witnessed such a grilling in such a short time. Cole finished and said, "Leona, thank you for co-operating and taking the chance that you did. You can go home now. Tomorrow Jane will meet with you about ten and I want you to work together to put the evidence in place."

When Spikel arrived with a young officer, Leona thanked Cole and left. Spikel said, "Don't worry about a thing. Nothing will leave this place unless you, or Jane, remove it."

Cole replied, "Call the office and tell them that Jane and I are going home."

Chapter 43 | Time to Relax

When they got to the car Cole asked, "How about something to eat? We can get cleaned up and walk over to Hibiscus."

"I'm game." she said. Then coyly, "I hope Phil won't get jealous."

Cole responded with, "I hope he does. There's nothing like jealousy to get a man to act!"

The two detectives did as planned and were welcome by Gart. The restaurant had quite a few patrons. Gart told them that the publicity about the raid had drawn people all day, and he was afraid he might run out of food, but he'd saved some fresh grouper just in case Cole should show up. He was surprised that Strong was not with Cole. Jane looked ravishing and Gart had a hard time keeping his thoughts clean. *'How many times have I seen successful married men walk into my place with a 'trophy' on their arm?'* he mused. Some patrons, especially the men took note of Jane as she walked to the table. A couple of ladies actually poked their escorts to make them stop gawking. Cole had fun teasing those women, as he gentlemanly pulled a chair from the table, and motioned for Jane to sit. She played her role and let Cole adjust the position of the chair toward the table. Gart enjoyed the action as well. Then he said, "If you have time, why not let me make this evening one to remember? I can choose some special wine and food and a beautiful desert. All you and Jane have to do is relax and enjoy."

Cole smiled. "Do your thing, Gart. Spoil us."

Jane looked at Cole, "My wound is healing fast. It doesn't hurt anymore. I could sit here all night and listen to your stories. You have no idea how much I admire you and what you have done at The Yard. You are a legend, and here I am, with The Great One. My dream has come true."

Cole raised an eyebrow. "I had no idea that someone thinks that I am The Great One. From what I've heard back home, and what I've seen in the short time you've been here, you are going to take over that role in a very few years. Thanks for coming to dinner, Jane. I am getting lonely and missing my wife. A man has to talk to a woman once in a while and you have stepped in at a very good time. And I'm glad you found Phil. He's a solid guy. He can fill the same void for you. And you for him."

She smiled and said, "I heard that one of your best strengths is analyzing people. You just proved it. I really like the man. But enough of mutual praise, tell me about some of your missions."

Cole knew that his will power was weakening, so he switched his mind to being a detective, not a sentimental target. He told Jane about capturing murderers and psychopaths as Gart kept bringing delicious food and keeping the wine glasses topped up. Three hours passed by before Cole and Jane finished eating. Gart offered them a liqueur, but the couple turned it down, thanked him profusely, and strolled across the road to Enchanted.

They were surprised that Strong was not there. Unawares to Cole, he had hooked up with the Taylor family, and did not get home until after eleven. Jane had gone to her room by then but Cole had stayed up to make sure his partner came home safely. He and Bill exchanged stories and finished the bottle of Pirate's Best.

Strong said, before parting for bed, "I can't believe Eisie was waiting for me to show up."

Cole replied, "I can't believe that I have so much self-control."

Both went to bed relaxed and feeling that they were lucky guys. Cole prayed thanks to the Lord for keeping all the agents safe, and asked for justice to prevail.

Chapter 44 | Wrapping up

Jane had gone to bed early because she had arranged to join Phil on his early morning walk along the beach. She tried to be quiet, but Cole was wide awake in bed and heard her moving about. He opened his drapes and saw a magnificent morning scene as the sea was calm and the birds were running along the beach. He thought, *'Maybe by tomorrow I'll get a chance to slow down and enjoy the sea and the sand.'* He knew today would be hectic as he and Strong would be interrogating the suspects non-stop. His focus changed abruptly. Jane was walking down to the water's edge and Phil was waiting for her. Cole smiled inwardly as the two met and kissed. *'I know where this is going.'* he mused. Now he was wide awake so he started a pot of coffee. Strong got the aroma and rolled out of bed to join his boss.

"Is Jane up yet?" Strong asked.

"She's up and in action, Bill. She just joined Phil for a romantic walk along the beach."

"Are you kidding me, guv?"

"Not at all, and I bet when they get back we'll see them holding hands."

"Well I'll be damned," Bill exclaimed. "Talk about a fast mover. It must be the weather here that makes the women so horny."

"Speak for yourself, Bill. You seemed to have caught island fever."

"Okay, okay, let's drop the subject. We have our hands full today, guv. Where do we start?"

"As soon as we get dressed we'll go to Carl's Treats for breakfast. By nine I want us to be at HQ. I've arranged for us to meet The Governor and The Premier at Curry's office at ten. I think we should request to have two judges sent in to handle the big cases. The local judge can set arraignment dates and trial dates. I want you to make sure that we have a complete list of subjects and locations of all crime scenes. Also we have to give the names of witnesses like Ted, Sheila, Gart, and Louisa. Then there is the question of which country gets the contraband goods and the physical assets. Make sure everyone is on track and ready to go to their assignments. When we finish at Curry's office, you and I will return to HQ and separately question each member of the police force and the staff. At thirty minutes each we should finish that exercise today. I want you to set up a meeting of Oakley's people and our people for tomorrow morning at ten. Finally, make arrangements for our group, except for Jane, to leave on the Tuesday BA flight to Heathrow. Can you think of anything else?"

Strong said, "Yes, what about Clifford Scott's accident?"

"You are right, Bill, I forgot about that. How about giving the case to Jane?"

"I'm not sure that Trump will agree, but it's a great idea."

"I'll convince Trump when I call him later. The Governor will back me up."

The day went along smoothly. After clearing Leona, Cole asked her to make arrangement to rent The Hibiscus Restaurant for Sunday evening. He had made a list of the agents, both British and American, plus the people who helped bring down Commissioner Black's operation. He felt that they should be publicly recognized for their efforts. He told her to make sure that the newspaper and radio reporters were welcome to attend.

On Friday, Cole spent the day at HQ writing up a detailed report to submit to The Governor and The Home Office. He had accepted an invitation to have dinner and spend the evening at the Governor's home. That left Strong to be alone that afternoon with Eisie, before partying with Jane and Phil, at The Cricket Club.

On Saturday, Cole kicked back and finally enjoyed the sea, sand, and sun. He had told the police officers to drop by anytime with their families or significant others as he would have non-stop pizza and drinks sent over from Hibiscus. Many of them came by with their kids. They had a great time swimming and eating. Comments were made about their new leader, The Interim Commissioner. They hoped that he would be affirmed for the full-time position.

On Sunday, Cole went alone to an early church service, and was recognized by the Pastor who offered up thanks and blessings to all of those involved with Cole's mission. Strong was a weak Christian, and he did not like listening to sermons. Cole met Harris at church and arranged a fishing trip to Rocky Palm. They caught several nice wahoo that Harris sold to Carl and Gart.

The Sunday evening party was a great success. Many attendees made congratulatory speeches. The media showed up and recorded the names of the people who risked their lives to help. The reporters were astounded by some of the stories. The Taylor Family sat with the DEA people. Strong invited Eisie, and Jane invited Phil. Both couples took a lot of ribbing, all in good fun.

On Monday, DEA agents Ian and Juan escorted the four Canadian suspects to the airport. They were put on a private jet that would skirt the United States air space by stopping to refuel in Grand Bahama Island and in Bermuda, before landing in Halifax. Oakley had convinced his boss Marcel Savage that the expense of the trip was nothing compared to the bounty they had seized. The Sun Airways flight was booked solid, so a private jet was their only alternative. Oakley explained that the men would be arrested in Halifax, thereby saving the expense of lawyers and security costs otherwise to be borne by United States taxpayers. As a U S taxpayer, Savage welcomed that idea.

Patton was up and able, so he and Oakley drove out to say goodbye to Billy Bob. He received them with a huge smile and made them stay while he pan fried Mahi-Mahi for lunch. They thanked him for his contribution to the mission. Oakley said, "We have never had a case finish like this! You are one hell of a guy, Billy Bob!"

They had also made arrangements with the P I Marine to take them out to the DIAMOND QUEEN. It was still anchored as a crime scene. Captain Marcus John on the Cutter Bradenton arranged for the agents to meet with Sally and Jan. They met in the Captain's quarters, and the women, with tears flowing, rushed into the men's outstretched arms, hugged them tightly and kissed them until they could hardly breathe. They spent twenty minutes together holding hands and talking. Tom told them not to worry, that Mancini was in prison on the Island and he could no longer harm them. Tom assured them that he and Willie would be keeping track of the ship, and the Cutter captain would notify him about the final destination of the DIAMOND QUEEN. Tom and Willie swore that they would be waiting there to greet their sweethearts. The men returned to shore with emotions running high.

Cole and Strong spent Monday at HQ with Herman Spikel. He seemed to have everything under control, but Cole told him to call, either himself, or Bill, at any time. Oakley and Patton arrived around four o'clock. They got caught up on what was going on. Cole felt that the four of them should go for dinner together. Strong said, "Why not go to the Seaview Grill where we first met?"

"Great idea," chimed in Oakley. "I'll drive, unless you sophisticated Brits need fancier transportation."

Cole responded jokingly, "I told you once before, up your bloody American ass!"

They all laughed. Oakley said, "Now that you mention it, yes I do remember."

That settled the idea and they drove to the Seaview Grill. They enjoyed the evening. Cole told the others that he would be leaving Jane on the island to investigate the death of Clifford Scott, the original owner of the mill.

Oakley and Patton dropped off Cole and Strong at Police Headquarters. They were very serious when they said their goodbyes. Cole invited the Americans to visit London. Oakley invited the Brits to tour the DEA facility in Miami.

On Tuesday morning The Outsider Cops were aboard the British Airways 747 – not in First Class, of course.

Epilogue

Police Commissioner Wharton Sylvester Black was met at Heathrow, on the airplane, by two friendly undercover Special Forces officers. Black assumed they were sent by The Commonwealth Police Commissioners' Association. Because he had taken advantage of the free liquor in First Class, he pompously addressed the undercover arresting officers, not knowing who they were. They played his game and led him to their waiting Land Rover, where he rode between the officers in the back seat. He wondered why the driver was not going directly to the hotel where he had a reservation. The officers told him they first had to stop at Charing Cross Police Station, and he was welcome to come inside with them to look around. He accepted the invitation and experienced his last few minutes of freedom. While one officer stood behind Black, the other officer showed him a copy of a warrant issued by the Palm Island AG. He told Black he was under arrest. He was read his Right to Silence, handcuffed, and led away to a cell. Screaming threats did him no good. The next morning he was taken before a magistrate and arraignment would be conducted when Detective Cole was available the next week. Detective Cole attended the hearing as a witness. He was armed with so much incriminating evidence that Black's solicitor offered no defense. The Magistrate ordered

Black to be extradited within one week, and was ticketed on the non-stop BA, Monday flight, to Palm Island. He was shackled and escorted by Detective Cole, and the same two Special Forces officers that had arrested him. A judge from The Cayman Islands was appointed to conduct the hearings. He sentenced Sylvester Black to eight consecutive 10 year terms, one each for the murders that Cole could identify. He was also given 40 years concurrent for drug trafficking and coercion of citizens. He is still rotting in the Palm Island prison.

Joey (Fingers) Black was convicted on six murder charges, and drug trafficking. He received 10 years, with no parole, for each murder. He was also sentenced to an additional 25 years for drug trafficking. He never recovered completely from a head injury and is in a prison mental care facility in Britain.

Drug kingpin, Romeo Balluchi, was extradited to the United States and is in prison in Miami, Florida. His Cigarette31 boat was sold for $60,000. The proceeds were donated to the Palm Island Police Benevolent Fund.

Homer Black was convicted as an accomplice for disposing of bodies before autopsy. He is serving 8 years in the Palm prison. His funeral home and crematorium operation was confiscated by the government, and is now a government business.

Detective Curtis Cole was offered a promotion to the rank of Senior Superintendent of Investigations, Criminal Division, New Scotland Yard. He declined, as he felt he could better serve at his current rank. He, and his wife Vickie, had a second honeymoon as the guests of Phil Russell.

Detective William Strong was promoted to Captain, Drug Investigative Division, New Scotland Yard. His romance with Eisie, the Palm Island beauty, ended after he invited her to London. He told her he was too old, and his lifestyle was too dangerous, for him to continue the romance.

Detective Jane Butterworth managed to prove that Clifford Scott did not have an accident but he was murdered by Black's henchman, Fingers. During the six month long investigation, she and Phil Russell fell in love. She moved into Phil's home and two months later they married. Her friend Darlene Clarke was the Maid-of-Honor.

Gart and Louisa Webber's Hibiscus Restaurant became world famous, and very profitable, when the magazine, World's Best Restaurants for Lovers, featured it with a cover story. The editor had read about The Hibiscus Restaurant when the Economist Magazine did a cover story about the Outsider Cops. He gave a five star rating for both the food and the ambience. Gart and Louisa continued to manage their restaurant for two years when they received a $1,500,000 offer from a Houston, Texas, oil magnate.

Tom Oakley and Willie Patton appealed to Citizen & Immigration Service, and permanent resident permits were issued to Sally, and to Jan. Oakley was given a senior rank and had to move to Dallas, Texas. Sally joined him there and they got married. Patton was promoted to Captain, Drug Enforcement Division in Miami, Florida. Jan was hired as an interpreter by a private investigation company. She married Willie. The two couples pledged to meet each November to celebrate the anniversary of their 'dive into love'.

The case received international attention when the Economist Magazine featured the story of The Outsider Cops. It won a Pulitzer Prize.

Comments appreciated at jgaryshaw@gmail.com. Watch for book #2. www.suckersgreed.com. Detective Cole goes to Canada.